THE
SEA
SPINNER

Julie Johnson is the No.1 *Sunday Times* bestselling author of *The Wind Weaver*. When she's not writing, Julie can most often be found sitting on the beach near her home in her native Massachusetts, adding stamps to her passport, drinking too much coffee and avoiding reality by disappearing between the pages of a book. She published her debut novel on a lark, just before her senior year of college, and she's never looked back. Since, she has written twenty novels, which have been translated into more than a dozen different languages and appeared on bestseller lists all over the world.

THE
SEA
SPINNER

REIGN OF REMNANTS,
BOOK TWO

JULIE JOHNSON

MICHAEL  JOSEPH

PENGUIN MICHAEL JOSEPH

UK | USA | Canada | Ireland | Australia
India | New Zealand | South Africa

Penguin Michael Joseph is part of the Penguin Random House group of companies
whose addresses can be found at global.penguinrandomhouse.com

Penguin Random House UK,
One Embassy Gardens, 8 Viaduct Gardens, London SW11 7BW

penguin.co.uk

First published in the United States of America by Berkley,
an imprint of Penguin Random House LLC 2026
First published in Great Britain by Penguin Michael Joseph 2026
001

Map designed by Julie Johnson and Alison Cnockaert
Book design by Alison Cnockaert
Title page art: Four elements © mountain beetle / Shutterstock
Printed and bound in Great Britain by Clays Ltd, Elcograf S.p.A.

The authorized representative in the EEA is Penguin Random House Ireland,
Morrison Chambers, 32 Nassau Street, Dublin D02 YH68

A CIP catalogue record for this book is available from the British Library

HARDBACK ISBN: 978-0-241-69475-6
TRADE PAPERBACK ISBN: 978-0-241-69476-3

Penguin Random House is committed to a sustainable future
for our business, our readers and our planet. This book is made from
Forest Stewardship Council® certified paper.

To the water signs, who feel everything with
the force of a stormy sea

KEY

LANDMARKS

1. Blister Bight
2. Forsaken Forest
3. Thawe Bridge
4. Avian Strait
5. The Vale
6. Frogmyre Bog
7. Red Chasm
8. Starlight Wood
9. Shadow Steppes
10. Soot Flats
11. Husk Desert
12. Howling Plains

CITIES / OCCUPIED PLACES

1. Windward Port
2. Leeward Port
3. Caeldera
4. Vintare
5. Coldcross
6. Acrine Hold
7. Hylios
8. Hollywell
9. Bellmere
10. Symmetria Keep

ANWYVN

THE NORTH SEA

① ③ DYVED

FROST LANDS

② ① PRYDAIN ISLE

THE NORTHLANDS

TITAN'S WAY

② ⑦ THE BAY OF BLOOD

REAVER TERRITORY

CIMMERIAN

④ ⑤

LLŶR

MOUNTAINS

③ ④ ⑥ ⑤

PLAINS OF ARANTHON

DAGGER POINT

WESTERLY SEA

⑥ ⑦

⑧

⑨

SEAHAVEN

⑧

EASTWOOD

SMUGGLER'S SOUND

THE MIDLANDS

WESTLAKE

ENDLESS OCEAN

LAKE LUMEN

NYTHIA

⑨

⑩

SHIFTING ISLES

LORDALE

THE REACHES

THE SOUTHLANDS

DYMMERIA

⑪

CARVAGE

⑫

⑩

IRON ISLE

DESERT DEPTHS

THE
SEA
SPINNER

PROLOGUE

LIGHT BRINGER

A CAELDERAN SONG OF BATTLE

Fyremas flames filled the air
An eve of joy beyond compare
Till skies flashed red at midnight's stroke
The wards came down and in they broke

Reaver blades, ice giant brawn
Would spare none to see the dawn
Arrows fell short, bolts flew astray
Defenseless, we made easy prey

But then she came to join the fight
Weaver of wind, bringer of light
Rhya the mighty, Rhya the brave
Eyes of storms, pale hair a'wave

Evil felled by a tempest's blows
Lightning flashed, a new day rose
Let none forget as time moves on
Caeldera's one true champion

CHAPTER
ONE

The metal handle sears my palm, a withering harbinger. One I ignore.

I step into the throne room and nearly double over. It's hot as a furnace, the heat a shock to the system after the chill of the corridor. At my chest, my Remnant mark burns with contradictory cold, stirring awake in response to the maegic shimmering in the air. It is thick as syrup, a vermilion haze that suffuses the entire space.

The doors close behind me with a resolute click. The sound makes me want to bolt straight back the way I came. I don't want to be here. In truth, I would rather be almost anywhere else, given the fiery reception I am no doubt about to receive, but the memory of Mabon's deep voice rumbles in my head, imploring me to try.

Maybe this time you can get through to him.

If anyone can make the man see sense, it's you.

Please, Rhya. You know I would not put you in this position without good reason. You know I would not ask this of you unless...

I take a deep breath, struggling to fill my lungs, tasting the distinct tinge of elemental power on my tongue. Flame and ash, pressing in from all sides. My knees threaten to buckle as I make my way down a short flight of stone steps onto the gleaming floor.

Set deep in the earth, the cavernous chamber was spared the wrath of the ice giants that ravaged Caeldera two months ago. While the rest of the city is an unrecognizable ruin of glass and debris—roofs caved in from massive boulders that rained down, storefront windows shattered with axe hilts, facade columns crumbled into dust—the throne room looks just as I remember it. Dark stone of pure, petrified lava, veined with red. Massive columns with bases of caged fire holding up a distant ceiling. Trenches of flame lining the perimeter floors, extending up the back wall.

But no people.

On the night of Fyremas, spectators packed inside, shoulder to shoulder, angling for the best view of the ward-charging ceremony. Now it is even emptier than the once bustling shops on High Street. My boot falls echo loud as cannon fire as I make my way down the polished aisle that halves the room.

On the lofted dais, the steward's seat Queen Vanora occupied during her reign is vacant. For one who ruled so long, and with such spectacle, her departure from this world was decidedly commonplace. Crushed to pulp in her gilded ballroom like so many others, then reduced to cinders alongside her most common of subjects on the mass pyre erected outside the city walls a week after the battle.

Were she there to witness it, she would have seethed at the indignity of sharing her last rites with the masses. No mournful bugles or waxing eulogies on her behalf. No rare flowers laid or grand portraits commissioned. But these days no one is inclined toward fanfare.

Not even for a dead queen.

My eyes move to the king's heavy metal throne at the center

of the dais. It, too, sits empty. Though I hardly expected to find him there. I doubt Dyved's new sovereign has spent more than a handful of minutes sitting down these past weeks—and certainly not in a stuffy ceremonial chair.

I skirt the platform and approach the back wall of the cavern. It is even hotter here, so near to the trenches of fire that leap high and hungry, so near to the source of the maegic that thrums unabated. One section of the wall juts slightly outward, concealing an old mine shaft that functions as a lift. I lay my palm against the warm stone where a peculiar pattern of gouges marks the surface—a glyph, carved there by some ancient ancestor. One short pulse of maegic is enough to activate it. A fiery glow filters between my fingers as the floor panel beneath me begins to rise swiftly upward.

I've grown somewhat more accustomed to using Caeldera's network of lifts over the past few months, but it is still never an entirely pleasant sensation. My innate predisposition toward claustrophobia is triggered anytime I find myself ensconced by earth. Even now, as I rise upward through the mine shaft, I'm itching for escape. The craving for fresh air, for sunlight and open sky, claws at my throat with razor-sharp talons.

The lift comes to a halt with a jolt that shakes my bones. I step out into a semi-enclosed chamber that overlooks the throne room far below and feel every hair on my body rise in response. This is a place of potent natural power, where the deep enchantment of Anwyvn's very core bubbles to the surface. Tears sting at my eyes, an irrepressible reaction to the thick cloud of maegic.

Around me, the curved walls and low-hanging ceiling are carved with countless glyphs. They are aglow, as though lit from within by pure power—the origin of which is crouched at the center of the chamber with his hands pressed flat to the floor of hardened lava, expelling pulse after pulse.

"Pendefyre," I call softly.

He does not look up.

"Pendefyre," I say again, louder. His head jerks, but he still does not look at me. In fact, he seems to redouble his focus, pressing even more firmly against the red-veined stone. Every knuckle of his strong, tanned hands is white from lack of circulation. Flames lick out between his fingers, burn twin paths up his arms, ignite a trail down his bare chest to where a dark design of whorls and spirals mars the flesh.

The Fire Remnant.

It is no less mesmerizing in this moment than it was the first time I saw it, furling outward across his right pectoral in a triangular pattern. But my awe is now laced with alarm as I watch Penn giving more and more of himself to the wards that shield his city from harm. For several long seconds I stand there, paralyzed, my vision consumed by the hungry flames that furl across his skin.

How much more can he give before he burns out completely? How much further can he push himself without causing permanent damage?

No wonder Mabon came for me. No wonder the Ember Guild is so concerned about their leader. The previous Fire Remnant, King Vorath, died here in this very room, doing this very thing. He reached for too much power, pushed himself too hard. And he lost his life because of it.

Angry as I may be at Penn for his attitude of late, I cannot stand idly by while he kills himself in his obsessive quest to make Caeldera safe.

Whether my efforts will be successful is another matter entirely. My teeth grit as recollections of the last time I found myself standing at this threshold—the result of Jac's relentless wheedling to accompany him a fortnight ago—sweep over me.

Penn made his position clear that day. Incontrovertibly so, seeing as he bellowed loudly enough to bring what remains of this keep down around our ears about how we should both mind our godsdamned business and keep our noses out of his affairs.

All hail King Pendefyre, the Pigheaded.

Swallowing down the irritation that lingers bitterly on the back of my tongue, I take another faltering step. "Pendefyre. Look at me."

But Penn is unreachable. He is entirely engrossed by his task, pouring every bit of his power into the wards. My heart pangs as I watch him draining himself dry. His expression is savage—a mix of determination and agonized desperation. His face is white as parchment. An overgrown curl of burnished chestnut hair falls over his forehead, concealing his eyes from view, but I know without seeing that they are alive with maegic, the irises burning like hot coals.

The steadying breath I pull into my lungs has the opposite effect. It shimmies through me with intoxicating provocation. Penn's maegic is affecting me more than I want to admit. The Remnant at my chest prickles relentlessly, awake and alert, eager to come out and play. I steadfastly ignore it. Adding air maegic to this scenario will likely have the same effect as dashing a cup of spirits on an open flame while attempting to put it out.

Combustion.

A fresh pulse of power rolls through the chamber. I watch it ripple through his body, the muscles of his bare back flexing, the tendons of his arms going taut as raw maegic transfers from him into the stone. The wards around us throb bright as starlight. My legs buckle as it hits me, stealing the breath from my lungs and sending me to my knees. I land with a bruising thud.

Blinking away the pain, I bring Penn back into view. A sharp blade of panic sluices through me. The fire snaking up his arms and coiling around his chest has grown. It now surrounds his entire form in a thick cloak of flames. He crouches there, within a blazing ball of heat, immolating as I watch. Through the white-hot flickers, I see blood beginning to pour from his pointed ears, dripping down the broad column of his throat, pooling in the rigid indentation of his clavicles.

"Penn!" I cry, a ragged plea. *"Pendefyre!"*

This time, he does not react at all to the sound of my voice. He is lost in the throes of his power.

I have to put a stop to this. Now. Before it's too late.

Before I lose him.

Gritting my teeth, I force myself forward inch by inch, half crawling across the floor toward him. It is like crawling into the midday sun. Sweat pours down my spine, slicks down my neck. The heat on my face is an unrelenting scorch. Any trace of the tears glossing my eyes evaporates in an instant. They are dry as desert sand, each blink of my lids an unpleasant scrape. My lashes feel like tinder, ripe for catching.

I wonder at what temperature my tunic will ignite as I drag myself across the blistering floor. The petrified lava is so hot beneath my fingertips, I think it might turn molten as it was a millennium ago, the last time this volcano erupted. I push past the pain, forcing myself to continue forward. Closing the gap between us, one excruciating sliver at a time.

It is not only physical pain that thwarts my progress. My very soul seems to sear, fueled by the Remnant bond that links me irrevocably to Penn. Usually I find our connection calming. Comforting. An unconscious tether in the back of my mind, letting me know where he is and, in rarer times of great emotion, what he is feeling. Like the scent of burning leaves on an autumn wind, I can sense him from afar and find my way to him if necessary.

There is nothing calming about our bond in this moment. Nothing remotely comforting. It is a charred current of unadulterated energy that scorches a path from his heart to mine. Within my own reserves of maegic, deep within the wild storm that swirls inside, I feel the placid waters of my power beginning to simmer beneath Penn's heat. All that is cold and controlled at the core of my being seems suddenly in danger of sparking. By the time I reach him at the center of the chamber, I am struggling to keep my own destructive abilities in check.

"Penn, you have to stop this." I lift a hand toward him but jerk it back from the flame as pain bites at me, a stinging lash across my fingers. Blisters bloom on my skin. "Please, Penn. Please listen to me."

The fire is so bright, so hot, it is hard to see and even harder to breathe. I try three more times to reach him through the ball of flame that surrounds his body, telling myself it is only pain, that any burns I receive will heal quickly, but I never manage to touch him before snatching my hand back, my singed flesh smarting in agony.

More blood is pouring from his ears, dripping down his chest in rivulets. Within the ball of fire, his skin is stark white. Corpse white.

Please, a small voice cries out from somewhere deep within me. *Please, Pendefyre. Hear me. Stop this.*

But he does not.

I cannot use my power to help him any more than I can use my hands. In desperation, I reach within to the bond that burns between us. I grab hold of that invisible tether that connects my heart to his, connects fire to air, and begin to tug on it, a spool of yarn without end, unraveling his psyche into mine.

I am not certain it will work. Not until I see the flames consuming Penn starting to disperse, weakening as I absorb some of the damage he is inflicting upon himself. I nearly bite through my lip as my nerve endings bake, as the marrow in my bones crackles with heat.

Skies, how much pain he is in, if this is but a shade of his power.

I cannot handle much more without doing myself serious harm. But there is no choice. Blood pours from his eyes as well as his ears now, trickling down his cheeks, dripping off his sharp jawline. And so, I take more. I pull his fire toward me, into me, until I think the blood will boil in my veins, until I feel my limbs turn to kindling, until each breath burns like my lungs are full of embers.

I channel every bit of heat and flame into the deepest recesses of my own power, where the air currents within me blow hard enough to extinguish them. Candles in the wind, no match for my storm. The flames around Penn weaken further, growing faint and translucent as they lick across his flesh.

More.

The heat is unbearable. I think my body will crack apart, think my mind will cleave beneath the force of it. The world fades around me, blackness closing in at my peripherals. I am losing the battle against unconsciousness. Just before my final shred of strength falters, my inner voice cries out one last time—a pained and broken prayer to the man crouched beside me.

If you die here, you take me with you.

He hears me. Somehow, someway, he hears me. The flames splutter out with a whooshing sound that echoes off the walls. The relentless wave of heat subsides so fast, I am certain I must be hallucinating. In a blink, I can breathe again. Ragged, desperate gulps of superheated air—but at least I am breathing. I stare down at the veined lava floor of the chamber where my hands and knees are planted. My arms and legs tremble with the effort to keep from collapsing entirely. The sleeves of the plain uniform I wear to treat patients at the infirmary are scorched beyond repair, the skin beneath flushed the angry scarlet shade of a fresh burn. My fingers are a mess of char, the tips blackened. I stare at the damage for a moment before my arms and legs do finally give out and, in an exhausted heap, I fall.

I never hit the floor. Two strong arms close around me before I make impact. Within the space of a breath, I am cradled against a broad chest, staring up into the King of Dyved's scowling face.

"What the bloody hell were you thinking?" he growls, fury staining every word.

"That's an odd way to thank me for saving your life," I snap hoarsely, shoving against his hold—a move I regret instantly, as it sets off a fresh wave of pain that racks me head to toe.

"Thank you? I'd like to shake some sense into you." His touch is utterly gentle, belying his enraged declarations. He holds me like I am made of glass, his large hands careful not to put undue pressure on my ravaged skin. "What you just did was beyond risky. I could have killed you."

"And, if I had not taken that risk, you would have killed *yourself*, you ungrateful lug!"

"Better me than you."

"Don't say that."

His eyes are still smoldering with maegic. They lock on mine, two embers, burning, burning, burning. There are deep, bruise-like shadows of exhaustion beneath them. Traces of blood still trail down his cheeks, drip onto his chest.

"I know you were trying to help," he murmurs after a long pause. "But you put yourself in harm's way unnecessarily."

"How was it unnecessary, Penn? You were lost in the maegic. The fire was consuming you."

"I had it under control."

"That's not what it looked like. Not to me, not to your men, not to anyone with eyes."

"You're exaggerating."

"Am I?" I shake my head. "I don't think so. I think, whether or not you want to admit it, you're playing a dangerous game. Pushing yourself so close to the edge, it's only a matter of time before you slip. You're driving yourself to your own death. Just like King Vorath did."

"As I said already," he grits out, "I had it under control. I would have reined it in before things went too far."

"Excuse me if I find that hard to believe when you're sitting here covered in your own blood."

I push against his hold again, and this time he lets me go. I scoot backward, craving a bit of distance. I haven't the strength to get far. I only make it a handful of paces before I stop to catch my breath, planting my palms on the warm stone to keep from toppling over. It will take a bit more time before I'm ready to find my feet, but already I can feel my body beginning to heal, the blisters and welts that bloom across my skin smoothing over into supple, unscarred flesh.

My eyes lift back to Penn. He is watching me, a grim set to his jaw as he examines my rapidly healing injuries. Through our bond, I feel a series of strong emotions. Guilt, pain, gratitude, rage, longing, self-loathing. And, beneath it all, a burning need for retribution that no amount of time will ease. The only thing that might do that is wrapping his hands around Efnysien's neck and squeezing until his life force flickers out.

"I'm worried about you," I whisper eventually.

He flinches and looks away, teeth clenching together. "You don't need to be."

"You're overly fixated on the wards, Penn. Obsessed, even.

It's not healthy, coming here every day. Draining your powers like this."

"I'm merely ensuring the city is safe. I would think after everything that happened on Fyremas, my efforts in that regard would be understandable."

"No one questions your intentions. And no one blames you for what happened that night."

He scoffs, a bitter sound. "No?"

"No," I echo softly. "No one. Except, perhaps, yourself."

His head whips back to me. "Who else should I blame if not myself? It was my wards that fell. It was my power that was extinguished. It was me who was left almost entirely useless in defending my people, my city, from slaughter."

"Even without your powers, you defended the city. You are the best warrior in Dyved. Perhaps in all the Northlands."

"Yet I could not keep them safe. I could not protect them."

"You did everything you could—"

"And it was not enough!" he roars, the sound reverberating against the walls. "They needed more, and I let them down. I will not allow it to happen a second time. Not while I still breathe. Not while there are still souls in this city who need my protection." He pauses, panting hard. "Not until Efnysien is dead and gone, his bones scattered to the most distant corners of earth and sea."

"Your people need you for more than just protection, Pendefyre. They look to you for strength, yes, but also for guidance. For leadership. To them, you are their hero and savior. You are their king."

"It is not my name the minstrels sing in the streets, but yours. Rhya the mighty, Rhya the brave."

My cheeks heat. I cannot contradict him. Since the battle,

there is an intractable sense of fascination where I am concerned. The story of how I thwarted the ice giants who otherwise would have happily butchered us all has been told and re-told so frequently—each telling, it seems, with additional embellishments—that by the time it reaches the farthest corners of Dyved, I fear they'll say I felled thirty foes with a single breath. That I can shoot electric bolts from my eyes and kill an entire army in a blink.

Wind weaver, they whisper when I pass by on the street. *Light bringer.*

Remnant of Air.

Champion of Caeldera.

I might laugh, if it were not so preposterous. I am no all-powerful deity, worthy of anyone's worship. I clear my throat hard to dislodge the lump of embarrassment. "The minstrels have a flair for the dramatic. Their accounts of the battle have exaggerated my role to mythic proportions."

Penn's expression darkens. "Don't do that."

"What?"

"Don't diminish what you have done for this city. Don't make yourself smaller to shore up my failings. It is unfair to you, and condescending to me."

My eyes narrow. "Perhaps the minstrels would not sing songs of my glory if you would show your face among them. Perhaps if their new king were not running himself ragged each day secur-ing the borders, or locked away all night in war councils with his advisers, or sequestered in this chamber pouring power into the wards in his every spare moment, they would see for themselves what you have done for them. How hard you are working to make them safe again. Perhaps then they would sing of you in-stead of me."

There is a heavy beat of silence. The very air seems to hold its breath as he gets to his feet. He does not move, does not pace. Just stands there, his hands clenched, his bare chest covered in blood, his face fixed in an expression of such ire, it makes me shiver.

"Is that what you think of me?" he asks finally, voice stark. "That I require songs of glory to remind me of my place in the people's hearts? Do you see me as so weak, so unsteady, I need heaps of hero worship to carry on in my responsibilities?"

"Just the opposite!" I cry, getting to my feet as well, ignoring the spasms of pain that seize my frame. "I think you are too strong. You shoulder too much of this burden alone, and will allow no one to help you carry it." My voice drops lower. "I think you need to remember there are more reasons to live than revenge. There are still good things in this world, Pendefyre. Good people."

"Most of them have fled."

"Some remain. Others will come back in time."

Or so I hope.

Only half the population remains by my count—some too sickly to make the journey, others simply too stubborn to cede their city to the violence of strangers. A mass exodus in the aftermath of the battle left the bustling capital but a skeleton of its former self. Citizens who once felt at ease in the warded shelter of the crater vanished seemingly overnight, piling their carts and wagons with as many belongings as they could, then setting their sights on distant reaches of the Dyvedi plateau, to live in isolation. And, perhaps, to try to forget the atrocities they witnessed. The friends they lost.

In my most spineless of moments, I have caught myself wishing I could join their ranks. That I, too, could flee under the cover of darkness and wake to a new vantage entirely—one where things like hope and joy and companionship do not feel so markedly out of reach. The urge arises, even knowing its futility.

There is no start fresh enough to erase what we have endured. There is no place remote enough to outrun the damage inflicted.

Wherever we go, we carry our scars.

I take a step toward Pendefyre, careful not to move too fast or push too far. He is still burning with anger, but I can see the effect my words are having on him. Some of the wrath is ebbing away, leaving in its wake a deep exhaustion from giving too much of himself these past months. He truly has run himself ragged. His reserves are empty. If I had not arrived when I did . . .

Just the thought of losing him makes my heart stumble.

"Pendefyre."

His eyes press closed as I say his name, his expression a war of conflicting emotions. Taking another step into his space, I reach out to him—slowly, so achingly slowly—and twine his fingers with mine. They are strong and callused and quite warm. His whole body shudders beneath my touch, as though his effort to remain stock-still is wearing thin. But he does not shake me off. No, his hand grips mine like a drowning man grabbing hold of a lifeline amid the rolling swells. The raw need in his grip, the flagrant urgency in it, makes my eyes sting.

"Come with me now." I squeeze his hand. At the same time, I send a pulse down the bond—a soothing shot of reassurance. "When was the last time you ate a proper meal? Or rested for more than a few stolen hours on a cot at the barracks?"

I do not wait for him to answer. I merely start walking, tugging him along with me as I make my way out of the chamber, to the lift, and activate the glyph that will bring us down into the throne room. He does not resist, shadowing my steps in silent compliance. And though I know he may never admit it aloud, through the bond I can sense the faintest furl of relief that this choice—this one singular choice—has not fallen upon his shoulders.

For they bear far too much already.

CHAPTER
TWO

We wind a twisted path out of the ruined palace, a journey that once took only minutes lengthened to nearly
an hour. Navigating the wreckage is no easy task. Hallways end
abruptly in piles of ruptured stone. The remaining staircases are
too structurally unsound to tread upon with any confidence. We
use a mix of servants' passages and debris-strewn corridors, following a series of lit torches from the throne room deep within
the bowels of the earth back toward the surface.

The air grows somewhat less stale as we progress, tendrils of
wind creeping in through cracks and crevasses in the keep's battered fortifications. I breathe easier as the constricting bands of
claustrophobia loosen their death grip around my chest.

Not much farther now.

We hasten our steps through the grand ballroom, scrambling
over loose stone and exposed mortar. A narrow path was cleared
during the desperate search for survivors—a mission of rescue that
all too quickly became one of recovery, for there was no one left
alive to dig out from beneath the rocks. Only corpses. The ceiling
is concave, a gaping hole open to misty gray skies. The detritus of
two collapsed turrets rests on the dance floor, where now only
ghosts twirl and pirouette.

With the bridge felled, the front gates demolished, and the main courtyard impassable, a new point of entry was forged by necessity through a seldom-used side terrace. Once used exclusively for the queen's garden parties and high teas, it now serves a far more pedestrian function. As we near it, we begin to pass burly soldiers in dusty brown uniforms, working to clear the rubble bit by bit. It is a grueling, monotonous task, one I do not envy as I examine their grime-caked faces and bloodied knuckles. Their muscles strain to lift gargantuan pieces of rock, often working in teams of two or three. They spare us no attention as we pass through their ranks.

I squint against the haze as we step out onto the terrace. It is eerily untouched by violence, its hedge topiaries green with new growth, its marble fountains still gurgling, its tile pathways unbroken. An aberrant sliver of normalcy amid the decay.

This section of the palace is the most intact. Its turret still stands, a lone sentinel piercing the sky high over our heads. From here, one could almost pretend that Fyremas had never happened. Even the lake looks almost normal. Almost. The illusion is marred somewhat by the pile of rubble that hashes a line down its center. That scar of tumbled rock and stone is all that remains of the fallen turrets, the bridge beneath. The *bodies* beneath.

So many lost.

Mist from the nearby falls hovers close over the water's surface, so thick it appears almost as fog. The familiar thunder of cascading water drowns out the grunts of the soldiers as they lug their heavy loads down a short incline, where a wooden access pier has been constructed atop an uneven pile of rubble. Several sleek wooden craft are tied there awaiting use, most bobbing low in the water as they are piled high with debris to be ferried across to the distant shore for removal.

As we make our way down the makeshift dock, Penn's grip on my hand tightens, wordlessly steadying me whenever my soles lose purchase on the damp boards. This close to the falls, everything is slicked with a thick coat of moisture.

After helping me into one of the unoccupied wooden craft, he climbs nimbly in after me and casts off our dock lines. For a time, there is no sound but the smooth dip of his oars as he steers us swiftly across the lake, the occasional puff of exertion between tight-pressed lips. Our silence strains with the weight of words left unsaid.

I feel Penn's eyes on me, but I keep mine fixed on the opposite bank as it nears. Teal waters lap gently at the sand. It is still strange to see the stretch of shore empty—no fishermen tossing weighted nets into the shallows or casting baited lines off the bridge. There are no fish left to catch. They perished along with the ice giants when the waters boiled. It will be generations before the lake teems with new schools. Even then, I doubt anyone will try their hand at luring them.

Who would dare plumb the depths of a watery tomb?

The rest of the capital feels hardly less macabre, in no small part because of the gloomy weather of late. Mist blankets the broken bones of the city. It never seems to burn off, even when sparse midday sunshine pierces the persistent cover of clouds that hangs over the crater. Unusual conditions for Caeldera in springtime—or so I am told. But then, nothing has been *usual* for several months.

Our silence endures as we walk toward my apartments. Penn seems content to follow me without question or complaint, lost in something of a daze, his thoughts distant as his expression as we wind through the marketplace. Gone is its buzzing energy, exchanged for the somber atmosphere of a graveyard. The cobblestones where citizens once traded crowns for all manner of goods are still stained with the blood of those who fell here beneath the cutting blades of Reaver battle-axes.

One day, I tell myself, the vendors will return, trading coin and gossip freely as their wares change hands, filling the afternoons with spices and laughter. For now, though, it, like much of this place, remains eerily vacant.

In unspoken agreement, Penn and I both increase our pace, not wanting to dwell any longer than necessary. I avert my eyes from the fountain where the old apothecary breathed his last; from the stretch of sidewalk where the cobbler and her wife met their sad end in each other's arms. But I do not need to look to see. Such memories are etched in my bones.

The worst of the glass and debris was swept off the sidewalks weeks ago, but the more substantial damage remains. Whole blocks are boarded up, their residents either dead or fled.

And even as traces of the slaughter are wiped away, even as the rubble is cleared and carted off... things are not the same. I fear they will never be the same. A grimness has settled over all of us, much like the unseasonable haze that clings to the air. Neither shows any sign of lifting.

So lost in my own thoughts, I hardly notice we've reached my front door until I am standing before it with my hand on the knob. I hesitate before I twist it open, eyes sliding to the man at my side.

"This is, um . . . where I've been staying," I say. *Astoundingly adroit, Rhya.* "Since I left the barracks, I mean."

"I know."

He knows? How can he know?

He's never once asked me about my sleeping arrangements, nor bothered to pay a visit. Farley or Mabon could've told him,

I suppose. Though I'm surprised he was curious enough to inquire. For weeks now I've harbored the rather painful suspicion that he's forgotten my existence entirely.

My tongue feels abruptly too big for my mouth, but I force it to form a handful of faltering syllables. "Right. Well, then . . . Come in."

I shove open the door and step into the dim shop without further delay. The soothing scent of dried plants and fresh linen envelops me instantly, a familiar perfume that reminds me of my childhood in Seahaven. The old apothecary's place on High Street was a natural choice of abode after the battle. He no longer has need of his tidy shelves of bottled tinctures or well-stocked inventory of hanging herbs. His spirit has fled to the skies, his ashes scattered on the winds. I hope, wherever he is now, he does not mind my continuing his work or making myself at home in his sparse apartments.

The back staircase is narrow and in need of a dusting. Penn's boots send up small plumes as he follows me up, each tread groaning under his weight. As we step into the parlor, my eyes scan the cluttered space, noting the books piled on practically every surface, the threadbare cushions of the sofa, the tattered edges of the rug. There is not much in the way of furniture or finery. Soft light trickles through the panes of the large picture window, the only source of illumination.

Penn stops just over the threshold. He says nothing, taking in my living quarters in silence, his eyes lingering on the crumpled throw I spend so many evenings curled beneath, the half-empty teacup I forgot to clear in my rush this morning. Chronicling each tiny trace of life like it is something worthy of acute study.

I examine him in turn, wondering why it is so difficult to find the right words to speak. Wondering why awkwardness has taken root in the space between us, and when the safe distance we've been keeping stretched into this insurmountable chasm of discomfort. Most of all, wondering how to possibly breach it.

Gods, I wish he would say something. His lingering taciturnity is beginning to unnerve me. It was my idea, coming here, and yet, now that we are . . . I feel as though I have brought a feral wolf into my living room without a proper plan as to how to domesticate him.

Those dark, intent eyes finish their investigation and shift back to fix on mine. I lose my breath when our stares lock, all the air in my lungs used up by a burgeoning flame that bursts to life deep within my gut.

"Wait here for a moment, will you?" My voice comes out strangled. "Make yourself comfortable. I'll be right back."

I escape into the kitchen like a fugitive on the run.

Cowardice, thy name is Rhya.

The old apothecary's larder contains nothing worthy of a royal feast. Yet I doubt Penn will mind the simple fare I've been living on lately. He may now be a king, but he will always be a soldier at heart. On the road, in the wild, I have seen him eat hare off the bone, watched him devour strips of venison and stale bannocks without a single murmur of complaint.

I pull together a simple dinner from my stores. While the rice simmers on the stove, I grab a dishcloth, run it beneath the tap, and carry it from the kitchen, dripping across the hardwood planks with each step.

Penn's eyes lift to me the instant I reappear, scanning me head to toe, seeming to catalog every dried bloodstain and singed tatter of my ill-fitting work uniform. It must have belonged to one of the young Life Guild novitiates at some point— probably an adolescent male, given its unembellished breeches and simple stitching. But it suits my purposes quite well. It is a rare day when someone does not cough, bleed, or vomit on me at some point during my time at the infirmary.

Penn is sitting on the worn sofa, holding the book I spent last night studying by candlelight—a heavy tome of medicinal herbs and their many uses. The bookshelves along the far wall are bursting with similar reading material. It looks odd in his hands. Those hands seem meant for gripping swords and throwing punches. I have rarely had an opportunity to see them do anything so mundane as turn a page or trace the shape of a word. The sight strikes me somewhere between the ribs, a direct blow to the heart.

He is still shirtless, clad only in black breeches. There is an ornate glyphed blade tucked into the top of his boot, twin to the one I so often carry. Even now, its comforting weight is sheathed at my left thigh. I rarely go anywhere without it. When I do manage to sleep, I do so with it close at hand, on my nightstand or tucked beneath my pillow.

"Here . . ." I lift the damp rag. "I thought I might . . ."

His brows rise in silent inquiry as I move to him and kneel on the floor at his feet. He sucks in a sharp breath as he registers my intention. Leaning forward slightly, elbows to knees, he brings his face down to my level. Our gazes tangle together for a charged moment. The depths of his eyes still smolder with banked heat. I do my best to keep my expression flat, calling on all my experience as a healer to remain composed. Still, it takes considerable effort to keep my hand from trembling as I press the limp washcloth to his face.

His teeth lock down tightly as I begin to wipe his skin clean of all traces of blood. It is crusted in the shadowed rings beneath his eyes, the fragile hollows beneath his ears. I am methodical in my efforts, moving from his cheekbones to his jawline, down the tanned column of his throat and across his chest. One singular drop of blood is dried directly over his Remnant mark, where the skin is slightly raised, like scar tissue from a brand. I wipe it away last, the whorls and spirals hot as a fever against my fingertips. His whole frame trembles as I do. The skin there, I know, is hypersensitive. By the time I am done, the white rag is red with blood and both of us are breathing fast.

"Finished," I murmur, for lack of a better thing to say. I begin to pull back, but find my wrist clasped within his hand before I've ever seen him move. My eyes flicker up to meet his.

"Thank you," Penn says haltingly. I know he is not only speaking of the washcloth.

"You're welcome."

I swallow hard. I have not been this close to him in more than a month. Since the battle, he has hardly crossed my path. If anything, he seems to be going out of his way to avoid my presence. Even so, there is no forgetting the last time we found ourselves alone together. The last time he touched me. The heated exchange we shared the night of Fyremas is scored in my mind too deep to expunge with any amount of avoidance.

Don't you understand? his voice whispers in my memory. *You have undone me completely . . .*

When I close my eyes, I can almost remember the taste of his mouth devouring mine. The feel of his callused hands, seeking out my most sensitive skin. The channel of need burning down our bond, an exquisite torment of lust neither of us was strong enough to deny.

I might convince myself I'd imagined it, if not for the strange new tension that charges the air between us now, with his hand on my skin and our faces a hairsbreadth apart. No, it was real enough. That stolen moment of passion on the lookout point above the city as fireworks exploded in the sky happened—whether he wants to own it or not.

My teeth dig sharply into my bottom lip as the memories flood me. Penn's eyes drop to my mouth, tracking the movement and seeming to get stuck there. I am blocking him as best I can, trying to keep my unruly emotions tucked behind my mental shields before they spill over into him, but the way he is looking at me has me questioning my own success in that endeavor.

While I am getting better at muting my emotions, I have not yet mastered it. Not like Penn. Except on the rarest of occasions—or when he is expelling so much maegic he can no longer afford to hold up those impenetrable bastions—he seldom gives me anything to go on. His true feelings remain an utter mystery. Whatever he feels for me, whatever he wants from me . . . he does not share. Not willingly, anyway.

A part of me longs to ask if my suspicions are true. If he laments letting his rigid sense of self-possession lapse long enough to expose his true desires. If he regrets how close we came to crossing an irrevocable line that night. But I find, when I try to ask, the words will not come out.

"I'll go take the rice off the stove," I say instead, voice thready. "You must be hungry. Mabon said you haven't been eating."

Penn grunts noncommittally as he releases me. The moment broken, I practically bolt back to the kitchen and turn my focus toward the meal.

Not a quarter of an hour later, I return to the parlor with food piled on a tray. Fresh bread, sliced cheese, a steaming bowl of long-grained rice, and a few of the apples I've been hoarding for a special occasion. Trade is finally starting up again, but for several weeks after the attack, no fresh produce moved in or out of the city. It will be some time before things are fully back to normal.

I freeze at the threshold.

Penn is fast asleep on the sofa, slumped over in what cannot be an entirely comfortable position, with his boots still tightly laced and his torso twisted against the cushions. The exhaustion on his face is so evident, I cannot bring myself to disturb him. I wonder how long it has been since he rested through the night. My own sleepless evenings have left me brittle and weary, but my burdens are nothing next to his.

Backing out of the room, I set the untouched feast on the counter with a soft thud. On the lightest tiptoes, I creep back into the parlor, drape a worn wool blanket over Penn's slumped form, and douse the gas lanterns. We will talk more in the morning, I resolve, as I get myself a helping of food and eat it in the darkened kitchen before retreating into my bedchamber to read until I fall into a fitful slumber.

Tomorrow.

Tomorrow, we will discuss our relationship and everything we've spent the past two months avoiding. Tomorrow, all will finally be resolved. I am certain of it.

But in the morning when I wake, the sofa is empty, the wool blanket neatly folded. Pendefyre is long gone—not merely from my apartments but from the city itself, no more than a hint of flame on a distant wind somewhere far beyond the crater's rim.

And growing fainter by the moment.

CHAPTER

THREE

It is not yet dawn, but already I am on my way to the infirmary. My boots are a steady rap in the eerie quiet, carrying me down darkened streets.

"You're about early," a voice says as its owner falls into step beside me. His gait betrays no limp despite the slim shin brace I know he still wears beneath his stiff leather boots—the final trace of a recently healed fracture. His copper hair is a dull flame in the dim light of dawn.

"So are you," I return, brows lifting. "Kicked out of bed by one of your many suitors?"

"You've got it all wrong, Ace. They beg me to stay. *Beg*. On their knees, tears in their eyes." Farley grins at me. "I thought I'd get an early start before reporting for duty at the barracks."

"Duty?"

"Didn't you hear? I finally got approval to rejoin active rotations. You're looking at a fully reinstated member of the Ember Guild." His chest puffs in self-importance. "I'll be leading my own unit."

"That's a big step."

"Not really. I have a wealth of experience in ordering men around."

"In the bedchamber, maybe. Not on the battlefield."

His grin turns impish. "They're not all that different, if you're doing it right."

My eyes roll at his innuendo. "Are you certain you're ready for this?"

"I've been ready since the day you first set my bones back in place."

"Just be careful—"

"*Och*, woman! Don't nag. I'll not ruin all your healing efforts on my first day back." He pauses. "You've got more important healing to do now."

My grip tightens on the basket hooked over the crook of my arm. It is full of salves, tinctures, and elixirs, the tiny bottles clinking musically with each step. I'd spent a good portion of this night in the stockroom, hunched over a mortar and pestle, grinding herbs until my fingers went numb. Just as I have every night this past week, since Pendefyre left the city. According to Mabon, he's gone to survey the plateau's pastoral provinces, where Dyvedi farmers are battling the blight like never before. He left no word as to when he'd return.

My irritation at that fact, along with my inability to sense his presence through the bond, has left me even more restless than usual. Though if insomnia has one benefit, surely it is productivity. The shelves have never been so tidy, the stores of herbal remedies never so well stocked. A good thing, as we are in sore need of them at the infirmary.

A nasty influx of spring flu has swept through the capital, sending countless patients into my care. At one point in my life, back when I was helping Eli heal sick folk in Seahaven, such rapid spread would've worried me terribly. Compared to battle wounds and crushed limbs, however, some mild coughs seem a flimsy threat.

I have lost count of the number of wounded soldiers and civilians I've treated over the past two months. I am not one of the Life Guild, with their austere sand-hued uniforms and rigorous apprenticeship requirements, who treated injured Caelderans in the time before the battle. But they need all the help they can get. With the old hospital ward buried beneath a pile of rubble, medical supplies are in short order. Healers who know how to administer those supplies are even more scarce, since the vast majority of them were inside when the walls caved in.

In the beginning especially, folks would stare at me with wide eyes and speak in hushed whispers whenever I came around to their cots to examine their wounds.

That's her.

The Remnant of Air.

See the storms in her eyes?

The chatter has died down recently. Or perhaps I've just gotten better at ignoring their awestruck murmurs as I change blood-soaked bandages and set bone breaks and check sutures for signs of infection. Much as I chafe against the growing myth that surrounds me, there is precious little I can do to set the record straight. And even less cause for it, according to my friends in the Ember Guild.

The people need something to believe in, Ace, Farley chastised me only days ago. *A god in their midst might just make them feel safe again. Let it alone, will you?*

"Have you seen Carys?" he asks now, as we approach the barracks. They are quiet this time of night—sparring pits empty, archery targets unoccupied, torches burning low.

My throat feels suddenly tight. "Only through the window."

"You should try again."

"She doesn't want to see me. She's made it quite plain. Or have you forgotten how she slammed the door in my face?"

"She's grieving, Ace." He sighs and shakes his head. "She lost her—"

"I know what she lost," I cut him off. "Just as I know who she blames for that loss."

"She needs time. She'll come around."

"Mmm."

"Doubt all you want. I'm right. True friendship doesn't disintegrate overnight."

I blow out a breath. "She's asked for space. I'm giving it to her. The best I can do for now is stay close enough to keep an eye on her and the baby."

The choice to dwell in the apothecary's home has as much to do with his mortar and pestle as it does proximity to my old friend, a stone's throw from her dressmaking shop on High Street. My large picture window offers a prime view of the blue building at the end of the block, where every so often a slender female figure in a dark cloak slips out the front door, a small bundle swaddled against her chest. Baby Nevin is growing rapidly and seems healthy enough, judging by the hungry cries I hear echoing down the lane from the open windows of his nursery.

I long for the days before Fyremas when I was welcomed in with open arms and a warm cup of tea. The last—the only—time I visited afterward, I saw the condemnation written plainly on Carys's grief-shrouded features, read the blame blazing in the depths of her green eyes, well before she had a chance to close the door.

"Ace, I just think maybe—"

"Enough, Farley." I shake my head. "If someday she decides she wants me back in her life . . . I'll be there. But I will not force her to forgive me merely to ease my own guilt."

"I've told you a thousand times, you have nothing to feel guilty about. No one blames you for Uther."

"Stop."

His mouth snaps shut at the severity of my tone. Despite his gentle prodding, Farley knows better than anyone that Carys is not yet ready to forgive and forget my role in her husband's death. For it was at my urging that Uther went into the palace; at my word that he raced headlong toward danger. If not for me, he would not have been on that bridge when the turrets crashed down upon it.

If not for me, he would still be alive.

It will take longer than a few weeks for such a wound to heal. I am not naive enough to believe Carys can ever forgive me, that our friendship will ever recover.

"I'll pop by her shop later, after my rotation," Farley assures me. "Make sure she's holding up all right. See if I can get her to rest for a span while I watch over the babe."

"You're a good friend, Farley."

"So are you, Ace. Only a matter of time until Carys sees through her grief and remembers that."

We go our separate ways, Farley disappearing into the barracks, me continuing on past the stables to the old warehouse we converted into an infirmary some time back. It is dark inside, the space lit only by a handful of candles flickering in their sconces. The air smells of herbs and sweat and days-old blood. Most of the patients are asleep in their cots, but some moan lowly in pain as they thrash, their foreheads dotted with perspiration from the fevers that ravage their weakened bodies.

By the far wall, I spot Lestyn, a scrappy, bespectacled lad several years my junior, in his tan Life Guild uniform. He is technically still a trainee, as he had not yet completed his decade-long novitiate when the world came apart at the seams, but his skill has grown by leaps and bounds these past two months. His quick, capable fingers are currently tending to a sol-

dier who took a Reaver axe to the shoulder—one of our last patients from the battle still to be discharged. Most would have
died from blood loss or infection, but the man is of strong stock.
He's lingered for weeks in increasing agony as his spliced muscles slowly stitch themselves back together.

Lestyn glances up when he hears me enter, nodding a silent
greeting, his elfin face hardly visible in the candlelight. I return
his nod as I slip off my cloak, trading it for a freshly bleached
apron on the hook beside the door.

Grabbing the salve of eucalyptus and camphor from my basket, I follow the sound of coughing toward the frail elderly
woman reposed on a nearby cot. She is unlikely to last the night,
her congested lungs failing a bit more with each passing hour. I
cannot save her. Not now. But I can rub salve on her chest to ease
her labored breaths and hold her hand as she slips beyond my
reach. I can sop the sweat from her brow and close her eyes when
they turn unseeing.

This is the hardest part of healing—knowing when it is time
to stop. Admitting that the battle, however hard-fought, has been
lost. Setting aside your tools and tonics to instead embrace the
uncomfortable truth about living: namely, that it always comes
to an end. Whether crushed in an instant beneath a fallen palace
or whittled away in sluggish increments by the passing years,
death is an inescapable inevitability. Try as we might to post-
pone its arrival, eventually it comes for us all.

I hope, when at last it takes me, I do not see it coming. I have
no desire to look death in the face. Not when I fear I might see
my own eyes staring back at me—two storm clouds of chaos ushering my shattered soul to the aether, no match for the maegic I
have unleashed.

Upon myself.

Upon the world.

"HOW MANY TIMES must I tell you, girl? My preferred poultice for infected wounds uses a pinch of ground marrow of mammoth. What is this you're using instead?" Osain takes a sniff from the jar of salve I've just finished bottling, and grimaces in distaste. "Plain comfrey? Marigold? Have you no respect for the wisdom of your elders?"

I bite back a retort. "My apologies, Osain. But in my experience, yarrow leaves are far more effective than marrow dust—"

"Your experience? *Bah!* If we relied only on your experience, we'd have no patients left. They'd all be ash on the pyre."

I press my lips together.

Muttering something about my general incompetence under his breath, the ancient healer hobbles away down the row of cots. He leans heavily on his cane as he goes, his arthritic fingers gnarled into a claw as they grip the handle. His spine is the shape of a crescent moon, a pronounced hunch rounding his shoulder blades.

Osain has been stitching wounds since well before I walked this earth—as he frequently reminds me—and was an active practitioner for decades before finally being forced into retirement several seasons back. When the city fell, he was all too willing to answer the call for aid.

He was altogether less willing to accept mine.

No matter how many fevers I ease, bones I set, brows I wipe, infections I lance, cuts I bandage . . . the old man seems ill-inclined to permit me into the lofty ranks of the Life Guild with any sort of grace. Left to his own judgment, he would have turned me away that first day I appeared at their makeshift field hospital and offered my healing services. I was no apprentice.

Besides, I am a woman. Suited for midwifery, in his eyes, but not the stomach-turning business of surgery.

It was Lestyn, with his quick wit, owlish glasses, and lopsided smile, who pointed out that they had more patients than sets of hands, many of whom would need weeks of treatment. It was Lestyn, with his quiet fortitude, who reminded his aged master that, in the years since he last touched his scalpels, the profession had evolved to accept female novitiates—many of whom were well on their way to becoming accomplished healers when the hospital roof crushed those dreams to dust.

Osain had little choice but to accept this—accept me—however begrudgingly. But old prejudices are more stubborn than whooping cough. He has not warmed to me in the slightest, and I highly doubt anything I do will change that.

While Lestyn is far more welcoming, he is only a novitiate, in many ways still learning his craft, honing his skills. He defers to his elder in all matters. Osain's word is law. Yet on the nights we find ourselves working without a hawkish, age-clouded gaze fixed upon us, I've found him to be a quick study, eager to learn my different methods and happy to listen whenever I have advice to dispense.

Most boys of thirteen are likely more concerned with courting pretty girls or practicing at the sparring pits. Not Lestyn. If he is not actively treating a patient, I'll find him in a quiet corner with a book, glasses sliding slowly down the bridge of his nose as he soaks in knowledge from the pages like a sponge.

When he heard of the apothecary's well-stocked shelves, he begged an invitation to my apartments. Now he is a near-constant visitor, ringing my bell at all hours, pounding down my door if I do not answer within the span of a breath. He bursts inside, uncoordinated as a newborn colt, his gangly limbs sweeping bottles off surfaces, his elbows knocking against doorframes and table corners, disturbing my peace and quiet.

In truth, I do not mind the disruption, however I might protest when he shows up unannounced, his face split by an unapologetic grin, his hands clutching the latest book he's conquered. For I have been undeniably lonely of late. With Carys still consumed by grief, Jac and Cadogan off to secure the borderlands, Mabon leading the capital's perimeter guard, and Penn thoroughly withdrawn in his own affairs, I have only Farley for companionship. And even he will soon be too busy for me, now that he is well enough to rejoin the Ember Guild ranks. His nights will be spent on patrol, not sitting in my parlor playing hands of twyllo, the tricky game of cards and wagers favored by Northlanders. A shame, as I'm finally getting skilled enough to win a few hands.

The day creeps on, hours sliding by in a blur of treatments and tidying. Lestyn catches my eye across the table where I am busy grinding herbs and boiling rags for fresh bandages. I lift one finger to my lips and wink as I tip a vial of rose-hip oil into the vat—an addition Osain would no doubt frown upon, purist that he is. It's a trick from the Midlands, one my old mentor Eli taught me. Infusing the bandages aids healing; it keeps air-starved skin healthy and hydrated upon removal. I'm willing to risk a tongue-lashing from Osain if it means my patients recover faster.

Lestyn's answering grin is a flash of white in the dim room.

Good lad. He will keep my secrets.

I grab the stirring stick and turn the bandages within the barrel-sized pot. Steam off the surface rises into my face, much like the persistent fog that presses against the infirmary windows. The strange weather has not yet broken, and the city is on edge because of it. Folks cast uneasy looks at the sky, muttering about ill omens.

Each morning, as I move through the misty streets, I see more carts piled high with belongings, more Caelderans fleeing to far-flung reaches of the kingdom. They are bundled in their winter cloaks, shivering against the cold. A strange sight for late spring. But there have been no sun-drenched afternoons to burn off the chill, no balmy evenings to usher in the first sighs of summer. We are trapped in a constant cycle of dreariness, caught in the grips of incessant cloud cover.

As always, those who spot me are quick to bow their heads in respect. Some cast the sign of the sacred tetrad in the air—two fingers, held aloft, moving in the shape of a diamond. I watch their lips form soundless words. *Wind weaver. Light bringer.* I watch their grave expressions flicker with hope. As though I might somehow save them. As though I might do something, anything, to banish the miserable cold and restore the warmth that once suffused their crater city, where traces of the long-dead volcano's heat linger in the stone even after a thousand years.

I want to stop and tell them the truth. That I am no savior. Not to them. Not to Penn. Not even to myself. But their misery is deep enough without my adding to it. So I merely nod and carry on my way.

Life is simpler in the darkness of the infirmary. Time slips away. Hunger pangs fade from focus, exhaustion is pushed to the back of the mind. I cease to exist as me, Rhya, a living being with needs of her own, and become no more than a set of hands. Mending and mixing, dressing and dosing. Tending to those in need with no heed to my body's urgings.

With an apron cinched around my waist and my pale hair plaited out of the way, I am unrecognizable as the Remnant of Air. It helps, of course, that most of my patients are caught in the throes of fever, too addled to pay much mind to the hands that sponge their burning skin or the fingers that check their racing pulse points. I may not be able to save the city at large, but I can save them. One at a time, cot by cot, body by body.

When the door swings open behind me around midday, I look up from the pallet where my latest patient, a boy of ten with a sore throat and swollen glands, is sleeping fitfully. Blinking to clear my thoughts, I wipe my hands on my apron as I cross to the threshold where a familiar figure stands in silhouette.

"Hello, Teagan," I say, smiling as I greet my former maid, now faithful friend. But my smile falters when I see she is dressed for travel, her slender form wrapped in a thick cloak, her back strapped with an orderly bundle. "No," I whisper in disbelief, shaking my head rapidly. "Not you, too."

She grimaces. "I've come to say farewell."

"You cannot leave!"

"Oh, Rhya, don't be upset with me." Closing the distance between us, her damaged hands reach out to find mine. The long puckered scar on her forearm—a souvenir from a Reaver blade, received during battle—peeks out from beneath her sleeve and snakes down her fingers. It's healed well enough but will never fully disappear, nor will she ever regain full function of the stiffened joints. And yet, the loss of dexterity is nothing compared to everything else that was taken from her that night. Her profession in the keep, the roof over her head, her sense of security. Above all, her closest friend.

Keda.

I witnessed her death, then avenged it—killed the Reaver who plunged his blade through her heart without blinking. But taking his life was little solace. No vengeance will bring Keda back. Just as no amount of salve or stitching will erase the jagged scar that mars the flesh of Teagan's arm.

After the battle, she spent several weeks here in the infirmary, under our care. Like many other survivors, her heart needed as much healing as her body. It was a time of great misery and pain for Teagan.

For Lestyn, though, it was love at first sight. The young novitiate took one look at my beautiful, heartbroken friend and vowed his everlasting devotion. He cared little that she is old enough to be his mother, hovering around her with the enthusiasm of an adoring puppy—and, thus, providing a source of much-needed amusement for everyone within earshot. He sulked relentlessly when she was discharged a month ago.

"You must understand," Teagan urges, blinking back tears. Brown curls escape her kerchief as she shakes her head. "There is nothing left for me here. Nothing but painful memories and broken dreams."

"But—"

"Please don't. Don't ask me to stay. You healed me after . . ." Her scarred hand jerks slightly as it clasps mine. "I owe you so much, I cannot deny you anything. So I hope you will not ask. I hope you will understand when I tell you I need to start over somewhere new. I hope you will wish me well and send me on my way."

My mouth opens, then shuts without a sound.

I *do* understand.

Too well, in fact.

Suddenly, I am also blinking back tears. I force my voice to level out as I pull her into an embrace. "Safe travels, my friend, wherever the road may take you."

"Our paths will cross again," she whispers back, her own voice choked with emotion. "I am sure of that."

"Where will you go?"

"There's a caravan headed north, toward the sea. It won't be hard to find work at a country inn or a wealthy estate. I can still scrub and fold, even if my hands aren't as quick as they used to be."

"It's cold as bollocks in the north," a sullen voice interjects. "You'll hate it."

Pulling apart, we both turn to find Lestyn glaring at us from the shadows, hands planted on his slim hips, eyes narrowed behind his thick glass spectacles. The copper skin of his cheeks is tinged beet red and, beneath the scowl, it is easy enough to detect the slightest wobble to his lower lip.

"I grew up in a northern province," Teagan tells him gently. "I know how fierce the winters are. But I appreciate your worry."

"I'm not worried!" he retorts. "Why should I care what you do? It's not like you came here to say goodbye to *me*."

I cough to cover my amusement at his display of righteous adolescent indignation.

Teagan steps closer to him, stooping a few inches to catch his eyes. "Of course I wanted to say goodbye to you, sweet Lestyn." She reaches out to cup his flushed cheek; it reddens even further beneath her touch. "I'll miss you."

"You—You will?"

"Very much."

He seems stunned by the news. So much so, he cannot even react as Teagan leans forward to brush her lips against his cheek in a quick kiss. He is still standing there, slack-jawed, when she turns back to me. Her mouth struggles to contain a grin. "Walk me out?"

Nodding, I fall into step beside her. We exit onto the street where a steady stream of carts and horses drift past. Most are headed toward King's Avenue, the main thoroughfare that cuts through the city center, but a fair few are bound for the barracks, which is serving as the main hub of activity until the palace is restored to its former glory. I feel many sets of eyes on us as they pass by, but keep my own trained firmly on Teagan.

"Write to me when you settle in?"

"I'll send so many ravens, you'll be sick of me," she promises. "I'll let you know where I end up, tell you all about my new life. And you can share news of everything here."

I blink rapidly, trying to hold my emotions in check. They are surging up inside my chest, an unrelenting tide of grief.

How many more losses am I to endure? How many more goodbyes can I utter before my voice breaks completely?

Teagan pulls me into one last embrace. Her mouth at my ear whispers a familiar refrain repeated often by Caelderans before a long parting. "By the warmth of the ember and the light of the flame, may the fire guide your path through the darkness."

I meet her eyes and, in a strangled voice, murmur, "Goodbye, my friend."

Standing in front of the infirmary, I watch her cloaked form meld into the street traffic until I lose sight of her. Until she, like the rest, is gone from me. And then, with a heart as heavy as the clouds that press down overhead, I go back inside and get to work.

CHAPTER
FOUR

The quake hits in the dead of night, startling me out of a dark dream. At first, I think I'm still asleep, that the shaking bed frame is another fragment of the horrible visions that haunt my subconscious—a sea of sand threatening to swallow me whole as carrion birds circle in a sky streaked with lightning, waiting to pick my bones clean. But as I jerk fully awake, I realize it's happening again.

Another quake.

A strong one, at that.

That makes three in the past month. It's hard to believe they were once a rare occurrence. Tremors plague us with increasing frequency as the blight spreads across Anwyvn, sickening the realm in slow degrees. Even here in the Northlands, where they were so long spared the grasping clutches of evil, it has begun to creep over the Cimmerian Mountains with skeletal fingers.

In response to this invasion, the earth heaves and shakes like a terminally ill patient too strong for his own good, fighting against that forthcoming doom with an obstinance that only drains his dwindling strength more quickly. For if the earth itself can feel pain, surely this is how it manifests—not with a quiet groan of acceptance but in great shudders that threaten to split the world in two. All of us along with it.

Bolting out of bed, I stumble toward the doorway. The planks beneath my feet are unsteady as a ship deck, pitching me to and fro against the walls of the narrow hallway. I drop into a crouch and scurry the rest of the way into the parlor. Lestyn is already awake, jostled out of the sound sleep I left him in on my sofa several hours ago, his book abandoned on the floor along with his eyeglasses. With sleep-tousled black curls sticking in several directions and his copper skin atypically pale, for once he looks every bit the boy of thirteen instead of the competent novitiate I've come to know over the past few months.

"It will be over soon," I call, gripping the doorframe as the quake begins to lessen in intensity. "Feel it? It's already slowing."

He nods, swallowing down his fright. After a few more moments of turbulence, the world stills and falls silent once more.

"There." I breathe deep. "See? It's done."

I walk over to him, one hand pressed to the fabric of my nightgown, as though I might subdue my racing pulse through sheer force. He looks faraway, his eyes not seeing me nor the room around him but something else. Something worse. Cautiously, I drop down beside him, mirroring his pose—back pressed to the sofa, knees curled to my chest, arms looped tight around them.

"Hey, now. It's all right. It's over."

Lestyn does not respond. His body trembles, as though still feeling the effects of the earthquake. His stare bores into the bookshelves, through them, reaching memories so painful I am afraid to pull him out of them.

There are things about the boy I've learned without needing to ask, without him explicitly telling me. I know he lost much in the battle—more than most. Just as I know he does not come to my apartments merely for access to the apothecary tomes, however he might pretend. He does not like to sleep at the barracks where other displaced orphans spend their nights. He prefers the lumpy cot we set up for him in the cold back room of the infirmary. Sometimes, though, he needs the semblance of home— even if he is not yet ready to express it. No matter how sharp-eyed or quick-witted, he is in many ways a lost little boy still learning to navigate this lonely new reality.

He is not alone in that.

We sit in silence for a while, until the aftershocks of the quake have subsided completely. When his breathing has evened out and his eyes have lost some of their bleakness, I get to my feet and pull him up after me.

"Come on. Get your boots on while I get dressed," I say brusquely. "Neither of us will be sleeping anymore tonight. No use sitting around here when we can be of use to others."

He nods, shoulders stiffening. "Okay, Rhya."

"Let's hope no more buildings collapsed under the tremors. The infirmary is finally clearing out. I'd like to see it remain that way for a few days before another disaster strikes. It would give us time to catch up on that pile of laundry in the storage room. If it grows any higher, it will rival the range."

His amused snort chases me down the hallway.

In a matter of moments, we are walking the dark stretch of High Street. We pass by Carys's dress shop. The windows are lit up, lanterns burning bright despite the late hour. If I strain my ears, I can hear the faint cries of a fussy baby being soothed back to sleep after an abrupt awakening. Longing ribbons through me. I wish I could knock on the door. Offer to make Carys a cup of tea and take a turn rocking Nevin back to sleep while she gets some rest. Perhaps begin to make things right . . .

"Are you okay?"

I glance over at Lestyn and find him watching me with concern. Wiping my expression clear, I force a smile. "I'm fine."

"Right." He shakes his head, muttering, "We're all just *fine*."

"Have you been tending Carys's garden, as I asked?"

"Every other morning."

"And bringing the care packages?"

He nods.

"Good lad."

I can practically hear his eyes roll skyward. "I don't know why you make me go there so often. I could just leave the packages on the stoop."

"What about the garden? Who will tend it if you don't?"

"I plucked all the weeds ages ago! And it will be months and months before anything's ready to harvest. Besides, why can't the lady who lives above the shop do it?"

How can I explain to a thirteen-year-old boy that my sending him there has nothing to do with the herb garden and everything to do with the woman who owns the courtyard in which it is planted? How can I tell him his visits are more about getting a set of eyes into a dear friend's world without intruding where I am no longer wanted?

I cannot.

There are no words for such matters.

"Because," I say stiffly. "The lady who lives there is . . . She's . . ."

"Sad," Lestyn finishes for me, exhibiting an insight beyond his years. "She's so, so sad."

I swallow hard. "How do you know that?"

"She doesn't cry or anything. She even tries to smile at me, some days. And she shared some slices of the apples you sent last week when I was done with the watering. But her eyes . . ." His slim shoulders move up and down in a shrug. "You can see it in her eyes. They're empty. Like a corpse at the infirmary after the fever's won. Except when she's looking at her baby—that's the only time she seems alive."

Gods.

My throat is so tight, it's tough to speak. "You should know . . . Carys, like so many of us, lost someone during Fyremas."

Lestyn glances at me sharply. He, more than anyone, understands the losses of that night.

"She's not sad. She's grieving," I continue. "And though some people may say those are one and the same, they are not. Sadness is a fleeting reaction; grief is a state of existence. One it takes time to work through."

The apple bobs in his throat. "Who did she lose?"

Uther's steady gray eyes flash inside my mind, a painful bolt of memory. "Her husband. He was a member of the Ember Guild. A good man."

"Oh."

We round the corner of High Street and cross onto the wider avenue that leads toward the infirmary. Every building—the few that are still occupied—is shuttered against the night.

"Anyway. That's why it's so important to keep up your visits." I force a brighter tone. "Come autumn, we'll have a whole stock of medicinal herbs to treat our patients. We're running low on just about everything and Osain isn't one to share his personal stores."

"Grumpy old bugger," Lestyn mutters.

That is the truth.

We walk the rest of the way in silence. He is long legged for a lad, easily matching my strides. All too soon, he'll be taller than me.

The barracks are abuzz with activity despite the hour. Foot soldiers in brown uniforms are streaming from their sleeping quarters, forming lines in front of the sparring pits. Their shields gleam in the torchlight, each bearing the sigil of Dyved—the flaming mountain. A dozen elite Ember Guild members are leading saddled horses from the stables, their deep maroon uniforms blending in with the darkness, their expressions solemn amid the chaos. I catch sight of a familiar face in their ranks and rush toward him.

"Farley!"

His head whips around at the sound of my voice. "Ace, what are you doing here?"

"That's what I was about to ask you. Is there damage from the quake?"

"Minimal. It seems we were spared this time."

"Then why the ruckus? It's two hours till first light."

"We're headed out. Cadogan has called for reinforcements by the North Sea. Apparently the Frostlanders have been even more aggressive than usual."

Behind me, Lestyn lets out a soft gasp. I grimace at the mention of Dyved's eastern neighbor—an ice-capped, inhospitable wasteland inhabited by marauding pirates, whose lack of fertile land leaves them more inclined toward raiding unsuspecting enemies than growing crops of their own. Usually they turn their opportunistic gaze to lands across the sea. Judging by the armed brigade gathering before me, they are taking a look at plunder closer to home.

"Their longships have been spotted not far off the coast," Farley continues. "They circle like vultures, thinking to strike when we are weak. We plan to remind them there is nothing weak about Dyvedi forces, even after Fyremas." He pauses, voice dropping with intent. "*Especially* after Fyremas."

"Will they truly attack us?" Lestyn interjects, sounding scared.

Farley's light green eyes flicker briefly to the boy. "Hard to say."

"Surely they do not court a full-scale war," I murmur.

"In the past, they have never been so foolish as to try. But we once thought the same about the Reavers. These are strange times. Our enemies seem just as unpredictable as the weather of late."

I glance up at the dark sky. Even now, in the wee hours, the clouds are thick enough to obscure the stars. "Who will protect the city with all of you gone?"

"Why, *you* of course." His expression turns playful. "For who would dare attack Caeldera with the mighty light bringer here to fry them where they stand?"

"I'm being serious."

"So am I! Between you and Pendefyre, no one would dare attack the capital again. Fire and air, together? Only a fool would court such an incendiary end."

Fire and air.

Together.

I very nearly snort, so absurd is the assumption. I have seen neither hide nor hair of the man in question since he returned from his most recent mission. He may now be back inside the crater, but if not for the bond, I would not know he was here at all.

"Even so," Farley hurries to add, no doubt seeing my dubious expression, "Mabon will remain behind with his unit to secure the perimeters and patrol the surrounding lands until we return."

"And when will that be? How long will you be away?"

"I don't know. Could be a fortnight, could be a year." His

lips tug up at one side. "Don't look so forlorn, Ace. You're damn near immortal, remember? Even if I hobble back home in a hundred years with gray in my hair and wrinkles at my temples, you'll still be the picture of youth. If anyone should be sad, it's me. I'm the one who'll be sleeping on a moth-eaten bedroll for the foreseeable future. Nothing but cook-pot porridge and saddle rash await on the road."

If his words are meant to cheer me up, they have the opposite effect. A horrifying flood of emotion gathers behind my eyes. I cannot help it—the thought of losing my last friend in this broken city is enough to rattle my precarious composure.

Farley gapes at me in horror, his expression somewhat blurry through my tears. "Gods, woman, stop that at once!"

"I'm sorry!" I cry, equally horrified.

"Don't be sorry, just don't *cry*!"

"I'm *not* crying!"

"Could've fooled me. Honestly, if I'd known you'd be so heartbroken I was leaving, I would've avoided you along with all my suitors. Clingy, the lot of them. I swear, nothing kills my affection quite so fast as someone expressing an overabundance of their own."

Despite my sadness, I can't help laughing. "You're awful."

"In demand, that's what I am. You may be the bringer of light, but I'm the breaker of hearts."

"*Dropper of breeches* might be more accurate."

Lestyn suppresses a giggle.

"Oh, good, she's back to insulting me." Farley grins. "She must be over her devastation."

I suck in an unsteady breath, desperately holding back the sob that's building in my throat. "I know the true reason you're leaving."

"Oh?"

"Now that I've mastered twyllo, you're afraid to play any more hands against me. You won't risk emptying your coin purse."

"Ah yes. That's it exactly." He reaches out and ruffles my hair playfully, mussing the plaited platinum strands. "How could I be so woefully transparent?"

Behind us, the foot soldiers are beginning to depart, streaming out of the barracks and down King's Avenue in orderly rows. I know the Ember Guild will be quick to follow suit. Already, half of them have mounted their horses. The night is full of jangling tackle and muffled whinnies.

Farley casts a quick glance over his shoulder, regret staining his expression. "Ace—"

Before he can say his goodbyes, I move forward and wrap my arms around him, squeezing so hard he lets out an audible whoosh of air.

"Be safe," I order gruffly.

He doesn't say anything. Merely hugs me hard before turning to haul himself up onto the back of a glossy speckled mare with a wavy black mane. Lestyn steps closer to me, as if lending me all the strength his slight form has to offer. Together, we watch Farley steer his mount to the front of the line. But the soft clop of his mare's hooves is quickly overshadowed by the piercing clangor of another horse charging down King's Avenue.

We turn to watch as the approaching rider, cloak billowing behind him in the darkness, jerks back his reins and clatters to a halt several paces away. His stallion's flanks are coated with lather—wherever he rode from, he did so at great speed. The beast swings its head back and forth in clear distress at the sudden stop, nostrils flaring, teeth bared against its bit. The rider makes no move to soothe his mount. His attention is reserved for the gathered company of Ember Guild. His scarred face contorts as he takes their measure.

General Yale, high commander of Dyved's armies, has arrived. And he does not look happy.

"What is the meaning of this?" Yale barks.

"What does it look like, General?" Farley's voice, only moments ago full of playfulness and good humor, is stripped bare. "We ride for the northern coast to lend aid to our fellow soldiers."

At this news, Yale's glare intensifies tenfold. I myself have been on the receiving end of that glare in the past—more times than I care to recount. I shy backward into the shadows, pulling Lestyn along with me.

"Go on ahead," I whisper in the darkness. "Head to the infirmary. I will meet you there."

"But—"

"*Go.*"

Lestyn, face set in a displeased pout, scurries off down the lane, his spindly arms holding the basket I shoved into them. I should follow him. If Yale sees me, it will only further blacken his mood. Yet my feet feel rooted to the street.

"I sanctioned no such deployment," the general growls at Farley, hazel-gold eyes flashing. The long scar that splices the left side of his face only heightens his wrathful look.

"With all due respect, General," Farley retorts, "last I checked, you did not command the Ember Guild."

"But I do oversee the legion of foot soldiers who march with you. No doubt that is why you chose to depart in the middle of the night." His gloved hands tighten on the reins. "So I ask again—on whose orders do you march north?"

"The king's."

A bitter scoff sounds in the night. "I see no king here."

Farley's mouth goes slack. A ripple of unease cuts through the gathered cavalry as Yale's words are repeated in hushed whispers and low grunts, spreading down the row of mounted Ember Guild fighters, gaining momentum as they move through the lines of foot soldiers who now wait, solemn and still, for permission to walk on. My own face pales. This is tantamount to open rebellion. To question the orders of the king shows a blatant disregard for the sovereign himself, as well as a more sweeping disdain for anyone who seeks to supplant the general's authority.

I wish, with a fervency that surprises me, that Yale had not been among the survivors pulled from the wreckage of the palace after the turrets came down. If anyone deserved to perish beneath tons of rubble and stone, it was him. He, who did not even fight with us in the streets, driving back the enemy with blade and bow. He, who instead hid in the safety of the keep as his battalions bled and died at the end of Reaver axes.

This is the man who now feels entitled to question Pendefyre's motivations? To sow seeds of doubt among his men?

No.

An uncontrollable surge of anger sweeps through me. I've taken several steps out of the shadows before I am even conscious of moving, my head craning backward to meet Yale's eyes, my voice cracking out like a whip.

"Careful, General. For someone who clambers so desperately for power, you seem perilously close to forfeiting yours."

His cutting gaze fixes on me immediately, gaining a vulturine edge. His mouth twists—half malice, half anticipation. "Well, well. If it isn't the Champion of Caeldera. I assumed you'd abandoned the city, I've seen so little of you. One might think you were avoiding my presence."

My teeth gnash. "For me to avoid you, I'd first need to consider your whereabouts. I don't make a habit of wasting my energy on such inconsequential matters."

Yale's cold stare chills to a temperature that rivals the Cimmerian summit. Digging his knees into his horse's sides to spur it into motion, he begins to circle slowly around me. I keep still, refusing to pivot with him, my gaze locked straight ahead. Farley and the rest of the soldiers look on, increasingly nervous. Their muffled shuffles are overshadowed by the steady clop of the stallion's hoofbeats against the cobblestones.

"None of this concerns you, wind weaver," Yale booms, loud enough for all to hear. "You may have wormed your way into Pendefyre's close counsel, but you have no authority here."

"Nor do you," I counter.

"Perhaps not over the Ember Guild, but the army is mine. And my foot soldiers will not be marching anywhere tonight—or any night—without my categorical permission."

I curl my hands into fists, trying to contain my anger. At my chest, my Remnant coils with serpentine menace, promising to put a lethal end to this conversation whenever I see fit.

You could send him flying into the stone wall with one flick of your wrist, a sinuous voice inside me whispers. *You could toss him the length of the sparring pits in the span of a single heartbeat. You could summon a power that would shatter his bones. You could starve the air from his lungs until he mottles purple with death.*

I shove down the voice and find my own. "Your orders are overridden, General. The king—"

"As I said, I see no king here."

"Then I suggest you look harder."

His brows shoot up, almost comically. "What did you say, girl?"

"*Look,*" I enunciate. "*Harder.*"

The words have no sooner left my mouth than the hoofbeats become apparent to all within earshot. They ring out in the night, a violent bellwether. A shiver of awareness races down my spine as I, along with everyone else on the street, turn to watch the King of Dyved steer his stallion out of the shadows, surely as if I have conjured him. And perhaps in a way I have. The bond between us is a precarious thing when emotions spill over unbidden. Penn seems incapable of feeling my distress without seeking out the cause and, whenever possible, mitigating it.

I had sensed his imminent approach, but still find myself affected by the sight of him. He cuts a foreboding figure against the harsh backdrop of night. Clad in all black, from the hilt of the broadsword sheathed across his back to the tips of his worn leather boots, it is difficult to see where his form ends and that of Onyx, his huge ebony stallion, begins.

"Soldiers," he bellows at the waiting battalion as he rides past. "On your way!"

The unit responds instantly, resuming their march down King's Avenue without another moment of hesitation. The Ember Guild is quick to follow, spurring their mounts into motion, taking up the rear of the procession toward the tunnel that leads out of the crater. Farley winks at me, a half smile playing at his lips, as his speckled mare passes by.

Penn pulls Onyx sharply to a halt beside me. The bond between us thrums like a lute string.

"General," he greets curtly.

Yale, who has finally ceased his slow circling, bows his head in a mockery of respect. "King Pendefyre."

"What an unexpected surprise. I thought you were busy securing our borders. Yet here you are."

"The surprise was all mine, I assure you. I was already on my way here bearing important news from the southern front." Yale's lips curl with distaste, as though he's swallowed something foul. "When word reached me last night regarding this deployment, I made extra haste."

"An unnecessary exercise."

"On that, we disagree." Yale's grip on his reins tightens. "Though we disagree on many things, it seems, if you've sanctioned more northbound soldiers without my input."

"Oh? Do you have a problem with my orders?"

Yale bares his teeth in a bitter smile. "I'm merely surprised that you did not seek my counsel on the matter. Our forces are already stretched thin. We lost so many at Fyremas."

"You do not need to remind me of those we lost, Yale. I fought alongside them as they fell. I watched the light leave their eyes, while others"—Penn pauses artfully—"sheltered inside the keep."

"I was defending our queen."

Penn scoffs. "You were defending yourself."

I suck in a breath at the vengeance that furrows the general's scarred features. The air between the men grows so thick and heavy, I think it will crystallize, then plummet to the cobblestones and shatter to pieces. My eyes move back and forth between them as they glare at each other from their mounts. A dozen paces divide them on the now empty street.

"Don't you two have more important things to do than bicker over old battles?" I interject when I can no longer stand the silence. "Fyremas is behind us. We should focus on the future of Dyved, not the past."

Yale's eyes move to me. "What I discuss and who I discuss it with is no concern of yours, child."

"You may outrank me in years, General, but if anyone here is acting like a child, it is you."

"How quickly you bite back! Rather like the rabid bitch that took up residence in the stables of my boyhood home one summer. It looked innocent enough from afar, but as soon as your fingers were within range . . ." Yale shakes his head mockingly. "Ferocious little thing. Far better for everyone at the manor when it found itself another place to live, where it could no longer distract our purebred hunting hounds from their duties."

Penn does not seem to enjoy the general's personal anecdote, nor the thinly veiled implications behind it. A pulse of anger shoots through the bond, nearly strong enough to knock me sideways. In my peripheral, his fingers tense against his strong thigh as he leans slightly forward in his saddle.

"A warning, Jareth," Penn says, the casual use of the general's given name somewhat at odds with his biting tone. "You have long held the reins that steer our armies. But those reins can be passed to another at a single word from me. It would be unwise to forget that."

"Just as it would be unwise to unseat the leader every soldier in Dyved has spent two decades looking to with trust and loyalty. You may now be their king, but it is me they answer to. It is me who ruled when your sister was otherwise occupied with the less bloody parts of sovereignty."

"Do not mistake me for my sister. Queen Vanora may have been more concerned with her garden parties and grand balls than the oversight of our armies, but I have no plans to continue that neglectful strategy. It has not served us well."

Yale reels back as though Penn has punched him, his expression stunned. "Are you implying that I am somehow responsible for the Reavers' invasion? That I somehow failed in my task as commanding general?"

"I'm saying that perhaps if Vanora had shown more interest

in the security of our borders, such a breach would never have occurred."

"I did everything possible—"

"And yet." Penn cuts him off. "Posts were attacked, our guards replaced in the dark of night by Efnysien's red army, without you ever sensing something was amiss."

I thought the air tense before, but it reaches new heights of animosity. Yale's scar is stark white against the deepening flush of rage blooming over his expression.

"How easy it is for you, *my king*"—he spits the title like a curse—"to make judgments about my choices. To lay blame at my feet. But you have no right to judge me. You were not here. You were off in the Midlands, scouring the realm for signs of your precious wind weaver. And you found her—but at what cost?" His gold eyes cut to me for a brief moment, brimming with dislike. "I hope she was worth it. For her, you forsook your kingdom. For her, you abandoned your people. For her—"

"Enough!"

I flinch at the brutality of Penn's roar as well as the shower of sparks that shoots from the tips of his fingers and scatters to the cobblestones between the two horses. Both stallions skitter nervously, widening the gap between the men as they shy away. Yale finally falls silent, perhaps wise enough to recognize he is treading on dangerous ground.

"You said you had an urgent missive." Penn's jaw is clenched tight with leashed fury. "Deliver it."

Yale's spine is ramrod. His voice is equally stiff. "Word arrived from Coldcross; scouts spotted the Llŷrian army passing through the Avian Strait at nightfall."

So Soren has returned.

My stomach flips.

"Do they have any prisoners with them?"

Yale shrugs at Penn's question. "I do not know."

"And the king?"

"If King Soren rode among them, my scouts did not see him. But if the Llŷrians have returned, it is safe to assume their business in the Southlands has reached a conclusion."

A current of foreboding sluices through the air.

In the wake of Fyremas, Soren chased Efnysien south, intent on bringing him to justice for his crimes. I've harbored stubborn optimism that he will succeed in catching the dark sorcerer before he disappears behind the impenetrable boundaries of Dymmeria, that shadowy desert realm he calls home. Pendefyre has been decidedly less optimistic about the Llŷrian king's odds.

If Soren's soldiers have returned north after such a short time without any prisoners in tow . . . perhaps I should've shared in his pessimism.

"Anything else to report?" he prompts Yale.

"The Reavers at the southwestern border continue to encroach," the general responds tersely. "We have driven the clans back onto the ice shelf time and again, but they persist. A strong show of force is needed to obliterate them once and for all. Instead, you've sent our troops marching in the opposite direction."

"I trust my lieutenants. They say the Frostlanders pose an imminent threat to the northern shores. I will not leave us open to an attack on both borders, not on some whim of revenge."

"Revenge?" Yale scoffs. "It would not be revenge to exterminate every last bit of Reaver scum from the face of this earth. It would be justice. Or have you forgotten they would have happily done the same to us? They will not stop until they have eradicated all fae. I merely suggest we return the favor in kind."

"The clans are not only warriors. There are children there. Expectant mothers. Elderly."

"Future and former monsters." Yale spits on the cobblestones. "I would slaughter every newborn babe on the ice shelf myself, given the chance."

My whole frame jolts.

Penn's eyes flash to me for a brief moment. He's sensed my sudden flush of horror through the bond. "Your appetite for vengeance is irrelevant, General."

But Yale is not finished. "There was a time, not so very long ago, when you would have been in total agreement with me in this regard. Tell me, Pendefyre . . . when did you become so soft?" His eyes pin me in place. "Or would the better question be *for whom*?"

"Tread lightly," Penn clips, his rage manifest.

"I see I've stumbled upon a sensitive topic." His golden eyes never leave my face, nor does his expression shift from the malicious sneer it has settled into. "I did warn you, wind weaver. Did I not? Are you so blind you cannot see how your position here compromises everyone in this kingdom? Or merely so selfish you do not care about the lives you put at risk?"

I flinch as his words make impact.

"Yale—"

The general cuts off Penn's attempt to interject. His tone is savage as he continues, "I think it must be the latter. Only someone entirely self-serving would be able to stomach standing so proud in the rubble of the city she made a target; walking among the survivors of an attack aimed at her." His lips flatten into a stern line. "Why do you think so many have fled? No one can stand the sight of you, so supercilious, so smug. Masquerading as a hero. We all know the truth. You are the root cause of every evil that plagues this kingdom. You are—"

"ENOUGH!"

Pendefyre's bellow is so loud, it pierces the sky. I flinch again as the sound of it rebounds off the walls of the barracks, echoes out over the lake.

Yale wisely stops talking.

"I will permit your insubordination toward me," Penn growls, fisting his reins in a white-knuckled grip. "I will even tolerate your attempts to undermine my authority in front of my men. But one more word spoken against Rhya and you will find yourself out of a position."

The general's teeth grind together in an effort to contain his anger. Even if he could not manage to remain silent, it scarcely matters. Penn is done listening. Using his knees to steer Onyx, he bends at the middle, reaches down to hook me beneath the arms, and hauls me up before him in the saddle. The move is so abrupt, I nearly cry out. My ass is barely settled when Penn's heels press to the stallion's flanks, spurring him into a gallop. Away from Yale. But I know, even as I am carried far out of earshot, his scathing words will follow me wherever I go.

CHAPTER
FIVE

Ⓦe ride for several hours.

I have not been beyond the limits of Caeldera for well over a month, and am surprised to see whatever odd weather patterns plague the capital city have spared the rest of the plateau. The kingdom is in the full throes of late spring. The deep snows I've come to expect have melted away, leaving behind a world of lush grass, flowering shrubs, and thickly leafed trees. After weeks spent beneath constant cloud cover, I find myself looking around in a mix of confusion and wonderment as we ride through the sun-dappled forest, passing the occasional guard tower and checkpoint. Each is outfitted with soldiers clad in Dyvedi brown, armed to the teeth.

King Pendefyre is taking no chances with another invasion.

The morning slips away. I do not ask where he is taking me, and he does not offer up the information. I content myself with savoring the rarity of the moment—pushing aside the obligations that await us both in Caeldera as I slump back against Penn's warm chest and allow his ever-present heat to sink into my spine. It is not enough to drive off the chill that has settled over me since Fyremas, but it helps.

I feel the maegic singing in my bones even before the forest yields to a craggy coastline where the wild ocean meets the western shore. It has been so long since I saw the sea. My heart cries out for the comforting rhythm of crashing waves and tidal breezes I knew for all my youth. But the strange cove that comes into view is as unlike Seahaven's white sands as I can fathom.

The frothing bay is ringed with dozens of oddly shaped tidal pools, the waters within them still and shiny and tinted a greenish-yellow hue. The air smells strongly of brine and sulfur, stinging my eyes until they gloss with tears. There is no dune, no beach. As Onyx slows to a stop his hooves crunch on crystalline salt deposits thicker than frost. Closer examination of the shallow pools reveals they are not home to any darting, jewel-scaled creatures or tough-shelled crabs; they are stagnant and steaming, their viscous surfaces belching occasional puffs of boiling vapor.

"What is this place?" I ask, tasting fumes on each breath as I look around.

"Blister Bight."

With that succinct answer, Penn swings down from the saddle, then offers me a hand to help me dismount. My fingers tingle with warmth as they clasp his, but he releases me as soon as my feet hit the ground. Leaving Onyx to wait beneath the battered trees at the edge of the forest, we pick a path between the bubbling vats, our boots crunching in the thick salt. Deep beneath the surface, a thick chord of power pulses through the earth, like a mallet on a drum. Like a heartbeat. Something alive, something ancient, vibrating up from Anwyvn's very core, creeping through the cracks between the pools.

I shudder as I gulp pure maegic into my lungs with each breath, feeling it fill my veins and permeate my bloodstream. The Remnant mark on my breast throbs with suppressed power, an icy burn against my flesh—so antithetical to the air, which grows hotter and hotter as we move deeper into the ring of odd sulfuric pools. I have been in places of natural power before, from Seahaven's Starlight Wood to the portal at the heart of the Forsaken Forest to the warded chamber tucked away behind Caeldera's great falls . . . but this is by far the most potent.

Penn's shoulders move visibly beneath his cloak as he breathes deep. The maegic is affecting him, too. I can see the flush of it on the exposed skin at his neck, reddening the sharp cut of his cheekbones. His hands are fisted tightly at his sides, and I know his control is being sorely tested.

"Is there a portal here?"

Without answering aloud, he points to the left. My eyes follow the gesture beyond the field of pools. I spot it almost instantly—a jagged arch of slate gray rocks, stacked one atop another to form a nondescript doorway. A faint shimmer disturbs the air around it, the only indication of the glamour that conceals it from mortal eyes.

"Are we using it?"

"No." Penn answers without breaking stride.

"Why are we here, then?"

"I want to show you something."

My brows lift. "What?"

"You'll see."

I heave a sigh.

"Not much farther," he notes, sounding somewhat entertained by my impatience.

We come to the largest of the pools, set at the edge of the bight, just out of reach of the waves' spraying foam. Twice as wide as the others and several feet deeper, it is a vivid orange color striated liberally with yellow and green. To my utter delight, it is surrounded by dozens of lounging lizard-like creatures with bodies of near-identical coloring to the pool. A natural camouflage. Some are small enough to fit in the palm of my hand, others are the size of a house cat. They pay us little mind as they doze on the superheated rocks. A smile stretches my lips wide as I watch one of their black tongues flick out—and, with it, a small fireball that floats up into the sky.

"Are they dragons?" I ask, enchanted by the sight.

"No. They are fymandridae. Fire salamanders."

I drop into a crouch, wanting a closer look, and am rewarded with fiery warnings from the creatures closest to me. Several tiny fireballs shoot in my direction and I jolt backward into Penn's legs, nearly knocking him over in the process.

"Sorry." I giggle as he helps me regain my feet. "They surprised me."

He stares at me for a long moment, his eyes intent. They are swimming with fire maegic, two pools of molten lava that scorch me where I stand.

"Don't apologize," he whispers. "It's been a long time since I heard your laugh or saw your smile."

The smile slips off my mouth. I swallow hard, ignoring the way my stomach clenches. "Is that why you brought me here?"

"Is it so inconceivable that I would seek to make you happy?"

"No," I murmur. "I just . . ."

He sounds suddenly tired. "Just *what*, Rhya?"

"You have avoided my presence for weeks now. For months, in fact. You have gone out of your way to create distance between us, ever since—" My teeth dig into my bottom lip, containing the rest of my words.

"Since?" he prompts.

Since you kissed me. Since I felt your body against mine, your hands in my hair, your fire in my blood. Since you held my pleasure in your callused palm, and I in turn stoked yours to a searing blaze I can still feel each time I close my eyes.

I want to say it, but embarrassment stills my tongue. My cheeks are burning. I tell myself it is from the heated air off the pools, not my deep mortification.

"Since Fyremas," I finish weakly. "Since the battle. It's like we are strangers again."

He is silent for a long time, absorbing my words. I can see the toll they take on him as much as I can feel his tension through our bond. Eventually, he breaks eye contact and looks out over the bight, his gaze scanning beyond the bubbling pools to the dark blue sea.

"It's not you I'm avoiding," he says finally. "It's everyone. Everything. The entire bloody kingdom. The entire bloody world, and all who inhabit it."

He shakes his head, weariness stealing over his features. The shadows beneath his eyes are so deep, I ache to trace my fingertips over the hollows, to soothe them away. I knot my fingers together behind my back to keep from doing so.

"Since that night," Penn continues in a rough voice, "all I do is replay my mistakes over and over again. Each failing. Each life lost. I cannot be in the present. Not while I am consumed by the past. Not while I am haunted by the future that still awaits."

"Efnysien, you mean." I chew my lip. "You want payback."

"He will pay for his crimes, Rhya."

"Soren has returned to the Northlands. Perhaps—"

"If Soren had succeeded in killing him, we would know about it by now. You think he would deny himself the opportunity to crow about his own success?" Penn shakes his head, still not looking at me. "No. Efnysien lives. Hidden away in his shadowy spires. Biding his time until he can strike at us again."

Anxiety stirs deep in my gut. "I know you fear another attack on your people. I know that's why you've been so fixated on strengthening the wards. But, Penn, surely we are safe. At least for a time. Surely—"

"*Safe?* We are not safe."

"But—"

"It's not just the threat of Efnysien or his red army. Violence gathers in the air. With the Reavers to the southwest and the Frostlanders in the northeast, we are penned between two enemies eager for our demise." His teeth grit together as his jaw ticks. "The blight worsens more each season. Our fields are failing, our crops dying on the vine. Between the increase in quakes and the influx of all manner of vile creatures coming down from the Cimmerians . . . we are vulnerable in ways we have never been before. Our troops are already stretched too thin as it is. I fear we are living in a house of cards. The faintest breeze will cast us into utter ruin."

"This burden is not yours alone, Pendefyre."

"No?" He scoffs bitterly.

"It does not need to be. Not if you would let me help you. Let me take a turn charging the wards."

His response is instant. "Absolutely not."

"Why?"

"You will not risk your life for my kingdom."

"But you'll risk yours?"

"As I said," he retorts flatly, "it's *my* kingdom."

I push aside the hurt those words—however accurate—births inside me. It is true, Caeldera is not my home. Not really. I do not have a home anymore. But his blunt reminder of that fact wounds me far more deeply than I will ever admit.

"Promise me," he demands. "Promise me you won't go anywhere near the wards. Promise me you won't put yourself in undue jeopardy."

"Fine," I agree grudgingly. "Then put me to work some other

way. I am not entirely useless with a bow. Let me help Mabon with the perimeter patrols. Send me to the front lines with Jac and Cadogan, so I may—"

He cuts me off. "Out of the question."

"Penn—"

"You are no soldier."

My eyes narrow on his profile, still turned away from me. "I've done battle before. I've taken lives. I've fought side by side with your men."

"That was not the same."

"What does that mean?"

He is silent for a long beat. "It means I want you safe. You have done enough already. Besides, you have your work at the infirmary to keep you busy. You are needed there, not on the battlefield."

"Most of our cots are empty. Only a handful of patients from Fyremas remain, and those will soon be discharged. Lestyn and Osain can handle whatever cases of summer croup arise without me."

"No."

I rear back at the flat rejection. "No? Just . . . plain *no*? We can't even discuss it?"

"Rhya, please. I did not bring you here to spar."

"Ah yes, I'm only here to giggle at the fire salamanders like a dim-witted schoolgirl."

"*Skies,*" he snarls. "You're utterly impossible, you know that?"

"Rich, coming from you."

"Bringing you here was a mistake. I thought I might give you a few hours' respite from your misery. Foolish of me to try. It won't happen again."

"Penn—"

"No. I was right before, to retain some distance between us. I do not have the energy to fight with you, and I do not have time to worry about you meddling in matters that do not concern you."

My hands plant on my hips as my eyes narrow to slits. My temper is flaring and, with it, my maegic. Air currents charge beneath my skin, struggling to burst forth in an all-consuming vortex despite my attempts to calm the raging storm within.

"Forgive me," I hiss, my voice cold as the wind that chases away all traces of spring warmth. "I did not realize my continued presence in your city was such a burden."

"Do not put words in my mouth."

"I would not need to put words in your mouth if you ever volunteered what you are thinking."

"You truly want to know?"

"Well, I did not ask the question merely to revel in the sound of my own voice."

His head turns as he finally looks back at me. When I see his eyes, I realize why he's been avoiding my gaze. They are so full of emotion and maegic, it steals my breath. His voice is raw.

"I worry about you. Is that what you need to hear? *I worry about you.* More than my city, more than my citizens, more than the fate of all Anwyvn. Every day, I worry what will happen when Efnysien returns. Every day, I worry that when he does, this time he will succeed in taking you away from me."

My anger dissolves, swamped by stronger emotions. I try to battle them back, but I am no match for them. "And what do you think I worry about, Pendefyre? My patients? My lack of purpose? My role in Uther's death? My ruined friendship with Carys? My future as a Remnant? The prophecy? The salvation of our entire realm?" My voice breaks on a brittle laugh. "No. Those are the things I *should* be worried about."

I take a step closer to him. My eyes never shift from his. My voice drops to a shattered whisper. "Instead, I worry about you, Penn. I am plagued by visions of you locked away in that ward chamber each night, a man possessed. Killing yourself by giving too much, just like King Vorath. I cannot sleep at night, tossing and turning, wondering where you are. Wondering if you even still live, or if you've finally succeeded in what seems to me a suicide mission."

"I will not repeat Vorath's mistakes."

"No?" Tears gloss my eyes. "That is little consolation when I have seen for myself how close to the edge you are walking. When I have pulled you back from the brink with my own two hands."

"I told you—"

"I don't care what you told me! Gods, Penn . . ." One more step brings us face-to-face. My neck cranes to hold his eyes, which are burning with flames that seem to ignite hotter with each word I rasp. "I cannot eat. I cannot sleep. I cannot focus on my tasks. I cannot even *breathe*, thinking that you may not. So please, do not speak to me of misplaced priorities. You are not the only one who lacks the luxury of choosing the things they care for, the reasons their heart beats, and the motives for which they want our world rebuilt."

His expression is a portrait of desperation, though his words are determined. "But I can choose. I *do* choose."

I flinch. "Your precious control."

"My city," he corrects, jaw tight as a vise. "My people."

I cannot fault him for that. I cannot even be surprised by it. For he has sung this refrain before, has made his position on this—*us*—more than apparent.

Emotions are a liability.

The things we want most in this world, the things that make us feel the most intensely . . . those are the things we cannot have.

Perhaps it is selfish of me to push the issue. Perhaps it is futile to ask him for things he cannot give me. Perhaps it is shortsighted to long so hopelessly for an ephemeral fix to an everlasting problem. But I cannot care about that. Not with him standing an arm's length away. Not with his eyes searing into mine. Not with the bond a live current of power and pining.

The emotions between us are a jumble—love, hate, regret, resentment. I cannot begin to sort out which belong to me and which stem from him.

A single tear streaks down my cheek. "You are many things, Pendefyre, but I never thought you were a coward."

Jerking my gaze from his, I turn my back to him and wrap my arms around my middle, as if to contain the relentless grief. My watering eyes fix on the salamanders basking by the viridescent pool. They blink back at me, translucent eyelids moving horizontally across angular pupils, turning their vibrant eyes opaque. As I watch, several of them scurry out of sight, retreating to burrows in the pitted rocks or slipping under the viscous surface of the pools. The sun has retreated as well, a dense bank of clouds swiftly casting the entirety of Blister Bight in heavy shadow. The hot, sulfuric air is suddenly thick with impending rain.

"Take me back," I say, my voice flat.

Not *home*. Just as Penn said, Caeldera is his home—his kingdom—not mine.

Two arms slide around me without warning. I do not resist as I am pulled back against a warm, strong chest. The bandolier of blades presses tight to my spine through my thin novitiate uniform. And though I try my damnedest not to listen, to shore up my heart with anger, a levee within me breaks wide open anyway as soon as I feel the brush of his lips against my lobe, as soon as I hear his deep, rasping voice in my ear.

"Skies, Rhya, if I could, I would lose myself in you. Utterly.

But in doing so, I would lose my grip on everything that allows me to wake up each day and walk the ruined streets of my city without cowering. I would lose my determination to set things to rights."

His lips skim the column of my throat, where my pulse pounds double time. His tone pitches even lower. "If I bury myself in you . . ." I shiver against him, powerless to stop the heat that furls through me. "I will never come up for air."

"So it must be all or nothing?" I whisper bleakly. "We must either be everything to each other or nothing at all?"

A low, tortured groan rattles in his throat. "*Yes*. Gods help me, yes. That's how it has to be."

"For how long?" I ask. "Forever?"

"Do not ask me that."

His clear devastation stirs mine. I feel it in the bond as plainly as I hear it in his voice.

"Infernal hells! I can't be—" He breaks off, control slipping. His fingertips dig into my skin. "I don't want—"

"You don't want what?"

He spins me around in his arms, the movement so fast I see stars. His expression is at war with itself, a plain divide of self-castigation and unflagging need. I cannot predict which will win out. Not until he mutters, "Forever can start tomorrow."

Then he yanks me fully against him, one arm a steely band around my waist, the other delving deep into the thick coils of hair at my nape. Before I can make a sound, his lips come down on mine.

Penn's mouth is hard. Unyielding. Almost angry. He kisses me like a punishment—whether for me or for himself, I'm not sure. Perhaps it is for both of us. Me for driving him to this state, him for caving to it.

For this is an unacceptable lapse of his rigid self-restraint, an abhorrent deviation from his plans to hold me at bay. A tiptoe into a forbidden pool of lust we've only just sworn never to submerse ourselves in.

And, gods help us, that makes it all the more glorious.

His lips set me aflame, fan the swirling ache inside me to a blaze that soon becomes a wildfire. Every kiss I've ever had before Pendefyre's pales in comparison. Not that I've had many. Tomas, the baker's apprentice back in Seahaven, was sweet. Kind. Slow, drugging kisses on summer nights, a flurry of buckles and bodice laces, quiet reassurances in the aftermath. His boyish love was a secret whispered into my skin.

Penn's touch is no murmured sweet nothing. No whisper. It is a scream. A shriek. A desperate heat that sinks into my bones. His fingers sear trails of fire across my skin. His mouth bruises. Passion ripples through me like supercharged air over a steaming kettle. I think I might begin to breathe pure flame like one of the fymandridae as our tongues and teeth dance together; as our heads slant this way and that, warring even as we yield.

My whole body trembles with yearning. I press myself flush against him, wind my arms around his neck, skim my shaking fingers along the sharp slant of his jaw. Craving a closeness that is not mine to claim. Pressing hard against his chest, as if physical proximity might somehow also permit me into the chambers of the heart beating within.

And yet, even in this moment, when I would happily throw all caution to the wind in favor of the less logical emotions thrumming through my body . . . When I would cast aside all my restraint, strip off any inhibitions along with my clothing . . .

Pendefyre rediscovers his own.

As I move closer, I can feel him retreating. His kisses slowing, his ironclad control supplanting the passion igniting in my very veins. My fingers dig into his shoulders, desperate to keep him, but I cannot. The tighter I try to hold, the faster he slips away. I feel the flames between us doused by harsh reality, the lust extinguished with a grim efficiency that leaves me clammy with cold.

He shutters the bond between us at the same instant his mouth breaks away. For no longer than a heartbeat, he allows his forehead to rest against mine. Then his arms unwind and he takes a purposeful stride backward.

That single step wounds me like a sword strike to the stomach.

He regards me with an expressionless mask—one that is all too familiar. The only sign he's at all affected by the kiss is in the teeth-grinding tightness of his jaw. The curl of his fists as they drop to his sides. And, perhaps, in the slight tremor in his voice when he speaks.

"The fymandridae have fled home. It's time we do as well. A storm is rolling in off the sea. We don't want to be here when it breaks."

I nod, for lack of a real response.

There is nothing more to say.

There is everything to say.

We walk in silence, our footsteps pulping the salt deposits. The sulfuric pools littered around us are dark now, steaming gray vats that reflect the overcast sky. With each passing moment, the air thickens with the promise of a downpour. By the time we reach Onyx, who is waiting dutifully beneath a scraggly tree exactly where we left him, the clouds are so black and ominous, it will take a miracle to make it back to Caeldera without getting drenched.

I hardly care. The idea of getting back on a horse, riding pressed close to Penn's chest for the next several hours when I can still taste him like blood in my mouth, while my skin still tingles from his touch, seems like a torture designed especially for me by the gods. The thought of a slow plod back to his city— back to a future that holds nothing but frigid civility and staunch self-restraint—seems the cruelest twist of fate I can conjure.

I feel, quite suddenly, that the star by which I have guided my life these past months since I came to Dyved has flickered out, leaving me alone in the darkness. My feet cease their approach without any cognizant decision to stop walking.

"Come," Penn orders flatly, gathering the reins in his hand. "Get on the horse."

In the distance, thunder rumbles.

I swallow hard. "No."

"What do you mean, *no*?"

"Just what I said. I'm not going."

"I do not have time for this. We need to get back. We've been away too long already. I have a meeting with the southern division leaders at dusk."

"Go, then," I say, feeling obstinate. "I'll find my own way."

Surely there is an inn nearby. A town where I can hire a horse of my own, or beg the aid of a kindly farmer who might let me hitch a ride on his capital-bound cart . . . *Anything*, to avoid getting back on Onyx in this moment.

Penn dashes my hopes in an instant. "This stretch of coast is desolate. There's not a single settlement for leagues."

Of course. That would be too easy.

"We are a four-hour ride from Caeldera," he continues flatly. "A full day's walk."

I confess, I do not much fancy an hours-long slog through the elements. My obstinance falters, my hope with it. Avoiding his eyes, my own sweep our immediate vicinity for another option. They widen slightly when I spot it on the other side of the pools, practically shimmering in welcome.

I look back at Penn. "I'll use the portal."

"Do not be reckless simply to spite me. You have never traveled by portal alone."

My teeth clench. "And?"

"Must you always be so oppositional?"

The thunder rumbles closer. "You and I have been bickering since the first moment we met. I see no reason to change that now. Not when everything else is to stay the same between us."

Penn runs his hands through his hair, tousling the sun-streaked strands. "I am not fighting with you about this. Not again."

"Again? You never fight about it at all! You merely shut it down. Then, you shut me out."

"I have no other choice."

My laugh is wintry. "There is always a choice. Perhaps not an easy one—but I have never asked for easy."

"Easy? You think this is *easy* for me? *You think any of my choices are easy?*" His words lift to a bellow. His eyes leap with fire as his fury rears its ugly head. "Gods, Rhya. Yale may be a consummate bastard, but he's right about one thing. When it comes to you, I cannot think straight. Cannot see straight. I cannot see anything but you. And that does no one any good—not you, not me, least of all my kingdom."

Something inside my chest crumbles to dust, pulverized by the devastating blow of his words. In my head, Yale's insidious whisper haunts me.

I hope she was worth it. For her, you forsook your kingdom. For her, you abandoned your people.

"So, he was right." I expel a fractured breath. "You see me as a liability."

Penn's jaw tightens. "I never said that."

"Not in so many words. Forgive me if I do not rejoice in

being described as a distraction to all you hold dear." My mind is suddenly spinning twice its normal speed, a match for the mad patter of my pulse. Beneath the strain of its frantic beats, my heart feels as though it is cracking into pieces—and, with it, everything I have come to know about my place in this world.

The one at Pendefyre's side.

"Rhya, just get on the horse."

"He said what happened on Fyremas was my fault," I whisper, as though he has not spoken. "That everyone blames me. That *you* blame me."

"I do not blame you. But—"

"But?"

He takes a shuddering breath. His brief pause is a fresh torment. "I will not lie to you in saying I have never considered the possibility that . . ."

"That what?"

"Maybe if I had been here instead of the Midlands, I would've—" He shakes his head. Swallows the words. Begins anew. "Maybe, once I returned, if I had been less distracted by—"

He does not finish the sentence. He does not need to; I read his intention in the silence, and finish it for him.

"By *me*." My voice is hollow.

A muscle leaps in his cheek as he works to control his emotions. He says nothing—either unwilling or unable to share his feelings on the subject. Holding me at arm's length.

As he always has.

As he always will.

Lightning splits the sky overhead as the storm finally breaks, a loud boom of thunder directly on its heels. I do not bother looking up at the bolts that streak over the sea as I turn my back on Penn and start walking toward the portal. Rain falls in a deluge, soaking me instantly to the skin.

"Rhya!" he yells over another guttural rumble of thunder. "Wait!"

I do not wait.

"Where are you going?"

"Away from here."

Away from you.

As I move, a small voice in the back of my mind pipes up that this is childish, that bolting from Penn's presence will not lessen the lash of his words. I silence that voice with a ruthless head-shake. The urge to flee, *now*, this very moment, has overridden any sense of logic that might normally guide my actions.

I increase my pace as I close the gap between me and the archway of stone. When I reach it, I pause to look back at him. He is six paces away, standing rigid with tension. His expression is even darker than the storm that looms overhead.

"What I said before . . ." He shakes his head swiftly. "You must know, I did not mean . . ."

"I know exactly what you meant, Pendefyre." My voice wobbles. I steady it, along with my shoulders. "Without me around, you might have seen the Reaver disaster coming and moved to prevent it. You cannot forgive yourself for letting me into your heart—not at the sake of your beloved self-possession." My rag-ged inhale is rife with pain. "More, you cannot forgive me. For it was on me that Efnysien set his sights that night. It was me who spurred him into action. I am the spark that lit the fire . . . and now your home is naught but ashes."

He pales as I speak the words, but he does not contradict them.

Lightning flashes again, splitting the sky. Thunder booms a ferocious response. I can no longer tell if the wetness of my cheeks is from the rain or my own grief.

Reaching out, I bring my palm down on the sharp edge of

one of the slate rocks. Blood spurts with a sudden slice of pain. It drips down the lengths of my fingers as I lift them into the middle of the archway. The portal activates instantly, a flood of pure daylight emanating from it. Tendrils of maegic reach out toward me, urging me forward. I resist for a moment—just long enough to glance back at Penn.

He is stock-still, watching me. His hair is plastered against his head, his saturated clothing steaming faintly as his immense body heat evaporates the cold water that continues to cascade from the clouds.

"Don't follow me," I tell him in a choked voice.

Then, I step through.

CHAPTER
SIX

I had forgotten the diaphanous delirium of traveling by portal. How it turns flesh and bone to dust and particle, how it reduces all that is solid into a disorienting state of nonexistence. All is light, all is aether, all is aglow. And I . . . I am nothing. An entity entirely distinct from my body. A wraith, moving at warp speed across the land.

The vast network of leylines is almost impossible to behold. It spreads across Anwyvn—through it, rather, like veins through a body. Gossamer as the web of a spider in sunlight, they branch off in all directions. Pathways of light, splitting and spiraling southward, beyond the borders of Dyved, beyond the range, beyond even the Midland kingdoms that lay on the other side.

The first time—the only time—I traveled thus before, it was at Penn's side. His hand holding mine, his soul a stalwart guide. No chance of getting lost, not with him. Still, he had warned me how important it is to know one's destination. To focus on it for the duration of your journey.

Only attempt to travel between portals when you know their precise locations.

I do try. Try to hold Caeldera in my mind, to envision the warded chamber atop the crater's rim where I intend to make my exit. Try to keep from getting distracted by the disorientation that grips me as I hurl through beams of purest light, a blinding symphony of white noise and leached color.

But I falter. For a split second, I allow my mind to muddle, my thoughts homed not on my task but, instead, caught up in the conversation I left behind at Blister Bight. In the man I left behind.

One fractured instant of inattention.

Still, it is enough to doom me.

My focus slips and, once it does, there is no regaining it. I lose my foothold on the path that guides me back to Caeldera and, faster than I would have thought possible, find myself completely unmoored. Flying through the aether without any true course, confronted with an infinity of unknown exits. None of which feels the least bit familiar.

Gods, what have I done?

Panic presses in, stealing even more of my concentration, making it all the more difficult to locate my intended target. Penn was right. This is reckless. I stare in increasing horror at the endless expanse of possible exit points, attempting to glean meaning like an astrologer picking out constellations in the vast blanket of stars. A handful terminate in bright orbs of light—the sign of a functional portal. Yet others appear sick. They flicker periodically, a weak throb of illumination that seems to dim with each passing moment. Many are entirely dark. Black and decaying, like the flesh of a gangrenous wound that requires amputation.

Dead ends.

These, I rush past without preamble, knowing they are not viable. Even if they are, I have a feeling they will not deposit me anywhere I want to be. For it would not serve me well to step out of a portal onto a Midlands battlefield where halflings are hunted on sight. Or worse, into the coarse sands of the South-lands where, by all accounts, my fate would be far more bar-baric. And far more swift.

My dissembled form is ferried like mist along a leyline that leads eastward, toward the heart of Dyved. So I think. I have very little concept of direction, very little cognizance at all.

How long have I been here?

Seconds, minutes, hours?

How far have I journeyed?

I feel I have been traveling for a single heartbeat and yet, also, an eternity. It is not merely time I am losing but ground. The earth slips by in a rush, leading me farther and farther from where I started.

I cast out my straining senses, trying to find some differenti-ation among the many options laid out before me. Trying to dis-tinguish some small nuance in the near-identical field of light orbs that dance on my periphery. I pass more and more dead portals, their rotten pathways a foreboding sight.

Would I, too, turn black and lifeless, lost here in an eternal loop? Unable to choose where to exit? Incapable of finding my way out?

Desperation mounts with each passing moment. If I could breathe, if I had lungs, I would be breathless, panting for air. If I had eyes from which to cry, I would weep. But my body is gone, no more than a memory. Reality is slipping away.

I am slipping away.

I cannot recall what I am doing here. I barely recall my own name. My very soul feels as though it is fraying at the seams as my frail mind struggles to contain the immensity of time's great fabric, the scope of a whole realm compressed into a single pane.

I have to get out of here.

Even if I end up in Carvage, my fate will be better than this slow atrophy into aether. I am prepared to choose at random, if only to escape the terrifying fray of my own consciousness. But then, finally, just as I have begun to lose all hope . . .

I feel it.

A pulse in the distance. Faint. Barely discernible at first. So weak I think it must be a hallucination born of delusional hope. Even if it is, I am too desperate to care. I follow it blindly, seeking out the current of familiarity.

Caeldera.

Please, gods, let it be Caeldera.

It is so far away. And I am so weak. The pathways before me diverge, branching in various directions. Dizzying directions. My mind is unable to think through the spinning.

What am I looking for?

Nothing.

Something.

The pulse.

Follow the pulse.

Where is it?

It's disappeared again.

Just as I will disappear.

Perhaps it never existed.

Perhaps you have gone mad.

No.

No.

There is somewhere I need to go.

There is someone I need to see.

A place of grief and ruin.

A man of fury and fire.

Caeldera.

Pendefyre.

The pulse comes again then, on the heels of my defiance. A

heartbeat in the abyss, leading me onward. The leylines branch and, at last, I see it. My exit. Far in the distance, brighter than the rest.

More vital.

More alive.

Almost like it is calling me.

Here.

Come here.

Come home.

I fix what little remains of my volition upon it, shut out every other possibility, and with a mental push from somewhere deep within, allow myself to be swept forward through the void. There is a rush of blinding white, a burst of nauseating speed, and then, with an abruptness that stupefies the senses, I am deposited out of the ephemeral plane and back into the real world. My bones reassemble, my tendons and sinews stitching back together in the space of a blink. Solid once more, I lurch forward out of the portal, landing hard on my hands and knees.

Bless the Goddess of Souls for not claiming mine this day.

For a few long seconds, I attempt to find my composure—dragging a series of tremulous breaths into my nose and out through my mouth, waiting for the nausea and disorientation to subside. Waiting for my scattered thoughts to sort themselves into something resembling normal cognition. When at last they do, I open my eyes to a luminous white floor of pure quartz. I blink at it several times, hoping it will shift into the solid, black-veined stone I expected to see. Hoping, gods, *praying* that my sight is deceiving me.

When several hard blinks do nothing to alter the smooth crystalline surface, I drag in a breath that is heavy with the intoxicating scent of jasmine, then force myself to look up.

Suspicion solidifies into reality.

Not Caeldera.

Not even close.

I am in a circular chamber, illuminated by flickering candle-light. Every surface is crafted from the same white mineral, from the walls to the ceiling columns to the expansive bathing pool that takes up half the floor. Moonlight suffuses the crystal, setting the entire space aglow. It is as if I've stepped inside an earthbound star.

The sunken tub is large enough to fit ten but, at present, contains a sole occupant—one who rises with breathtaking slowness from the steaming water, plants his hands on his naked hips, and stares down at me sprawled on his floor with unguarded amusement.

"If you were so desperate to see me in the nude, skylark, you merely had to ask. No need to sneak into my bathhouse in the middle of the night."

Still sprawled on my hands and knees, I can only gape up at the King of Llŷr. Water sluices down his muscular form, dripping from his dark head of hair, running off long, tanned limbs. It beads on his broad chest, where the dark whorls of his Remnant spiral outward across one well-defined pectoral. I watch several droplets descend past the mark, beyond the rippled indentations of his abdominal muscles to the line of hair that trails down toward his—

Skies.

My eyes jerk upward. Color sears my cheeks, hot as a flame. "Soren!"

One dark brow arches. Otherwise, he moves not a muscle. "Yes?"

"You—You're—" I scramble to my feet, heart pounding hard enough to bruise the inside of my chest cavity. "You're *naked*," I hiss, finally finding my voice.

"Mmm. I generally do not bathe fully clothed. Rather defeats the purpose."

Staunchly refusing to look lower than his chin, I splutter, "That's not what I—I did not mean—"

His other brow arches sardonically.

"Could you *please*," I force out firmly, "cover yourself with something?"

"Why? Is my nudity bothering you?"

My teeth clench. I turn my head so I am looking at the wall. In the flickering candlelight, the shadows dance across the quartz's many facets like players on a stage.

"My, my." He makes a *tsk* sound. "What a prude you are. I'd have thought after all those years of stitching wounds and soothing fevers, a bit of male flesh would not fluster you so."

My head whips back around to glare at him—a mistake, for he is still standing tall in the bathwater, his manhood completely exposed. I clap a hand across my eyes.

"I am not a prude. I simply have no wish to witness such an unattractive form at this proximity."

He chuckles at my bluster. For it is, in fact, bluster. His form looks as though it has been personally carved by the gods themselves to torture womankind.

"Please," I repeat, hand still tight over my eyes.

I hear a heavy sigh. Then, the sound of a large form disturbing the lapping water as he stalks to the edge of the bathing pool. Then . . . nothing at all. The silence is so complete, I can hear only my own pulse roaring between my ears and the occasional sputter of flame as a warm night breeze disturbs the wall sconces. If he moves, he does so in total stealth.

I very nearly jump out of my skin when he speaks again. His voice comes from less than a pace away. "You can open your eyes now."

I do not move; I do not trust him.

A large hand manacles my wrist and pulls it from my face. I find myself looking directly into the broad column of Soren's throat. The golden skin is damp, as is the dark hair that curls around it, the ends nearly kissing his shoulders. It has grown long since I last saw him. My eyes flicker down to examine the thick bath towel slung low on his hips—a meager concession to my request.

"Big of you," I snap.

His mouth twists. "So I've been told."

"The *towel*," I clarify, cheeks flaming even redder. "You could've put on some breeches, at the very least."

"People who storm into my private chambers unannounced do not get a say in what I choose to wear—or, more often, not wear."

I roll my eyes to cover my deep embarrassment. And for a momentary respite from looking at his face. I had somehow forgotten how arresting his features are, how startling he looks up close. On anyone else, such beauty might have a softening effect. Make them more approachable. Somehow, on Soren, it does the opposite. Makes him all the more lethal. Beauty is another weapon in his vast arsenal, each line of his chiseled features designed to ensnare and bewilder his opponents.

But then, the loveliest flowers are often the most poisonous.

"Rhya." All traces of amusement are gone from his voice. "Delighted as I am to see you here . . . would you care to explain your rather abrupt arrival through my personal portal?" His pause is intent. "A portal, I might add, only a handful of living souls even know exists?"

Truly? I suck in a soft gasp as I meet his gaze.

He is still holding my wrist. The bones feel very breakable

in his grip. "Is an explanation forthcoming, or must I strip to the skin to get you to speak again?"

"I got lost," I blurt when he starts reaching toward his towel.

He stills. "You got lost."

"Yes. In the leylines. I was . . ." I shake my head. "It was foolish. I thought I could take a portal back to Caeldera by myself. I should've just gotten on the godsdamned horse like Penn told me to, but I was so angry and—"

I break off before I can spill too many unnecessary details. Soren's eyes sharpen with curiosity nonetheless—two ocean-blue blades, cutting into me with lethal perception.

"You and Pendefyre are not, perchance, fighting, are you?"

"That is not, perchance, your business, is it?"

His mouth twitches. "Fair enough. But you still have not answered my question."

"Which one?"

"How did you find yourself *here*? Even if you were lost in the leylines, as you claim, I find it hard to believe you chose this particular portal at random."

"I never said it was random." I glower up at him. "Like I told you, I was lost. I was starting to panic, thinking I'd never find my way out. Some of the exit points looked . . . *sick*. Some looked dead. But this one looked different—felt different—than the rest."

"Different how?"

"I don't know how to explain it."

"Try anyway." It is not a request.

"It was . . . It felt . . ." I hedge. "Alive."

"Alive?"

"Brighter. Almost . . . beckoning me in, like a torch in the darkness." I shrug. "I thought it was Caeldera. Obviously I never would've selected it if I'd known it was going to spit me out on your bathhouse floor."

I look around, taking in the full scope of the chamber for the first time. Spherical in shape and exquisitely designed, with few furnishings to detract from the natural beauty of the moonlit quartz. The domed ceiling is open to the night sky, a perfect circle cut out of the center. Through it, I can see a waxing moon and a phenomenal spread of stars. If one were to lie back in the bathwater, the constellations would be directly overhead, a glorious tapestry for viewing.

"Are we in Llŷr?"

"Yes." Soren's voice warms a shade. "Hylios welcomes you, little wind weaver—even if you are several weeks ahead of schedule. I did not expect to see you until Arwen's wedding at midsummer."

"As I told you before, coming here was not my intention."

"And yet, here you are." He pauses. "Your timing is fortunate. I myself only returned earlier this very night."

Night.

I jolt in realization. It is full dark outside. That means I was in the portal network not seconds, not minutes, but hours, for it was not even midafternoon when I departed Dyved.

Time passes differently in the leylines—something to keep in mind for my next journey.

I tear my attention away from the stars and find Soren studying my face in the candlelight. His casual expression belies the intensity of his eyes.

"And how did you find the southern kingdoms?" I ask, forcing a light tone.

He scoffs. "The Midlands remain a misery. The Southlands fester like a sour wound, ripe for lancing."

"How delightfully descriptive." I grimace. Given his attitude, I assume the mission to hunt down Efnysien was unsuccessful. I ask anyway. "And what of your . . ." My brow furrows as I attempt to recall the twisted familial ties that once made the sorcerer his relation. "Your brother-in-law, is it?"

"Stepbrother," he corrects, voice losing some of its levity. "*Former* stepbrother. For the past century. Ever since I cast him out of my kingdom."

"Ah." I gulp delicately, sensing this topic is a sensitive one. "Right."

Soren blows out a short breath. "Regrettably, Efnysien is elusive as ever. We chased the coward southward beyond the Cimmerians, cut a path clear through the realm. In Eastwood, the woods are so thick there is no possibility of speedy pursuit. In Nythia, the woods may not be thick, but the fighting is. Their king has dragged his people into yet another bloody skirmish with Carvage. Let's just say, it is difficult to cover much ground when said ground is littered with freshly slain bodies."

I shudder. I do not miss the Midlands, with its endless bloody wars and power-hungry kings.

"Glamoured uniforms may conceal fae features, but that matters little when traversing indiscriminate killing fields," he mutters. "The mortals swing their swords at anything that moves. We were lucky to make it through at all. By the time we crossed into the Reaches, Efnysien and his army had already disappeared into the Shadow Steppes."

The name is unfamiliar. "Shadow Steppes?"

"A region of near-constant sandstorms, stirred by violent winds that whip through malformed rock formations." Soren shakes his head. "A shroud of darkness blankets that place. The air is thick with sand and ash. Even with a face-covering, after a few hours there your lungs feel gritty with debris, your eyes caked shut, your skin cracked and raw. Still, we pushed on, pursuing them all the way to the edge of Dymmeria."

My brows lift. "But no farther?"

"I will not lead my soldiers into the Husk Desert. No valor awaits there. Only slaughter."

"You have tried before," I surmise.

His nod is tight. "Many times over the years, we have attempted to infiltrate that dark dominion. I have sent scouts, spies, full squadrons. No matter the approach, the results are always the same. None ever return. There is no breaching even the outskirts of the drifts that surround Efnysien's keep. There are no roads to follow, no landmarks to orient oneself. Even if you make some headway without dying of thirst, the creatures who burrow beneath those black sands are more effective than any archers or infantry."

"No wonder Efnysien feels so at home there. A monster among other monsters."

"Mmm. Though I think his selection of the desert had more to do with me than any arachnidae lair or abyss pit."

I make a mental note to ask about the unfamiliar terms later. "You?"

"Of all the locations my stepbrother could have chosen to build his empire, do you think it is a coincidence he selected the one place in the realm my powers are at their weakest?"

"Water has no place in a desert," I murmur, following his logic. I think of my own clawing claustrophobia each time I am suppressed beneath deep earth, and wonder if Soren's physical reaction is similar when he steps foot in the parched sands of the Southlands. "He hides from you where you cannot follow."

"Rare are the occasions he leaves his own borderlands. Before Fyremas, he had not been spotted beyond the Symmetria Keep for nearly a decade. I cannot begin to express my frustration that I failed when given such an opportunity."

"I'm sorry."

His head cants to one side. "Whyever are you sorry?"

"I know how badly you wanted to catch him. To make him pay for all he did to us at Fyremas."

"My issue with my stepbrother long predates what happened in Caeldera. I should've killed him a century ago, when I had the chance. At the time, banishment seemed a more humane option." His voice is light; his eyes are not. "In the years since, whatever merciful instincts I possessed back then have been whittled away. When next I find occasion to wrap my hands around his throat, I will not squander it."

"Are you very different, then?" I cannot help asking. "From who you once were?"

"Far more handsome."

I cast my eyes heavenward. "I'm being serious."

"As am I." He smirks at my scowl. "Truthfully? I barely remember the man I was a hundred years ago."

"I doubt that."

"Oh?"

"You remember everything." There is an accusation in my voice. "You just do not want to tell me."

"I have always been honest with you. Since the first day we met."

"There is a difference between honesty and transparency."

"Yes. One is expected, the other earned. I will always tell you the truth when you ask for it. But I'm afraid you have not yet earned my secrets, skylark."

Skies, I had forgotten the vertiginous nature of conversing with him. How he uses conversation like another battle tactic, to disorient and disarm his opponent. How he talks in circles until you can no longer remember what you asked in the first place.

"It's late," Soren announces, eyes flickering to the arched

doorway where a gauzy white curtain flutters in the night breeze. "We can talk more in the morning."

With that, his fingers—which are still looped around my wrist like shackles—slide down the length of my hand and intertwine with mine. He walks toward the archway, dragging me along after him. My thin boot soles slip uselessly against the glowing floor when I attempt to dig in my heels, finding no purchase on the smooth white crystal.

"Wait!"

He halts, half turning to look back at me. For the first time, I notice the deep shadows beneath his eyes. "For . . . ?"

"I cannot stay here. I have to get back."

"To Caeldera."

I nod.

"Because your last journey through the portal was such a stunning success?"

Heat steals over my cheeks. "I was thinking . . ."

"I could see where that would be exhausting for you," he says drolly when I trail off.

"I *thought*," I restart, annoyed, "you might be a friend and take me back through."

"A friend?" His tone is wry. "Is that what we are?"

"I suppose that depends on whether you help me."

"Ah. Yes. *Blackmail.* The bedrock of all true fidelity."

"Are you going to take me back or not?"

"Not."

"Why?" I exclaim.

"For several reasons."

"Several?"

"Three."

"Which are?"

"Firstly," he says, calm in the face of my vexation, "because you look like you are about to collapse at my feet at any given moment. Tell me, have you eaten a single godsdamned meal since I last saw you, or are you intent on withering away to a skeletal corpse like some boring, self-flagellating martyr?"

My chin jerks higher. "I'm fine."

"You don't look fine," he says bluntly. "You look . . ." His eyes scan my face, then move down my form, seeming to take in every dried bloodstain and frayed seam, lingering on the narrow slope of my hips, the sticks of my legs in the tattered uniform.

I know, since Fyremas, I have grown too thin. But even when I find the time to eat a proper meal, I rarely manage to muster the appetite for it. Some days, if Lestyn does not shove a cup of stew or a baked bannock into my hands in the infirmary after a long shift, I do not eat at all.

Something dark moves in Soren's eyes—a flash, there and gone too quickly to properly decipher—as they shift back to mine. "You would be most unwise to travel by portal in such a state. The leylines . . . they take a toll. More than the blood you spill to activate them. Given the chance, they will pull at the loose threads of your psyche. Unravel you."

I purse my lips, unable to contradict him. The terror I felt during my doomed attempt to reach Caeldera is fresh in my mind. I have no desire to ever experience such a thing again.

"*Oblivion.* That's what we call it. A state deeper than amnesia. One that erases all that you are, undoes the stitches that hold your very self together." He shakes his head. "Portal travel is not for the casual voyager, and definitely not for the unprepared one. At the very least, you require a warm meal and a decent night's sleep before we pass through again."

"Fine," I begrudgingly agree. "I can see the sense in that."

"A first for you?"

I pointedly ignore his sarcastic comment. "You said there were three reasons."

"Did I?"

"Soren, you cannot detain me here without cause—"

"My second reason involves my own exhaustion, not yours. I myself traveled a very far distance by portal only hours ago. I am not altogether eager to make another trip so soon—especially when a brooding Pendefyre no doubt awaits on the other side, full of acrimony and accusation."

My teeth sink into my bottom lip. I've not thought of Penn since my arrival. Is he already back in Caeldera? It's nightfall. Surely, he is back by now. Has he realized I have not returned? Does he think I have deserted him on purpose? Gods, he will be worried . . .

Or relieved, a bitter voice whispers from the back of my mind. *He wanted peace of mind. Your absence, however unintentional, may well be a gift to him.*

"Tell me." Soren cuts into my unpleasant thoughts. "How fares our fiery king?"

I swallow hard. "Take me back to Caeldera and see for yourself."

"Clever. But no."

My sigh is resigned. "And your third reason?"

He hesitates, staring at me for a long beat. "Consider it an unearned secret."

"You truly aren't going to tell me?"

"I would, were you ready to hear it."

"Soren—"

"We can resume this squabble in the morning. But for now, I have not seen my bed in well over a month and I am most eager to reacquaint myself with it."

"I am not sleeping in your bed," I grouse at the back of his head when he starts walking again, dragging me along in his wake. His hair is still dripping wet, sending droplets down the back of his neck, the blades of his shoulders, the defined divot of his lower spine where the towel is slung.

"Did I invite you to sleep in my bed?"

My eyes narrow. "Then where am I to sleep?"

"This is the Water Court. We have no shortage of rooms. Pick one."

He stops, shoves aside the curtain, and, like a partner leading the steps of a waltz, spins me through it, into the night.

CHAPTER
SEVEN

The drugging scent of jasmine drenches the darkness. Beneath it, I taste a kiss of salt on the breeze. I haul gulps into my lungs as we ascend a set of stone steps from the round bathing chamber. Soren is close on my heels as I climb, for the way is narrow and there are no railings to speak of. Not far below, I hear the gentle slosh of water against rock.

Not a stairway, then, but a bridge.

The water is a dark spill of ink all around us, indecipherable to my eyes, which are slowly adjusting to the dimness. When we reach the top, I glance back at the bathhouse. It is a tiny island unto itself, aglow at the center of a large natural spring. In the shallows, dozens of phosphorescent frogs sit upon lily pads, their croaks a throaty chorus.

Soren says nothing as he moves ahead, leading the way down a path that rounds the edge of the spring. His bare feet make no sound on the smooth slate. Lanterns hang interspersed in the darkness, illuminating a lush garden of night-blooming white flowers. Phlox, jasmine, wisteria. A few more I do not recognize. Palm trees sway overhead, their fronds thwacking melodically.

Fyrewisps flit everywhere, some weaving lazily while others zoom at speeds I am unable to track. I have only ever before seen the vibrant red variety that populates Dyved's deep forests, and the even more muted kind that inhabit rare stretches of the Midlands. These are a strain I have never encountered—not one shade but many, changing color as fast as they change flight direction. Yellow, blue, green, purple.

Like fireworks.

The instant the thought crosses my mind, I am thrown back in time. Back to Fyremas, back to Caeldera. Back at the top of the crater, watching fireworks explode over the city. Back with Pendefyre—

I banish the memories with a firm headshake. I have no desire to relive that moment, nor anything else that followed that terrible night. If I have learned anything during these past months of bleak survival, it is that I cannot reshape my past by dwelling on it. Reliving my losses will not dull them. Endlessly replaying past darkness does nothing to ensure a brighter future.

Better to live in the now. One day at a time. One breath at a time. Until, someday, I no longer have to remind myself to breathe.

The path slopes upward to a large terrace, and an impressive building comes into view. More than a mere house, yet not quite a castle. It sprawls with palatial grace around the gardens, all white walls and stately columns, with a pagoda roof of silver tiles that curves up at the corners in a way that is reminiscent of the floating lotus flowers I've seen sketched in some of the apothecary's oldest botany texts. Torches burn bright in welcome along the terrace, casting a luminous glow across the impressive facade. There is no door; the main entry is an archway wide as a wagon and twice as high, completely open to the night.

"This is my villa," Soren announces, walking between two marble columns thick as wine barrels. They are covered in intricate carvings I wish I had the leisure to examine.

"Yours alone?" It is big enough for fifty.

"I enjoy my space." He pauses a beat. "When you've met Arwen, you may understand why."

"She lives in Hylios?"

"She does, along with a few of my other siblings. There are several villas scattered around the royal grounds for visitors and family members. It will be easier to show you in the light of day."

I nearly trip on the threshold, not watching my feet with my head tipped back to take in the soaring ceilings of the atrium. The gardens have followed us indoors. Potted palms tower along the perimeters in vases large as I am tall. Vines of a variety I do not recognize creep up interior columns and bloom with glowing blue flowers.

"You have other siblings?" I manage to ask once I've stopped reeling.

"Arwen is technically my only full-blooded sibling, resulting from my parents' marriage. The rest are a result of my father's many dalliances." There is a smile in his voice. "I gained a handful of stepsiblings from his subsequent marriages, along with a whole brood of bastard half-siblings. And those are just the ones we know about. The only pastime King Manawydan enjoyed more than bedding his wives was bedding women who *weren't* his wives."

I swallow a startled laugh.

"Of course, many of his progeny are long gone now. Old age, illness, what have you. The handful who remain—those of strong maegical lineage—are elderly and ill-tempered despite their age-resistant appearances. Keep that in mind when you inevitably cross their paths."

My stomach clenches uncomfortably at the thought of meeting Soren's siblings. The last time I was introduced to a Remnant's kin, it did not go well. If they are anything like the late Queen Vanora . . .

"They tend to come and go as they please," Soren continues. "Especially Vaughn. But the doors of Hylios are always open to my siblings, should they desire a visit." The smile disappears from his voice. "Most of them, anyway."

"Efnysien, you mean."

"Yes. But even he was welcome, once. A long time ago."

He slows his pace, falling into step beside me. The lofted ceilings are cut with skylights, allowing shafts of moonlight to slice down around us. A beautiful fountain gurgles at the center of the atrium—two mythical merpeople locked together in a passionate embrace, mouths fused, hair flowing. Their naked forms are so realistically chiseled, it is difficult to believe they are not flesh and blood. Their scales possess the luster of abalone shells, shining bright despite the shadows. Water spouts from the tips of their intertwined tails and the length of the merman's trident, showering them in a constant waterfall. I can hardly tear my eyes away, but Soren pays the fountain no notice as we pass by, seemingly immune to its beauty.

"What did he do?" I ask softly, almost afraid to know the answer after wondering for so long. "To warrant banishment?"

Soren sighs. "That is a story for another night. One bolstered by copious intake of Titan gin."

We pass beyond the atrium into a wide corridor that runs the length of the villa, splitting off into darkened rooms we do not pause to explore. Eventually, we reach a separate wing that houses a half dozen doors. They are all crafted of the same pale wood—bamboo, I think, or teak—but unique in their designs. Some are carved with feathers, others seashells. The one on my left looks like a setting sun; the one on my right captures the crest of a perfect wave.

My eyes move over them as we walk, studying the ornate craftsmanship, until we reach the very end of the hall. There sits another door, set quite a distance away from the rest. A grander entryway, double the width of the others. Not wood. It is a solid slab of crystal—cleaved, like the bathing chamber, out of pure, opaque quartz. It glows faintly. I sense the unique signature of Soren's power rolling off it and know, even at ten paces, that it is warded shut.

Soren stops at the center of the corridor, finally pausing to look at me. "Feel free to choose any of the bedrooms that most appeals to you. They are all vacant and well maintained. That one"—he gestures toward the door with the sun—"the Sunset Suite, has a particularly nice view of the Westerly Beacon. The Gull Suite"—he points two doors down, to the one with feather elements—"faces the interior gardens."

I jerk my chin toward the crystalline threshold. "And that one?"

"My bedroom." He pauses a beat, head canting sideways as he stares at me. "You are welcome to wander wherever you please for however long you are here—with the exception of that door. No one enters but me."

I scoff. "I have no desire to spy on you."

"Says the woman who interrupted my bath."

"Spare me your belated—and, might I add, *false*—modesty."

His lips twitch. His fingers lightly graze the fabric of his low-slung towel. "Oh, I think you know I have nothing to be modest about."

Color hits my cheeks. I ignore it. "Trust me, even if I wanted to see inside your personal chambers—which I do not—I can tell just standing here that the door is heavily warded. I doubt I could get through it if I tried."

"Let's not test that theory, shall we? We don't yet know what you are capable of, little wind weaver."

"As always, you overestimate my powers."

"And you, as always, underestimate them." His eyes flash, sudden flecks of silver striating the blue. "How long will you deny your own abilities? How long will you run from who you are? From what you are capable of?"

I blink, startled. His furl of temper is unexpected, a rogue wave lashing out of calm waters. But as quickly as it arose, it is gone again. The silver fades from his irises. His voice drops to a mutter I am not sure is meant for my ears. "Just as well you've come on your own. Spares me the unpleasant task of dragging you out of Dyved by force."

Surely I have misheard him. *"Excuse me?"*

"It's past time we began. Well past."

"Began what?"

He does not answer, merely turns on his heel and walks to his door. "We'll discuss it in the morning."

"I'm leaving in the morning," I remind him. "You're to bring me back to Caeldera at first light."

"Like I said, we'll discuss it in the morning."

"Soren!"

"Good night, skylark."

"Wait—"

Ignoring my protests, he lifts one hand to the door. It glows brighter under his touch, then swings inward. I do not even have time to call good night back to him before he vanishes into the dark chamber beyond. The door closes after him with a re-sounding click, its glow dissipating instantly.

I have half a mind to march straight up to it and attempt to unlock the wards myself, simply to be obstinate. Instead, I sigh and turn to face the other doors stretching out before me. It is beyond late. I am bone weary. And I have a sinking feeling that whatever Soren aims to discuss with me tomorrow, I will need a full night's sleep to face head-on.

Setting my shoulders, I stomp to the nearest suite and shove its door open.

I AWAKEN TO a symphony of crashing waves carried on the wind. It is the song of my youth, a refrain so familiar to me while growing up, I often felt my heart's every beat synced in time with the tides. For a few dazed moments, as I cross that liminal threshold from sleeping to waking, I can almost convince myself I am back in Seahaven. Curled on a narrow cot in a cozy cottage at the edge of a strange silver wood, a stone's throw from the ocean. But the down mattress beneath me is far too soft, the duvet blanketing my limbs is of a quality so far beyond that of my flimsy childhood bed, I'd never consciously confuse the two.

I open my eyes to study the darkly coffered ceiling. It is somewhat obscured by panels of sheer fabric that drape artfully over the four-poster bed. They flutter lightly in the breeze; I left the balcony doors open last night when I finally fell into bed with the force of an anvil. I slept too deeply even to dream, my mind as exhausted as my body.

After a cursory examination of the available suites, I'd chosen the one with a seafloor theme. It is painted in the deepest shades of the ocean—navy, teal, black—and styled with a simple motif of bottom-dwelling creatures. Coral reefs, urchins, anemones. While not half as large as some of the other suites, there is something soothing about its dark palette, its sparse yet sumptuous decor. It also happens to be the farthest from Soren's private chambers, tucked at the opposite end of the hall in a forgotten alcove, well away from the other, more extravagant rooms.

What mine lacks in size, it makes up for in style. A tapestry depicting the waterlogged remains of a sunken ship hangs over the filigreed writing desk. The indigo walls are textured like sand, but somehow soft to the touch. The black marble floors are veined with jade and, when I push off the covers and hop out of bed, they are warm beneath my bare feet despite the lack of rug. I cross to the balcony doors, step through them into the daylight . . .

And gasp aloud.

Hylios.

In the dark, I was not able to make out much beyond a few distant flickering lights. I had assumed—quite wrongly—that the villa was located at sea level. In actuality, it is perched on a precipitous rise at the island's highest point, like the crown atop the city's head, overlooking everything. My eyes drink in the splendor on display, spellbound by a labyrinthine sprawl of white sandstone buildings with tiled pagoda roofs in every conceivable shade of blue. Even from this vantage, I can see the bursts of color where gardens contrast with the pale architecture: the arresting pink of bougainvillea creeping up facades, the shocking green of palms swaying against the sky.

It's no great secret that Hylios is an island city, set some distance offshore, surrounded on all sides by ocean. Naturally, I expected water would have a prevalent presence here. Expectation falls short, however, for water is not just present. Not a characteristic or a dominant trait.

The city *is* water.

In place of roads there are canals, curving out in semicircular arcs like aqueous ribs of a great skeleton. Some are wide and busy with boat traffic, others so narrow they seem impassable by anything larger than a dinghy. Twin lighthouses bracket the city—one facing east, the other west. The renowned Beacons of Hylios. They are taller than any structure I have ever beheld before. Taller, even, than the Spire of Bellmere, which I thought must be the highest tower in all of Anwyvn when Eli first brought me to see it. Like massive sundials, their tall forms cast long shadows even as their bright beams sweep far out to sea, guiding homebound ships back to port.

Beyond the towering stone walls that surround the network of canals, there is nothing but ocean flowing for leagues and leagues in every direction. It is a stunning shade of blue, nearly turquoise. The mainland is a distant smudge on the horizon.

There is not even a bridge to connect the capital to the rest of Llŷr. I wonder how they manage to conduct trade, how anyone who lives here ever pays visits to their relatives in shore-bound stretches of the kingdom. By ship, I suppose. There are plenty of multimasted sailing vessels bobbing in the great harbor at the city's mouth, where the many canals funnel into one.

I squint at the indistinct fae-shaped forms moving along the sidewalks and crossing the footbridges that arch gracefully over the waterways below. Perhaps they do not leave at all. What person lucky enough to live in such a place would ever want to abandon it? It is incomparably beautiful—even on a day like today, when clouds obscure much of the sun, stealing a shade of the vibrant natural splendor.

I allow myself a few more moments of silent appreciation before I tear my eyes away and move back into the dark suite. I slept deeply, and for far longer than anticipated. It is already midmorning—past time I head back to Caeldera. By now Lestyn will be well into his routine at the infirmary. He'll be worried when I don't show up.

As for Pendefyre . . .

I can only guess at his reaction to my abrupt disappearance. It is strange, after so many months spent sensing his every pitch of temper and unchecked spike of pain. Yet here, a whole kingdom away from him, our bond feels stretched thin, the most friable of tethers. His emotions are as distant as the ruins of his royal palace.

Was he anxious when I did not return? Or angry?

Does he assume I've abandoned him on purpose?

I should've written to him last night. Informed him of my whereabouts. Assured him that I am safe and still breathing, at the very least. But frankly, the thought did not even occur to me until well after I'd locked myself inside my suite and slipped beneath the silken sheets. Guilty as I felt for my lack of communication, I could not quite summon the fortitude to climb back out of bed, stalk down the hall, rap on Soren's door, and demand access to a slip of parchment and a serviceable raven. Not in the middle of the night, in any case.

Perhaps not ever.

I have no desire to unearth whatever secrets he's locked away behind that thick crystalline barricade.

I make use of the suite's adjoining bathing area, which houses a tub hewn from one massive chunk of midnight marble. The sink and toilet are cut from the same dark stone. I grimace when I catch sight of my bedraggled appearance in the vanity mirror. My platinum mane is mussed, my skin wan and pale. Pinching some color into my cheeks, I plait my hair into the thick, serviceable braid I've made a habit of while healing the wounded. There is nothing to be done about the sorry state of my uniform, but it matters little.

I'm leaving—just as soon as I locate Soren, that is.

With one final glance around the cozy chamber, I step into the silent corridor. I stare for a beat at the king's quartz door at the end of the hallway, wondering if he is inside. I feel not a trace of him anywhere. It's possible our bond is still too new, my ability to sense him too underdeveloped. That or he is blocking me intentionally.

I have a feeling it is the latter.

Retracing last night's steps through the villa, I strain my ears for sounds of life. It is even lovelier in the daylight. Grandiose ceilings, peppered with skylights, soar overhead. Open-air archways lead straight out into the tropical gardens of the royal grounds. There are no signs of Soren in the atrium, with its magnificent fountain and potted palms. Nor do I find him in the gallery room, with its vast art collection and mural-covered ceiling. Oil paintings span the lofty walls—landscapes and portraits and still lifes, some large as a ship sail, others smaller than my palm. Many depicting unrecognizable settings and subjects. A whole universe of brushstrokes.

I force myself to keep walking, resisting the urge to linger as I pass beyond the gallery into a grand library that rivals even that of Seahaven's most prestigious university. Its floor-to-ceiling shelves are stocked with leather-bound books and all manner of intriguing artifacts, accessible via rolling ladders bolted on oiled tracks high overhead. The furnishings are as sumptuous as everything else in the villa, but look better used—the leather sofa by the fireplace broken in, the pillows still bearing the indents of a resting head. The taper candles are more melted wax than wick.

Someone spends many nights in this room.

I can easily picture Soren here, lounging on one of the chaises, reading by candlelight. His body still, so very still, even as that meteoric mind of his races over the pages . . .

I jerk my eyes away and carry on.

Once before, I visited another Llŷrian estate. The Acrine

Hold, a sterile stone fort at the base of the Cimmerian Mountains. The two dwellings have precious little in common when it comes to structure or design, yet they do share one attribute: a strange lack of staff. No guards are posted at exterior doors, no soft-footed pages carry parchment scrolls down corridors. Even the kitchen is empty of the usual chatter of cooks and clatter of ladles in pots.

Admittedly, my experience with royal households is limited . . . but certainly a king's home would have a whole fleet of footmen and scullery maids? Before Fyremas reduced the castle to ruins, Vanora's court deployed an invisible army that moved through the keep, prepared to fulfill her every whim at a moment's notice.

If Soren has a similar legion, they do not reveal themselves. The only sound that disturbs the quiet is the patter of my boots on the polished marble as I walk across the vacant kitchen. Like many of the rooms, it is open to the air at one end with a vast columned archway that allows a crisp breeze to blow in, carrying currents of jasmine and sea salt.

As I wander out onto the terrace, my eyes sweep the inner courtyard, following the slate paths that lead down into the lush gardens encircling a spring-fed pool. At the center sits the bathhouse, connected by a curved stone bridge. I study it from afar, allowing the pulse of pure power it emits to wash over my skin. The mark at my chest prickles in response.

The portal there is highly concentrated. I assume that's why I was pulled here, instead of to Pendefyre.

"If you're hoping to catch me in the nude again, I'm afraid I'll have to disappoint you."

I spin around at the sound of Soren's liquid lilt. He's appeared behind me without any warning at all. As though he's materialized out of thin air.

"I wish you'd stop doing that."

"Bathing?"

"Sneaking up on me."

"Your inability to sense me has less to do with the skills I possess and more to do with those you lack." His eyes dance with humor as he watches my lips flatten into a frown. "Did you get any rest?"

"More than I've had in a month."

His humor vanishes. "You've been wearing yourself down to the bone. Not eating, not sleeping. I fear if I let you return to Caeldera, you'll desiccate entirely."

"If you *let* me? It's not your decision."

"My, my, you're cranky in the morning."

"I am not cranky."

"That statement might be more convincing if it weren't coming at me through clenched teeth."

I forcibly relax my jaw and smooth the glower from my face. "I'm sorry. I am merely eager to get back to Dyved. I've been away too long already, and sent no word about my abrupt disappearance—"

"I sent word."

My eyes widen. "You . . . *What?*"

"To Pendefyre," he explains, unperturbed by my shocked reaction. "I sent a raven to Caeldera late last night, informing him of your rather . . . serendipitous . . . arrival during my bath. I'm sure, once the firestorm of temper subsides, he'll be relieved."

"*Firestorm?* What else did you say to him, exactly?" Gods, I can only imagine. The man takes every given opportunity to goad Penn . . .

"Don't fret. I left out the more salacious details." Soren appears to be fighting a grin. "Wouldn't want to incite any international incidents, would we?"

My eyes press closed for a long moment as I attempt to summon a sense of calm. "I appreciate you sending word that I have not been lost forever in the leylines. That said, it changes nothing. I still need to return as soon as possible. So if you would take me through the portal, as you agreed—"

"Tell me . . ." He cuts me off, folding his arms across his broad chest. His shirt is rolled to the elbows and crafted of a pure white linen that accentuates the deep golden tan of his skin. "What is it you are so eager to get back to?"

"It's—Well—I—"

His dark brows arch as I struggle.

"There are people there who count on me."

"Pendefyre?"

I try not to flinch, but I cannot quite conceal my reaction. A sharp pain vaults through me.

No.

Not Pendefyre.

He does not allow himself to count on me for anything.

Soren easily reads the truth from my silence. "Mmm. I thought not."

"Feel free to keep your thoughts to yourself."

He promptly disregards that suggestion. "If it is not the new king calling you back, whyever the rush to return?"

"Have you so easily forgotten the damage wrought on Fyremas? Even now, the city sits in ruins. There is much to rebuild."

"And they require you to clear the rubble yourself, piece by piece?" He answers his own question. "No. Dyved has a large army capable of setting the court to rights without the aid of the Remnant of Air."

Blood rushes into my cheeks. "I have other responsibilities."

"Such as?"

"Not that it's any of your business," I say stiffly, "but I've been working with the Life Guild. Healing those wounded in the battle."

"I suppose that explains the drab attire."

I make a vulgar hand gesture to illustrate precisely how little I care about his opinions of my threadbare uniform.

Soren chuckles, more amused than offended. "While healing is a valiant pursuit, it's been months since the battle. Most of the wounded have either vacated your infirmary or fled to the skies by now."

"Regular illnesses and injuries still occur every day."

"And you are the only one in Dyved with healing skills?"

"Well, no, but—"

"Then your responsibilities are not, perhaps, as restrictive as you would have me believe."

"You may presume to know everything about my life, but presumptions are only as strong as the actualities behind them."

His fingertips dig into the fabric of his shirtsleeves, a reflexive indication of annoyance that does not show in his expression. "The only thing that can turn presumption into actuality is time," he rebuts softly. "Something I rarely have with you."

We stare at each other for a long moment, until the air grows charged with a thick tension that makes me look away. My eyes skate across the inner courtyard, tracing the twisting vines of jasmine, the sloping grace of the palm trees, the dizzying blue of the spring. The quartz bathing chamber at its heart is a striking sight in the light of day, though nothing can compare to its luminous beauty in the cast of the moon.

"Your home is beautiful," I murmur, not certain why I feel so compelled to share that with him but unable to resist the urge all the same.

There is a pause. "I'm glad you think so. Though it pales in comparison to the rest of the capital."

"Yes, from my balcony it looked . . ." Hearing the dreamy quality of my own voice, I swallow hard and clear my throat. "Anyway. I'm sure I'll see more of it at midsummer when I return for Arwen's wedding."

To this, Soren does not reply.

I continue staring at the bathhouse. "You should take me through now."

He says nothing.

When I finally glance back at him, he is standing there staring at me like I am a puzzle for which he cannot quite work out a solution. A lock of dark hair falls over his forehead, where a furrow mars his perfect brow. His eyes are the same shade as the sapphire spring water.

"Well?" I prompt. "Will you?"

"No."

"No?" It is a struggle to keep my voice even. "I've rested, as we agreed. It's time to go."

"I believe our terms included a good meal in addition to a good night's sleep."

My teeth grind together. "Are you joking?"

"I never jest about breakfast."

"Soren, I mean it."

"As do I. You must be hungry. Admit it."

As it happens, I am hungry. I haven't eaten for . . . Actually, I've lost track of my last meal. I only know it was far too long ago.

"Don't make me beg, skylark," he cajoles. "Come now. Wipe that frown off your face and follow me."

My lips press together, deepening my frown, but the sight only makes his own tug up into a half smile. I cast my eyes heavenward, seeking divine intervention. When none arrives, I heave a sigh. "Fine. Feed me if you must."

He laughs at my undisguised annoyance. Then he turns on

his heel and walks back into the villa. I have no choice but to scurry in his wake, resigned to my fate. Frankly, I am tired of arguing—with him, with Penn, with Yale, with Osain . . . with everyone in my life. On this one thing, I will yield. It is only a meal, after all.

What can one meal change in the grand trajectory of my existence?

I catch up to Soren in the kitchens. He does not slow his pace to accommodate my shorter strides, nor does he pause when we pass beyond the cold hearth into a wide hall littered with more art and artifacts. An impossibly beautiful runner rug stretches the length of the corridor. It is soft even through the soles of my boots.

"Um . . . Soren?"

"Mmm?"

"The kitchens are back there."

"Astute observation. Gods, you're sharp."

My hands curl into fists. "How do you plan to cook my breakfast without making use of your gargantuan range?"

"I don't plan to make your breakfast at all. Not when there are so many skilled vendors down in the city eager to do it instead."

"But—What—" I shake my head as though that might clear it. "I never agreed to traipse through Hylios."

"You agreed to let me feed you. You never specified where said meal was to take place, or that I was the one who'd prepare it."

"That's a technicality and you know it."

"Then let this be a lesson. Your first of many. Next time you strike a bargain—with me or anyone else—be more specific on the terms."

My eyes narrow at his back. "What do you mean by that? My first lesson of many?"

He does not answer except to slow his pace somewhat, so we are side by side as we exit the villa through another wide archway onto yet another terrace. This one does not face the interior courtyard but the city itself. A near identical vantage to that offered by my balcony, perched high above a swath of rooftops and canals. Soren hears my breath catch as I take in the view and smirks at the sound, but blessedly refrains from comment. Perhaps he knows I have reached my limit for teasing for the day.

As it is not yet noon, this does not bode well.

CHAPTER
EIGHT

We walk in silence, following a downward-sloping trail of slate paths, and eventually reach a sharp set of steps hewn directly into the bedrock. It, like the rest of the royal grounds, is entirely deserted.

"Where is everyone?" I blurt, unable to contain my curiosity.

Soren glances over at me, brows aloft. "Whatever do you mean?"

"Butlers, porters, scullery maids . . ."

"Ah." He shrugs. "The villa does not require much in the way of maintenance. There are groundskeepers to tend to the gardens and cleaning staff to corral the occasional dust bunny. Otherwise, I see no need to keep a fleet of servants at my beck and call."

"Not even a cook?" I press. A king would keep a kitchen staff at the very least . . .

"I enjoy cooking."

"*You* cook." I cannot hide my skepticism. The towering, battle-hardened warrior . . . the bloodthirsty killer-king, feared by all in the Midlands . . . *cooking*? I try to picture his hands—hands I have watched snatch the life from men with an ease that speaks of long practice—dusted with flour, maneuvering a rolling pin across a countertop, steering a whisk. It is not an image I can reconcile with reality. Rather like trying to envision a shark climbing a tree.

"You'd be surprised by the hobbies you find time to pick up when saddled with the curse of immortality," Soren says lightly. "Give it fifty years. A hundred. You'll be far more eager to hardboil your own eggs than have them hand-delivered to you by someone you have watched wither beneath the weight of age during their years of service. Just as you watched their predecessor—and their predecessor, and *their* predecessor—lose the battle against time." His pause earns a wry edge. "Somewhat spoils the taste of one's breakfast. You'll see."

I fight a shiver. "I should hope not."

"In any case, I do cook. I'm even rather good at it. Maybe I'll give you a demonstration at some point."

"You could've given me a demonstration today if you'd made breakfast," I grumble. "Thus eliminating this little quest to town."

"And miss an opportunity to annoy you?" His lips twitch. "Never."

My sigh is martyred.

We reach the bottom of the stairs and continue onto a forked path that winds through a grove of lemon trees. Their scent is both crisp and mellow, a suffusive cloud of citrus. At the end of the grove, nestled on the cliffside, sits another villa. Like Soren's in style, though smaller and less stately.

"Arwen lives there when she's not out on campaign," he informs me, noticing the direction of my gaze. "She's the best general in Llŷr, as well as the best strategist. She's been leading my armies in battle for longer than you've been alive."

Not quite the picture I'd had in my head of Llŷr's crown princess.

"We'd have been invaded ten times over without her aptitude for strategy and surprise attacks," he continues. "Don't tell her I said that. If her ego gets any larger, I fear I'll need to expand her villa to accommodate it."

I suppress a laugh. "I look forward to meeting her."

"I'm not certain you should. Arwen can be a bit . . ."

My brows lift.

". . . abrasive," he finishes finally.

"A dominant trait in your bloodline, it would seem."

He looses a huff of amusement. "You have not seen my abrasive side yet, little wind weaver. Consider yourself lucky."

I bite back a retort.

As we slowly descend toward the city proper, I come to realize the royal grounds are stacked like layers of a tiered cake, each housing different groves and gardens, springs and waterfalls. Each home to mysterious inhabitants of which there is no earthly sign. I struggle to take it all in while keeping pace with Soren's long strides, curbing my impulse to bombard him with questions. He does not offer much in the way of conversation, though occasionally as we pass by different dwellings, he will murmur a name associated with whoever lives there.

Tethys.

Melité.

Vaughn.

I try to keep them straight in my head, but in truth it is beginning to spin from both information and overexertion. I've lost count of the endless stairs and pathways. My thighs are aflame, my breaths reduced to choppy pants by the time we reach the final set of steps that brings us down to the edge of the grand canal that wraps the base of the royal grounds. A beautiful bridge, crafted of an unfamiliar metal—pale and refulgent, much like the inside of a seashell polished to a shine by a thousand ocean caresses—curves before us.

Soren pauses briefly at its foot. "Ready?"

"For what?"

He grins, a flash of white there and gone. Then, he crosses the canal into the heart of his city.

AFTER THE UTTER desertion of the royal grounds, Hylios is a veritable melee of life. The throngs of civilians are so thick, it is difficult to forge a path forward. I make myself Soren's shadow, keeping close to him as he moves unhurriedly past innumerable outdoor cafés that line the canals, where people are crowded around tables eating breakfast, drinking coffee, smoking tybae leaf from braziers fitted with pipe hoses. I drag in a lungful of the familiar smoky scent and my eyes water as it burns a path down my throat.

I have never felt more drab in my colorless uniform than I do as I survey the citizens of Llŷr, in their flamboyant silks and elaborate embroideries. A pigeon in a menagerie of beautiful peacocks. It is more than mere clothing. Until I walked among them, until I heard their carefree conversations and easy laughter, I did not realize how foreign such things have become. These past months, the cobbled streets of Caeldera were silent as a crypt. Misery oozed from the pavestones.

Yet here is Hylios. Untouched. Unscarred. A lively port brimming with vitality.

A constant stream of boat traffic flows beneath countless curved bridges. In every direction, couples stroll with arms interlocked, families pick powdered sugar pastries from shopwindows, elders hunch on benches, feeding scraps of bread to rainbow-hued finches.

I am so parched for normalcy I want desperately to drink it in; to suck it down in great gulps as if to fill myself up before life once again becomes about bandages and tinctures and inflammation and death. This craving within is followed swiftly by a paralyzing guilt.

How selfish am I to dream of sitting at a bistro table with a cup of something warm clutched in my hands, when those I've left behind are barely scraping by? How dare I even contemplate a wasted afternoon of people-watching when, back in Dyved, joy is such a scarce commodity?

"Are you all right?"

My eyes flash up to Soren's. He's paused beneath a large lemon tree, standing in the shadows with his back to the bustling sidewalk. He is so tall, I find myself mostly shielded from the prying eyes that press upon us as people amble past, no doubt curious about the pale blond stranger who shadows their king's every step.

"I'm fine," I whisper.

"You're not."

My retort dies on my lips when I register the awareness in his eyes.

The godsdamned bond!

Infernal hells. Of course. I should have realized. He can feel my emotions cresting and crashing like sea upon sand, a relentless riptide of grief and guilt. Instantly, I throw up more mental blockades, building an invisible fortress around my mind so he cannot read the feelings that spill down the tenuous thread that connects his maegic to mine. I thicken the air shields that surround the center of my power until they are denser than stone. Impermeable. All the while, I glare defiantly into Soren's face.

Try to invade my private thoughts now, I challenge silently. *I dare you.*

He does not. Emotions swirl in the depths of his deep blue eyes as he stares down at me, but I cannot read them with any more success than I can his empty expression. Before I can even attempt it, he glances away.

"The floating market is just around the corner," he says, as though the last few moments have not happened. "Fair warning, it can be . . . chaotic."

I say nothing as I fall back into step beside him. My tongue feels thick and useless inside my mouth. Every now and then, I sense his gaze on me as we cross a nearby bridge and turn the corner to a wider waterway than any we have yet come across, where several main canals intersect. I stop in my tracks, staring at the myriad boats crisscrossing before us. There are so many, the surface is barely visible.

Every city has a central marketplace of some kind. A hub of trade, where citizens can barter for goods in exchange for precious coin. But I have never seen one like this. Its name is apt, for it is indeed a floating market. In lieu of carts or stalls, dozens of barges are moored in the middle, plus more tied to heavy cleats along the canal-side. Flatboats ferry willing shoppers between them, steered by sternmen with long oars wearing striped blue shirts.

Vendors shout out their wares in booming voices, urging passing craft to stop at their barges. There seems no end to their inventory. I struggle to pick out individual calls in the clamor.

"Apples by the bushel!"

"Fresh figs, get your figs here!"

"Eggs by the dozen!"

"This morning's mussels, still breathing!"

"Salted cod, straight from the North Sea!"

"Daggerpoint lager by the barrel!"

"Titan gin, direct from Prydain!"

My eyes cannot take it all in fast enough. My head whips back and forth from barge to barge, each painted a different attention-catching color, some flying embroidered flags, others displaying wooden signs that advertise their stock. I hear Soren speaking to someone in measured tones close beside me, but I pay him little notice, even as his hand lands on the small of my back and he guides me down onto the deck of a flatboat. The sternman grins at me as it bobs under our sudden weight. I grab at Soren's arm for balance, fearing we might pitch over. He chuckles as he settles us onto the cushioned bench seat.

"We'll have to work on your sea legs."

I narrow my eyes at him. "I've not spent much time on boats."

"Define *much*."

Flames of embarrassment scorch the back of my neck. "Essentially none."

"I thought you grew up by the sea."

"By the sea. Not on it."

He suppresses another chuckle. "Don't worry. I have no plans to bring you into the Bay of Blood for a clash with Frostlander longships." He pauses. "Not today."

With that rather foreboding remark, Soren turns his attention to the ruddy-cheeked sternman—who introduces himself as Deke—as he guides us swiftly out into the constant stream of boat traffic. They chat animatedly about a mutual acquaintance's most recent trade run to the Southlands, which is due back with several months' worth of coffee, sugar, tybae leaf, and other imported pleasures. Enough to keep citizens stocked for the summer. I am content to sit back and listen, well occupied by observing the bustling marketplace that streams to either side of our small vessel.

Occasionally, Soren directs our smiling captain to approach a barge, and he steers us in close enough to barter. Each vendor we visit beams with unguarded pleasure at the sight of their king. Soren greets most by name and speaks to them with a familiarity that surprises me—asking after family members' health, joking about the unseasonable conditions when they clutch their thin cloaks tighter and grumble about the chill. Though they make a fuss about not accepting payment, Soren continuously forks over fistfuls of coin in exchange for all manner of things—which, in turn, he promptly shoves into my hands for consumption, along with a one-worded order.

"*Eat.*"

I happily comply, if only to have something to do with my mouth besides gape at him. Who is this man? I thought I knew, but the mercurial monarch who smiles and laughs with his people is a stranger to me. For their benefit, he tucks away the darker side of himself I know exists—the one that bubbles up from the depths on the rare occasions he allows his charismatic facade to slip—and gives them a lighthearted version of himself instead. Showering them with his favor.

Two things become inarguably clear as the morning progresses. First, that King Soren is utterly beloved by his people. And second, that he is treated less like a sovereign than any I have ever met. Even Pendefyre, for all his hatred of royal protocol, is greeted with a grave sort of reverence when he walks the streets of Caeldera. Bowed heads and downcast gazes of respect. Yet every Hylian we come across acts as though the man seated so close beside me is a long-lost friend, not a liege lord. Despite complaints about the pervasive cloud cover, whenever Soren appears, those who spot him light up like the sun has finally emerged.

I lose count of the barges we stop at, of the delectables I consume. I scarcely have time to swallow before Soren deposits something else into my hands. A cup of green tea so flavorful it makes my tongue tingle. Two hot pink fruits I have no name for. A handful of steaming nuts seasoned with fiery pepper. A crispy seaweed wrap stuffed with rice and crabmeat. A skewer of succulent grilled shrimp that the vendor assures us he caught just before sunrise.

The shrimp in particular are so delicious, I very nearly beg our sternman to go back for a second helping.

I am too busy chewing to talk to anyone, but Soren does enough for the both of us. Even after Deke steers us out of the market onto a quieter canal, Soren continues to call out greetings to people walking along the banks, passing in their own craft, and, a few times, throwing open their second-floor windows to wave and smile at us.

Swallowing the last sip of my tea, I set down my cup on the low-slung table bolted to the boat's bottom and press my hands to my stomach. I feel full enough to burst. It's been a long time since I've eaten so much, and so well.

"So? What's the verdict?" Soren asks, settling back against the cushions beside me. His arms snake along the top of the bench, his boots cross at the ankles—a position of utter repose. "How was your first Llŷrian breakfast?"

"Unlike any breakfast I have ever had before."

He grins.

"Can I ask you something?"

The grin fades somewhat, but he nods. "You can ask me anything."

"How is it you can do this?"

"I'm not certain I follow."

"How can a king move so freely through his city, as though . . . well, as though he is not a king at all?"

"I didn't realize you were acquainted with so many kings."

"You know what I mean."

He sighs. "You would have me—what, exactly? Hide out in my villa? Live entirely separate from the people I am meant to rule? Lord over them from above without emerging from my privileged cocoon long enough to learn who it is I am responsible for? Make decisions for them without bothering to ask about their needs and desires and fears?"

I blink at him, stunned. "No. No, of course not. I only meant . . ."

His brows rise.

"Where is your royal guard?"

"I don't have one."

"You don't have one," I repeat, voice thick with disbelief.

"Haven't you heard? I'm by far the most menacing thing in this city." He winks playfully. "Perhaps in all the realm, if you put much stock in Midlanders' rumors."

"Why is it so difficult for you to give a straight answer?"

His eyes earn a shade of solemnity. "If someone aims to kill me, I stand a far better chance of stopping them than any hapless soldier with a sword in his hand."

"That smacks of hubris."

"If my pride provokes the gods, so be it. I see no need to prop my kingship up with superficial spectacle, surrounded by fawning courtiers and guards armed to the teeth, simply to prove my own power. So far as I can tell, my citizens are happier to find their own debauchery down here in the city than manufacture it for the sake of foolish court politics. And my soldiers are certainly better served at the borders, protecting those in Llŷr who cannot protect themselves, than posted outside my villa at night."

"So you have no court here?"

"You mean with a golden throne carved specifically for my ass? Tumbling jesters and warbling minstrels, performing for my pleasure? A gilded banquet hall stuffed with sycophants?" He snorts, as though the concept is preposterous to him. "No, we have no court. Not in any official sense. Occasionally, folks from across the kingdom will gather in the capital for festivals and momentous events. Arwen's wedding on the coming solstice, for instance, will temporarily double our population. But as a whole, Hylios does not hold much favor for the pomp and circumstance of other strongholds. We do not specify courtier from commoner. We are all equals here."

"Even you?"

"Especially me."

I do not know how to respond to that, so I tear my gaze away from his and direct it ahead. The canal we are on is off the beaten path; only a handful of other flatboats drift by as we pass beneath bridges and wind by buildings blanketed with blooming flowers. My eyes catch on several glass-fronted boutiques, their displayed finery reminiscent of Carys's once spectacular atelier on High Street. Resplendent gowns of gold and silver, feathered frocks with remarkable stitching, whalebone cages for formal hooped skirts, glyphed fabrics that lend their wearer a mortal glamour . . .

Skies, she would love to see this place.

I have no idea where we are in the city. It is a beautiful maze—one I have no real desire to escape at present. The only thing to mar the perfection of the day is the lack of sun. It is nearing midday, but the air is nearly as cold as Caeldera. A clammy mist coats my skin without a cloak to insulate my limbs. I fight a shiver in my thin uniform.

"I thought Hylios was supposed to be sunny," I huff, rubbing my hands up and down my arms to inspire warmth.

"Oh, it is," Soren murmurs absently.

"This is abnormal then? The mist?"

"Most abnormal. And most unpleasant. If you plan to stay with us, I'm going to have to ask that you put a stop to it."

I jolt in surprise. My head whips around toward him. *"Me?"*

"Yes, you." He sounds highly amused. "Or were you unaware that this pall is your doing?"

"Certainly not—I would never—" I stammer. "I do not control the weather!"

"Not intentionally, no. But your dark mood is manifesting quite plainly." He cants his head back to stare up at the sky. "I, for one, don't mind the occasional cloudy day. Reminds me not to take the sun-drenched ones for granted. But I fear my merchants will have to import far warmer fabrics if you don't cheer up soon. Otherwise, we will all freeze to death by autumn."

I do not have the heart to laugh. My mind is reeling. *My doing?* Absurd! I would know if I were manipulating the weather . . .

Wouldn't I?

I think back over the past few months. The overcast gloom that settled over Caeldera in the aftermath of the attack. The pervasive chill that seems to follow me wherever I go. Surely, I am not responsible for that. Surely, I cannot be inadvertently influencing the very skies.

And yet . . .

Yesterday, when Penn and I left the city, I was startled to see the rest of Dyved in the full bloom of spring, while Caeldera lingered in perpetual winter. When we'd arrived at Blister Bight, the fymandridae were basking in the sun. Not ten minutes later, they fled as clouds moved in and mist blanketed their steaming pools. And as Penn and I began to bicker . . . as my emotions heightened to a breaking point . . . a wild storm had been unleashed.

Gods above.

I look over at Soren. My heart is a riot in my chest. "I had no idea. I did not even know it was possible to do such a thing."

"Your power, when suppressed, will find other ways of expressing itself," he says. There is no judgment in his voice, only bare fact. "I told you once before: you cannot live as Pendefyre does. A life of repression and restraint is not what you were created for. The more you push down your grief instead of processing it, the more you bury your guilt instead of exposing it to the light, the longer it will fester in the shadowy corners of your mind. And the worse the ramifications. Not only for you, but for everyone in your path." He pauses. "Or, at least, everyone who shares your immediate climate."

He seems to find this horrid state of affairs trifling. I am too alarmed by my own unconscious actions to muster a response.

"Don't fret, skylark. When I was six years old, I had a temper tantrum after my father forbade me from swimming out beyond the sea gate without supervision. I flooded an entire region off the northern coast in my rage. Ruined an entire harvest's worth of crops and nearly caused a famine. *That* was a cause for concern." He shakes his head. "A little cloudy weather won't doom the realm."

Soren, age six.

What an unfamiliar image. I try to picture it—him, young and coltish, overcome by his own abilities—and find I cannot. I blow out a breath. "How do I stop it?"

"Being aware you're doing it is a good first step."

"How can you be so flippant about all of this?"

"Would you rather I yelled at you?" he asks, tone mild. "Railed once again about your need for proper training? Frankly, I have grown tired of berating you in the hopes that you come around. It doesn't seem to work anyway. I figure you will either accept that you need to master your abilities . . . or you won't." His eyes slide closed. "Just let me know whatever you choose. I'll be here when—if—you decide you are ready for a real lesson in Remnant power."

I mull over his words as Deke steers our flatboat down countless canals. Soren seems perfectly content with the silence. He remains statue-still beside me on the bench seat, his eyes closed, his posture relaxed. I wish suddenly that he was not so adept at shutting me out. His emotions are locked away in an inaccessible vault, secure as the warded door of his bedchamber. It is especially frustrating, seeing as the man always seems to know exactly what I am thinking and feeling—sometimes even before I know myself.

After nearly an hour, the waterways spit us out into the expansive harbor I saw from my balcony. It is much larger up close than it appeared from a distance, dominating the southernmost quarter of the island. There are larger vessels here than any we passed by in the canals—bulky, triple-masted tall ships with carved figureheads at their bows and bundled white sails on their booms; sleek schooners with shallow drafts, fully outfitted with battle-ready cannons. Sailors scurry across long wooden sprits and climb up netted rope riggings as they prepare for departure.

A sudden loud groan of metal shakes the sky. I sit straight up, certain we are under attack, yet neither Soren nor Deke reacts with the slightest bit of alarm. It is not until I locate the source of the racket on the far side of the harbor that I relax. Two massive waterwheels, each taller than a warehouse, start to turn, churning the surface to froth. A second later, the city walls split at the center as the gargantuan sea gate inches open in smooth jolts, permitting entry into the port's protective embrace.

Everyone from the sailors in the rigging to the bystanders on the docks turns their attention toward the new arrival. Even Soren cracks his eyes open long enough to examine the fishing rig that is making its way through the ever-widening gap. His relaxed posture shifts in the space between one blink and the next. He abruptly sits up, frame taut with tension. I do not understand the intensity of his expression until I see that the outrigger is towing a much larger vessel behind it, thick ropes straining under the load.

A merchant ship, from the looks of it. I am not familiar with boats, but even I can tell something is wrong from no more than a cursory examination. The sails are not rolled neatly around their booms but flutter loose in the breeze, tattered and wind-torn. No crew scrambles in the rigging, no one races along the decks. No captain stands proudly at the wheel. It appears to be unmanned.

A ghost ship.

"Strange," Soren mutters. Glancing around at Deke, he jerks his chin to the side of the harbor, where many rowing craft are tied to cleats embedded in the stone. "Take us to the tie-up, will you?"

Deke nods. He, too, bears a strangely unsettled expression—ruddy cheeks gone pale, dark eyes darting continually over to the harbor mouth even as he steers us toward an open spot at the end of the dinghy dock.

We glide to a stop and, with a murmur of thanks to our sternman, Soren hops out, then offers me a hand to follow after him. I barely have time to wave goodbye before I am dragged away. There is an uncharacteristic speed to Soren's steps, contrary to his typical smooth pace, as we round the harbor.

"What's going on?"

His hand squeezes mine once, then drops to his side. His eyes do not shift from the main dock where a flurry of sailors are securing the towed vessel to knee-high bollards with thick braided lines.

"I don't know yet. But that ship—the *Selkie*—was due in from the Southlands weeks ago. We assumed it was caught in the doldrums in the Endless Ocean, or run aground in the Desert Depths off Carvage. It's not uncommon—the drifts from the Husk Desert blow far offshore, creating league-long shoals that shift with every major storm. Makes it damn near impossible to navigate that coastline."

"But you don't think that's the case now?"

"No, I don't. I know the captain personally. Her crew has made that run a dozen times without incident. To see her limping into port on a fisherman's towline . . . no crew in sight . . ." He trails off as we cut through a swarm of sailors and civilians, all stretching their necks to stare. They part to give us a path as soon as they recognize Soren in their midst.

We are still a fair distance away, but even from here I can see dockhands positioning a gangplank against the starboard side. A young man, hardly older than Lestyn, races up its length the second it is secured, an anticipatory grin splitting his face. A pair of older men follow after him, their own steps tempered by experience. Or foreboding. They disappear out of sight as soon as their boots hit the deck.

I study the sails as we close the final stretch of distance separating us from the vessel. There is something odd about them. I thought, at first, they were shredded by strong winds. But a closer examination shows more than mere tatters. The thick canvas material appears almost translucent in places. Too thin to effectively catch a breeze. It reminds me of the gauze I use to wrap wounds. Wafer-thin. Filmy. Like . . .

Cobwebs.

"Soren—" I start.

But my warning is overshadowed by a piercing scream of utter horror. Even from inside the bowels of the ship, it is loud enough to bring all activity on the docks to a standstill.

"What in the deepest hells?" a nearby soldier coiling a length of rope mutters. His voice is drowned out by yet another scream. This one is harrowing enough to electrify the gathered crowd. Some spring into action, others start to flee the scene. But most stand stock-still, staring up at the ghost ship with equal parts trepidation and fascination.

My chin tips up to Soren at the same instant he glances down at me. The look lasts no longer than the length of a heartbeat, but I know what he is going to suggest long before he speaks.

"We should probably—"

"Let's go!" I yell as I take off running.

Soren matches me stride for stride as we race toward the ship. We fight the thick crowd as we go. Soren starts shoving people physically out of our path to get through. We reach the bottom of the gangplank just as the young sailor reappears at the top. Blood is sprayed down his left side. It doesn't look like his. His face is white as a sheet. His bellow is one of unadulterated terror.

"ARACHNIDAE!"

Gods.

The word echoes across the harbor, setting off a chorus of fear that rises sharply at our backs from the bystanders. People disperse like they are being shot at with crossbow bolts, scurrying off the docks and away from the harbor as quickly as their feet can carry them. Only a few leather-faced sailors remain, eyeing the hull with a wariness that makes my throat convulse.

The youth barrels down to us, each word cracking with hysteria. "Top deck was abandoned, so we went down into the hold. Thought the crew were asleep in their berths! Wasn't till we got close we saw they weren't in their hammocks at all!" He shoulders past Soren, so terrorized he doesn't even realize who he is pushing. "Cocooned in webs, they were! Blood sucked out!"

Suppressing a shiver of horror, I grab the boy by the arm. "Wait a minute, you're covered in blood."

"Not mine!" His eyes fly to my face, only half focused. I can see the whites on all sides, they're so wide. "Marcus and Emil! Dead, both dead! Didn't even see it happen, the fiend was so fast! Just a blur in the dark! I barely made it out of there!" His throat works as he rips out of my grip and ducks behind a barrel. "Gods, we're all going to die!"

"Perfect," I mutter.

Evidently, even idyllic Hylios is not exempt from life's miseries. Death has followed me here as well, effectively as the ugly weather.

Soren is busy barking orders at the few remaining dockhands who have not fled in terror. "You! Get to the tower guards, tell them to close the sea gate. No boat traffic in or out until we have this contained. *Now*." He points at another man. "You, get a message to the beacon lighters. Emergency lockdown protocol. I want everyone off the streets, shutters drawn." His gaze swings to a female sailor. "You, run to the hospital. Tell them to have the antivenin on standby. As much as we have." He drops down into a crouch to speak to the young man, who is hyperventilating. "You. Get ahold of yourself. I need you to take a message to the barracks and bring a full unit here, battle ready, as soon as they're able. Make sure they fill their quivers with immolating arrows."

The boy takes a tremulous breath. His eyes widen as he finally registers he is staring at his king. He squeaks out a faint agreement before he finds his feet, then takes off in what I can only hope is the direction of the barracks.

I watch him go, then glance back at Soren. He is still

crouched, but his head is angled up to mine. When our eyes meet, his are glowing bluer than ever, awhirl with maegic. I can feel it gathering inside him like a storm, triggering a swell of power in my own chest. It presses violently against my rib cage, a wild animal ready to be unleashed.

I square my shoulders, trying to appear unfazed, though I am relatively sure my expression is pale as the spider silk cloaking the ship's masts. I brace myself for the inevitable explanation that this situation is too dangerous for me; the subsequent suggestion that I retreat to the villa, where I'll be safe from harm while he handles whatever horrors await inside the ship. Instead, his lips twist into the specter of a smile as he rises back to full height.

"*You!*" he barks in the same gruff tone he used with the sailors. "You're with me."

CHAPTER
NINE

No sooner have we stepped on board than Soren unhooks the gangplank and lets it drop into the water. When I ask him if he's trying to prevent anyone from following us, he shakes his head.

"If we're eviscerated, it's better to contain the bloodshed to the ship. That way, they can just burn the damn thing and sink it, bodies and all." I must look horrified, for he tacks on, "Oh, relax, skylark. When death finally comes for me, it will take far more than a few hound-sized arachnidae." He pauses, crossing his arms over his chest. "You, on the other hand, appear to be the perfect size for a spider's snack . . ."

I make a crass hand gesture.

He chuckles, but all humor flees as we turn our attention to the ship. Up close, the signs of infestation are far more apparent than they were from the docks. We follow the bloody trail of footsteps the young soldier left toward the stern. A suspended corpse hangs from silken threads between two lashed barrels by the main boom; another lies by a ventilation hatch, an abandoned sword still in hand. Not the sailors from the docks—these have been dead months, not minutes. Their mummified skeletons stop us both in our tracks.

"Skies." Soren whistles lowly from my side. He is so close, our arms brush. For once, I am grateful for his proximity. My fingers lift automatically to trace the sigil for the Goddess of Souls in the air. My throat is too thick to speak the invocation aloud.

May you meet the skies with swiftness. May the aether offer eternal peace.

Soren's gaze follows my hand movements, but he does not mimic them. The grim set to his mouth mirrors the tension in his shoulders as we continue toward the stern. Webs coat everything in sight—clinging like moss to the masts, creeping over rigging lines. They drape the dual stairways that lead to the upper deck where the unmanned steering wheel creaks back and forth in the current. The round portal windows that lead into the captain's cabin are so thoroughly filmed over, it is impossible to see inside.

We check there first—Soren taking point, me close on his heels. A potent mix of apprehension and fear races through my blood like an elixir. My legs tremble with it as I step over the threshold. The interior is bizarrely untouched by disaster. The desk is cluttered with navigational charts and correspondence. A quill, slicked with dried ink, sits atop the stack, as though someone has only recently set it down. The bed is unmade, blankets rumpled, pillows askew. A pair of boots sit by the foot. A woman's, judging by the size.

"Imeera," Soren says, glancing around the empty cabin. "What the fuck happened to you?"

My eyes are on the weapon rack by the bed. Several weighty maces are on display, replete with spikes. I'm not a master swordswoman by any stretch of the imagination, but I figure even an unwieldy blade is better than none at this point.

"Don't you think we should arm ourselves before we—"

A low thud startles me into silence. Not the distant rumble of the sea gate ratcheting closed across the harbor, but something closer. Far closer. So close, in fact, I suck in a breath as my gaze drops straight to the wood plank floorboards. I cannot hide my flinch when a second thump echoes up at us from belowdecks, followed by a low hiss that makes all the hair on the back of my neck stand on end.

"There's something down th—"

"Quiet." Soren's whisper is barely audible. *Their hearing is nearly as good as their eyesight.*"

My mouth slams shut.

He jerks his chin toward the door and moves to it. I look longingly at the weapon rack for a few scant seconds before I follow, attempting to copy his soundless gait. No matter how carefully I tread, the soles of my boots boom against the floor.

One day, I will force him to teach me how he moves with such stealth.

My heart pounds faster and faster as we retrace our steps out of the cabin and onto the main deck. We pass several more mummified bodies hanging from the rigging, draped over supply crates. The young sailor's bloody footprints come to an abrupt end midship, at the shadowy steps down to the crew quarters on the lower level.

I have not forgotten the boy's words on the dock. *Cocooned in webs! Blood sucked out!* They ring in my head like a death knell as we approach the dark gap. Gods, I wish I had my bow in hand. All I have is the rather pathetic dagger I keep sheathed at my thigh, but that is better suited to harvesting medicinal herbs than dealing physical damage. Still, I feel a shade better with its glyph-covered handle gripped in my palm.

Soren looks entirely too nonchalant, given the circumstances. I swallow hard against the lump in my throat as I follow him, reminding myself with each step that panic is, above all, a paralytic.

No poison in the world more lethal than the fear running through your own veins, Eli used to say.

In my experience, the only known cure for fear is to grit one's teeth and carry on in the face of it. Be scared; live regardless. For it is always better to die swinging at an enemy than cowering in a terrorized ball in the corner.

In theory.

But theory only goes so far—a truth I have never felt quite so acutely as the moment Soren draws up short. I slam straight into the broad planes of his back. He doesn't spare me a glance as I step to his side. He is staring intently at the opening to the lower deck . . . where several long, serrated appendages are emerging one by one from the darkness.

Oh, hell.

The arachnida appears slowly, then all at once. With a tandem flex of eight double-jointed legs, it vaults like lightning from the hold. For a few breathless seconds, it is fully airborne above us. I gape up at its enormous body, unable to decide which of its characteristics is the most ghastly: the segmented abdomen, black and covered in coarse hair; the dozen orb-like eyes, shiny as mirrors, reflecting my horrified expression in miniature; or the fangs, coated with a viscous white venom, clacking together as the beast hisses a foul breath that reeks of rotten flesh.

This is no hound-sized arachnida. *Horse*-sized comes closer— and that does not even account for the leg span. Stretched end to end, it would almost be capable of straddling the ship. I am so stunned by its unexpected scale, I don't realize it's coming straight down at me until it is far too late to move.

Soren's body collides with mine as he tackles me to the deck. The impact steals the breath from my lungs and slams my head so hard I see stars. There is no time to process the pain. His arms are like metal bands, pinning me to his chest as he rolls toward the port rail. We lurch to a stop the same instant the arachnida crashes down. Its immense weight drives its legs into the boards like nails, splintering the wood by several inches. A guttural scream emanates from between its fangs as it realizes it has lodged itself.

Soren drags me to my feet, not squandering the brief moment we have before the creature pulls itself free. I glance around for my dagger, which flew from my grip when he tackled me, but it is nowhere to be seen amid the lines and webs that cloak the deck.

"Forget the damned dagger!" Soren snaps. "You have better weapons."

Even as he chastises me, he is lifting his arms, summoning two great globes of water from the harbor, each wider than the average soldier is tall. They rise up over the railing and hover there, suspended, for several seconds. I can feel the maegic surging through him, but his face shows not a ripple of expended effort as he holds his position, attention fixed on the foul, hissing monster not ten paces from us.

It has finally managed to work the last of its legs free of the deck. I swallow a curse as its inverted joints compress like springs, launching it straight into the air again. I think for sure it will come for us, but it has higher ambitions. Spinnerets on its underbelly shoot sticky white fibers at the booms overhead, adhering to the shredded sails with staggering speed. It begins to scurry upward into the rigging, all eight legs working together to climb faster than its size should allow.

I crane my neck to watch, mouth parched. "Soren—"

The second his name leaves my mouth, he flicks his wrists forward. Both water globes sail directly at the arachnida, enveloping it in midair. Its hiss of rage bursts out with a furor of bubbles. It attempts to climb, but its sticky web is floating, slack and useless, in Soren's trap.

"This shouldn't take too long." There is a smug note in his voice. "Most everything drowns eventually."

"It doesn't look like it's drowning," I can't help pointing out, eyeing the thrashing creature. "I think you're just pissing it off."

Soren grunts noncommittally. But as the minutes drag on and the monster continues to flex and flail its many legs, a faint line of strain appears on his forehead. More bubbles stream out between the thick black jaws that chomp relentlessly against captivity. Its beady eyes remain trained on us with unsettling wrath.

"Infernal hells."

I glance over at Soren's low curse. "What is it?"

"It should've run out of air by now. Damn thing must be from the Desert Depths. An amphibious varietal."

"What does that mean, exactly?"

"It means I can't drown it." For the first time, I detect a bit of exertion in his voice. The effort of holding the massive globule overhead while the arachnida fights with all its might is beginning to take a toll. "It means, once I let it out of this water cage, we're next in line for mummification."

"Perhaps we should pivot to an alternative plan," I suggest.

"I don't have an alternative that doesn't involve water powers."

"Fantastic."

"Don't suppose you can spare some of your lightning?"

My brows arch, aghast. Has he forgotten the utter calamity in Caeldera, when I unleashed my electrical storm on the lake? "Only if you want me to fry everything and everyone in this harbor."

"That would be less than ideal."

"Let me run and grab a bow. I'll find some soldiers, someone who can help . . ." I trail off as his eyes begin to glitter with familiar calculation; a new plan is taking shape in his mind. "What? Why are you looking at me like that?"

His pause is full of implications I do not fully understand. Not until he says, "You have other powers, skylark. Beyond the lightning."

My shoulders stiffen. "Powers I have not used in months."

"Great. You'll be fully charged."

"You cannot be serious." My heart thumps so hard, I'm surprised my ribs haven't cracked. "I can't control my maegic, Soren. Look what's been happening with the weather! You said it yourself, it's manifesting in dangerous ways. Even when I do access my powers intentionally, they're totally out of control."

"Probably because you're too scared to use them properly."

I cast a glance at the suspended arachnida. Is it my imagination, or is the water cage lower than last I looked? "This really isn't the time to discuss this."

"Actually, I disagree. It's the perfect time."

"Soren, I can't do what you think I can."

"You can do far more than I think you can. Better—you can do far more than *you* think you can."

Beneath the thin tunic, my Remnant licks out across the skin of my upper chest, frosty with cold. It, like Soren, seems to have a mind of its own when it comes to dealing with the situation at hand. Or maybe it merely wants a chance to come out and play after so many months kept suppressed beneath the weight of mourning.

My fingertips tingle as a chasmic reserve of untapped maegic spirals through me. A storm is gathering within. One that never goes away—merely ebbs and flows from the forefront of my mind to its deepest recesses. Most of the time, I do my best to banish it there. I can count the number of times I have called the wind willingly on one hand, for I know the risks. Penn has made them abundantly clear, over and over again. His mantra on the subject is so familiar, I can almost hear his voice inside my head.

You must contain it, Rhya. If you don't, it will consume you.

Yet here is Soren, so casually asking me to do just the opposite. To summon a power I scarcely understand. A power that, unchecked, is far more likely to kill me than save me.

"You must be mad," I say, shaking my head rapidly. "I realize you want to help me master my powers, but surely you don't expect me to start with an impromptu trial by fire."

"Not by fire. By spider silk."

"If you make one more jest, I swear to the gods—"

"Now or never, skylark."

"Fine!" My throat is tight. "I choose never."

"*Now.*"

His arms come down—and, with them, the water cage. It smashes into the deck, through it, to the lower hold, sending up a splash that douses us both. The arachnida disappears beneath a pile of splintered wood, but I am not fool enough to think it was mortally wounded by the impact. I stand, tense as a bowstring, waiting for it to reappear with the quicksilver speed I witnessed before.

This time, when it vaults up into the air, I am prepared. Time slows to a crawl as it springs at me, fangs clacking, forelegs extended, lethal stinger jabbing from its undercarriage. Beads of water fly off its hairy body in all directions as it sails across the deck. I take a breath, raise my arms, and blast outward. A shock wave of pure, solidified air.

The arachnida reverses course, caught in the wind current, flipping end over end until it lands in the ratlines that run the height of the mast. Any satisfaction I might've felt is snatched away as, less than a breath later, the creature's spring-loaded legs bend and it launches itself straight back at me.

"Skies!" I yell, diving sideways onto the deck, narrowly avoiding a fatal jab of its stinger. I tuck my body into a quick roll and spring back up—a move Jac spent weeks drilling into me over the course of our many sparring sessions. With a normal opponent, I'd be well out of range of sword or fist. Not so when it comes to this foe. The very instant I find my feet, I'm jerked off them again. I scream as I realize a thick web has snared me around the midsection. The giant beast is steadily winding me in as a fisherman might his reel, forelegs jerking the tendril closer and closer to its snapping jaws.

My fingers work to peel away the sticky silk, but it is fused to my tunic. I nearly lose my footing as the creature gives another strong tug, my boots scrambling for purchase on the slippery deck.

"*SOREN!*"

"Mmm?"

Gods, the man sounds positively bored. Meanwhile, I am staring into the festering maws of certain death. No amount of advanced healing will save me from this end. My own horrified expression is mirrored back at me in the collection of dark eyes lodged in the arachnida's misshapen head as the distance shrinks from paces to handspans.

"*HELP ME, YOU PRICK!*"

I hear a sigh from somewhere behind me. Then, a thin shot of water sails arrow-like through the air and severs the spider's web. I fall abruptly onto my ass, then scramble backward until my back hits a pair of black leather boots.

"You're welcome," Soren says from above.

Had I possessed the courage to take my focus off the hissing arachnida, I might've glared at him. As it is, I keep my eyes locked on my target, even as Soren's hands slide under my armpits and lift me up onto my feet. Across the deck, the foul beast is skittering from side to side, agile legs clicking against the splintered wood. I get the sense it is evaluating us—or, more specifically, contemplating how best to wrap us in its webs and suck us dry.

When it springs again, I am ready with a counterattack. My chest flares with ice as I summon another blast of wind that bursts forth in an indiscriminate—and ineffectual—wave. Not only does it miss the arachnida entirely, it manages to crack the foremast clean in half. The rigging comes down on the bow in a tumble of canvas and line and fragmented timber. Before it can be crushed, the creature scurries up the central mast, spewing sticky webs from boom to boom as it ascends toward the crow's nest.

"Damn it!"

"Are you even attempting to aim?" Soren drawls. "As a reminder, you're meant to eliminate the venomous spider, not the ship."

"Feel free to pitch in anytime," I growl without bothering to look at him. I'm trying to keep the enemy in my sights, but it's moving so fast I catch only blurry glimpses of black among the tattered sails.

"Oh, I think we've ascertained I'm quite useless in this fight." There is a smile in his voice. "Besides, you've got it well in hand."

Well in hand?

Is he insane?

"Soren, would you just—"

"Incoming," he warns lightly.

I intercept the spider's attack by the skin of my teeth, throwing up my arm to blast it backward at the last second. It gets so close, I can make out the white froth of venom around its pincers, the chunks of desiccated tissue caught in its coarse hair. I shudder in horror as it is flung into the rigging. While it is briefly tangled up in the lines, I spin around to face Soren.

I am fuming.

He, on the other hand, is leaning back against the rail looking for all the world like a man at utter ease. His lips twitch when he sees me glaring daggers at him. "Do you always use your powers like this? With the light touch of a battering ram?"

"I don't use them at all," I grit out. "Not since Fyremas."

His ocean eyes swirl with dark currents. "And why is that?"

"Do we have to talk about this now?"

"What else would you like to talk about?"

Peering over my shoulder, I see the spider's bulbous body dangling from a fresh web near the crow's nest. No doubt preparing a sudden descent onto my head as soon as my gaze is averted. "Perhaps the giant, unkillable monster intent on exsanguinating us."

"Oh. That."

"Yes, Soren." I send another blunt air blast at the rigging. "*That.*"

"It's not unkillable."

"It seems pretty godsdamned unkillable to me."

"Try some finesse."

"You want finesse? *Get me a bow!*"

"A bow is merely a tool that fires a projectile. You don't need a tool when you are fully capable of firing projectiles with the flick of your fingers."

My teeth gnash together. "You are the most asinine—"

"Incoming."

Swallowing a scream, I again whip around just in time to fend off another assault. The arachnida hisses as it is hurled back into the air, legs pinwheeling like hairy scythes, shredding through sails and halyards as it goes.

"How many times are you going to do that?" Soren asks.

I'm out of breath, my voice hoarse. "As many as it takes to kill it."

"Ah. Well, so far, you've only succeeded in giving it a severe case of windburn. I actually think it's enjoying itself."

"As I told you before," I seethe at him, "I don't know how to wield my powers!"

"Try harder."

That is easy for him to say. Too many times in the past, I'd pushed myself too far—my power too far—and paid the price for it with a bout of days-long unconsciousness. Already, my rib cage is beginning to ache with the effort to contain the gathering wind within me. The storm inside swirls faster with each passing moment, maegic mingling with fear and frustration and fury until I am a living, breathing maelstrom.

You cannot put yourself at risk, Rhya! Penn is shouting from my memory. *Rein it in before you lose control!*

Twice more, the spider comes at me. Twice more, I rebuff it with amateurish air blasts that send it spiraling up into the rigging—each less accurate, and less powerful, than the one before.

Despite my best efforts, the creature seems no worse for wear. I cannot say the same for myself. Blackout looms, the telltale signs too apparent to disregard. My chest burns with a cold I feel down to my marrow. My head pounds, static waves pressing in at my peripherals. My breaths shred in my throat.

I cannot keep this up.

Not for much longer.

A web shoots suddenly down from above, snaring me around the head and shoulders, wrenching my braid with scalp-searing pain. I cry out as I am jerked off my feet, the sound somewhat muffled by the thick film cloaking my face. The arachnida manages to pull me quite a ways into the air before Soren waves his wrist and frees me with another sluice of speeding water. I collapse at his feet, breathing hard as my trembling fingers rip the sticky silk from my skin, my nose, my mouth. My whisper, when it comes, is directed at his boots.

"Are you trying to get me killed? Is that it?"

Two fingers slide beneath my chin, tilting my face up to his. He is crouched before me. His eyes are deadly serious, not even a trace of teasing humor in their depths. "I think the more appropriate question is, why are you fighting like you want to die?"

I jerk my face from his grip. "I am not the one with a death wish here!"

"No?"

"No."

"Then why do you keep repeating an approach that is clearly not working?" He shakes his head slowly. "If you attempt to fill a cup from a roaring waterfall, you'll never drink. Likewise, if you attempt to snare a spider with a tornado . . ."

"I understand the issue," I say tersely. "It's the solution I'm struggling with. I don't seem to be able to summon the wind without . . ."

"Blasting with brute force? Mmm. I've noticed."

"I'm not in the mood to be teased. I'm tired. I'm—" I bite back the word *terrified* before it can escape. "I can't seem to do anything but blast at it, which is clearly not working. And I don't know how much longer I can keep trying before I—before—"

"Rhya."

I swallow hard. He so rarely says my real name—and never in a tone like that. Never soft. Never . . . *gentle*. "What?"

"You have everything you require to win this fight."

"How can you say that? I do not possess whatever *finesse* you use to so easily drown your enemies on dry land and shoot water-arrows and orbit droplets around goblets!"

He stares at me for a long moment. Calculating something. Turning over options in his mind. Eventually, he shrugs with a casualness I do not believe, even for a second. "Then borrow some."

"Excuse me?"

"You envy my finesse?" Pushing off his heels, he rises to full height. His hand extends down to me. "Borrow some."

I look from his hand to his face and back, somewhat baffled by the proposition. "What do you mean, *borrow some*?"

"Channel me."

CHAPTER
TEN

Channel him?

He truly is mad.

I shake my head rapidly back and forth. "Soren, I can't possibly—"

"You can. You will." Impatience flaring, he grabs my hand and pulls me up. Our fingers interlock in a grip so tight I could not escape it if I tried. "Even the best natural rider learns better on a training saddle."

"Are you the saddle in this analogy?"

His smirk is dark. "I'm the stallion."

I don't know how to respond to that, so I ignore it outright. My head tilts up to the rigging. The arachnida has momentarily retreated into the crow's nest, folding its long legs into the lofted lookout perch like a born sailor. I doubt it will stay there for long.

"I'm guessing we have about two minutes before that thing comes at us again. So whatever you're suggesting . . ." I eye him warily. "Do it already."

"I'm not the one who has to do it. You are."

"Me?"

"You."

"Because I'm doing so well with the basics." My words drip sarcasm. "You want to attempt an advanced maegic lesson right now?"

"I would not be attempting but succeeding if you would focus."

"You know, not two hours ago you claimed you weren't going to force me into Remnant lessons."

"I'm not forcing you. You have a choice." He shrugs. "Learn to channel or continue to bat the arachnida about like a child with a toy ball until you eventually drain your reserves, pass out, and find yourself sharing the same sad fate as the crew of the *Selkie.*"

"You call that a choice?"

"I never said it was a good choice."

Gritting my teeth, I grip his hand tighter. "Fine. Tell me what to do."

"You're going to tap into my power through the Remnant bond."

"Right." I scoff. "You're so adept at blocking me, I can barely feel our bond, let alone tap into it."

He stares at me for a long moment before the admission. "For this to work, I'll be forced to drop my mental guards. Just as you'll drop yours."

I suck in a sharp breath. I'm not sure I like the sound of that.

Soren in my head.

Me in his.

"The bond between us has . . . a certain elasticity, if you will. When I yield my grip, you can pull the slack into you. Pull my maegic into yours." He pauses, gaze flickering up to the crow's nest. Several legs are creeping over the sides, coarse hair scraping unpleasantly against the wood. "As this is your first time, I'll make sure not to give you too much. Just enough to shore you up while you finish off our eight-legged friend up there."

"That simple?"

"Hypothetically." His eyes find mine again. They are very blue, very bright. "It's been quite a long time since anyone's channeled me."

"What do you mean by—"

"Incoming."

There is no more time for discussion. The arachnida is out of the rigging, descending at us with unnerving alacrity. I feel the moment Soren drops his impenetrable mental guards, the ones I have never before been able to breach. One moment, I am standing on dry land, parched for connection; the next, I am drowning in him. His maegic swells, infusing the bond with so much raw strength, my knees buckle beneath its force. It is like a rogue wave that sweeps you out to sea without warning. But his grip is firm on mine, holding my body up even as my feeble mind strains beneath the influx of power.

I have no real instruction, only instinct as my guide. Blindly, I pull at the bond. Pull his maegic into mine. Into me. Much, I realize belatedly, as I did the day I extinguished Penn's fire in the ward chamber.

Unlike Penn, Soren does not resist me. He flows in like water, his mind closing around mine as the ocean does after a dive into the depths. Cool and crisp and calm, churning through me with melodic currents.

I gasp at the unfamiliar sensation. My own maegic—always so wild, so untamable—feels somehow soothed into quiet, subdued by his steady tides. Like a tight embrace that settles a ragged sob; the strong arms that squeeze until hysteria subsides.

I am still me. Still Rhya. But somehow, I am Soren, too. I can feel him there, inside my mind. Around it. Encompassing it. And for the first time since I tapped into my Remnant, the frenetic chaos of my inner wind does not seem like something to fear. Through Soren's eyes, I see it differently. It is not one entirety, one unstoppable tempest. Just as the most fathomless ocean could be broken down into tides, then currents, then individual droplets, so, too, could the storm inside me be dismantled into manageable pieces. I sense them all there inside me, together and yet separate, functioning as a whole and also as singular fragments. From the swirling black clouds of condensation to the ribbonlike breezes that whip beneath. From the strongest gusts to the thinnest wisps to the tiniest, individual, invisible particles of air.

I cannot say why this revelation makes such a difference in my mindset. Perhaps there is a certain comfort in knowing that while I might not ever wield a tempest with any grace . . . a handful of particles are a far more manageable feat. Something I can bend to my will. Something I can shape and steer with, if not Soren's elegant insouciance, at least a semblance of it. Perhaps it is his unshakable confidence I am feeling, not my own.

Whatever the case, as my free arm lifts up to the rapidly descending creature, it is with an assuredness like never before. I call the wind and it comes to me—not as an uncontrollable shock wave, not as a clumsy blast that more often than not misses its target. No. This time, when it leaves my fingertips, it is as one single stream of air.

The condensed shot strikes the arachnida in the center of its abdomen. A direct hit. It shrieks, a sound of pure agony, as the impact penetrates the dense flesh of its exoskeleton. The force of the blow rockets the spider back several paces before it drops like a stone to the deck with a thud that makes the boards creak. Black fluid spurts from its wound. I think it is blood, but it froths like acid, chewing through the wood in a matter of seconds. Both Soren and I vault several steps out of range of the deadly spray.

For a moment, I stand utterly frozen, watching the foul creature twitch in pain. Once the shock wears off, a wave of undeniable exhilaration sweeps through me.

I've done it.

I've actually done it.

My head whips toward Soren. The grin on my cheeks is so wide, it almost hurts. "Did you see that?"

He looks like he's suppressing a smile of his own. "See what?"

Scowling at him, I squeeze his fingers hard enough to turn his bones to dust. He doesn't seem to notice. He is already turning his attention back to the arachnida.

Wounded it may be; defeated it is not. Even now, it is pushing itself upright, shaking off the stupor of its fall to fix its myriad eyes once more in our direction. An irate hiss vibrates from between its jaws as its forelegs dance menacingly against the ruined deck.

"You're not finished yet," Soren says. "Don't celebrate prematurely."

"I wasn't," I grumble.

The arachnida musters enough strength to attack. As it comes at us, I feel oddly calm—a feeling I have not experienced since we first stepped foot on this cursed ship. Actually, if I look a bit deeper . . . It is a feeling I have not experienced for far longer than a few moments. For months now I have been on edge, living in constant anticipation of new threats materializing around every corner. A state of perpetual vigilance. But now my mind is bathed in the cool waters of Soren's maegic. My breaths are even, my pulse steady. My hand does not even shake as I lift it once again and fire another concentrated air missile.

The infernal creature learns all too quickly. It manages to sidestep at the last moment, taking the hit on its left flank instead of directly to the abdomen. One of its eight legs falls to the deck, still spasming as it spurts more toxic black ichor that erodes into the lower hold. The spider's anguished screech is at such a decibel, it raises all the hair on the back of my neck. It lurches sideways, unaccustomed to its mismatched gait, but soon finds its balance. Before I can blast again, it stages a quick retreat, spinnerets firing web after web as it ascends up the mast.

"Stop it before it gets to the crow's nest," Soren orders, his grip tightening on mine as more of his maegic flows into me. My whole arm tingles with it. "Otherwise we'll never get the damned thing down."

I shoot off another air missile, but the bulbous body is moving too fast for it to do more than clip a leg at the joint.

I expel a frustrated breath. "It's too fast!"

"Again, might I suggest *aiming*?"

"I'm trying!"

"Remind me to add target practice to our long list of necessary training exercises."

A vexed growl rattles in my throat. But the sound turns to a surprised gasp as Soren drops my hand. My fingers flex at empty air, desperately seeking a severed connection. The sudden loss of his maegic, his mastery, hits me like a punch to the gut. I think my legs will collapse, that the new void in my chest might stretch and stretch until it swallows me from the inside out.

"Wait!" I cry. "You can't just leave me!"

"I'm not."

"Then what are you—"

My protests dry up as he moves behind me, fitting his broad chest tight to the planes of my back. I want to ask what he thinks he's doing, but my throat effectively closes up as his arms slide around my waist. His hands skate down the length of my forearms to find mine again—palms cupping the backs of my knuckles, lacing our fingers together. His mouth is at my neck, his warm breath stirring the feathery hair of my nape as he speaks.

"I'll show you another way, skylark."

His maegic jolts through me again, an even stronger pulse than before, as we begin to channel anew. His mind settles over mine, steady and strong and so very, very different from my ever-spiraling self-doubt. I am a puppet under his control as he guides our joined hands into the air.

We do not need words. I know his intentions as clearly as if they were my own, see his plans forming in my own mind without any need for vocalization. Tendrils of air shoot from each of my fingertips and ribbon up into the sky. They are not piercing, but soft. At first, I fear they will be ineffectual against such a gargantuan creature. But as they wrap themselves around the monster's body, snaking up its remaining legs, snaring it by fang and stinger, I realize what Soren is attempting to illustrate.

There is a beautiful strength in this quiet power, an astonishing advantage to my slow-motion assault. The beast cannot fight. It cannot even flinch as I render it totally immobile in a set of invisible shackles.

"You know what comes next?"

Soren's deep voice rumbles through my head, plainly as if he's spoken aloud. I flinch within his arms, unable to conceal my shock at the sudden invasion. It is one thing to see his thoughts as images; it is another to hear them in psychic conversation. I had not known such a thing was possible.

I swallow hard. I cannot speak—neither in my head, nor aloud—so I merely nod.

"Good."

Soren's torso twists toward the bow, and I turn with him. Our lofted hands steer the immobilized arachnida through the air until it is poised directly over the toppled foremast, which protrudes up through a mess of torn rigging.

"Now," he whispers in my head.

His voice, which has always reminded me of falling water on the bed of a river, sounds different this way. Smoother, somehow. More intimate. A timbre reserved for secrets. I can feel his heart pumping, hear his pulse racing.

Or is that my own frantic pulse, pounding in my veins?

"Let's finish this."

At his command, I bring down our joined hands in one fluid motion, impaling the arachnida on the splintered base of the mast. The thick shaft pierces cleanly through its abdomen. A death blow. Black fluid explodes across the entire bow, dissolving everything it lands on in seconds. A smattering of holes appears across the foredeck as the hissing and bubbling subsides. The creature convulses violently, and then, with one final haunting shriek, falls utterly still as its life force flees.

Leaning back against Soren, I expel a long, tremulous breath. "Please, for the love of the gods, tell me it's dead."

His chest rumbles with a laugh that echoes in the farthest reaches of my mind. *"It's dead. You can relax."*

Easier said than done. Energy churns through my veins along with Soren's maegic. Deep currents wash through me, rhythmic as the tides. We are still channeling, though there is no real need for it anymore. Our hands are still joined tightly. Neither of us moves. I don't even think I blink.

It is Soren, finally, who severs the connection. He extracts his hands from mine and steps away at the same moment his mental guards slam back into place. I do the same, summoning internal shields around my thoughts. Yet the strangest sensation grips me when I find myself alone in my own head once more. Not the solace I expected, but a hollow disquiet. I take a series of uneven breaths, waiting for the discomfort to subside.

"I confess, that was a more eventful morning than I'd planned for your first in Hylios," Soren says wryly.

How odd to hear him speak aloud again.

I dig my fingernails into my palms in an attempt to focus and force a flippant tone. "You mean you don't subject all your guests to the most vile monsters Anwyvn has to offer?"

"Only the ones I like." His voice loses a bit of its humor. "No doubt you'll be running back to Caeldera even faster now that I've traumatized you."

I jolt.

Caeldera.

Right.

Only a few hours ago, returning there was my primary objective. In the madness of the past few moments, I had forgotten my determination to leave. Soren's offhand remark is a harsh reminder of reality.

I have to get back.

I have responsibilities.

I gather the courage to glance over at him. He is watching me carefully, his eyes locked on my face.

"Why are you looking at me like that?"

His answer is almost inaudible. "How, exactly, am I looking at you?"

Like you're still inside my head, perusing all my private thoughts.

I grit my teeth and jerk my gaze from his, back to the bow. The ship is lilting slightly forward as we take on water below. I have no doubt the black ichor has burned a path straight through the hull. I wonder how much time we have before we sink. Long enough to retrieve the bodies cocooned in the crew quarters? Maybe if we get some sailors from the docks to help . . .

Movement in my peripherals draws my attention to the port rail. All thoughts of body recovery falter as the breath catches in my throat. Something is crawling through a jagged hole in the deck. It is small—no larger than my fist, with a light brown exoskeleton, spindly legs, and finger-length fangs—but it is not alone. Everywhere my eyes move, I see more legs creeping up from the flooding hold.

"Soren . . ."

"I see them." He sounds grim as he steps up beside me. Our shoulders press together as we take in the sight of dozens—no, there must be *hundreds*—of arachnidae scurrying onto the upper deck. "Gods damn it," he mutters. "The fucking thing reproduced."

I'm already reaching for his hand, bracing myself for another fight, when a battle cry splits the sky. My head snaps up in time to see them drop out of the thick clouds above the sea gate. Five winged horses, flying in tight formation. My heart stumbles inside my chest as the impossible becomes possible.

Paexyri steeds.

The stuff of legend. Livings myths, every one of them. For though I had never before laid eyes on such magnificent beasts, though I had not even been sure they truly existed outside the pages of children's books, I know without question that these can only be the fabled faery mounts that ferried riders across Anwyvn before the Cull.

Their feathered wingspans stretch wide, gliding effortlessly through the air as they swoop toward the harbor. The five flying stallions in the V-shaped order are each a different color. At the rear, a dapple gray flanks a gingery roan. At the middle, a chestnut bay speeds opposite a piebald black. And at the very front, a mount of pure white dominates the pack. Each carries a rider on its back clad in navy blue flight leathers.

Soren's colors.

Not enemies, then.

The riders duck low over air-whipped manes as they descend rapidly toward us, but sit up in their saddles once they are within firing range. With the upper half of their faces fully obscured by goggles, their identities are a mystery; their intentions are not. A volley of immolating arrows rain down on the foredeck as they shoot sleek silver bows with effortless coordination, instantly igniting the swarming spiders.

I backpedal away from the quick-spreading flames. The webs that cloak the deck go up like a wine-soaked torch. In seconds, the whole ship will be engulfed.

Soren's hand finds mine. "Time to go."

We run for midship, fire at our backs roaring as it rips through wood and canvas. The hissing shrieks of the burning arachnidae grow to an earsplitting pitch as the creatures are consumed. When we reach the starboard rail, I see a crowd has gathered at the docks below. Sailors and soldiers, all staring wide-eyed at the inferno as well as the Paexyri steeds, who continue to circle the ship. Each pump of their impressive wings serves as a bellows, fanning the flames.

"Cut us loose!" Soren calls.

The sailors below instantly spring into action, untying the coiled bowlines from their bollards and tossing them into the water. The moment we are free, maegic thickens the air. I glance over at Soren in question, but he is occupied—his eyes are on the harbor, surveying everything in our immediate vicinity.

"You might want to hold the rail."

"What?" I'm thrown off by his casual suggestion. "Why?"

His answer comes in the form of a violent lurch. I grab the rail by the tips of my fingers before I go down on my ass. The wave Soren has summoned lifts us straight up into the air, several feet above the surface. The listing ship groans like a dying man as he maneuvers us across the harbor, strained by the excess water in its holds as well as the fire consuming its bow.

It is a jerking, uneven sort of slog. I cling to the wooden railing as the vessel seesaws from side to side. Soren guides us to the center of the harbor, well away from the other ships and the docks where so many onlookers are gathered. Intent on his task, he does not seem at all bothered by the spreading blaze. The fire has consumed the entire bow and central mast. Flames jump from ratline to ratline, turning canvas sails to cinders, reducing thick rope rigging to ash. The crow's nest is no more than a memory. And as the Paexyri continue to circle, their wingbeats only heighten the fire's fury.

"Soren—"

"A little busy here, skylark."

Fair enough. He is, after all, moving a full merchant vessel. I'll have to take matters into my own hands. Ignoring the nagging exhaustion that tells me I am nearing the bottom of my maegical reservoir, I summon a dense air shield to hold back the encroaching heat, along with any of the arachnidae offspring who manage to flee its deadly embrace. It is the sort of blunt, brute-force power I am accustomed to—none of Soren's finesse required— but it gets the job done. The fire ceases its forward march. It licks and lashes at the impenetrable wall like a living thing, testing my strength, demanding more of it.

I give all I have left. But I am already weak—I have pushed my maegic further today than ever before—and only grow more so with each passing moment. The toll on my mind, on my body, is greater than I can pay with my flagging reserves. My teeth sink into my bottom lip as I struggle to fend off the raging flames.

Only when the ship is at the very center of the harbor does Soren lower his arms. We bob back to sea level as he releases his hold, sending swells rippling in all directions.

"It's deepest here," he says with a nod, talking more to himself than me. Even in profile, I can see a faint crease of concern on his brow. "We'll let it sink after it burns."

"Sounds like a plan," I mumble. Waves of black are pushing in at the edges of my vision. I am seconds from losing consciousness. "But, uh—"

"I'll deal with the wreckage tomorrow."

"Sure, but—"

He finally turns to look at me. His face morphs into a mask of pure shock. For a split second, he looks almost afraid. But that is impossible. The ruthless King Soren of Llŷr? *Afraid?* He isn't afraid of anything.

"Gods, Rhya, what the hell are you—"

"Fire," I manage to say. My lips are numb. My fingers tingle with what feels like frostbite.

His eyes flash over my shoulder, widening fractionally as he sees how intense the fire has grown. In an instant, he's standing directly in front of me.

"Tell me you know how to swim."

I nod.

He grabs my hand and tugs me toward the gap in the railing where the gangplank typically rests. "We're going to have to jump."

I eye the harbor below. It is a long drop. I think there's a rather solid chance I'll be out cold before we hit the water, but I don't see much point in telling him that. My only other option is to remain on the ship to be cremated like all the other corpses.

With a sharp exhale and a flex of my fingers, I release my flagging command of the air shield. The fire, freed from its confines, howls as it closes in at our backs. It is close enough to make my neck slick with sweat. Close enough to make my skin prickle with the promise of pain. Above the growing roar, a loud crack rings out as the central mast snaps in half. It falls, a pillar of pure flame, toward the deck.

Toward us.

"Fuck," Soren curses. "Jump!"

Together, we leap from the ship. A shower of sparks fills the air as the mast crashes through the hull, chasing us all the way down. There is a rush of air, a blinding free fall. When my feet break through the surface, the force of it is enough to knock the remaining air from my lungs. I take an involuntary breath as the water closes over my head and a cold mouthful surges down my throat. Gagging on the brine, I kick blindly at the dark depths. Our combined weight has plunged us far deeper than I anticipated. My limbs scream for relief as I try to propel myself toward the light that leaks down. Even underwater, the red glow of the flames is visible overhead.

Soren locks one arm around my midsection; the other knifes through the water like he is the direct spawn of the God of Seas until we resurface. I intermittently choke out seawater and haul in broken gulps of air, clutching him like a life ring to keep from slipping back under. He spares a brief moment to examine me, the maegic in his eyes churning like typhoons as they scan my face. His dark hair is damp, plastered against his forehead in a way that makes him look almost boyish for once. His mouth grows tighter the longer he looks at me.

"Breathe," he orders rather sternly. "And hold tight."

Adjusting his grip on my body, he rolls onto his back and begins to tow me back to dry land. In truth, I am too exhausted to do much more than comply. I watch the burning ship grow smaller and smaller as we cut across the harbor with impossible speed, his strong kicks and one-armed strokes smooth as silk. The entire deck is engulfed now, bowsprit to stern. By the time we reach the docks, it is no more than a fireball.

Soren passes me into the helping hands of several sailors, then hauls himself up after me. We are both sopping wet. His white shirt clings to every muscular line of his body. The linen has gone totally transparent, clearly revealing his Remnant. His dark breeches are soaked to the skin. His leather boots squelch with every step. I am no better off. My thin uniform is plastered to me and torn in several places. The tip of my messy braid drips steadily down my back.

But we are alive.

And that is something.

There are words of congratulations and concern from those gathered. Yet they are quickly overshadowed by a commotion on the smooth stone street that butts up to the docks. The flying squadron of Paexyri lands with a clatter that draws every gaze. I can only stand there, shaking, as the five riders dismount and stride in our direction.

The flight leader from the white mount leads the way. Her stride is authoritative, boots rapping against the dock like a cavalry charge. Her navy leathers are gorgeously crafted—feminine enough to show off her curves but made of armor thick enough for battle. She is laden with weapons, from the twin throwing stars at her hips to the silver bow at her back to a wicked-looking scimitar slanting over one shoulder. Her dark hair is cropped short at the temples but kept long otherwise, and currently plaited into dozens of tiny braids. Her startling blue eyes never shift from me. Not at twenty paces, not ten, nor two, when she and her squad finally come to a stop.

"Brother, please tell me this quivering little dock rat is not the supposed salvation of the realm?"

I jolt in surprise.

Beside me, Soren heaves a sigh. "Rhya," he says, sounding like he doesn't know whether to smile or scowl. "Meet Arwen."

CHAPTER
ELEVEN

Soren's hand is a steady weight at the small of my back as he guides me through the endless maze that is Hylios. I'm too exhausted to ask where we are going, or even to take much notice of my surroundings with any real attention to detail. All my strength is used to keep my legs beneath me and my eyes from slipping closed.

I blink hard to clear the haze from my mind, trying to get my bearings. We've long since left the harbor behind, skirting the congested center of the city in favor of narrower alleys on the outskirts, in the long shadow of the perimeter walls. I spot the unmistakable sprawl of soldiers' barracks along with some industrial buildings—a smithy, an armory, a sailmaker, a brewery. This part of town is less populated, its civilians shut away indoors. Those we do pass on the streets clutch their colorful cloaks tighter, casting worried looks at the sky as they hurry home to escape the dreary weather.

My dreary weather.

I chew my bottom lip, wishing I knew how to dispel it. It is not yet twilight, but the sky is dark. Thick black clouds billow in on the heels of an all-too-familiar misty haze. The palm trees look out of place without a vibrant blue backdrop, the sandstone buildings around us no longer white but ashen gray. Even the waterways have dulled, from radiant turquoise to a darker teal.

Surprisingly, Soren makes not a single snarky comment on the subject. He seems content with our silent stroll. His gait is leisurely, his expression relaxed. He does not even look at me—something I find shockingly irritating.

An hour ago, he was inside my head, his intentions so interwoven there was no untangling them from my own. Now, from the bond, there is resolute silence. More than silence. A void. I can sense nothing at all. Normally, that would not bother me in the slightest. After today . . .

Nothing feels normal.

This muted censor is such a stark contrast to the intimacy of channeling, it gives me whiplash. Curiosity claws at me. I want to crack open his skull and peer inside, if only to cast some illumination on his thoughts.

Are they back at the docks?

Back with Arwen?

As introductions go, ours could have gone better. I have no real explanation for her instant dislike. So far as I can tell, I did nothing to inspire her wrath. Yet the mere sight of me standing there beside her brother, dripping wet from the harbor, hair a sticky mess of webs and snarls, made her bristle like a guard dog scenting an imminent threat to its master. She'd taken one long look at me—evidently finding me lacking—then turned on a booted heel and stalked back to her magnificent white winged steed without a word of farewell. Her squad instantly fell into step, leaving Soren and me staring after them.

"She never can resist a dramatic exit," he muttered, watching the five riders mount and, with a swift press of knees to flanks, take off at a gallop down the docks, then launch into the sky.

"*Exit?* What about her entrance?"

He glanced over at my incredulous comment, lips twitching as he read the clear awe on my face. His eyes slid to my sodden, snarled hair for a long beat. With a sudden flick of his fingers, a wave of maegic washed over me. When it receded, I found my clothing completely dry, as though every particle of water had been sucked out of it.

I was still reeling when Soren further stunned me by reaching up and pulling a thick, sticky web from where it was fused near my temple. My muscles locked, rendered utterly immobile as he worked it free of my skin, his fingers moving with a gentleness I had not known him capable of, slowly peeling the adhesive spider silk off my face, my neck, my collarbone.

It was a task I easily could have done myself, but I did not tell him that. I could not seem to find the powers of speech. My lungs were paralyzed, my throat lodged. I did not take a breath until his hand dropped back to his side and he turned away to speak to the dockhands. And, even when I did manage to inhale, the air felt paltry in my lungs.

Aftereffects of the seawater I choked down.

Or so I told myself.

"Where do you think you're going?"

I jerk out of my memories at the sound of Soren's voice. In my dazed state, I failed to notice he stopped walking several paces back. I look around, startled to see we are at the base of the Easterly Beacon. The lighthouse is embedded in the city walls, but double their height. Even with my neck craned back, I cannot make out the roving beam affixed to its top.

"Erm . . ." I shuffle from one foot to the other. "Back to the villa?"

"Not that way, you're not. You'll never make it up all the stairs, and I for one don't fancy carrying you. Might pull a muscle."

My eyes narrow at his teasing tone.

"Glaring at me, when I'm about to show you a shortcut home?" He tsks, head shaking.

Before I can retort, he turns away and steps through a doorway at the base of the tower. With no other option, I trail after him into the dark, circular space. It takes my vision a moment to adjust to the shadows. When it does, I see Soren standing beside a thick wooden ladder bolted to the far wall. My gaze tracks its rungs endlessly upward, until I lose sight of them at the very top of the monolith, where a weak ring of daylight marks the exit to the lightkeeper's quarters.

"You expect me to climb all the way up there?"

"Not all the way to the top." There is a brief pause. "Halfway."

That is hardly better. Halfway is still an unappealing distance.

"I don't suppose you'd care to fly instead?"

I scoff. "Amusing."

"I wasn't joking."

My head swivels his way. He does not, in fact, appear to be joking. "But—"

"Or, I could call Arwen back," he continues, bemused. "She might give you a lift to the royal grounds on Atyr. No assurances she won't dump you into the sea on the way there, though, if the mood strikes her. The Paexyrian riders are as high-strung as their mounts."

The climb, however daunting, suddenly seems the safest option. Lips pursed, I shove past Soren and grab the first rung. His chuckles follow after me as I haul my aching body upward, rung by rung, cursing him with each minute gain in elevation. My thin soles feel dangerously slippery on the wood. I keep my eyes fixed firmly ahead, not chancing even the tiniest of glances up or down.

It is a long climb.

"How . . . much . . ." I wheeze. "Farther?"

"We're about a third of the way there," Soren returns from below, sounding not at all winded.

Only a third?

Skies.

"I must say, I'm enjoying the view. Those shapeless breeches of yours are much more flattering from this angle."

I ignore his commentary, along with the resulting heat in my cheeks. We are getting closer. The light grows brighter as we approach the midpoint of the tower. I hear a torch crackling somewhere nearby, smell the faint whiff of smoke over the scent of damp stone.

"At least," I pant, lungs burning as I grab another rung, "if I lose my grip"—I haul in a gulp of air—"you'll break my fall."

"Glad to know you find me good for something."

By the time we reach the middle of the beacon, where the ladder splices at a landing, the last of my energy has whittled away into nothingness. Kicking off the final rung, I heave myself onto the stone platform and promptly collapse in a heap, my muscles screaming for reprieve. For a few moments, I lie there with my eyes closed, wheezing audibly.

A shadow moves over my face. My eyes sliver open to see Soren standing directly over me, his tall form blocking out the scant light.

"We need to work on your stamina," he says lightly. "I'll add wind sprints to our training program."

I can only glare at him in response.

He gives me a few more seconds to catch my breath before he drags me to my feet. There are two doors at opposite ends of the landing, each bracketed by wall-mounted torches. Soren leads me through one, and we step out of the beacon onto a wide rampart.

We are atop the towering city walls, I realize with a lurch. To my right, beyond the waist-high parapet, is a precipitous drop straight down to the sea. To my left, the canals coil below us with serpentine grace. My eyes follow the gradual curve of the wall from our position all the way to the northern end of the city, where Soren's villa sits like a white diamond atop the terraced rise.

"See? What did I tell you?" He winks at me. "Shortcut. Leads straight to the royal grounds. No stairs required."

My eyes continue their sweep along the curve, following the walls to the other side of the city, where the Westerly Beacon spears up into the sky directly opposite our position. If I squint, I can make out several shadowy forms moving behind the parapets.

"Can you walk around the whole city this way?"

Soren nods. "All the way to the sea gate. Comes in handy when you're in a rush. The canals are beautiful, but they get unbelievably congested at times."

I do not doubt that.

It takes about a half hour to make the journey along the top of the walls, a time we pass mostly in companionable silence. I am distracted by the sheer beauty coming at me from every direction, incapable of keeping my eyes from roving over every proffered angle of Hylios. Soren seems amused by my undisguised fascination, studying me as I study the bird's-eye view.

There, out to sea, three triple-masted merchant vessels race along the waves like gulls in flight. I hope they have a less violent voyage than the *Selkie*. *There*, in the middle, the floating market, still a mishmash of barges and flatboats. I wonder if they are moored there permanently or move each day. And *there*, fading out of view behind us, the great harbor, not even a smudge of smoke rising off the surface to indicate the ship that sank at its center. How long will its skeleton rest there before being hauled away?

We are not the only ones enjoying an afternoon stroll atop the walls. We pass many Llŷrians as we go. Couples strolling arm in arm. Families with fleet-footed children. Painters with easels, their brushstrokes painstaking as they attempt to capture the precise shade of the cresting sea, an unusually stormy palette. They are friendly, greeting Soren with the same warmth I witnessed this morning, but do not intrude with more than a wave or head bob.

"Admit it," he says finally.

"Admit what?"

"You like my shortcut."

I press my lips together to contain a smile. "It's not terrible."

"I'll take that as a victory." He pauses, gaze moving past my face to the city sprawling below. "Is it what you expected? Hylios?"

"I did not know what to expect. How could I?"

"If I recall, the book I gave you has an entire chapter dedicated to the Water Court."

My stomach flips at the mention of the book he gifted me during our first encounter. The one he'd annotated in the margins, his innermost—and often amusing—thoughts scrawled throughout the chronicle of Remnant lore. I lost it during the Battle of Fyremas when the castle collapsed, along with just about everything else I'd called my own. It is one of the few possessions I actually miss.

"Your book is at the bottom of the lake in Caeldera, I'm afraid, buried beneath a ton of stone and rock."

He heaves a sigh. "This is precisely why you should never

lend your books to anyone. You never get them back in the same condition."

I roll my eyes. "Regardless, reading your informative guide—or your pithy commentary—is no longer an option."

"That's okay. I'll give you something better."

"Another book?"

"Not quite."

"What, then?"

"Me."

"You," I say, dubious.

"I can't exactly trust you in my library, given your track record. You'll have to ask me directly when you have questions. Or when you find yourself in need of more . . . How did you phrase it? *Pithy commentary?*" His lips twist into a mischievous smirk. "Not only do I have two centuries of knowledge to offer, I can take far more rough handling than any old tome."

"I think I'd prefer to remain in the dark," I mutter, tearing my eyes from his. I quicken my pace along the ramparts as I hear his answering snort. We are nearly at the royal grounds. The city walls snake behind them, a continuous ring that runs along the back side of the gardens. There are no guards posted, no signs to warn away the riffraff. A nondescript gate with a glyphed handle offers entrance into a grove of wide-trunked olive trees, their slender leaves fluttering in the breeze.

Soren unlocks it with a quick pulse of maegic and it swings inward on soundless hinges. He bows mockingly, allowing me to precede him into the grove. I breathe deep, pulling in the scent of bark, the fainter notes of honey and floral. The dirt path slopes sharply upward, then winds around a bend, and soon we are stepping into a familiar courtyard, the earth beneath my feet replaced by the smoothest slate. As I walk through thick, creeping shrubs of jasmine, my eyes drift past the spring with its glowing water lilies and viridescent frogs to the opalescent bathhouse at the center and, eventually, to Soren's villa. It looms against the gathering twilight sky, ethereal and empty.

All I can think of is getting inside, stripping off my dirty clothes, collapsing into the plush bed of my suite, and sleeping for a week straight. My tunic reeks of smoke and sweat and arachnidae breath. Sticky silk is snarled in my hair, plastered to the fabric. With each stride, the adhesive residue tugs at my skin. My hands skim down my sides, trying to pry the webs loose. They're everywhere, covering my shoulders, my waist, my hips. At my thighs, clinging to the empty holster—

Stopping short on the path, I suck in a severe breath.

"What is it?" Soren asks, hearing it.

I look at him, feeling oddly bereft. "My dagger. I—I lost it on the ship."

"We have smiths here in Hylios. The finest in the Northlands. I'm happy to have one of them—"

"No."

His dark brows quirk up toward his hairline.

"It's not . . ." I swallow harshly. "You don't understand. That dagger . . . it was special to me. It was . . . a gift."

"Ah." His pause is knowing. "From who, pray tell?"

My lips press together.

"Pendefyre," he guesses, gleaning the answer from my silence. "Of course. That explains the look on your face."

I bristle. "What look?"

He doesn't answer. Merely reaches up absentmindedly to peel a particularly sticky tendril of spider silk off the column of my neck. My pulse leaps along with my annoyance. I slap his hand away and backpedal out of reach.

"I am perfectly capable of grooming myself."

He scans my disheveled frame top to toe, no doubt amused by the contradictory statement.

"And I plan to," I tack on, glaring back at him. "Just as soon as I've located a bathtub."

"I'd take you to the Kettle, but I think you've had enough shocks for one day."

The Kettle?

"You're welcome to use my personal bathhouse instead," he continues before I can ask, gesturing toward the spring. "It's big enough for two."

"It's big enough for *ten*, but I still have no plans of sharing it with you."

"Fine by me. I prefer my bathwater sans cobwebs."

I scoff.

Grinning, he tugs a lock of my hair. I reach up, fully prepared to slap his hand away again, until his grip changes from playful to . . . something else. As do his eyes. They shift over my face and an altogether different emotion moves in their depths as he tucks the tendril gently behind my ear, his fingers a fleeting brush against its pointed tip. His voice pitches down an octave. "Perhaps I could make an exception. This once."

My mouth parches. Undeterred, I bluster on, "I'm surprised you'd allow me alone in the bathhouse at all. You seem determined to delay my leaving Hylios. How do you know I won't slip through the portal at the first possible opportunity?"

His lips press together. For some reason, I get the sense he is trying not to laugh. What is amusing about this particular situation, I have no idea, and Soren does not seem inclined to share. Without another word, he turns and walks away.

Fighting the bubble of annoyance expanding inside me, I

trail after him in resolute silence. I swear, the man's moods are more mercurial than the tides he commands. And far less predictable.

My stride falters when he does not climb the stairs onto the terrace but, instead, turns down a narrow side path that snakes out of view. I'm not sure he means for me to follow until he pauses to hold aside a large palm frond that blocks the way forward. His lips twitch as I slink past, careful not to invade his space.

Just around a bend, we come to a tall glass enclosure tucked beneath an arbor of creeping wisteria. I think it's a greenhouse at first, but the ceiling is open to the sky and in lieu of garden beds or potted plants there are several scarred wooden perches, along with elevated feeding troughs and water bowls.

An aviary.

As I watch, a bird of the deepest blue-black sweeps down from the boughs and settles onto one of the perches, its talons scoring deeply. Another raven, this one the darkest shade of scarlet, is already inside, its elegantly plumed beak tucked under one wing. It pauses its preening as we approach, cocking its head in tandem with the more recent arrival. Two sets of canny eyes never shift from Soren as he strides into the enclosure. I hang back, watching as he gently removes the thin scrolls of parchment tied to the birds' proffered legs.

My eyes fix intently on the scarlet raven. I have seen that unique coloring before. A breed distinct to Dyved. An emissary of the Fire Court. I wonder who sent it here, and what the small roll of parchment it ferried all this way contains.

A response from Pendefyre?

One about me, even?

Whatever the missive, it makes Soren's face ripple with

displeasure and his shoulders go stiff. His gait is hesitant as he makes his way back to me.

I wait for him to speak. To share, though he has no real cause to do so. His private correspondence is no business of mine. Still, my fingers twitch with the effort to keep from snatching the scroll from his grip. My lips press together to contain my curiosity.

Such efforts at self-discipline are rendered ridiculous only seconds later when Soren reaches down, grabs my hand, and presses the parchment into it.

My eyes jerk up to his, startled.

"This was sent to me, but it's you who should answer," he says softly. Almost solemnly. "It's your reply he wants."

With that, he takes his other scroll and disappears down the path, leaving me alone with only the rainbow-hued fyrewisps and glossy-eyed ravens for company. The paper in my hand feels like it weighs a thousand pounds as I raise it to my eyes. Only a few sentences are scrawled across it in messy, hurried hand-writing.

Penn's handwriting.

The sight of it makes my foolish heart vault straight up into my throat.

> Soren,
>
> What do you mean, Rhya is in Hylios with you?
>   I expect a more thorough explanation is forthcoming—more than the three scribbled lines of snark you were benevolent enough to send last night.
>   Though, frankly, I am less concerned with how she came to be there than why

she remains after a full day in your
company. I cannot think of a single good
reason she would choose to stay there.
    Not of her own volition.
    When she entered the portal yesterday
at Blister Bight, her intentions were to
return to Caeldera. Until I hear
otherwise, I will assume those intentions
have not changed.
    I swear to the gods, if you are in some
way preventing her return to me—

There is a dark blot of ink where the words abruptly taper off. As though his quill rested on the parchment for a long stretch while he gathered his thoughts. As though he had not quite known how to ask for a favor from his oldest enemy without resorting to threats.

In the end, he did not.

Only a handful more words stain the page, tacked on near the very bottom, just above the official seal of Dyved.

    Just... send her back here.
    Give her back to me.
    Please.

It is the *please* that breaks me. The formidable Pendefyre of Dyved, begging. Begging *Soren*, no less, a man he loathes.

Begging for me.

I know what that plea cost him. I know the weight of it. I feel the weight of it, too, behind my eyes. A burning precursor that couples with the bone-deep exhaustion already eroding my composure. I cannot hold it back, not for long. Sorrow swamps me along with a hot flood of tears that blur my vision, rendering the page unreadable.

All the feelings I've been suppressing since I stepped into that portal yesterday return with a merciless vengeance.

Pendefyre.

Blister Bight.

The fight in the rain.

Our broken potential.

Our precarious future.

I cannot even think of crafting a coherent response to the letter.

Not now. Not yet.

I am grateful Soren possessed enough compassion to leave me alone. Losing the battle against my melancholy is horrendous enough without him here to witness it.

Clutching the scroll tight to my aching chest, I run back to my dark, cozy suite inside the villa and bolt the door. But even the heavy wood paneling cannot keep out the sound of the storm that splits the skies outside my balcony windows, nor of the torrential downpour that pelts the tiled roof overhead as I sink down onto the veined marble floor and press my forehead to my knees to muffle my sobs.

CHAPTER
TWELVE

I'm running.

 Running so fast, I am practically flying, my strides lifting me into the air higher and higher with every desperate bound. Something is on my heels, closing in. Chasing me across this unfamiliar terrain of sand and ash.

 But I am faster.

 I move on wings of air.

 My blood sings with the very wind.

 Until my foot comes down, one faulty bound, and the earth opens up beneath me. Swallowing me whole. Plunging me into darkness. The walls close in around me, shuddering, shaking—

I wake with a start, jolting out of the disturbing nightmare. As the haze of sleep clears, I realize the shaking is not confined to the realm of dreams. The doors of my balcony are rattling, the wardrobe on the far wall knocking violently against the indigo sandstone. My ears pick up the faint wail of a warning siren being blasted across the city by the beacons.

Another earthquake.

Sliding out of bed, I keep low to the floor as I make my way to the door. The robe drags around my feet. It is a man's, far too long for me. I found it hanging in the back of the wardrobe after my bath and fell into bed wrapped in its plush warmth, wishing it could counteract the icy pall Penn's letter placed around my heart.

The tremors continue to rattle the chamber as I pull open the door and station myself at the threshold with one hand gripping either side of the frame. Past experience has taught me this is the safest place to stand until the shocks pass.

However, no sooner have the last of the rumbles faded and I have dared rise to full height than I am knocked flat on my ass again. Not by an aftershock but by a huge surge of maegic. It sweeps over me in a wave, raising every hair on my body to attention. My Remnant mark sears, responding instantly to the influx.

What the skies is happening?

Another wave crashes over me, pressing me to the floor. I fight against its crushing weight, knees creaking as I drag myself upright. Power tinges the air, flowing thickly all around me, catching me in its clutches. My feet move of their own accord—down the hallway, around a bend. I throw one hand out to the wall for support as I am pulled along like a tiny minnow caught in the deepest of currents.

The periodic surges continue as I move through a nondescript doorframe, then up a set of narrow, spiraling steps to a landing where a short ladder spears upward through a hatch into open air. I am incapable of resisting the mammoth outpouring of maegic that continues to crest and crash, a sea of sensation that heightens my every faculty. I sweep the dragging hem of my robe aside and climb without thought, without question, through the hole in the roof where the trapdoor is thrown wide, and step into the shadowy night.

By the time I reach the source of the relentless onslaught, I am out of breath—not from the climb but from the effort to keep my own power from responding in kind. Wind batters at my inner reservoirs, thrashing me from the inside out, eager to escape.

Breathe, Rhya. Just breathe.

But I cannot breathe. For all the air in my lungs vanishes as I catch sight of the man standing at the precipice, where the flat section of roof tapers sharply off into a slope of interlaced silver tiles.

I come to a sudden stop, staring at the bare planes of Soren's back as they ripple beneath the strain of his task. He does not turn to greet me. He does not even seem to know I am there. His arms are lifted out in front of him. His attention is fixed on the dark sea—as is his maegic.

My wide eyes follow the surge and what I see makes my whole body tighten with apprehension. Despite the darkness of the hour, the night is clear and the moon is bright. Bright enough to illuminate the crest of a great wave building on the horizon, where the Bay of Blood fades into the Endless Ocean. A wave that, even now, is headed straight for the city walls.

A tsunami.

I've heard of them before, these city-leveling aberrations, in Eli's old history tomes and cautionary tales told by the hearth. But I have never seen one for myself. At first, I do not understand how we could be so unlucky. Two natural disasters in the span of a few moments? It seems an ill omen from the gods.

As the beacon sirens fill the air once more, alerting the city below to the incoming danger, I realize the two incidents are irrevocably linked. The tsunami is a side effect of the quake, triggered by the shifting of the earth somewhere far out to sea. A swift and deadly ripple, looming in the distance.

To my straining eyes, it looks impossibly large. Large enough to devastate every town and village along the Llŷrian coast.

Large enough to break against the highest ramparts of Hylios and sweep us all away. And there is nothing to stop its advance.

Except for Soren.

Standing alone against the impossible. Protecting his kingdom even if he has to use every ounce of his power to do so. Pulse after pulse, he pushes back against the tsunami. Against the ocean itself, like some divine ruler of the tides.

I feel awed by him in this moment, lit by moonlight, his sleep-mussed hair somehow darker than the night itself. Such strength, such immense control, even in the face of certain defeat.

And yet . . .

Not so certain, after all.

For as I watch, the wave on the horizon stalls in its roaring approach. I cannot look away, cannot even spare the time to blink, as gradually it begins to recede—pushed back by the uncompromising strength of the Remnant of Water. He has fallen to his knees, his physical strength flagging, but his maegic remains immovable as he singlehandedly holds off the ocean's wrath, compelling distant currents to change course.

After a few moments, the mountainous crest has shrunk by half. Another few, and it has been compressed down into a swell that, while still tall enough to douse the sea gate, will not smash it off its hinges. By the time the wave finally reaches the city, it is hardly distinguishable from the others that crash rhythmically below us where the stone walls meet the sea.

I watch its final spray of foam fade into darkness, then take my first gulp of air in what feels like ages. My entire body is covered in gooseflesh. My blood churns with maegic as the night falls utterly quiet, the sirens keening off into a definitive hush.

Only then does Soren relent. His arms lower back to his sides as his maegic shudders to a stop. His head hangs down, drops of blood dripping from his eyes and spattering like tears against the silver tile. His breaths are labored. Even at ten paces, I can hear them moving in and out of his lungs. I have the strangest urge to close the distance between us, to do . . .

Something.

To *say* something.

But what could one say in a moment like this?

Where did you learn to wield your power thus?

When will you teach me to do the same?

In the end, it is Soren who speaks. His voice is thicker than usual, a throaty rasp that lacks all levity. "Spying on me, skylark?"

"No." I swallow hard against the lump in my airway. "I merely . . . I heard the sirens after the quake. Then I felt your maegic and . . . It was like I was compelled to seek it out. A tether, pulling me in. I could not seem to—" My teeth dig into my bottom lip, locking in the rest of my incautious words before they can escape.

Must I tell the man every thought that pops into my head?

As for Soren, he says nothing. He is unnaturally still, his body a gargoyle of stone on the edge of the roof. Suddenly feeling like the most voyeuristic of intruders, I begin to backtrack toward the trapdoor. I should've resisted the strange pull that led me here, even if I had to lock myself in my suite to do so. I should've—

"I'm hungry."

I halt, startled into stillness by Soren's abrupt announcement. "Sorry?"

"Famished, actually." His voice is back to normal. In a heartbeat, he's risen to full height and crossed to my side, moving like a phantom. The only indication of his recent maegical expenditure is his eyes. He's wiped away the blood, but his irises are nearly pure silver as they lock on mine, streaked sparsely with his typical sapphire. Only once before have I seen them like that—the night of Fyremas, as he fought the ice giants and drove back the Reaver clans.

"What about you?"

I blink stupidly at him. "What?"

"Are you hungry? You must be. You went to bed without dinner." He doesn't wait for me to follow him, merely prowls toward the hatch that leads back into the villa on bare feet. "Come on, then. I'll make you a midnight snack."

His tall form ducks down into the darkness as he descends the ladder out of sight.

After a brief moment of befuddled hesitation, I follow.

I SIT ON a stool, watching Soren move barefoot around his kitchen through slitted eyes, intermittently sipping wine from the crystal goblet he poured for me. I'm not entirely sure what to make of the sight of him huddled over a skillet, his large hand gripping a spatula. Gone is the man from the roof, with his quicksilver eyes and immeasurable power. Here is a new creature— one that sets my teeth on edge.

He moves with confidence as he collects ingredients from the larder and tools from his cupboards, as he cracks eggs into a flour-filled bowl. He did not lie this morning. The man does indeed know how to cook.

I sip more wine, hoping it might soothe the fluttering anxiety within. It is more than his ease in the kitchen that's making me nervous. After what I witnessed with the tsunami, I don't know quite how to talk to him anymore. Wariness lodges in my throat, so thick I'm certain I will not be able to get down a single bite of food despite the gnawing hunger in the pit of my stomach. I should tell him not to bother making me a helping. I'll simply go back to my room and—

Soren sets down a plate in front of me.

My mouth fills with a rush of saliva. I stare, astonished, at the perfect stack of griddle cakes, golden brown at the tops and bursting with purple berries. They smell heavenly, like butter and sugar and sweet cream. I am abruptly ravenous.

"They're no good cold," he says, taking the stool across from mine at the heavy oak table.

I nod, still staring at my plate.

He douses his own with a pour of syrup from a porcelain tureen, then sends it sailing across the smooth wood surface with a sharp flick of his fingers. Jolted out of my trance, I catch it reflexively before it topples off the edge onto my lap.

"If you're not going to use that mouth for conversation, you should use it for nourishment." His lips twitch as he pauses with a forkful held aloft. "I must say, I find you strange when star-struck into silence, skylark. I much prefer you snappy and snarling at me to tongue-tied and taciturn."

Gods, this man.

I shoot him another glare as I aggressively cut into my meal, my knife scraping the plate with a piercing shriek. All annoyance vanishes the instant the first bite hits my tongue. The syrup's sweetness mixed with the unfamiliar tang of tart berry juice is a revelation. I thought the sensory feast I experienced at the floating market would never be topped, but this is the best thing I've ever eaten in my life. I cannot stop a low hum of pleasure from escaping the back of my throat as I chew.

Soren's gaze flickers up to mine at the sound. "Satisfactory?"

I manage to swallow, still reeling from the flavors bursting across my tongue. "What kind of fruit is this?"

"You've never had a seaberry before?"

I shake my head and take a sip of the crisp, floral wine—a perfect pairing for the tangy berries—to wash it down. "They do not grow in the Midlands. Not anywhere I've been, in any case."

"Ah." He saws another forkful off his stack. "I sometimes take the Llŷrian climate for granted. We have a long growing season on the mainland. What we cannot produce ourselves, we import from the Southlands or across the North Sea. And here in the capital, we have several greenhouses that keep us in plentiful produce during the colder season. They're not far from the Easterly Beacon, if you feel the urge to explore tomorrow."

Tomorrow.

Will I still be here tomorrow?

Everything inside me feels tangled. Decisions that once seemed clear as the crystal of my goblet are veiled with hesitancy. Penn's letter should've made the choice simple. He wants me back. I should return to Caeldera. There is no reason for me to stay.

There is no reason for you to go, a small voice whispers at the back of my mind. *There is nothing down that path but pain.*

The silence stretches as we eat for several minutes. Soren's eyes linger on me across the table as he takes long sips of his wine. Studying me as I clear my plate, bite by bite. As usual, he discerns the direction of my thoughts without my ever sharing it.

"Have you replied to him yet?"

I stiffen on my stool, fork frozen halfway to my mouth. "No."

"You don't know what to say."

My teeth grind together.

"I suppose I cannot blame you there, given his rather incendiary reaction to things that do not go his way." Soren pauses. "Maybe a love sonnet to soften the blow?"

My grip tightens on my fork; I am surprised it does not bend in half.

"No, Pendefyre doesn't seem the type for poetry . . ." Soren pops a berry into his mouth, chewing slowly. "You could sketch him a picture. That might better suit his reading level anyway. How's your hand at drawing?"

I frown at his mocking grin. "This is not a joke. Nor is it your business."

"Oh, but it is," he counters, flattening one hand against the tabletop. His index finger taps absently as he speaks. "The last time he thought I'd taken you against your will, he showed up at the gates of the Acrine Hold with a battalion of soldiers, fully prepared to start a war to get you back."

Some of my anger ebbs. Trepidation washes in to replace it. Surely Penn will not actually show up in Hylios looking for me . . . Surely he does not really believe I remain here as a captive . . .

"I like to think you're wise enough to realize you have to stay."

My eyes fly back to Soren's at his unexpected announcement. He's abandoned his meal, not even keeping up the pretense of eating as he fixes every ounce of his attention on me. The force of that stare is astonishing. It is all I can do to remain in my seat.

I clear my throat. "I may be tired now, but by the morning I'm certain I'll be rested enough to survive a portal journey. If you'll only—"

"I don't mean stay because you're tired or hungry," he says, cutting me off. "And I don't mean stay for another few hours or another night. I mean . . . *stay*. Stay here."

My inhale is audible, my reply instant. "I can't."

"Why? You were to come here at midsummer anyway for Arwen's wedding. That is less than a month from now."

"Exactly. I'll be back at midsummer, as scheduled."

"You're already here."

"I wasn't meant to be."

"What's meant to happen and what actually happens rarely align in this life. And we are usually better off for it, in the end." His fingers flex against the tabletop. "Do you think people have any true concept of what is best for them? Of what will make them happy?"

I huff softly. "Because you are some great expert on happiness?"

"I never claimed to be. I'm merely pointing out that, more often than not, those who get precisely what they want in this world are disappointed to find it does not live up to expectation, let alone provide fulfillment. It is the things that surprise us, the things we never see coming, that make this slow march toward death even remotely enjoyable."

"Careful, Soren. If you carry on with these sentimental worldviews, people will start to see you as an optimist. However will your fearsome reputation survive?"

He does not even crack a smile at my flippant remark, clearly not in the mood for levity. He takes another swallow of wine, eyeing me over the rim of his glass as his throat works. "Tell me honestly. What is so pressing back in Caeldera?"

"The restoration efforts—"

"Will take years. And are not your burden."

"The citizens—"

"Are fleeing in droves, according to my sources."

"I have patients—"

"Who will surely get on without you as they did before."

"That may be true," I reluctantly concede. "But there are also threats to the borders, which are—"

"Being dealt with by Dyved's highly capable armies. And, it bears repeating, no burden of yours. Unless you plan to venture onto the ice shelf arm in arm with General Yale." He pauses. "I cannot quite envision such a partnership, given the commander's outright hostility when it comes to you."

How is it that he always seems to know everything?

My nostrils flare on an exhale. "Reavers aside, there are other pressing threats. The Frostlanders—"

"Will turn their gazes back across the sea to easier prey after one strong show of force. They're scavengers, not occupiers." His fingers tap out a new pattern on the tabletop. "Now. Any more excuses to spin for me, or have you finally run dry?"

"You don't—I just—" I take another sharp breath. "Pendefyre will be—"

"What?" he clips when I trail off, a flash of impatience in his face. "Angry? Jealous? Fuming at the loss of his possession?"

I set down my fork, hand shaking. "I am not his possession."

"He keeps you like one."

"I am not his to keep."

"Aren't you?"

My eyes narrow to pinpricks. "No. I am *mine*, and mine alone."

"Right." His voice drops lower, to a blatant imitation of Penn's rumbling tones. *"Give her back to me."*

The words he wrote in his letter.

Soren's scoff is scathing. "What are you, a misplaced hat? Some lucky trinket he keeps in his pocket?"

"You have no idea what you're talking about when it comes to my relationship with Pendefyre."

He scoffs again. "Clearly."

"I will not be relegated to the role of a toy without autonomy, caught in some ridiculous game of tug-of-war between the two of you. I have my own mind, and make my own choices. Always."

"Always?" Then why do your decisions hinge on his desires?"

"You don't know anything about my desires!"

"Don't I?" His eyes hold mine as his head cants to one side, regarding me. There is an awareness in their depths that makes my stomach clench. "You want to stay."

"I don't."

He drains the rest of his goblet. "In two centuries, I've never met a worse liar."

I shoot to my feet, anger surging. "I am not lying."

"You are." He rises as well, then rounds the table toward me in slow, deliberate strides. "I can read your emotions behind those flimsy little shields you put up, but I don't have to. The truth is written all over your face."

Nearly tripping on the too-long robe, I backpedal away as he comes closer, my pulse spiking in alarm as I make efforts to so-lidify my—apparently ineffective—mental shields. Whether it's the effects of the wine or a leftover rush from his battle against the tidal wave, there is a disconcerting energy swirling around Soren. Not the frothy, playful waves at the surface of his person-ality. No, we are deep in uncharted waters. The look in his eyes makes my heart thud, my nerves ignite. My hands come up as if to ward him off.

"Soren, stop."

Yet he keeps coming, crowding me back until I've retreated all the way across the kitchen. His voice is calm; his expression is anything but. "Do you think you can hide from me?"

I do not answer.

The air between us grows denser as it compresses to an arm's length. Charged, like the sky before a storm. Every particle of it seems to sizzle in my lungs.

A messy lock of hair falls into his face. He does not pause to push it away. "Do you think your guilt is thick enough to obscure the things you want?"

"Guilt?" My back hits the wall, halting my retreat. "I don't feel any guilt."

"Again, with the lies."

My teeth clench. "You're being an ass tonight."

"Just tonight?" His smirk is dark. Dangerous. He takes another step—a final step—and my heart stumbles a beat.

I clear my throat nervously. "I don't know what's come over you, but—"

"Perhaps I'm tired of this game."

"I'm not playing any games."

His body stops just short of mine, so close we are very nearly touching. My head tips back to keep him in view. His eyes at such proximity are impossible to escape, the blue piercing straight through me, the dark lashes fringing them thick enough to make any kohl-clutching courtesan jealous.

I press my spine so hard against the wall, I'm certain it will bruise. I do not dare breathe. I fear if I do, the slightest expansion of my lungs will cause our chests to brush.

"If you're trying to intimidate me," I hiss, "it's not working. You can be the pushiest prick in the realm, I'll not cower before you like some wilting flower."

His lips twitch briefly with amusement, but soon twist into the cruelest of smiles, his humor vanishing so quickly it gives me whiplash. "Pushy I may be, but at least I'm honest. Can you say the same?"

My lips part, but he cuts me off before a single retort escapes.

"You want to be here. Whether you can admit it or not . . . I can *feel* it. Today, when we channeled . . . That high, that rush . . . You've never felt anything like that before. And I didn't need the godsdamned bond to tell me that." His face swoops down so it is aligned with mine. His cheekbones are sharp as blades; his words somehow sharper, though they come out in a whisper. "I know because I've never felt anything like that before, either. Not in my exceedingly long lifetime."

My lungs seize, incapable of function.

"Even now, beneath your annoyance, I can still feel traces of it," Soren continues. "Your mind moving with mine. Your heart pounding in perfect sync." His voice, always so melodic, turns serrated. "Connected. *One*. You felt it, too. I know you did."

"I didn't feel it." A friable declaration.

He grins darkly. He knows I'm lying. He does not call me out on it. Instead, his hands come up—one bracing on the wall behind me, the other collaring my neck. I suck in a startled gasp as his strong fingers wrap like a featherlight noose. He can no doubt feel my pulse racing under his fingertips. But then, he does not need to feel it.

Not when he is inside my head.

I tell myself to pull away, but I am oddly paralyzed in place—by his body, by his touch. By his words most of all.

"You are a bird that's been kept in captivity for far too long, skylark." His mouth is so close, I can feel his breath on my lips, sweet with berries and wine. "It's time you try out the open skies for a change. If you go back to Caeldera, you go back to your cage."

"And you'd rather keep me here? Another bird in your aviary?" I croak. "That's just swapping one set of bars for another."

His jaw tenses with uncharacteristic tightness, a fissure of pure frustration. He quickly smooths it away. "Is it easier to paint me the villain in your story than to admit I might be right?"

"But you aren't right."

"No?"

"You don't know anything about me or my life."

"I know a great deal more about you and your miserable life than you can imagine." His eyes glitter ominously. His fingertips glide against my throat, a lethal caress. "I know you spend your days toiling at the sickbeds of strangers. I know you spend your nights locked away, alone, in the apartments of a dead apothecary. I know you rarely eat, rarely rest, rarely speak, and never smile. I know your friends have fled to every corner of the Dyvedi plateau, and the few who remain in the city are none too eager to pass hours in your company. I know you are deeply lonely, little wind weaver. And that loneliness has cut you to the bone, chiseled away your wild, reckless spirit into a melancholy skeleton."

The words lash through me, devastatingly honest. I cannot refute them. They are true, every one.

"You are disappearing before my very eyes. You paint the skies with your sadness. You walk through this world, wings clipped. A ghost, terrified to make any impression. Afraid to offend or draw attention." His sigh is laced with displeasure. "Gods, you cannot fault me for trying to prevent you from returning to that dismal fate."

"You . . ." My face slackens with shock as his words trigger a new realization. "Have you been . . . *watching* me?"

"I have eyes everywhere. Even the Fire Court." He sounds completely unrepentant. "Especially the Fire Court."

"But that's—" I shake my head. "I don't understand. *Why?*"

"I have made it my business to know about you since I first heard of your existence. Long before you arrived in the Northlands."

I flinch.

Before?

What does he mean, *before?*

"No. No, that's not . . ."

"Oh, yes. From Thawe Bridge to the Cimmerians. From Vintare to Coldcross to Caeldera."

"The mountain. The wildfire. You *were* there," I breathe, staring at him. "You helped me ford that river. The day we met."

He does not answer. His jaw is tight. His eyes are swimming with maegic and something else. Something deeper. Something downright terrifying.

"Why?" I ask, practically panting.

"Why what?"

"Why were you there?"

He does not answer this, either. Not verbally, anyway. But as his fingertip traces the thudding pulse point at my neck, I feel his maegic whisper through me, a silken blow that makes me quake.

"If you would rather dwell in your own darkness over things you cannot change, that's your choice," he says, eyes locked on mine. "But if you let it, it will eat you alive. You will lose yourself in your grief. Your regret. Your losses."

His mind brushes sinuously against my mental blockades. His maegic threads deeper into mine.

"You blame yourself for Fyremas, though it was not your fault," he says inside my head, seamlessly shifting to a psychic connection. *"Worse, you fear that Pendefyre blames you, too. If he does, he is an even bigger fool than I previously believed him to be."*

"Get. Out. Of. My. Mind!" I grit aloud.

"Make me."

I'm trying—not very successfully. "Back off, Soren. I mean it."

His mocking laugh reverberates inside my skull. *"Well, if you mean it . . ."*

"I am finished with this . . . this . . . whatever this is. Or . . . was." I swallow hard. My heart is pounding too fast inside my chest, and my body—my maegic—is intensely awake, as though it might explode out of my skin at any moment. "I'm going back to Caeldera. Now. This very moment. Take me to the portal."

"Is that really what you want?"

Yes.

No.

I am no longer sure.

My chin jerks. "You expect me to stay here and allow you to invade my head without permission anytime you see fit?"

"Do you think our enemies will ask nicely before tearing through your mental guards? Do you think Efnysien will tread carefully on your precious need for privacy?"

The blood drains from my face.

His eyes never shift from mine, boring into me as his voice batters at my resolve. *"You believe you do not need lessons. You believe you can face this coming war with sheer bluster, because that's worked for you in the past. It will not work in the future."*

"You don't know that."

"Oh, but I do."

The challenge in his voice—in his eyes—is unmistakable. His maegic sings even more strongly through me as he drops his guards, releasing his steely grip on the bond that is stretched taut between us. The slack rushes in, swirling through me, uprooting my control. I try to push it back, but it's impossible. Like trying to scoop water from a flooding boat with your hands alone.

I am sinking.

"You want me out? Prove it. Push back."

"GET OUT!" I shriek down the bond, finding my inner voice for the first time. It is surreal, but somehow deeply significant, to speak thus. Like a hushed conversation that happens under covers in the middle of the night. Something halfway between dreaming and daylight. Even screaming cannot dispel the intimacy of it. *"GET. OUT. OF. MY. HEAD."*

"But I'm not just in your head, skylark," Soren whispers back, a taunting rumble that shakes me from the inside out. *"I'm under your skin. Admit it."*

Operating on pure fury, I throw up a fresh mental air shield, the strongest I've ever conjured, and shove with all my might. I am determined to drive him out of my thoughts, to sever the connection he's forced. To prove him wrong at any cost.

Pain vaults through me, battering my temples, but I keep pushing, pushing, *pushing*, just as he did with the tsunami, until I feel the water recede. Until I am alone again in my head.

For a moment, I actually think it's worked. I think I've succeeded. I pant, spent by the immense effort, but proud of myself nonetheless. Until I see the look on Soren's face as he leans deeper into the wall, fully dwarfing me with his frame. A familiar predatory glint creeps into his eyes. There is a flash of silver in the blue, like the whitecap of a wave.

Then I feel it.

Feel *him*.

His mind, pressing against the perimeter of mine. Soft at first—a caress, testing my newfound fortifications. The faintest brush. And then, with a swiftness that makes my whole body spasm, he tears through my mental barricade like it is made of paper.

The mark on my chest burns, a cold flame, as he invades, engulfing me where I stand. The calm waters of my mind's eye, where my power is centralized, flood with him instead of me, his maegic instead of mine. Physically, I am still breathing, yet I feel like I'm drowning, like the oxygen inside my lungs has been swapped out for ocean. He swamps me with a laughable lack of effort.

Not that I am laughing. A scream builds in my throat as all that is Soren sweeps around my head, overturning memories, unearthing secrets. It is not like the first time we channeled. This is not a bolstering gift of strength, a buttress to my inherent limitations. This is an invasion. A hijacking. A full-scale assault of the mind, the maegic, the soul.

There is no possibility of resistance. No chance of fighting back. I stand there, flayed open to him, the depths of my mind painfully accessible. For some reason, he does not dive deep. He stays on the surface, floating high above the recesses that house the darkest parts of me. I wait for the humiliation, for the violation that will surely come.

It does not come.

Staring into my eyes, he lets me drown in him for three endless seconds. A tiny eternity in which I do not draw breath, in which my very heart ceases to beat. Long enough to let me know, if he wanted to, he could take everything from me without batting an eyelash. And then, just as quickly as he pushed in, he extracts himself. His water recedes and my mind is my own once more. My maegic is my own.

Yet in the shuddering, knee-shaking aftermath, I know *nothing* is my own. Not really. In the space of a heartbeat, he has effectively proved that everything I hold dear, every private memory and close-guarded confidence, is *his* whenever he chooses to reach out and snatch it away.

Pushing off the wall, I plant my hands against his bare chest and shove him back with all my might. He barely budges. But his hands drop to his sides, so he is no longer touching me.

"If you ever do that again," I hiss, voice breaking with rage, *"I will kill you."*

A humorless smile twists his mouth. "You are welcome to try. Many have before. None have yet succeeded. Not even me."

Some of my anger slips a notch at that admission. I refocus, intensifying my glare. "Are you determined to make me hate you?"

His eyes go carefully blank. "You may hate me. But the truth is, you need me. That may piss you off, but it doesn't change the facts. A war is coming. It has been brewing a long time, and when it finally reaches us, you must be ready. Body, mind, maegic." He pauses to expel a breath. "I am not Pendefyre. I'm not going to coddle you or keep you behind glass like some dainty fucking butterfly. *You are a Remnant.* It's time someone reminded you of that. And since I'm the only one capable of it—or because the gods have a twisted sense of humor—that unfortunate task appears to be mine."

I say nothing. I cannot. My words are caught in my throat, as conflicted as my emotions.

With another harsh exhale, Soren turns and walks away. I watch him go, my spine still pressed tight to the wall, each breath in my lungs sharp as shattered glass. When he reaches the archway that leads out onto the dark terrace, he pauses with his back to me. A towering silhouette, half painted in candlelight. His voice is barely a whisper, but I flinch as though he's shouted.

"The next time you ask me to take you back to Caeldera, be certain you truly want to go. Because I will comply." There is a brief pause. Even from this distance, I can see the tension rippling through his shoulders, the tight furl of his fists at his sides. "I cannot be the only one fighting for you to embrace your potential. Not anymore."

My mouth opens to tell him to take me back now, this instant. But no words come out. Not even as he steps over the threshold. His voice carries to me one last time as he vanishes from sight, a low purr in the night air.

"Our choices are all we have in this life, Rhya. No one else can make them for us. So ask yourself what you want. Not Pendefyre, not me, not another living soul in Anwyvn. *You.*"

CHAPTER
THIRTEEN

I lean against the feather-strewn desk in the corner of the aviary, eyeing the scarlet-plumed raven. He eyes me back, shrewd gaze all-seeing in the dull midday light. His talons are longer than my fingers, curled around the scarred wood perch like black blades. I take a calming breath before I summon the nerve to approach, imagining how easily he could scratch out my eyes, but he obediently lifts his leg, where a leather cord is affixed, for my use.

I work methodically, hyperaware of the sharp beak a handspan from my face as I bend in to attach the scroll. It is slightly crinkled—the parchment I found in the desk is old and curling at the corners. I think back over the message I scrawled inside as I slowly tie it in place.

Pendefyre,

I am safe. And, for now, I am staying.
I will see you at midsummer.

Rhya

A handful of words that had taken me hours to compose. I'd tossed and turned all night, agonizing over how best to respond to him. In the end, I went with bare facts, excising my feelings from the missive. It's better that way. My feelings are too tangled to sort into rational sentences, an unruly knot of regret and remorse and rage, all of which is threaded through with irrevocable longing.

I miss him.

I miss his heat and his fire, his burning eyes and that way he looks at me—like I am the spark that sets his very soul aflame. But I learned the hard way that a fiery passion can sear the heart from your chest if you are not careful. I got too close, and it burned me out. Something inside me singed into ashes that day at Blister Bight. I fear I cannot rebuild it, even if I were brave enough to try.

Perhaps time away will lend me the clarity I need. Perhaps some space from the flames that flare so brightly between us will be enough to soothe the scorch—aloe on a wound that will never heal in his presence, for seeing him rips it open again and again and again.

Arriving in Llŷr was an accident . . .

But it could also be my salvation.

Though it would be foolish to mistake Soren's presence for a balm to one's damaged soul. He pushed me last night—mentally, physically, elementally—crossing boundaries I am still furious about, overstepping in ways I will not soon forgive. He seems to enjoy meddling in my life, as well as testing my capabilities. And while a part of me chafes against that, another part, deep down inside, knows he is right.

If you go back to Caeldera, you go back to your cage.

I made more progress with my power in a single day in Llŷr with him than in all the days I spent in Dyved combined. I am not so pigheaded as to pretend otherwise. Nor am I able to deny that I have a lot further to go before I begin to approach mastery. And I desperately need to master my powers. There is no more time to waste.

For a war is coming, of that I have no doubt. The Midlands are poised on the brink of utter carnage. The Southlands are in worse straits. And then there is the not-so-insignificant problem of Efnysien. There is no telling how long it will take for the weasel to pop his head out of his den again so we might lop it off.

Before Fyremas, he had not been spotted for nearly a decade, Soren told me.

Pendefyre will not wait a decade. His need for revenge is insatiable. His anger is inextinguishable. It is only a matter of time before he launches a campaign into the black sands of the Husk Desert with his broadsword aimed at the Symmetria Keep.

The only question is: will Soren march with him?

Llŷr and Dyved are allies in war, pledged to defend the Northlands against invasion. But this is untested territory. To seek out the enemy, to invade the most inhospitable stretch of Anwyvnian soil . . .

Soren himself said it is nearly impossible.

Where his stepbrother is concerned, his motivations are murky at best. He wants revenge, that is clear enough. But for what? How deep does his animosity run? Deep enough to take up arms with Pendefyre? Deep enough to set aside all previous failed attempts at conquest and try again?

I suppose we will find out in three weeks, at midsummer, when Pendefyre arrives here. I know him well enough to realize his upcoming visit to Hylios is about far more than attendance at a royal wedding. He will not squander the opportunity to sit down with Soren and sketch out a strategy of attack.

I do not know the King of Llŷr half so well. I cannot say

whether he will be willing to wade into war. For now, I do not care. His willingness to teach me to wield my maegic is a far more immediate bridge to cross. Despite my initial resistance to the idea, long hours of restless contemplation in bed last night ultimately led me to a conclusion Soren no doubt reached the moment I tumbled out of his portal.

I have to stay.

Moreover . . . I *want* to stay. To train my skills, to improve my control. To learn from him any way I can. Only a fool would walk away from such an opportunity.

I am many things, but I am not a fool.

So, for the time being, I will remain in Hylios. I will soak up Soren's knowledge like a sponge. And come midsummer I . . . I will . . .

I shake my head.

That bridge is one I am not going to even think about crossing.

Not yet, in any case.

Scroll affixed, I step back and watch as the scarlet raven takes flight, spreading its dark wings against the gray skies and swooping up into the heavy cloud cover. I try not to imagine Pendefyre's reaction when he receives my message. I have a feeling the paper will burst into flames the second his eyes spot my handwriting.

When the bird is out of sight, I leave the aviary, brushing at the downy feathers that cling to my fitted navy tunic and trousers. I found a pile of fresh clothing waiting for me outside my bedroom door at noon when I finally dared to poke my head outside my suite. They fit perfectly, as do the soft leather boots that lace up to my knees. The trousers are similar to the ones I saw the Paexyrian riders wearing yesterday, with built-in sheaths for weaponry, though lacking the inner thigh padding. I was surprised to find one of the sheaths contained a dagger.

My dagger.

Soren must've retrieved it from the water sometime in the night. I cannot fathom why he went to such effort, nor how long it had taken him to locate it at the bottom of the harbor. I traced its familiar glyphs, wondering what sort of man mercilessly invades your mind, then swims to the depths of a shipwreck to retrieve one of your lost possessions.

A man I do not understand in the slightest, that is certain.

I make my way back through the gardens toward the villa. I am nearly there when I hear the sound of raised voices spilling from the terrace. Slamming to a halt, I duck behind a large palm frond before I am spotted.

"—subjected to yet another day of this miserable weather! How long will you allow her to pollute our skies unchecked?" a female voice snarls. "The earthquakes and tsunamis are bad enough. Now we must contend with pervasive cloud cover courtesy of that temperamental airhead, who shows no aptitude for—"

A heavy male sigh cuts her off. "Arwen, your Paexyrian can fly through the pitch-black night and gale-force winds. I doubt your training schedule will be interrupted by a smattering of clouds."

"It's not the Paexyrian I'm concerned with. Are you so wrapped up in her you've forgotten I'm to be married in under a month's time? Half the bloody kingdom is coming, if my bridegroom has his way. And by the looks of it we won't be celebrating out of doors! Not when the heavens threaten to pour buckets whenever Miss Misery twists her nose out of joint or, gods forbid, gets a hangnail!"

"I wouldn't think you'd be concerned about the wedding at

all. You put up such a fuss about the ceremony, I assumed you'd be thrilled the day was spoiled."

Clearly, he's struck a familiar nerve. Arwen's voice goes glacial. "You know how important this alliance is. I will not jeopardize our relationship with Daggerpoint. If I have to put on a frilly dress and spout vows before every lord and lady in Llŷr, so be it."

"I'm certain Alaric won't mind if you get married in your flight leathers. The man worships the ground you walk on."

"As he should."

Soren sighs again. "Arwen—"

"Look, brother, I understand your head's been turned by the stormy-eyed chit, but is it too much to ask you to speak with her about the weather that is poised to ruin a day that has been in the making for longer than she has walked this earth?"

"Ask her yourself" is Soren's reply.

I go stone-still.

"What?" Arwen asks.

"You can come out, skylark." He sounds amused. "I promise my sister won't bite. Hard."

Attempting to smother the blush that is overtaking my cheeks, I slink from behind the palm tree and step back onto the path. Not a dozen paces away, Arwen and Soren are standing by the top of the stairs, gazing down at me from the terrace. They look almost like twins, with their blue eyes and dark hair and identical poses—arms crossed over chests, feet planted wide. They possess the same vicious beauty. Those cutting cheekbones, those elegant jawlines. There is not much softness in either of them, though Arwen's expression holds none of her brother's warm amusement. She studies me like a cockroach as I approach, her angular features pinched in blatant dislike.

"Hello," I say tentatively, ascending toward them. "You must be Princess Arwen. We didn't have a chance to officially meet yesterday on the docks."

"What, no curtsy?"

I freeze at her tart question. I thought Llŷr did not practice the traditional royal protocols. My eyes shoot to Soren for confirmation.

He shakes his head lightly. "Ignore her. The delightful *princess* here would sooner arm wrestle you than observe proper etiquette."

"As if she could arm wrestle," Arwen mutters. "Her limbs are like toothpicks."

"Sister, you are about three biting comments away from me having the armorers fashion you a muzzle."

Ignoring her brother, her eyes narrow further on me. She is an intimidating sight, clad in leather top to toe. I count a minimum of four lethal blades tucked at various places on her person, along with the set of silver throwing stars at her hips. The shaved sections of hair at her temples lend her an additional air of menace, as do the inky tendrils of a tattoo that corkscrew up the side of her neck. She is tall for a woman, with curves almost as ample as her muscles. Besides the silver hoop in her septum, her only accessory is a pair of flight goggles that hang down around the sculpted leather bodice like a necklace.

She uses the opportunity to study me in turn. "So, this is the famed Remnant of Air. You do look like a gust of wind might blow you away, I'll give you that." She pauses, eyes flickering down my form. "That, and not much more."

I grit my teeth and strive for calm. "I'm Rhya."

She continues to stare at me in silence.

"Though you seem to have several other names for me already," I go on, never breaking her gaze. *"Quivering dock rat? Temperamental airhead? Stormy-eyed chit?"*

"Don't forget Miss Misery," Soren adds, crossing his arms over his chest as he leans against the railing. "I quite liked that one."

We both ignore him, still glaring at each other.

Eventually, Arwen shrugs. "That's what you get for eavesdropping. Don't listen in on other people's conversations if you are not prepared to hear things you do not like."

"Are you always this caustic toward strangers, or am I a special case?"

"That depends on how long you're planning to stay in my city."

"Don't you mean *my* city?" Soren mutters.

"Why would I want to leave when my reception has been so warm?" I ask her, voice saccharine. "I wouldn't want to miss a moment of your wedding festivities." I pause, all sweetness draining from my tone. "A real shame about the weather. If only there was something I could do about it . . ."

Arwen's blue eyes flash with annoyance. She turns to her brother as though I no longer exist. "I'll be at the barracks. Harpina and Bretiax are due back from Windward Port with a briefing from Vaughn. Come find me when you're ready to discuss it. And do me a favor? Leave the runt at home."

With one last scathing look at me, she turns on a bootheel and trots down the steps, following the path that leads toward her villa. I watch her go, my expression pinched into a scowl.

"Who on earth would marry her? A bridge troll?"

Soren lets out an unbridled laugh. "You'll meet Alaric soon enough. He and his fleet are due to arrive from Hollywell next week with half the wedding party and a metric ton of lager."

Our eyes meet, and an unspoken understanding passes between us. He does not ask if I will still be here in a week; I do not tell him I have decided to stay. Admitting it aloud feels, somehow, like admitting he was right to do what he did last night—invading my mind, pushing my limits. I would sooner choke on my words than make such an admission.

"Llŷrian garb suits you," Soren says, shattering the silence. His eyes sweep me up and down. "Though you did look rather fetching in my robe."

"*Your* robe?"

He nods, lips twitching.

My eyes widen. "I did not realize. I found it in the wardrobe in my suite . . ."

"That room was mine as a boy."

I rock back on my heels in surprise.

His room.

As a boy.

I sometimes forget that Soren was raised here, in this very house. Unlike Pendefyre, he is royal not only by birthright but by blood as well. He and Arwen sprang from one of the strongest fae lineages in history, which dates back to the time of the emperor. His father was a king long before he was born, and continued to rule for a long stretch after.

King Manawydan was reputedly even more fearsome in battle than his son. He steered the Water Court through the bloody aftermath of the Cull, all while holding back the grasping Midlanders, Frostlanders, and Reavers who sought to eradicate his kind in the years that followed. Not to mention raising a Remnant and a brood of other children.

Questions bloom inside me, a garden of curiosity. How old was Soren when his father died and passed on the crown? How old was Arwen? She must be nearly as old as Soren, though she looks not a day over thirty. Was she raised here as well? And what of their mother?

I will have to explore the library later in search of answers, for I do not feel quite brave enough to pry into Soren's personal life by asking him directly. Bad enough to learn my beloved bed-chamber is, in fact, *his*. I fear I cannot take any more earth-tilting information today without falling over.

"I didn't know," I say stiffly, "that it was your childhood room."

"Really? I assumed that's why you picked it."

My mouth drops open. "It was not! I picked it because it's the farthest away from yours, you self-obsessed—"

His laughter interrupts my diatribe. "Gods, you're easily riled. I'm teasing you."

I do not know whether to laugh with him or gut him with my dagger. Since I am rather grateful for the fresh clothing and un-willing to spatter it with blood, I decide to practice mercy.

"I can sleep in a different suite, if—" I break off. After an awkward swallow, I try again. "Now that I'll be here for a longer stretch, I could find another place to sleep."

He waves away my words. "Don't be ridiculous. I meant it when I said the villa is yours to explore for however long you are here. Make yourself at home."

"Right." My throat feels oddly thick. "Thank you for the clothing. And . . . the dagger." I finger its ornate handle. "It means a lot to me."

There is a charged beat of silence. Soren's mouth opens, then shuts again. As though he was about to say something, only to reconsider his words. When he does speak, his tone is decep-tively light. "Yes, well. You're lucky dark blue favors your col-oring."

"Your people wear many shades of color," I point out.

Yesterday, the streets were a rainbow of skirts and cloaks, with both men and women in all manner of dress. I saw every-thing from pale yellow breeches to a gauzy gown of aquamarine that reminded me ever so much of the one Soren gifted to me all those months ago at the Acrine Hold. It, like so much else, was lost to me at Fyremas. But I have not forgotten how it felt to wear it. How the many shades of blue rippled with each stride, so I felt like a shore-bound sea creature.

"Those associated with the royal family or who work in an official capacity in the capital typically don the Llŷrian standard." Soren shrugs. "You are free to wear whatever you'd like. There are plenty of shopkeepers down in the city who would be thrilled to outfit you. There's enough coin in your desk drawer to purchase anything your heart desires. Or, if you'd rather not spend your days shopping, simply ask one of the staff. They'll provide whatever you need."

"I thought you did not keep a staff."

"Typically, I don't. But the upcoming wedding will require more than even my sublime cooking skills to keep everyone fed."

I arch my brows. "*Sublime* seems a stretch."

"Must we have another conversation about your penchant for lying?"

"No." My eyes shoot daggers at him. "Though I would like to have a conversation about your behavior last night. If we are to do this—if you are to train me—it must be with the understanding that some things are off-limits."

He considers this for a moment, then shakes his head.

"Why are you shaking your head?"

"No limits. No boundaries. And no more bloody restrictions." His voice goes slightly rough. "I would think you'd had your fill of those in Caeldera."

"So you are to . . . what? Invade my mind every time you please?"

"Hardly. Last night was a lesson. One I did not undertake lightly, and one I would not have resorted to unless I felt it was truly necessary. As you are now, you lack the strength to guard your mind against threats, as well as control your own power. We may channel, but I will not invade your thoughts again. Not until you invite me in."

"Don't hold your breath."

He carries on as though I have not spoken. "That said, for this to work, for you to make progress with your power, you must open yourself up to everything. Let go of this incorrectly ingrained idea that you ought to lock your thoughts inside your head and your emotions inside your heart. You must allow yourself to feel everything, without limit. Without recourse."

My pulse picks up speed as I contemplate that. It is contrary to everything I have been taught to this point. "Penn says emotions are a liability."

"Pendefyre is a bloody idiot." Soren pushes off the terrace railing and crosses to stand before me. "The king of restraint has no business giving lectures. Emotions are not a liability; they are a limitless resource. You want to wield your power like me? You need to *feel* it. All of it. Every damn bit of pain and passion and desire." His eyes glitter as they hold mine. "Repression never got anyone anywhere except dead."

We stare at each other for a long moment. Eventually, I clear my throat. "Where do we start?"

My whole frame tenses as he reaches toward me, but he merely plucks a wispy raven feather from the sleeve of my tunic and holds it between us. His mouth tugs up at one side. "With something small."

CHAPTER
FOURTEEN

After the chaos of my first day in Hylios, my second is rather dull by comparison. No monster attacks—assuming one does not categorize Arwen as such—or tsunamis or mind invasions. I spend most of my afternoon in the aviary, annoying the ravens as I attempt to float feathers.

"Now that you know what finesse feels like," Soren tells me at the start of our lesson, "it's time for you to find some of your own."

Standing at my back with his fingers interlaced with mine, he allows me to borrow a bit of his proficiency as I direct thin streams of air to steer molted feathers into the sky. They orbit around us, a tornado of maegic moving faster and slower at my command. Sometimes just hovering there, like dandelion wisps in the wind.

Soren gives occasional instructions, mind to mind. *That one there, on your left. Float it higher. Flip it on its end. Spin it twice clockwise.* For the most part, though, he allows me to play at will. After a while, I actually begin to enjoy myself. I lean back against his chest, relaxing as tendrils weave from my fingers with an elegance I never thought I'd achieve.

"You're getting the hang of it now," he says after nearly an hour.

I nod absently, most of my focus caught up in my task. My teeth sink into my bottom lip as I spin a vortex faster, elongating the pillar of feathers until they reach through the open ceiling. I'm so intent, I don't realize Soren's stopped channeling until my tiny tornado sputters suddenly into stillness. The feathers flutter back to the earth, scattering before my boots. The lack of his power is a dull void beneath my ribs.

"Hey!" I half yell, whirling to face him. "You disconnected!"

He looks amused by my accusation. "You don't need my maegic for this anymore. You've had enough practice that you should easily be able to achieve the same kind of control on your own."

"Easily?" Historically speaking, nothing about using my powers has ever come easy.

He flashes an unconcerned grin. "Just remember to focus on your breathing, like I told you. The air that moves in and out of your lungs is the same air you manipulate with your hands. Shaping it to your will should feel as effortless as an exhale."

"But that's impossi—*Hey!* Where are you going? We aren't finished!"

To my dismay, he's already turned and started walking away. "You're not; I am. I'm late to meet Arwen. Keep at it while I'm gone, skylark." Over his shoulder he calls back, "And do try not to murder any of my ravens. My correspondence is tardy enough without the need for a newly trained flock."

I glare at his back until he disappears around a bend in the garden path.

Without him there to channel, I am not nearly so successful, nor half as graceful in my efforts. It takes far more energy to isolate the vastness of the wind into maneuverable streams. Several times, I accidentally disturb the ravens with rogue blasts of air, which results in them retreating up into the wisteria to plot my demise. And yet, I am not a total lost cause.

Now that I know how control feels, I can mimic it. It is a bit like retracing steps through a city you've been led through blindfolded. My feet know the way even if my eyes do not. While my feathers do not dance and flutter in perfect sync, as they had with Soren, I do manage to levitate them one by one, up and down, side to side. A headache gathers at my temples as I repeat the moves again and again and again, until they are fluid as the breath in my lungs.

By the time I quit for the day, I am physically exhausted yet my mind is uncannily energized. The successful use of my maegic puts a spring in my step as I make my way back to the villa. It is abandoned, no signs of Soren or the staff he has supposedly enlisted.

Stomach growling with hunger, I raid his larders, helping myself to an apple, freshly sliced bread, soft cheese, and some more of the crisp wine I sampled last night. It's barely sunset; far too early to go to sleep. Instead of heading to my suite, I wander the villa.

Without Soren there to oversee me, I snoop freely through his galleries. His home is like a museum, stocked with artifacts and intriguing baubles, many of which look old enough to predate the Cull. Vases and statues and masks, varying widely in color and craftsmanship. Some are from distant places I've never even seen on maps.

The shelves are stocked with strange things—vials of gritty black silt from the Shadow Steppes, tattoo pots from the famed ink mavens of Carvage, fist-sized Dyvedi rubies, a luminous bottle of liquid starlight that can only be from Lake Lumen. He even has a gold-leafed branch from the mythical Aurea Tree in Seahaven. Seeing it makes my heart ache for my childhood.

The artwork on the walls is extensive and extraordinary. I could easily spend hours walking with my gaze cast upward in awe, captivated by the collection.

How surprising, then, that the piece that stops me in my tracks looks, at first glance, rather mundane. It is a portrait. Not particularly large nor particularly vibrant. In fact, its paint is faded with age, its gilded frame dulled and cloudy. Nothing special in the midst of so many grander works. Still, it holds me captive, as though the woman depicted within has reached straight from the canvas and seized me by the soul.

I cannot tear my eyes away from her. An angelic figure, backlit by a blazing sky. She is in the heat of battle—arm cocked back, coiled whip held aloft—but her expression is one of total serenity. She wears golden armor, sculpted to her body like liquid. It is nearly the same shade as the mane that streaks out behind her as she flies. Not a leap off the ground, nor a jump from great heights.

She is *flying*.

My heart lodges in my throat as I bend close to read the etching at the corner of the frame.

"THE GOLDEN GODDESS"
QUEEN ARIANRHOD
HOUSE OF TARANIS

I'd read of her before. The famed sovereign of the Sky Court, struck down defending her kingdom when mortals sacked the stronghold and slew everyone within. Judging by the smile on her face in this painting, I think she would not have chosen an easier end. For this was a woman born for battle.

What would it be like to fight in flight, I wonder? To take to the sky like a bird, so in command of your own power you do not question it as the earth falls away, as the heavens press close? The mere idea is equal parts exhilarating and terror inducing.

Arwen and the other Paexyrian riders seem fearless as they ascend atop their winged mounts, but this . . .

This is another feat entirely.

My thoughts remain distracted as I finally tear myself away from the gallery and resume my wandering. I determine to learn more about Arianrhod of the Sky Court. The little I know about her—the strongest sylph ever to weave the wind, from one of the oldest fae bloodlines ever to rule—only increases my curiosity about her grim demise.

How had one so powerful fallen so fast? What happened to her court after her soul returned to the skies? Was her maegic like mine, or somehow different? Was she a distant ancestor, some severed branch of my unknown family tree?

I stack those questions atop the growing mountain of others in the back of my mind about Soren's homeland, his family dynamics, his history . . .

It is growing rather cluttered in there.

My feet subconsciously steer me toward a solution to my curiosity. The library. It's dark when I enter, no fire in the grate or signs of life amid the many shelves. After lighting a handful of sconces, I peruse the books for a long time. There are more than I could read in a lifetime, many written in foreign tongues I do not recognize.

Despite the vastness of Soren's literary trove, my search for material related to the Sky Court turns up empty. Instead, I select a thin tome that chronicles the history of the Water Court and its ruling family, and settle in on a chaise lounge to read. I make it through approximately five pages about the geothermal springs that heat the turquoise waters of Hylios before my eyes slip shut and I tumble into dreams.

THE LUXURIOUS WEIGHT of a down duvet settles over my prone form. I jolt into consciousness, my sluggish eyes adjusting to the darkness of my bedchamber. As the cobwebs of sleep clear, I see a shadow sitting on the edge of the mattress.

"Soren?"

"Shh, skylark. Go back to sleep."

Oh, gods, he must've found me asleep in the library, book askew on my chest, and carried me here. My cheeks flame with embarrassment. "Sorry. I was reading. I must've nodded off . . ."

"Mmm. Probably something to do with your choice of material. Not the most enthralling historical account, as I recall. It would have even the most disciplined scholar slack-jawed and drooling by the second chapter."

I push up into a seated position against the headboard. "I was not drooling!"

"On my favorite pillow, no less." There is a teasing note in his voice. "I'll set out some better books for you tomorrow, ones that won't bore you into slumber. We can't have you ruining the furnishings."

"I thought I was not to be trusted with your books after the castle incident."

"Thank you for reminding me." His eyes gleam, inquisitive. "What were you hoping to learn, anyway?"

My blush intensifies. I hope he cannot see it in the dark. "Oh, nothing in particular."

"Skylark."

Sighing, I hurry on, "I was curious about Hylios. How things function here."

"Things?"

"The royals. The armies. The citizens." I clear my throat. "You."

There is a loaded silence. "Me."

"Yes, you. You are a king, after all, even if you don't act like one. Is it so shocking I would be curious about your long reign?"

"No, I suppose not. But I was not joking when I said you merely need to ask. I will happily answer anything you want to know about me." Another short silence descends. "Almost anything."

I shouldn't pepper him with questions. It's late, and he has better things to do with his time than indulge an inquisition . . . But before I can stop myself, I've blurted out, "How old were you when you took the throne?"

"Seventeen," he answers immediately.

"So young."

"At the time, I felt ancient, trust me."

It is as difficult to imagine him as a teenager as it is to imagine him at six. Hell, it is difficult to envision him at any age remotely close to my own. There is a timeless air around him, a self-awareness accumulated by centuries on this earth.

My mind stalls on thoughts of a very different Soren. One less in control of himself, one more on par with my own floundering skills . . .

Incomprehensible.

My brows lift. "The crown passed to you when your father died?"

"When he was killed, yes."

"*Killed?*"

His jaw flexes. "Poisoned. We never discovered by who, but I have long held my suspicions. His last wife, Duvessa—my step-mother, Efnysien's mother—was fond of alchemy and fonder of the riches she drained so proficiently from the royal coffers. I would stake my life that it was her hand that tipped the vial into his glass and stole him from us."

I swallow a gasp. "Skies, Soren. I'm sorry."

"It happened nearly two centuries ago," he says, shrugging. Yet I can hear the grief buried not so deeply beneath his words and know he is still pained by the loss. "My father was gifted the luxury of a long rule, and an even longer life. He died with a smile on his face, ready to meet the aether, even if he did not fall in the glory of battle, as he anticipated . . . or while bedding one of his many conquests, as the rest of us assumed he would." He chuckles darkly. "I like to think he had no regrets in either life or death. He certainly never acted like he did, given his wild enthusiasm for all of the world's many pleasures."

"How long, exactly, was his reign?"

"Manawydan ruled Hylios for nearly four hundred years after Emperor Belenus elevated him to the throne. Before the Cull, the two men were evidently close personal friends. The emperor was gifted with two maegics—"

"Fire and air," I interject, nodding. "Penn told me once."

He stares at me. "What else did he tell you?"

"Not much." I think back to the conversation. It feels so very long ago. Another lifetime. "He said the emperor was conceived from a union of two exceptionally powerful parents. Born the product of a soulmerge—and, thus, blessed with the ability to wield two distinct elements. A powerful combination that has not been seen in all the years since."

His throat works on a swallow. "Yes. That's true enough."

Enough . . . but not everything. Not the full of it. I get the sense there is much more to this particular chapter of Anwyvnian history than I've been told.

Soren shifts the conversation forward before I can press.

"Emperor Belenus valued my father highly for his formidable water powers. Manawydan could spin the seas with a twitch of his finger, could command the tides and influence the currents like none ever before. Or after."

"Until you."

He shakes his head. "Remnants possess but a vestige of the old maegics. We are an echo of what once was. Before the uprising, before the blight that followed on its heels, Anwyvn was a land of abundant elemental power. Each of the four courts brimmed with gifted sky sylphs, water nymphs . . . flame breakers, earth turners . . ." His eyes narrow a shade. "It is difficult to imagine, even for me. By the time I was old enough to comprehend, things were already so irrevocably changed."

Soren's birth, I know, coincided with the Cull. With the imperial execution itself. As the first Water Remnant—the only Water Remnant—his soul reputedly entered this world at the precise moment the emperor's fled it. His, along with King Vorath's and those of two unknown others, scattered in distant spots across the realm. The original four of the sacred tetrad, prophesized to someday restore the balance, should they ever find their way together.

So said the oracles, anyway.

I wonder, not for the first time, about the first wind weaver, birthed in the same breath as the man sitting before me. Who were they? Where did they live? When did they die? How many others existed in the time between their demise and Enid's discovery, seventy years ago?

The one person in the realm who might know the answers is seated mere inches away.

"Were there others before Enid?" The question flies out. "Other wind weavers, I mean?"

"Two, to my knowledge."

Two!

I lean toward him, interest piqued. "Did you meet them?"

"Not personally, no." He frowns, thinking back. "About ninety years ago, one managed to send a raven north to Dyved—a desperate plea for extraction. She was dead by the time Pendefyre reached her in the Soot Flats of Nythia."

I grimace, saddened but not surprised. Nythia is one of the worst stretches of the Midlands. The fighting there has raged continuously for two centuries.

"A few decades before that, around a century and a half ago, another made it nearly to the Avian Strait, where my armies were camped. At the time, we were embroiled in a decade-long conflict with a particularly persistent king from the plainlands." A muscle ticks in his jaw, expression darkening. "She got close. Achingly close . . . only to be struck down by a group of bloodthirsty culling priests and made into a depraved spectacle for the amusement of the Aranthonians."

My whole body trembles at the thought of such an end.

Damned culling priests. Hypocritical monsters, the lot of them. They wrap their dark hedonism in false holiness, a shroud for acts of such evil only a blind man could mistake them for anything remotely divine.

"I pulled her down from the iron crucifix where they'd nailed her body," Soren says, voice thrumming with untempered distaste. "Gave her a proper pyre. Then, I razed the priests' temple to the ground—with them inside it."

A fresh shiver moves through me at his admission. At the wrath in his voice, still fresh despite the lifetime that's passed since the atrocity occurred. I feel no condemnation for his actions, only horror at the barbarity that necessitated them.

He forces a lighter tone. "It is good you were born where you were. Seahaven's sheltered shores gave you a chance most others did not live long enough to take."

I blink, concealing my surprise. I cannot recall ever telling him where I come from. Evidently, he was not exaggerating when he said he'd made it his business to learn about my life before I journeyed north.

"Any other questions?" he asks.

Only one I can think of.

"Did . . ." I pull in a breath. "Did they look like me? The others?"

His head tilts, examining me in the darkness. "Not really. Similar coloring, perhaps, but different builds, different features . . . The crucified one in Aranthon was far taller than you. And Enid was all curves whereas you are . . ." He trails off, then grins. *"Not."*

I fight the urge to throw a pillow at him.

His grin widens, noticing my annoyed expression. "I'd say a passing resemblance, at best. Well. Except for . . ."

I wait, brows high on my head.

"Your eyes," he finishes. "Every wind weaver has those stormy irises." The grin fades into a new smile—less sardonic, more sentimental. One I've never seen on his face. "Even Enid, in all her softness, could unleash a tempest with her gaze alone."

My stomach twists into a knot. "Penn said—" I start, then falter.

His expression clears. "Go on."

I gather my courage. "He said she was beautiful, but . . . broken by all she had endured. The slaughter of her family. The loss of her home."

"Beautifully broken. Mmm, that was Enid. Wildly intellectual, but exceptionally introverted. It was difficult to draw her out of her shell. Unless you wanted to discuss whatever book she had most recently devoured—in which case, it was impossible to stop her chattering. She spent hours and hours in my library when Penn brought her here to visit."

The unguarded fondness in his voice makes the knot in my gut twist even tighter. Speaking of her feels intrusive, somehow. I begin to regret my own insufferable curiosity, and wish I'd never broached the topic of my venerated predecessor.

For who can ever live up to a ghost?

"What else did Pendefyre tell you about her?" Soren asks, gaze sharpening on me when he notices I've fallen silent.

Only that he believes himself responsible for her death.

And that you both thought yourselves in love with her.

I bury the words deep inside. "Not much of anything."

He looks as though he does not quite believe me, but blessedly does not push.

"So . . ." I swallow hard. "Besides those two wind weavers who died in the Midlands, you have no record of any other Air Remnants?"

I do not ask about Earth. I know better. Whoever they are, wherever they are . . . they have never been located. Not once in two hundred years.

"No, unfortunately not," Soren admits. "I did not begin to search in earnest for other Remnants for several decades after I became king. Frankly, whispered prophecies simply were not a priority at that time. *Survival* was our priority. War raged on a grand scale for a dozen years after the Cull, in every corner of the realm. It had died down slightly by the time I took the throne, though not by much. My formative memories are of bloodshed and death."

I tense at the thought of such an upbringing. While my own childhood had hardly been one of privilege, it was safe enough until, at last, war overtook us. But for twenty years, Eli had carved out a quiet life for us in Seahaven. Like Soren said, the peninsula's shelter gave me a chance never afforded to my fellow wind weavers. I was lucky to have experienced relative peace, away from the brutality encompassing other stretches of the Midlands.

Soren crosses his arms over his chest. "Llŷr lost so many of our strongest fighters in those first years of battle. My father proved formidable enough to hold off the encroaching mortal armies . . . but only just. Much of our population was lost even before the oldest bloodlines began to falter."

I nod, for this is not new knowledge. I had read of the slow erosion of maegic. How our strongest fae families began to produce maegicless children, how the divine gifts of our people slowly died out. Advanced healing, long life, enhanced eyesight, attuned hearing . . . all of it, lost within the space of a few generations.

And Soren had lived through it all; had watched so many perish, as he remained. He and Arwen and a handful of others from the oldest bloodlines are all that is left of a bygone era.

"The Northlands were different then. Pendefyre's predecessor, King Vorath, was not interested in an alliance. He closed the borders of Dyved, would not discuss trade or combine forces in battle." A shadow of irony creeps into his tone. "It would be another half century before change arrived in the form of a young boy at the city gates, demanding to see the king."

Pendefyre.

"A warrior from the start," I say without thinking.

"And yet," he counters, "so rarely fighting for the things that truly matter."

A thick silence descends as we both contemplate the King of Dyved. We are now traipsing on unsteady ground. I suddenly find it difficult to breathe around the tension in the air.

Clearing my throat, I look around the dim chamber and ask, "What time is it, anyway?"

"Moving on midnight."

"Were you at the barracks all this time?"

He nods. "Yes. A long day, and not a particularly pleasant one, as I spent the majority of it buried under a mountain of correspondence. There is much to sort out, with Arwen leaving."

"Leaving?"

"After the wedding she'll be moving to Hollywell with Alaric. Ruling with him from Daggerpoint. Raising her family there, assuming they decide to have one."

"Oh. I did not realize."

"She'll still command my armies and serve as flight leader for the Paexyrian riders. But she'll be doing it from a portal away, instead of a few stairs. It will be an adjustment for both of us." His voice pitches lower, as though his next words are not meant for me. "After two centuries, you grow accustomed to doing things a certain way."

Skies, he sounds almost . . . *vulnerable.* I have never heard that from him before. But then, I've never had a sibling. I cannot begin to understand how it would feel to lose one. Certainly not one I'd lived with, fought with, laughed with, for hundreds of years.

The faint shaft of moonlight on Soren's face is enough to highlight the frown at his lips, the furrow of his brow.

"You will miss her."

His eyes find mine in the darkness. "Yes," he says simply.

"Can you not ask her to stay?"

"If I asked, she would. But I cannot. I will not. Not when I know she wants to go. Asking her to choose between me and Alaric would be like asking her to cleave the heart from her chest for the sake of duty." His fingers rake through the hair that has fallen into his face. "When you see them together . . . how they look at each other, how even across a room they seem to move in the same orbit, like two tethered stars . . . you will see what I mean. I would never deny her that chance at happiness. She has waited nearly as long as I have for it."

I digest his forlorn confession in silence, my thoughts spiraling in directions they have never dared before. If Soren was a friend, I would attempt to comfort him in a moment like this. If he were Jac or Farley, I might crack a joke to lighten the mood. If he were Carys or Lestyn, I would wrap my arms around him in a warm embrace until the shadows retreated from his eyes. But Soren is . . .

I do not know what he is. I do not know how to comfort him, or how he would react if I tried. My fingers unconsciously clutch the duvet. With effort, I force them to relax their death grip. The air between us has grown markedly heavy.

"You said it was a long day. Did something happen? Do you . . ." I am out of my depth, but bluster on anyway. "Do you want to talk about it?"

He stares at me, saying nothing. Just studying me intently, his gaze roving over my features. The silence stretches on and on, until I begin to long for powers of invisibility rather than endure one more moment of scrutiny.

"What is it?" I scrub at my cheek with one sleeve. "Do I have dried drool on my face or something?"

His chuckle is subdued. "No. It's just been a long time since someone was in a position to ask me about my day."

My stomach flips. Surely that cannot be true. He is a king. Beloved by all. Revered by his people.

And yet . . .

He lives in this big house all alone, looking down over his city like some distant god. Never quite connected, never fully a part of the fabric, even when he takes the time to rub shoulders with those at sea level.

Only last night, he spoke of my deep loneliness. As I look at him now, for the first time I consider the fact that Soren might be deeply lonely, too.

"And how was *your* day?" he asks, skillfully shifting the conversation around the awkward tension.

"I am a master of feather levitation," I inform him, tone glib.

"Is that so?"

"You don't believe me?"

He shakes his head. "You'll have to prove it, I'm afraid."

"I'm not going to the aviary right now. It's the middle of the night and, besides, I think the ravens are angry at me for—*Hey!*" My words cut off in a squawk of alarm as Soren's arm darts behind me and extracts one of my pillows so fast, I barely see it happen. A low tearing sound precedes an explosion of downy white feathers as he rips the plush cushion clean in half. They rain down in a cloud that covers everything—the bed, the marble floor, Soren's white linen shirt. They have no sooner settled than he reaches down, grabs two fistfuls, and tosses them straight back into the air.

"Soren!" A shocked sound—half laugh, half gasp—explodes out of my lips. "What is wrong with you?"

"Show me." He's grinning, tossing more feathers. "Come on, levitation master. Let's see those much-lauded skills of yours in action."

The stilted atmosphere is swept out of the room by a chorus of chaos and laughter. I set about demonstrating my newly minted skill set, manipulating several streams of air at once in a slow spiral that lifts all the fluffy white feathers into the air. Soren's eyes crinkle at the corners as his gaze tracks the vortex that swirls through the suite, from the veined marble floor to the richly coffered ceiling.

"See?" I, too, am grinning like an idiot. "I told you. Master of levitation."

He looks at me for a long beat. There are feathers stuck in his hair, clinging to his shoulders, smattered across his shirtsleeves. He does not brush them away or even seem to notice them. The lonely look is long gone from his eyes; they now hold only amusement. And, perhaps, a hint of pride.

"There may be hope for you yet, little wind weaver," he murmurs. Then, pushing to his feet, he walks through the floating sea of feathers to the door. "Tomorrow, we shall test what else you excel at manipulating."

After the door clicks shut behind him, I release my hold on the feathers. They flutter to the floor, a blanket of white settling over everything. In the morning when I awaken, it looks like snowfall on a cold winter's day. But outside my windows, shafts of warm spring sunshine are creeping through the dense clouds.

CHAPTER
FIFTEEN

T oday's lesson is about trusting your instincts."

I tilt my head to one side, confused by Soren's announcement. "My instincts?"

He smiles mysteriously.

We're on a pebbled spit of beach just outside the city walls, accessible via a narrow cut-through at the base of the Westerly Beacon. A set of salt-crusted steps hewn directly into the foundation lead down to a cove so tiny, it is hardly more than a tidal pool even at high tide.

Too shallow for ships, the Hylians use it as an underwater vineyard of sorts. Not far offshore, vintners on flat-bottomed barges use rope-and-pulley rigs to haul sealed casks from the sandy bottom, where they have spent several months fermenting, then lower fresh ones down with heavy anchors for next year's vintage.

After spending some time in Llŷr, I'm learning that the sea touches every facet of life here. Every industry, every livelihood. Even winemaking. And I must confess, however foreign the means of production seem to my eyes, the wine inside those barnacled casks is beyond reproach. It has become a nightly indulgence after long days of training.

Sometimes, when he is not occupied by his kingly duties, Soren is there to drink with me. Other nights I sit alone on the inner terrace or my private balcony, sipping slowly as I flip through one of the books he has taken to leaving out for me, savoring the fruity bouquet as I scribble letters to Lestyn.

Our correspondence began on my third day in Hylios. The first raven I sent was merely to inform the boy not to worry when I do not show up at the infirmary these next few weeks. To my surprise, a scarlet raven was waiting for me with a response the very next morning in the aviary. He'd written me back—and continued to do so throughout the following week, his messy, boyish scrawl a perfect suit for his boundless energy, whether he was chastising me for abandoning him or complaining about Osain's overbearing dominion.

Don't let the old badger boss you around too much, I wrote to him last night in response to a long-winded missive that detailed their latest clashing of minds over leg-cast preparation. *And please don't forget to check in on Carys . . .*

The letters are my one true touchstone to Caeldera. For Penn does not write again.

At first, I wondered about him constantly, worrying about his reaction to my absence, his fixation on the wards, his tendency to push himself too far . . . But as time slipped by, the days lengthening into a week, then stretching toward two, I grew less preoccupied by the life I left behind and more consumed by the new one I am carving out in Hylios.

I am too busy to mark the days as they pass and too tired to second-guess my decisions by the time I crawl into bed at night. My daily lessons have progressed from levitating feathers in the aviary to swirling fallen branches from the olive trees to juggling the heavy lemons that pepper the grove outside Arwen's villa. The last, in particular, won me no favors with Soren's snarling sister, who, when she caught me decimating her produce, made it clear I am not welcome in her section of the royal grounds, no matter what her brother says.

I have not gone back to the lemon grove since.

Eventually, I graduated to flinging smooth stones from the spring against the targets Soren set up for me in his courtyard— my favorite of the lessons so far, even if it did disturb the phosphorescent frogs that dwell in the still waters around the crystalline bathhouse. I am finally beginning to grasp what he meant during our battle against the arachnida.

I do not need a weapon to fire a projectile.

I *am* the weapon.

Yesterday, after another eclectic breakfast at the floating market, Soren took me out sailing in the Bay of Blood aboard a trim skiff. I had never been sailing before, and found myself undeniably nervous as we passed beyond the towering sea gate. But with Deke at the helm, steering us capably into open waters, I did not panic. Not until Soren positioned me at the bow and ordered me to fill our square-rigged mainsail with currents of wind, commanding changes in our speed and direction every few moments like the most incorrigible of admirals.

This was unquestionably the most challenging training exercise I have yet attempted. Several times, I miscalculated my own strength, nearly tearing our sails and sending our shallow-keeled vessel careening into the rocks, boom swinging precariously, water spilling in over the gunwales. I swallowed down bouts of nausea each time we pitched riotously amid the swells, trying to keep a handle on my errant tendrils of power despite the distractions.

Not an easy task.

Even Deke, seasoned seaman that he is, grew a bit green around the gills after we nearly capsized the second time, thanks to my use of a bit too much force when we tacked rapidly around a sandy shoal halfway between Hylios and the mainland where dozens of sea lions were basking in the midday heat.

Of the three of us, only Soren appeared to truly be enjoying himself. He'd lain back against the cushions along the starboard rail, arms folded across his chest, face angled up to the sky, eyes closed. Soaking in the sunshine like another lazing sea creature.

I could hardly fault him for it. Fair weather has been something of a rarity in Hylios of late. In recent days, though, it does seem to be creeping more boldly between the clouds. Today, in fact, the sun is only partially obscured by hazy mist. Visibility across the water is clearer than I've witnessed since my arrival in the city.

From Vintners' Cove, I can make out a good stretch of the mainland in the distance. A pitted strip of coast leads from Daggerpoint in the south up to Titan's Way, the heavily traversed channel that runs along the northern length of the kingdom between Llŷr and Prydain Isle. Connecting the North Sea to the Bay of Blood, it is one of the most important passages in all the Northlands, for without it one would have to sail all the way around the large island the Titans call home.

No sailor would risk such a journey if it could be avoided. The Titans' hostility toward strangers is almost as notorious as their immense size.

Eyes narrowed in a squint, I watch several ships chart a course toward the high walls of the capital. Their progress is slow in the light wind, barely enough to push their heavy cargo across the turquoise waters of the bay. They are the latest in a long string of arrivals, with berths full of guests for the wedding and holds laden with foodstuffs and decorations. Not to mention the gifts from Llŷrians who cannot attend in person. There has not been a royal wedding for several decades. Excitement is high, and the generous tithes reflect it, with folks from all across the kingdom lavishing their warrior princess with tribute.

Each evening, I watch more ships appear on the horizon as I walk the ramparts, tiny from that vantage, their masts like matchsticks, their crews ants scurrying about as they douse sails and drop anchor outside the sea gate, where a temporary mooring field has popped up seemingly overnight. There is no room for them in the harbor. Every slip and tie-up is occupied, along with every inn and canal-side café.

The city feels near to bursting already, and the wedding is not quite a fortnight away. I can only imagine what it will be like when the groom's party arrives from Daggerpoint. They are due in later this afternoon, according to Soren.

I catch myself wondering when the Dyvedi contingent will put in their own appearance. Probably not until the very last opportunity, given Penn's reluctance to leave Caeldera unprotected.

I cannot say whether the thought of several more weeks of separation from him inspires trepidation or impatience within me. Somehow, both in tandem. My heart, like the rest of my world, feels ever so slightly out of sync. As though time is moving simultaneously too fast and too slow for my liking.

I tell myself that when Pendefyre finally does arrive, so will clarity of thought. And yet, the mere prospect of him in Hylios makes my breath shorten and my mind spin.

It seems incongruous.

I cannot properly picture it.

Penn, here.

A spark amid the sea.

A sputtering flame against endless blue.

A crab scuttles over my foot, startling my focus back to the cove. I nudge it away with the tip of my boot, avoiding its clacking claws. It is a beautiful spot, secluded from the frenetic energy of the canals. The waters are calm today, the waves a gentle lull in lieu of their typical violent crash against the walls. Schools of colorful minnows dart around in the shallows. Mossy orange algae cling to the rocks where exposed beds of black mussels await harvesting before the tide sweeps back in.

It's quite warm in the sunshine. Sweat slicks down the back of my neck, drips into the collar of my close-fitted cotton shirt, beads beneath the supple gray leather of my pants. I'm hit with a fierce urge to strip off my clothes and jump into the shimmering sea. I have not been swimming since I fled Seahaven last autumn.

Gods, was that only last autumn?

I feel I have lived several lifetimes since then.

Above the quiet slosh of waves, my ears pick up the strains of music nearby. It sounds almost like wind chimes, but deeper in pitch and not perfectly rhythmic.

An organ?

"Soren, what is that sou—"

A huge water ball slams into me without warning, knocking me backward into the shallows. My whole body is submerged for several seconds before I splutter back to the surface. Utterly drenched and gasping for air, I claw my way to my feet, my fingernails full of sand and pebbles. I am slicked to the skin, water pouring off me in rivulets.

"Infernal hells! What was that for?"

My shriek draws the attention of the vintners offshore, but I am too angry to care about causing a scene. I stomp out of the shallows with my glaring eyes fixed on Soren. He is still standing precisely where he was before, arms crossed over his chest, booted feet planted on the beach, enigmatic smile on his face.

"Instincts."

I blink. "What do you mean by—"

Another mammoth ball of water clips me in the chest. I tumble backward again, ass over elbows, and hit the water face-first, ending up with a mouthful of briny seaweed. Choking and spitting like an enraged beast, I burst out of the bay intent on murder. My clothes are plastered to every curve of my body as I slog back toward the beach. To my great annoyance, the waves seem to be ferrying me along, kissing at the backs of my knees.

Soren's doing.

"So help me gods," I thunder, storming toward him the second my sodden boots hit the rocks. "This is not amusing!"

"I fully agree," he says solemnly, though his lips are twitching.

"Do you care to explain what that was about?"

"*That* was you failing to trust your instincts."

I gape at him, totally confused. "Have you gone insa—"

Another water ball slams into me. This one is smaller. It does not take me down, merely douses me where I stand.

"Stop that!"

He just stares at me, watching the water course down my body. I can feel it dripping off the ends of my hair, pooling in my socks, saturating the leather strappings of my thigh sheath. My anger is matched only by my mystification.

Why is he doing this?

I thought Soren and I were becoming, if not friends, at least . . . Close acquaintances. Comrades in arms. Allies of a sort, beyond mere teacher and pupil.

With the exception of our maegical lessons, we do not spend an exceeding amount of time together. He is, after all, rather busy with the business of running a kingdom. But on the occasions he is not meeting with Arwen or consulting his advisers or mingling with his people, he is at the villa. He does not go out of his way to avoid my presence. Often, he actually seeks me out—

joining me on the terrace for a glass of wine at sunset, or in the library where I am reading by candlelight, or in the kitchen where I am fixing myself a meal.

Sometimes he cooks. Sometimes I do. He is undeniably a dab hand with a whisk or a spatula, but I am not completely incapable of pulling together a passable dinner. As we eat, he tells me stories about the happenings down in the city—Arwen's warpath regarding the rapidly approaching wedding, the grueling process he's been overseeing to remove the burned-out wreckage of the *Selkie* from the harbor floor, the mediation of several trade disputes between rival merchant companies. In turn, I tell him about my progress with my powers, brimming with excitement over my increasing control.

He never pushes me to reveal anything beyond what I offer willingly, nor does he share much of anything personal. I think we both feel safer that way. Keeping conversations light, never straying into deep waters. Superficial though it is, I cannot deny it feels . . .

Restorative.

There is a part of me that craves normalcy. Lightness of being. Levity. Before I arrived in Hylios, I could not recall the last time I had a conversation with anyone that did not reference war or wounds, devastation or death. To have someone to simply chat with about nothing of any real importance . . .

It is like a gift.

One Soren has given to me, one for which he does not expect anything in return. And that, in itself, is another kind of gift. For it is perilously rare to receive something without any expectation of reciprocity.

But now, as I stand here on the beach, sopping wet and mad as a hornet, I cannot help but question our burgeoning camaraderie. Perhaps I have been mistaken. Perhaps we are not as close as I've presumed. If he thinks torturing me for sport is an amusing diversion . . .

"Look," I grit out, still seeing red, "I don't know what you think this is accomplishing, but . . ."

My words falter into silence. Because, suddenly, I *do*. I feel the faint surge of maegic stain the air between us the instant before he summons another water ball, before his fingers so much as twitch to send it flying. One split second of awareness. Hardly enough to process what is about to happen, let alone dodge out of the way . . . but long enough to counterstrike.

My anger thrums close to the surface. I do not tamp it down. I use it like fuel. The very moment he blasts me with another globe, I fling out my hand and send it barreling straight back at him. He grins as it misses him by a large margin, already summoning another from the shallows. It hurls at me quicker than should be possible, but I'm prepared. I call a current of wind and catch it, an invisible hand closing around the ball. Then, with all my might, I lob it at Soren's head.

He deflects it easily, sending it splashing onto the rocks.

"Good." His eyes are glittering. "Now you're getting it."

I'm panting too hard to respond.

"You have sharper senses than most, but they're only good to you if you use them," he says, not at all winded. "Once you can recognize the telltale signature of impending maegic, you can stop it before it is used against you."

I raise my brows. "Are you planning to use it against me?"

"I am not the only one with maegic in this kingdom. Llŷrian bloodlines are strong despite the blight. Arwen herself has minor water powers. Nothing like mine"—his words gain a wry edge—"but enough to do some damage."

I have no difficulty envisioning an attack from Arwen. The

ice between us has not thawed since my first day here. If anything, it is thicker than ever.

"With focus, you will be able to sense far more than just maegical threats. As a wind weaver, you more than any of the Remnants are innately attuned to body and breath. You can sense the smallest hitch in a throat, the quickest intake into lungs. These are telltale cues from your enemy." He takes a deep breath that broadens his whole frame, as if to underscore his point. "You can feel an arrow as it flies at you through a sightless sky, can perceive the swing of a soundless blade as it arcs toward your neck. Think of it as an internal alert system. One that will protect you from harm, if you put it to use."

Soren calls another globe of water from the shallows. Shafts of afternoon sun pierce through it, refracting in all directions like a diamond in the light, as he sends it hurtling toward me without warning.

But then, I do not need warning. Not this time. In addition to the brief swell of maegic in the air, when I hone my attention I can indeed sense the slightest change in his breathing—the infinitesimal huff that escapes his throat as he heaves the heavy water my way.

I cast out my arm and watch the ball careen off course under a wind current, splashing harmlessly into the shallows.

"Well done." Soren's smile is anticipatory. "But can you do it at double speed? Or how about two at once?"

His next few attacks come at me twice as fast and twice in number. I dodge a strike coming at my face only to be struck from behind; duck an inbound volley only to be clipped in the shins. Predicting his moves takes every ounce of my focus. Despite my best efforts, he manages to douse me multiple times.

"I suppose there was no other way for you to teach me this

lesson?" I grunt as I stop an incoming globe, holding it still between us. "One that did not involve me ending up soaking wet?"

From my peripheral, I see a secondary ball sailing straight for my head. I manage to stop it at the last second, throwing up a wall to shield my right flank.

Soren grins as he neatly sidesteps my retaliatory shot, his boots kicking up a shower of sand. "None that would be half so effective at drilling it into your head. Or half so amusing to witness."

I respond by way of an eviscerating glower.

Unbothered, he sends a pulse of pure maegic my way. I am instantly dry, every particle of water leached from my skin and clothing in the time between two blinks. The sudden change is disorienting.

"Uh . . . thanks." I run my hands through the wild tangles of my hair. It, too, is bone-dry, but still holds traces of salt, sand, and seaweed. "I don't suppose you have a comb handy . . ."

He does not chuckle at my low request. He does not hear it at all. His eyes are fixed over my shoulder, far out to sea. I turn to follow his gaze. At first, I see nothing. Nothing but a haze along the distant horizon, emerging from the mist that shrouds Prydain Isle in the north. After another moment of squinting, I am able to pick out the familiar shape of matchsticks moving toward us.

Ship masts.

Many of them.

I look at Soren. "More wedding gifts for the blushing bride?"

He shakes his head slowly, eyes still riveted.

The look on his face is making me nervous. My heartbeat picks up speed. "The fleet from Daggerpoint, then?"

"No. Alaric's ships are larger." His voice is tight. His eyes finally cut to mine and, when they do, they are rife with fervor, all traces of humor stripped away. "Those are Frostlander long-ships."

My lips part to ask a question, but it is drowned out by the sudden blare of the Westerly Beacon overhead. And then, there is no more time to ask anything. Soren has my hand in his and he is running—pulling me across the rocky beach, up the narrow stone steps, into the dark passageway that cuts back into the city proper.

THE SOARING WALLS of Hylios are something of an architectural marvel. Since my arrival in the capital, I have spent many twilights strolling along the ramparts, admiring the view of the labyrinthine canals below, the endless expanse of ocean that stretches as far as the eye can see. The true marvel is not in the lofty sightseeing spots atop the walls, however.

It is within the walls themselves.

A series of ladders, trapdoors, and narrow corridors cut through the thick stone, leading to hidden battlements built at strategic points around the perimeter. It is dark and narrow inside. Only the occasional slotted window allows shafts of sunlight to pierce the shadows, cleverly angled so an archer might take aim without exposing himself to return fire.

Navy-clad members of the Hylian Guard are taking up their positions even as Soren and I race southward in the direction of the sea gate. We pass six water cannons, by my count. The massive metallic beasts are the city's strongest fortification against incoming ships, sending out huge streams of pressurized spray over the bay—or so I read in *Historical Battles of Hylios: Waging War from Behind the Walls*, a sharp-tongued account Soren left on my bedside table for perusal several days ago. The pages within detail all of the capital's many unique methods of defense, from the sea gate to the beacon lights to the nearly invisible tidal shoals that ring the outskirts . . . All solid protection measures in their own right, yet none half so effective as the water cannons.

They'll take down anything in range, a boasting soldier told me just last night during my stroll atop the walls. *Brigs, schooners, dinghies. Doesn't matter the size. Our cannons can smash 'em to bits, simple as that. Keeps most marauders from even thinking to raid us.*

I confess, I have been eager to see them in action. To witness their hull-crushing capabilities firsthand. But in this moment, as I watch teams of two working in tandem, using brute force to turn wheels wider than I am tall in order to pump streams of water up from the bay, my enthusiasm is tempered by reality.

The closer we get to the sea gate, the more crowded the battlements. Armed soldiers are everywhere, strapping on bows and quivers, sharpening blades on whetstones, loading crossbows with sturdy bolts. Everyone is in motion, climbing ladders up to the ramparts or down toward the canals, depending on their orders. Overhead, the blaring of the beacons is a distant drone, warning civilians to take cover in their homes.

We reach the end of the passage where a thick spiral staircase leads up to the top of the walls. Soren scales it quickly; I follow close behind. He's tense. I can see it in the lines of his broad shoulders just as I can feel it thrumming down the bond. The fact that I can feel him at all is indicative of the situation's severity. For once, he is too preoccupied to bother blocking me out.

We burst into the hazy daylight, searing after the darkness. I blink rapidly as my eyes strain to take in all that I am seeing. The upper fortifications are lined with soldiers standing shoulder to shoulder. They stare out at the horizon, looks of foreboding on their faces. A similar pit of dread opens in my stomach as I follow their worried eyes out to sea.

Beyond the merchant vessels at anchor, and rapidly closing in, are more ships than I can count in a single glance. Now that they are somewhat closer, it is hard to believe I ever mistook them for Alaric's fleet. These are clearly warships, not trading vessels. Built for speed and stealth. Their distinctive curved bowsprits slice the waves like blades, gaining unnatural speed as the Frostlander rowers heave their oars in perfect unison.

"They're after the anchorage," Soren mutters, hands bracing on the parapet at our waists as his eyes scan the horizon. "Probably heard about the wedding and thought to help themselves to the cargo in those holds."

My gaze flickers down to the dozens of vessels bobbing unprotected beyond the heavy stone of the sea gate. "Will they attack the city?"

"They have no interest in conquest. But they will pillage everything on those vessels, given the chance, before they set them aflame." His tone pitches lower. "And they will slaughter every sailor and civilian on board to do it."

I swallow harshly.

I have heard tales of Frostlander raids. Their swiftness, their savageness. Their tendency to take no prisoners, wiping out whole villages in the span of a single night, hauling off everything of value, leaving none alive to tell the tale. In the past, they've aimed such plundering pursuits across the North Sea, rather than at their neighbors. But their strategies are changing. Only weeks ago, Cadogan called for reinforcements, fearing an imminent attack on Dyved.

I did not think Llŷr would face a similar threat—certainly not here in the capital. Not with Soren's menacing presence to keep them at bay. The prospect of so many stocked ships, sitting ducks ripe for shooting, must have proved too difficult to turn down.

Over the drone of the beacons and the din of soldiers running to their battle stations, the clipped bark of a woman's orders carries on the breeze. Soren takes off like a shot toward the source. I follow more sedately, a silent shadow trying not to lose him in the melee.

The line of soldiers continues all the way along the top of the sea gate, some fifty paces across. At the midway point, straddling the seam of the two great doors, a female figure with a sleek silver bow strapped to her back is standing atop the waist-high balustrade, bellowing at everyone with a set of ears.

"I want those tower cannons firing the minute they're in range!" Arwen's braids fly as her head swivels back and forth, surveying the scene. Her flight goggles swing around her neck. "Wheelmen, work in shifts. If you get tired, tap out and let someone else take over. Those pumps need constant pressure on the valves to be of any use to your gunners!"

To either side of the sea gate, perched on flat lookout platforms that protrude from the parapets, sit a pair of matching water cannons. *The Twins*, as the soldiers so affectionately refer to them. They are double the size of the ones we passed by inside the wall battlements. Each requires a team of four men to manipulate the horizontal wheel that powers its pump.

"They will use the mooring field as cover!" Arwen flings a hand toward the bobbing ships behind her—prime targets for the raiding party. "You have to sink them before they make it into the anchorage or we'll lose our chance!"

Soren slams to a stop just before his sister, head craned back to capture her gaze. "How many longships?"

"Fifty, maybe sixty." Arwen's tone is blunt. "About five hundred men."

"How the bloody hell did they get here without detection?" Soren's eyes flash to the incoming horde.

They are still quite a distance away, but making good headway. The armada is fanning out, splitting into two distinct prongs with the clear aim to surround the temporary mooring field on all sides. Like a noose tightening around a neck, they will close in all at once to take their bounty, then flee before the blood runs cold.

"They came around the back side of Prydain. Must've taken shelter on one of the islands off the coast overnight." Arwen sounds more annoyed than angry. "If the Titans saw them hiding out, they did not feel inclined to warn us. I'll be having words with Vaughn about that, trust me."

"Vaughn is not solely responsible for all that transpires on Prydain, as you well know." Soren shakes his head. "What of your scouts? Were they all asleep on their watches?"

Arwen scoffs, a biting sound. "Even if they were, it would not have mattered. You know how fast those ships are, brother. They can outrow even the swiftest ravens."

"They still never should've made it this close to the city. They're at our godsdamned gates."

"For that, you can blame the bloody *mist*," she seethes, eyes flashing over to me for a glacial instant. "The beacons cannot detect incoming threats if they are ensconced in constant cover."

My stomach drops to my feet, a leaden ball of guilt. "I . . . I . . ."

"Do not speak," Arwen hisses. "You have done quite enough here without adding your inane commentary to the mix."

I recoil as though I've been struck.

Soren's hand catches my arm before I make it more than a step, stilling me so I cannot retreat.

"Arwen," he says with a frigidness that stuns me. "You embarrass only yourself when you act like a schoolyard bully instead of the leader I need you to be. Take your anger out on Rhya again and you will feel the brunt of mine."

His cold chastisement snaps her focus back to the impending battle. Her blue eyes narrow as her mind turns over a thousand warring thoughts. "We need to cut them off before they reach the anchorage. The Twins alone will not keep them back. Not all of them. Not for long. We are already deploying soldiers to the exposed ships and evacuating the civilians, but . . ."

Her eyes drop down to the sea. Far below, several midsized rowing craft are making their way around the anchorage, letting off contingents of armed soldiers at each vessel, taking on the unarmed passengers in their stead.

"Where are the other Paexyrian?" Soren asks.

"Harpina and Thisobei traveled to Coldcross yesterday to confer with our Cimmerian scouts. They will not be back until this evening. Bretiax and Yara flew out to meet the Daggerpoint fleet at daybreak."

"Any idea when Alaric is due to arrive?"

"It could be anytime now." Her face ripples with a shadow of concern. "Let us hope it is sooner rather than later. We could use his artillery at our backs."

Soren stares at his sister for a long beat before his eyes shift again out to sea. The Frostlander longships are halfway across the bay, close enough that I can see the froth stirred up each time their oars dip into the swells, hear the rhythmic chants that carry across the water as hundreds of men grunt in concert.

Pull! Pull! Pull!

"We cannot count on timely arrivals to stave off this battle," Soren says, voice low.

Arwen bristles. "I know that."

"I never questioned otherwise."

"They will strike here, at the anchorage, but I have deployed squadrons stretching all the way back to the beacons. The inner battlements are ready as well, though I doubt the longships will come close enough to make use of the smaller cannons. The Frostlanders may be shit for brains, but even they are wise enough to stay beyond the spray."

"And the Twins?" He jerks his chin toward the colossal cannons perched to either side of the sea gate.

"I leave their oversight in your capable hands, brother." A smile creeps over her face. "I plan to greet these visitors personally."

Soren shakes his head. "You cannot mount an aerial assault without another rider on your wing, covering your blind spots."

Her shrug is unconcerned as she fixes her goggles over her eyes. "I can sure as hell try."

"Arwen—"

"Atyr and I have faced worse odds, as you well know."

His frown is severe. "Do not put your life at risk to prove some asinine point."

She stills. "And what point would that be, brother?"

His voice lowers a shade, so none of the nearby soldiers can hear. "That this marriage will not change you. That being in love has not softened you."

She glares at him, not dignifying his observation with a response.

"We could use you here, flying around the perimeter," Soren reasons. "Ensuring no one makes landing at Vintners' Cove or by the sea organ or at the Kettle."

"The Hylian Guard is well trained. They will cover our weak spots well enough without me." Her grin widens. "Besides, if things go my way, the Frostlanders will never get close enough to toss their spears."

"Arwen—"

But she has already turned away from her brother. Bringing her hand to her lips, she lets out a sharp whistle. Then, in a move that makes my heart seize inside my chest, she begins to run down the length of the balustrade, her feet nimble as they dance across the stone. With no railing to shield her, one wrong footfall will send her plummeting straight down into the sea below. A height so great no one—not even the strongest fae—seems likely to survive it.

"What is she doing?" I cry, horrified.

"Showing off," Soren mutters. "As usual."

There is a sudden gust of wind that makes every archer cover their eyes, such is its force. I think it will knock Arwen off-balance, but she does not fall. Instead, with a grin and a running start, she *leaps*—straight off the balustrade's edge, into thin air.

CHAPTER
SIXTEEN

A scream gathers in my throat as Arwen plunges toward the water. It never makes it past my lips. For her descent is halted by a winged white horse, rising up to meet her.

Atyr.

Arwen lands in the saddle with a practiced maneuver, fingers delving deep into the flowing white mane, heels slamming home into the stirrups. She crows with pure delight as feathered wings pump her higher into the sky, sending gusts of air washing over everyone watching from the ramparts. A cheer goes up as the magnificent Paexyri steed coasts straight out to sea, into the direct path of the longships.

I cheer, too. I can't help it. When Soren hears my whoop, he casts an amused look my way.

I shrug sheepishly. "Her attitude leaves something to be desired, but even I can admit that was incredibly epic."

"Skies, don't tell her that. She needs more confidence like I need a Frostlander ice-arrow through the heart."

My gaze tracks her for a moment, then moves beyond to the approaching armada. "Can't you summon a tsunami?" I ask. "Take them all out at once before they can do any harm?"

He snorts softly. "Much as I appreciate the vote of confidence in my abilities, summoning a wave of that magnitude would require strength beyond even mine."

I look at him, brows lifting. "But I watched you dispel one just last week."

"Dispelling requires far less effort than conjuring. The ocean's weight is . . . *immense*. Even for me. Still waters do not easily shift. Those already in motion are far more malleable."

My lips purse.

Shaking his head, as though he finds my disappointment charming, Soren turns to stroll the length of the sea gate. He examines the soldiers as he goes, occasionally stopping to give a low order or point out an untied bootlace or clasp a shoulder in greeting.

It is clear the Hylian Guard has been drilled for this exact occasion. There is no chaos, no confusion. They take up their posts and gather their weapons with an ease that speaks of long discipline. Unlike in Dyved, which clings to more rigid gender roles, the Llŷrian ranks are a near even split of males and females. When I look behind us, I see navy-clad forms of many shapes and statures lining the ramparts from our position all the way to the beacons halfway around the city. Down at the inner harbor, a sparser secondary squadron is stationed along the docks, prepared to stop anything from advancing into the canals.

Not that anything will breach the sea gate. It is nearly as thick as the walls themselves. As large as it seems from harbor level, one cannot appreciate its true scope until you are standing upon it.

"Longbows, hold steady!" Soren calls, coming to a stop at the very center. His voice rises to a boom that carries into the distance. "Main cannons, engage!"

At his signal, the teams of four brawny men stationed at the Twins on the lookout towers brace their hands against the spokes of the giant wheels and begin to push in slow, backbreaking circles. It is a punishing task, one that requires brute strength and total synchronicity. I watch them make two full rotations, waiting breathlessly for something to happen. Finally, there is a metallic groan, then a rumble that rattles the city's foundations. A ripple of awareness moves through the Hylian Guard, but no one even flinches as the water cannons begin to blast monumental streams out over the bay.

Even having read about it beforehand, it is an astounding sight. The sheer volume of water that comes out, the stupendous force of the spray . . . Like two horizontal waterfalls, they shoot well above even the tallest masts in the anchorage. Where they strike down, the ocean turns to pure lather, stirred into a frenzy beneath the cannons' might.

My gasp is audible.

"Impressed?"

I nod, not looking over at Soren. "However do they aim?"

"Swiveling bases beneath each cannon. You see that man— the stocky one with the gauntlets?" His shoulder brushes mine as he lifts his arm to point out the man taking up position on an elevated perch directly behind the cannon. "We call him a gunner. He's the cannon's eyes. There are two levers he can use to pivot the stream back and forth. It's not instantaneous, but it works well enough. Usually."

Even as he speaks, I am watching it happen. The gunner on the tower to my left is turning his cannon, shifting the stream of water across the ocean's surface. A moving barricade. It is a brilliant way to do damage from the safety of your defensive lines.

The Frostlanders are not yet within striking distance, but given their speed, they soon will be. If the sight of the Twins pummeling their path forward intimidates them, it does not show. Their rowing pace only seems to increase. They are so close, their low chants can be heard even above the constant rumble of the pumps—a chorus of deep grunts, one for each oar pull.

Fearless, Arwen flies ever nearer, the silver glint of the sun catching on her bow as she swoops low over the water. Atyr's coat is brilliant white beneath her hunched form.

"She shouldn't be out there alone," Soren says tightly, eyes on his sister. "She's going to get herself killed."

"Then go to her."

He glances over at me, brows lifting. "She'll be furious."

"She'll be *alive*," I counter.

His eyes flare with warmth, there and gone in a flash. "And leave you up here alone?"

"Alone? Hardly. I am surrounded by scores of highly trained soldiers. I think I'll be fine." I roll my eyes. "If they get close enough, I'll show off some of my new skills."

His mouth twitches. "Beware the fearsome levitator of lemons."

"*Ha!*" I shove his shoulder. "And here I was, actually worried you might die at the end of a Frostlander spear! That's passed. Feel free to perish."

He grins at me as he braces one hand against the top of the stone balustrade. "You'll regret that when I'm no longer around to cook for you."

I would miss the griddle cakes.

I do not tell him that. I make a sweeping gesture, indicating he should make haste. "Go on, then. Arwen has nearly reached the front of the fleet. It's going to take you an awfully long time to catch up by skiff, so—"

Suddenly, Soren moves. He does it so fast, my eyes do not register it happening. Yet there he is, standing a handspan in front of me. My words cut off at the look on his face as it comes close to mine. Closer than it has ever been before, closer than I ever thought it would be.

Before I can brace for it, his lips hit the side of my neck, just below the fragile hinge of my jaw, where my pulse is pounding twice its normal speed. My mind blanks, every coherent thought sweeping straight out of my skull in the single heartbeat his mouth lingers against my skin.

It ends almost before it's begun. Pulling back from me, he turns on a heel, plants his palms flat atop the balustrade, and heaves himself up onto it. Frozen in place, I watch him straighten to full height. I cannot seem to speak a single word. My throat is effectively sealed shut, preventing all airflow.

Soren glances down at me. His mouth is set in that sardonic grin I have come to know quite well. But beneath the playful guise, his eyes are swimming with emotions I have never encountered in all our time together.

"In case I really do die," he says in a whisper meant for my ears alone. "I had to do that. At least once."

Turning, he swan dives off the top of the sea gate.

My heart drops straight to the harbor as he vanishes from view. My blood runs cold as ice.

Is he utterly insane?

To jump from such a height . . .

Flying to the balustrade, I peer over just in time to see Soren's tall form disappear below the surface like a hot knife cutting through butter. There is hardly even a splash as he disappears into the blue depths.

I do not breathe for the endless seconds it takes for him to resurface. When he finally does, he is much farther out to sea than I expected—nearly halfway through the anchorage, his swift strokes carrying him with blinding speed into open water. Around him, the swells surge, buoying him above the waves, rippling outward to rock the boats on their chains.

I let out a ragged breath, watching his form growing smaller and smaller as he heads toward danger. No hesitation, no fear. He and Arwen have that in common—two gallant hearts wrapped in sea urchin spines. I cannot decide which of the two is more reckless. Or more dauntless.

My fingers reach up to brush the hinge of my jaw, where I can still feel the shadow of a kiss. Below the skin, my pulse is a mad tattoo of anxiety and anticipation.

About the battle.

Nothing more.

I shove aside the storm of feelings swirling inside me as it begins in earnest. It is hardly a fair fight—one winged mount against sixty longships. I, along with every soldier on the ramparts, watch with my heart in my throat as Arwen engages them. Her bow twangs again and again, silver flashing in the sunlight, as she picks off Frostlanders. It is difficult to make out precise details at such a distance. Only the splashes of the corpses falling overboard indicate her arrows have found their marks as Atyr dips and banks in dizzying loops, pulling up to avoid the retaliatory spears that whiz toward the woman on his back.

Despite the casualties, the ships come ever closer.

Arwen is not battling alone for long. Panicked screams echo back to us across the water as rogue waves begin to swamp sections of the fleet. I've momentarily lost sight of Soren amid the rolling swells, but he is out there somewhere, using his maegic to sink ships and drown every Frostlander in his path. The bond between us is an open current of power, flowing straight to the center of my chest as he systematically sends his enemies to the bottom of the bay, one after another after another.

Still, it is not enough to stall them all.

The remaining ships advance. There are simply too many of them, even for Soren and Arwen attacking in tandem. The breath catches in my lungs as the first of their curved bows row into range of the Twins. Two streams of water are now all that separate them from the spoils of war. As though they can taste it, their oars increase speed.

Pull!

Pull!

Pull!

But the tower gunners are ready for them.

More screams ring out as wood splinters and hulls are pummeled under the roaring surge. There is no resistance, no fighting back. A single sweep of each cannon can obliterate an entire line of longships. The soldiers around me cheer with each direct hit, filling the air with the song of victory.

For a moment, I allow my heart to brim over with hope. The second line of longships slows, oars pulling back to avoid the fatal spray. The front line is no more than driftwood, much of the crew no longer breathing. A smattering of survivors swim for rescue and are promptly hauled aboard.

"They'll turn tail now," a soldier close by says under her breath, leaning against the parapet. "Thieving cowards."

I hope she's right. The anchorage is not yet fully evacuated. Panicked civilians are crammed into lifeboats, rowing frantically for the safety of the city walls.

"Bet you fifty farthings we will not even need to nock arrows," another soldier responds. "They're no match for our—"

His words are buried by a shuddering wail that shakes the world into deafening silence. We all turn as one toward the left Twin, collectively horrified by the sight of it hissing to a halt. The thunderous hose of water shuts off; the team of four steps back as the wheel ceases its rotations. Their expressions no doubt mirror the one on my own face.

Unguarded doom.

The loss is incalculable. The consequences unthinkable. With the cannon down, our entire left flank is exposed. Long-ships start to slip through the gap unchecked, rowing with re-newed haste. Though the still-functional right Twin attempts to cover the entire anchorage, it is impossible. There are too many ships, all moving with lethal precision toward the exposed vessels. Toward the innocent civilians in those lifeboats.

I watch Hylian soldiers stationed on the outermost ships un-sheathing swords and raising crossbows as the enemy moves in. There is nothing more to keep them at bay.

We need that cannon back.

We need it *now*.

I move on wind-propelled heels, eyes on the left tower as I shove my way down the length of the sea gate, then sprint up the short set of stone steps. There is not much room to move up here. The horizontal wheel-pump takes up most of the platform. Elevated on a cramped dais behind it, its metallic swivel base soldered straight into the stone, the cannon is steaming faintly but otherwise deathly still.

"Hey!" one of the burly wheelmen barks at me. "You're not meant to be up here!"

"Leave off, Erdin," another voice cuts in. "She's authorized to be anywhere she likes."

I turn to the sound of the voice and see a familiar face sta-tioned by the steps. It's Roq, a guardswoman I've met several times on my evening strolls—the one who so enthusiastically explained the city's fortifications. She winks at me when our eyes meet; I nod in thanks.

"What's going on here?" I ask, turning back to the wheelmen.

They are an intimidating crew—barrel-chested with bulging muscles and thickly corded necks—but I do not cower. "Why did you stop firing?"

"Oh, thought we'd take a little break," one of them drawls sarcastically. "Gods, woman, are you blind? It's broken down."

"What's wrong with it?" I look from him to the gunner on the dais.

The smaller man leans close to the levers, his face contorted in frustration as he attempts to repair whatever is broken. "Swivel mechanism is jammed," he mutters morosely. "Can't aim."

"So . . ."

"So, we're fucked." The biggest of the men, the one called Erdin, grunts, shaking his beefy arms to dissipate the strain in his muscles. "Unless you have a mystical wrench up your sleeve, you're not needed here."

I ignore him. My eyes are on the cannon. I do not question myself as I hop up onto the dais, where the gunner is hunched, and elbow him aside.

"Move."

His head jerks up. "Excuse me?"

"Move," I repeat, less kindly.

"Look, you can't just—"

"The rest of you, get that pump going," I call, cutting him off. "Now."

When nothing happens, I glance over my shoulder at the four wheelmen. They're staring up at me, looking mystified. Except for Erdin. He looks more like he wants to tear my head from my shoulders for daring to give him orders.

"Woman, I don't know who the hell you think you are, but—"

"I am the Remnant of Air. You need aim? *I will be your aim,*" I hiss, infusing my voice with as much authority as I am able to summon. "Now, do you want to stand here debating with me or do you want to destroy those longships before they reach the anchorage and slaughter a harbor full of innocents?"

There are several long heartbeats of absolute silence as my words hang in the air. It is broken only by a constant refrain of Frostlander chants—*Pull! Pull! Pull!*—which grows louder as they near. Finally, Erdin clears his throat and reaches for the sedentary wheel.

"You heard her!" he barks, spurring the others into motion. "Let's blast the godsforsaken bastards out of the water!"

LATER, WHEN I looked back, I would have no real idea what came over me; wherever I got the confidence to even attempt it. And yet, in the moment, there is absolutely no doubt in my mind. As the pump engages, water begins to cascade from the cannon with such ferocity, it vibrates the entire tower, shaking me to my very bones.

Ignoring the full-body rattle, I turn my focus inward as I call the wind. Soren may have teased me about lemon levitation, but I am grateful for all those hours I spent lifting objects with tendrils, flinging them with stinging gusts. For though the water is a soul-rending force . . .

So is my wind.

I shape it to my will, using drafts to point the lethal stream wherever I want. Bending it with a downward gust until it pierces through an encroaching ship, I grin as I watch it explode to pieces, strangely apathetic about the entire crew I've just sent into the bay. My Remnant burns cold as I wrench the water to the left with a huge gust that takes out three more ships, sweeping bodies overboard like leaves scattering across pavestones. The manual swivel mechanism could not pivot half so fast as my maegic.

Someone shouts an oath of surprise from somewhere behind

me. I think it is Roq, the friendly guard, but I don't turn to look. My eyes are locked on the harbor.

Arwen and Soren are far out to sea, forcing a good chunk of the fleet into a swift retreat toward Prydain. The other tower is keeping up a constant barrage, holding back the right flank. With my cannon back in action, the Frostlanders finally sense the foolhardiness of their plan. The remaining longships on the left flank turn tail, fleeing back in the direction from which they came. All too soon, they will be completely out of range, slipping away into the mist to rape and pillage and plunder another city or township—one that, more than likely, will not have such strong defensive protections.

My blood boils at the thought.

The water roars in my ears, matching my roaring pulse, as I watch them retreat.

I could let them go.

I *should* let them go.

But I am caught up in the power that surges through me. A limitless resource, fueled by pure fury. Mine for the taking . . . if only I am brave enough to reach for it. Before I consciously know what I am doing, I loose more wind, twisting ribbons of air along the torrent of water. Elongating it farther than would be possible on its own power, until the spray reaches a distance the pump alone could never achieve.

There are more shouts of surprise behind me, which quickly morph into alarmed yells as the wheel spins faster and faster. No longer in the control of the wheelmen, but under my command. The men cry out, jumping back to keep from being battered as it begins to whirl independently. I no longer need them anyway. My air is everywhere, all around me—driving up through the pipes from the harbor, lending more pressure to the already immense surge, carrying that blinding pressure outward.

More wind, more water.

More.

The fleeing ships stand no chance. I take them out one by one, relentless in my pursuit.

Smash.

Sink.

Smash.

Sink.

Smash.

Sink.

Over and over, until none remain.

As I do this, I feel nothing. Not a shred of remorse. It's as though that constant coldness centered at my Remnant has spread through me, an icy elixir in my veins, strong enough to block out any other emotions. Strong enough to block out everything—the world around me, the people watching. There is nothing in that moment but me and my maegic, a malevolent maelstrom unleashed upon the world.

It is not until I feel a disturbance in my wind that the ice encasing my mind cracks open. There is a distinctive pump of wings gusting across the ramparts. The following clatter of hooves as landing is made. Two sets of boots dismounting. Footsteps crossing up onto the tower platform. And then, a voice.

"Skylark. You can stop now."

He sounds close. He feels close. I blink, staring at the horizon. There are no ships intact on the left flank. Only indistinguishable flotsam and jetsam, drifting on the frothy surface in the distance. Splintered oars, smashed hulls. Casks and crates, weapons and water jugs. The detritus of a ruined fleet. And bodies. So many bodies, floating face down. No longer swimming or kicking for shore. No longer doing anything at all.

Because they are dead.

They are all dead.

Gods, what have I done?

The cannon splutters to a stop as I release the wind. I take a deep, tremulous breath as I turn slowly around. Soren is there, hair tousled from the sea, body rigid with tension. He is staring at me—as is every other living soul on the city walls. The silence is deafening. A lump lodges in my throat as I meet his eyes. They are fathomless, holding all the secrets of the deepest oceans. Holding things I am not yet ready to see. More evidently than anything, though . . . the distinct sheen of pity.

"It's over," he says with halting gentleness. "It's done."

My fingers curl into fists at my sides. I want to put them through something. To beat them against a stone wall or a hardwood floor until they are torn and bleeding, a physical reflection of the invisible blood staining my hands.

I do not know what to say to him. How to explain what I am feeling. The guilt of it. The horror. Worse, the unquenched thrill that races, even now, through my veins.

What kind of monster am I becoming, to kill with such abandon? To take lives without even a beat of hesitation? What happened to that noble healer from Seahaven? She would be horrified to see me as I am now.

An object of utter destruction.

"Rhya," Soren says. Soft as a blade sliding between two ribs, and equally lethal to my resolve. He sounds poised on the knife's edge of his own control. It is my fault, for I am not shielding from him at all. He can feel everything I'm feeling. The rawest self-loathing tangling with shameful chords of self-satisfaction.

"I'm fine," I say in a hollow voice that sounds nothing like my own.

He continues to stare at me. He opens his mouth, as if to say something else, but it is Arwen's booming voice I hear instead.

"Skies, why's everyone so bloody quiet?"

Leaving Atyr on the rampart at the base of the steps, she strolls up to stand beside Soren on the platform. Her eyes find mine and in their depths, for the first time ever, I see the shades of something like respect there, instead of unveiled disdain. She says nothing to me, merely gives a shallow jerk of her chin, then turns to face the crowd.

"We won the battle, did we not?" Her voice carries far into the distance as she turns to look out over the sea of silent soldiers and lifts a fist in the air. "Tonight, we drink to Hylios!"

A cheer goes up from the crowd, undulating from the sea gate all around the walls, then spreading down into canals until it encompasses every stone of the city, and every soul therein.

CHAPTER
SEVENTEEN

Steadfastly ignoring the weight of many curious eyes aimed at me across the bar, I take a fortifying sip from my mug. The mulled wine is a fragrant and flavorful varietal made from sea grapes. It tingles a fiery path down my throat, then spreads slowly outward, warming me from the inside out.

I keep my gaze trained out over the maze of blue rooftops, but no matter where I look I see the same thing. Those floating bodies. Those splintered ships. I am alone in my horrified reflections, for no one else is the least bit upset about my wanton disregard for Frostlander lives. In fact, the massacre has earned me a certain amount of esteem among the soldiers. I was clapped on the back more times than I could count as I made my way through the crowd atop the ramparts.

It's been several hours since the battle ended, but the celebrations show no signs of waning. The crowd at my back is boisterous, and growing more so as the night creeps on and drinks flow freely. I just hope no one falls over the rail. It is a long drop down to the canals.

Aptly named Ledge for its unique location, the open-air veranda juts out from the inner wall below the ramparts in the shadow of the Westerly Beacon. Not far from the barracks, it is frequented mostly by Hylian Guard and Paexyrian riders. It offers a variety of unusual libations and unparalleled views of the rest of the city—which, currently, is in an equal state of frivolity.

All up and down the canals, cafés are bursting with patrons, sidewalks spilling over with revelers. The floating market is even more crowded than usual. Music thumps from somewhere below, a driving beat of drums accompanied by a lively fiddle. If there was room, I'm certain the crowd behind me would be dancing to it. But there is hardly space to stand; spinning is out of the question. Every table is jammed with men and women in the navy standard of Hylios, along with the lighter blue-gray of Daggerpoint. Their laughter and chatter spills through the twilight, the graceful extension of their vowels a fluid contrast to the more clipped Dyvedi accent.

I'd spotted Ledge several times during my nightly strolls along the walls, and wondered how one got in. My answer came in the form of a trapdoor entry embedded in the stone floor in the corner. A near constant stream of newcomers scamper through it, undaunted by the precipitous ladder climb from canal level. Those rungs are hard enough to ascend sober; I doubt the descent is easier after copious mugs of mead. But the arrivals never cease as the sky streaks with the telltale shades of sunset.

How many more can possibly squeeze up here before the whole place comes crashing down? It is not a particularly large bar. Despite the crush, the rest of my bench remains unoccupied. If I didn't know better, I'd think I might be casting an unconscious air shield to keep everyone at arm's length. Then again, my introspective disposition alone is likely enough to ward off approach.

The thud of a mug hitting the table makes me flinch violently. Warm wine sloshes over my fingertips and I curse.

"Jumpy one, aren't you?"

I glance over at the chuckling woman as she drops beside me on the bench. Her frame is petite, but every inch of it is packed with corded muscle. Her flaming red hair is shorn at the sides and braided in the back in the battle-ready fashion the Paexyrian favor. I wonder if it is because their heads are so often strapped into goggles. She smiles wider when our eyes meet, seeming oblivious to my unapproachable attitude as she settles back in her seat.

"I'm Yara," she greets. Her chin jerks to my other side, where another rider is hopping up to sit on the railing, long legs dangling in front of her. "That's Bretiax. Don't be offended she doesn't speak to you. She lost the ability as a young girl."

The second woman winks at me over the rim of her mug as she takes a long sip. She has warm tawny skin and the glossiest hair I've ever seen, flowing in wild waves down her back.

I give a small wave. "I'm Rhya."

"Oh, we know who you are." Yara leans in conspiratorially. "Everyone does. The whole city is talking about what you did with that water cannon."

My lips press together. "I wish they wouldn't."

"Why's that?" She sounds genuinely baffled. "Frostlanders have been a thorn in our backsides for ages. Do you know how many villages we've seen on the mainland torn to shreds by their night raids?"

Bretiax signs something in agreement.

Yara snorts and signs back at her.

I watch their silent volley of curious gestures. The few times I've seen them in flight, I've noticed them communicating with similar hand signals from their saddles. I imagine it is the only way to pass messages in the sky, for even a shout likely could not be heard over the roar of the wind while on the back of a soaring Paexyri steed.

Yara glances back at me. "Don't let the deaths of a few scavengers spoil your evening."

My brows lift. *A few?* I singlehandedly took out half the fleet. Some two hundred souls.

"Okay. More than a few." Yara grins. "My point stands. Getting blasted out of the water was no more than they deserved. They should've known better than to attack us so brazenly. Taking an anchorage a stone's throw from the capital . . ." She shakes her head. "I knew they lacked all morals; I didn't think they lacked all logic."

"Have they tried to attack Hylios before?"

"Why do you think we have so many cannons?" She chuckles softly. "The raids were more frequent when I was a girl. In recent years, they have not been so bold. Not until today, in any case." Yara leans back against the bench and takes a sip from her mug. "I have to say, when Bretiax and I were flying back earlier, we had no idea what we were seeing at first. Took a few low loops over the surface before we realized where all that driftwood had come from. Isn't that right, Bre?"

The other rider nods.

"Could hardly believe my eyes when I looked up and saw *you* were the one responsible for such carnage." Yara's distinctive almond-shaped eyes are tinkling at the memory.

I swallow hard, not sharing her amusement. It is a memory I am working to forget, not reminisce over.

Yara and Bretiax returned to Hylios on the heels of the battle, their winged mounts descending on the ramparts before we'd even had a chance to disperse. I was emotionally numb, still processing my own actions, when they clattered to a halt beside Atyr.

Arwen's large white beast may dwarf every other Paexyri in size, but certainly not in beauty. Yara rides a chestnut bay with red-tipped wing feathers the same scarlet hue as her own hair; Bretiax favors a piebald mount with feathered white hooves. Had I not been so caught up in my own inner turmoil at the time, I would not have squandered the rare opportunity to get a look at them up close.

Their arrival was quickly overshadowed by that of Alaric's fleet. The crowd, still buzzing from the aftermath of the battle, pitched up to a dizzying decibel of excitement as five double-masted brigs made their approach, traversing waters that only moments before had been filled with our enemies. Cheers went up as Daggerpoint horns blew from the bows.

The wedding party had arrived.

Double the reason for celebration, as far as the Hylians saw it. Soldiers streamed from the battlements, headed down into the city in search of libations. Soren ferried me along with them, his hand firm on mine to keep me from getting lost in the crush. We did not wait for Arwen. She remained pressed against the balustrade, fighting a smile as she watched her fiancé drop anchor and row ashore. It was strange to see her like that, her rough edges softened by anticipation, her sharp features almost . . . *sweet.*

Even now, after several hours of watching them from the corner of my eye across the bar, I have not quite grown accustomed to the sight of her standing close to the tall blond man's side as they converse with Soren and several of the broad-shouldered men from Hollywell. Every few minutes, my gaze moves that way of its own accord, noting the way Alaric's hand skims over her hip, the way Arwen's head falls onto his shoulder when she forgets to act indifferent, the wordless looks they trade when they think no one is watching.

He is not what I'd pictured for Arwen. She is such a natural warrior, so fearsome and bold. I'd expected the man she loves to be similar in both stature and disposition. But with his neatly trimmed facial hair, light coloring, and refined features, Alaric reminds me a bit of Cadogan—albeit, much less somber. He smiles often, laughs frequently, and moves with a refined elegance totally opposite Arwen's volatile energy.

"Attached at the hip, those two," Yara remarks, noticing the direction of my gaze. "Wasn't always the case. When they first met and Alaric proposed marriage, I thought Arwen would gut him for daring to ask."

Bretiax signs something that makes Yara giggle. Kicking her feet up to rest on the railing, she drains her mug in one long sip. Her boots, like the rest of her uniform, are designed with flight in mind. The soles are tapered to fit seamlessly into stirrups. When she crosses her legs, I see padding runs up the inside of her thighs where the saddle chafes. Her abdomen is cinched tight with an armored corset.

Bretiax is in a near identical uniform, though the glyphs stitched at her collar are slightly different. I want to ask about the mysterious symbols, but Yara is stuck on the topic of their ornery flight leader.

"The two of them are about as different in temperament as they are in looks," she tells me, staring unabashedly at the lovesick couple. "Thankfully, that means he's got all the patience in the world. He waited almost a decade for her to finally look his way. The moment she did, that was it. She fell head over heels. Surprised the hell out of all of us. Though, I suspect, not as much as it surprised her."

"When she moves to Hollywell, what will happen to the Paexyrian? Will you all go with her?"

"We riders would follow Arwen anywhere in this world. But it's not only our decision. Our mounts have minds of their own, and tenets of steel. If Umyr will not stay in Daggerpoint, I cannot force her. She goes where she will, when she will."

Umyr is her chestnut bay Paexyri.

"But they stay here," I point out, brow furrowing. "In Hylios."

I have seen the stables myself, several times now. They encompass a large section of the royal grounds not far from Arwen's villa. I sometimes wander there in the evenings, eager to steal a glimpse of the winged horses who graze on the lush seagrass, wings tucked in close to their bodies, manes blowing in the breeze. No saddles to diminish their magnificence. Something about them captivates me in a way I cannot quite explain.

"The Paexyri stay here by their own leave," Yara tells me. "They are not captives, nor pets. The moment I lost her respect, Umyr would fly back to the highest reaches of the mountains she calls home and never return."

"I'm not sure I understand. Is she not yours? Could you not stop her?"

"The Paexyri do not belong to us. We belong to them." Yara taps the unique glyph stitched at her collar. "This sigil means I was chosen to ride her. To do so is the greatest privilege of my life. A life, I might add, that will end long before hers ever does. She will have another rider someday when I am a shriveled old crone and my hands are too arthritic to grip the reins."

I contemplate that for a time, somewhat stunned by the deep reverence with which she speaks of her winged companion. It is hardly uncommon for soldiers to feel a kinship with the horses that carry them into battle, but this is something else. Something beyond simple loyalty or affection.

"It is difficult to explain with words alone. Next time you come to the stables, don't spy from the shadows of the lemon grove. I will introduce you to Umyr." Yara quirks a brow at my surprised jolt. "What? Shocked to learn your furtive surveillance was not as discreet as you believed?"

"Hardly. I simply wasn't expecting an invitation to anything involving the Paexyrian. Your flight leader has been somewhat less than welcoming."

Yara merely waves away my worries. "Don't take Arwen to heart. She's not a big fan of change, whether it's in the form of a midsummer wedding or a new wind weaver. Not to mention, she's overprotective of her brother."

"You don't say."

My sarcasm is not lost on Yara. Chuckling, she signs something to Bretiax that makes the other woman grin.

"Why she thinks her brother needs protection from *me*, I can't imagine," I mutter mostly to myself. "I'm not exactly a threat to the King of Llŷr."

Yara's eyes drift back to me. Her voice softens. "There are many ways to hurt someone, Rhya. Not all of them physical."

What is that supposed to mean? I could not wound Soren if I tried.

I take a large sip of my wine, savoring the burn as it slides down my throat. The mug is nearly empty. I will need a refill soon.

Bretiax signs something, her fingers moving rapidly in the air.

"You're right, Bre." Yara nods, then looks back at me. "She says to remind you that Arwen hated Alaric at first, too. The longer you stick around, the better your chances at winning her over."

"Maybe I don't want to win her over."

Her lips twitch. "Word of advice?"

"If you insist."

"You may not want to win her over, but you need to. After Soren, Arwen is the most powerful person in all of Llŷr. As your ally, she will save your life a thousand times over. As your enemy, however . . ."

My temper flares despite my attempts to tamp it down. "I didn't do anything to earn her wrath besides exist."

"When it comes to Arwen, sometimes that's enough."

I narrow my eyes at her.

"Glare at me all you want. I'm just trying to be a friend because . . . Well, frankly, you seem like you need one. Don't say we didn't warn you. Arwen is not someone you want on your bad side."

I lean forward a few inches and hold her eyes. "Neither am I."

At that, Yara throws back her head and roars. I think she's laughing at me until she slings an arm around my shoulders. "Gods, maybe we should try you out for the Paexyrian. You're scrawny, but so long as you can keep your saddle seat, you'll fit in with the rest of the riders perfectly." Her arm squeezes affectionately. "A certain amount of blatant disregard for reality is encouraged in our ranks."

I shove her off, acting annoyed, but am forced to hide my smile behind my mug. Something about Yara reminds me of Farley. Not only the red hair, but the playful temperament and tendency toward teasing comments.

I wish suddenly that my old friend was here with me instead of a whole kingdom away. Farley would love everything about Ledge, from its intriguing method of entry to the strong ale to the abundant supply of fit soldiers to flirt with. If he were here, he'd have half the establishment in stitches of laughter by the end of the night—and, more than likely, the other half trying to drag him into bed.

My smile slips as longing sweeps through me. I do my best to banish it, draining my last sip of wine in one large gulp.

Time for a refill, unquestionably.

I open my mouth to ask if Yara or Bretiax needs a fresh pour, but never get the question out. A sudden silence descends over the boisterous bar, lively chatter ceasing without warning as mouths snap closed and minds clear of thought.

Instantly alert, I jump out of my seat and turn to confront whatever new threat has materialized. What will it be this time? More arachnidae? Giant wharf rats? Mutated seagulls? Another fleet of Frostlanders, out for vengeance?

But no.

It is only a woman.

She weaves through the crowd like a needle through fabric, footsteps smooth and sure. She is clad in a scandalously sheer gown made of a unique Llŷrian fabric finer than the smoothest Midland silks. It flows around her legs in panels of many different hues, dips low between her breasts to display her generous cleavage. Her hair is the inky blue-black of a midnight sea, cascading down her spine in a riot of lush curls. Her pale skin shimmers in the fading sun, like the light catching the scales of a fish in the shallows.

I cannot tear my eyes from her. Nor can any other living soul in the bar. Her magnetism is absolute, unwavering. I swallow hard, mouth parched.

"Melité," Yara says tightly. She is standing at my side; I did not even hear her rise from the bench.

The name is familiar to me. It takes a long moment for it to surface from the back of my foggy mind. "Soren's half-sister?"

Yara nods. Her eyes are locked on the woman, her cheeks flushed red as her hair. "And half-siren."

Half-siren.

That explains her allure. No one at Ledge seems entirely immune to her presence, but some are clearly more affected than others. Men are tugging at their collars and curling their hands into fists; women are crossing and uncrossing their legs, shifting in their seats. A few reach out toward her as she drifts by, desperate for the whisper-soft caress of a curl against their fingertips, the fleeting slide of silken skirts brushing against their own legs. Those not close enough to reach for her reach for one another instead.

In a shadowy corner by the taps, a couple presses against each other—hands sliding up skirt hems and slipping under waistbands. One table over, I watch two Hylian soldiers join eager mouths, their tongues dancing together with delirious abandon. Alaric's hand is no longer at Arwen's hip but sliding up her rib cage to cup her breast through the sculpted leather of her uniform.

Gods, what is happening here?

A drowsy, damp heat begins to gather between my own thighs. My nipples harden through the fitted fabric of my shirt. I tell myself to look away, but I cannot quite manage it. The more I stare at the half-siren, the more my blood sings in my veins, an escalating need I cannot explain, cannot deny, cannot—

"Melité, that's enough."

My eyes tear away from the siren at the sudden boom of Soren's voice. He has not moved from the barstool where he's been camped out all evening, conversing with Arwen, Alaric, and a rotating parade of soldiers.

Our gazes lock instantly, and I suck in a sharp breath at the thick silver maegic churning through the blue of his irises. Even he is affected by the siren's thrall. I have never seen that look before—not on him, not on anyone.

Dark lust.

Driving need.

It is there in the tightness of his grip on his glass, the sharp set of his shoulders beneath the linen. In the line of strong white teeth sinking hard into a full bottom lip. More still, it is there in the bond.

His hunger, flooding into me.

Mine, whispering back to him.

His teeth sink harder into his lip.

My stomach drops straight to the floor as I stare at him. Stare and stare and stare, unable to shift my eyes even as the rational part of my brain screams at me to look away. Look anywhere else. Anywhere but at him. But my body is not complying with my mind's demands. My heart is rampaging inside my chest, my core throbbing with a violent surge of pure desire.

It doesn't matter that it was manufactured by Melité. It is there all the same, shimmering through my bloodstream. Surely Soren can see it written on my face as plainly as I see it on his. Mortification rises up, tangling with the coursing need within me.

Skies, make it stop.

Soren's nostrils flare. A muscle jumps in his cheek as his jaw flexes. His throat works on a thick swallow as he speaks again. "I mean it, Melité. Quell it. Now."

At his harsh order, the lust-drenched haze clears from the air. Melité is tamping down whatever power she exudes to inspire such animalistic attraction. All around, people are blinking at one another, looking dazed and disoriented as sanity returns. Pairs of lips part, hands cease their wanderings.

I jerk my eyes from Soren and direct them to my feet. My pulse is thready. My lungs scream for air. Squeezing my thighs together against the unabated throb, I take my first true breath in several moments. It does precious little to soothe the raw feelings within me.

The half-siren heaves a dramatic sigh. "Ever the spoilsport, brother."

Her voice is just as melodic and enticing as one would expect. There is a breathy quality to it that steals over my skin with impossibly corporeal weight. Beside me, Yara shivers and stares hard at her boots. Her breathing is as uneven as mine. Bretiax is gripping the stone rail so hard, her knuckles are white.

"If you care to spark an orgy, stick to the thermal baths and pleasure clubs," Soren says, sounding like his fury is in jeopardy of escaping. "Do not use your siren song on the unwilling. Not unless you want me to ban you from public spaces."

Melité comes to a stop a few feet from Soren's barstool, skirts swishing around her shapely legs. "The *unwilling*? How absurd. I do not cause any harm, nor inflict any pain. I merely lower inhibitions. I liberate the chaste from their tedious shackles of convention."

"Not all inhibitions are meant to be indulged."

"That's not the refrain you sing when you visit the pleasure clubs. Not according to my sources. I've heard you've quite the appetite . . ." She is practically purring. "You like to sample a wide variety of flavors. Isn't that right, O mighty king?"

"Who I fuck is really none of your business, *sister*," Soren snarls softly. "If you've a point to make, either make it or get out of my sight."

An enticing laugh tinkles from her throat. "You were much more fun fifty years ago. When did you become so repressed?"

"What I am is tired, Melité. We have had this conversation too many times already." His voice hardens to stone. "I will not repeat myself again. Next time I witness you influencing my citizens into acts they do not have the cognizance to consent to, you will find yourself without a villa in the royal grounds. And not even Tethys will stand by you if you're forced to return to that seaweed-covered cave your mother pushed you out in."

Fury flashes over her face. Her eyes turn completely black, the whites around her irises swallowed by ink. But her voice reveals not an iota of her rage as she says, "Fine. I'll behave . . . for tonight."

Leaving those rather threatening words in the air, she makes her way to the opposite end of the veranda. I quickly lose sight of her in the crowd.

Yara blows out a breath. "Fuck, I need another drink. You want one?"

She doesn't wait for me to answer, merely starts walking toward the bar with Bretiax. I follow in their wake, cutting through the thick crowd, winding around the mismatched hodgepodge of tables and chairs strewn about. The atmosphere slowly comes back to life, conversation restarting in lurches and lulls as the moment of Melité's influence passes. By the time we reach the bar, it is as though nothing happened.

"Titan gin, and make it a double," Yara instructs the barkeep, squeezing in between two other Paexyrian who are nursing frothy pints of Daggerpoint lager. I know their names are Harpina and Thisobei, though we have not yet been introduced. Harpina has pale freckled skin and honey-hued locks that hang to her chin; Thisobei's hair is so close-cropped she is nearly bald, and she sports a perpetually impish grin.

Yara glances over her shoulder at me, brows arched. "Another round?"

"She's had enough," Soren cuts in before I can say a word.

I spin around as he comes to a stop before me. He is standing close—it is quite crowded by the bar—and does not move away, even when I tip my head back to glare at him.

"Have I?"

He leans forward into my space, not stopping until his mouth is at my ear. His hushed words are for me alone. "If you want another drink, that's your prerogative. But Titan gin is three times the strength of that mulled wine you've been nursing for the past two hours. The Paexyrian may guzzle it like water, but if you plan to make the climb back down the ladder to the canals, I suggest you quit while you're ahead." He pulls back a few inches—just enough to align our faces, so his eyes stare directly into mine. "Unless you'd like me to carry you back to my villa."

My teeth grit. "That will not be necessary."

His smirk is there and gone, disappearing in the time it takes him to straighten back to full height. I look at Yara and shake my head. She rolls her eyes knowingly, then turns to chat with Bretiax, Harpina, and Thisobei.

Soren hasn't moved. His arms are crossed over his chest as he stares down at me. A lock of dark, lush hair is falling across his forehead. I have the strangest urge to push it back for him.

"You look like you're about to fall over," he informs me, voice blunt.

The urge fades instantly.

My reply is acerbic. "Such flattery! I may swoon."

"I just meant . . ." He pinches the bridge of his nose, an uncharacteristic display of unease. "Look, if you want to drown your sorrows, that's fine. All I ask is that you wait until you're back on solid ground."

"Who says I'm drowning my sorrows?"

The awareness in his gaze sets my teeth on edge. "What happened earlier, with the cannon . . ."

I flinch at the soft compassion in his tone. His flippancy is easier to withstand. "I don't want to talk about it. I don't even want to think about it," I whisper quickly, before he can say anything else. My words pour out faster as the feelings I've spent the past few hours suppressing bubble to the surface. "Right now I just . . . I want to forget. I *need* to forget, Soren. Because if I think about it for too long I might—I might start to—"

"Rhya."

My heart stumbles. "Y-yes?"

"I have been around for two centuries. I am an expert at forgetting. But . . ." His eyes striate like stars. "There are better ways of distracting your mind than dulling it with drink. More . . . *pleasurable* . . . options for untangling that knot of tension inside you."

What sort of ways?

One part of me wants to ask; the other part is wise enough to keep silent. No verbal response feels entirely safe at this moment. My emotions are frazzled from Melité's thrall, my body not fully back in my control. My whole frame is strung tight.

His tone turns to gravel. "Would you like me to show you?"

My lips part, but no sound escapes.

Soren does not seem to be breathing. He is perilously still, awaiting my answer. Only his gaze shifts—dropping down to watch my throat as I swallow against the thick lump lodged inside it. My skin tingles under the weight of his heated stare. He's never looked at me that way before.

The cursed siren song!

Clearly, its effects have not yet waned.

"*Oi!* Rhya!"

When Yara calls my name, I whirl toward her so fast I nearly snap my own neck. I could not be more grateful to see her flaming red hair and sly grin in the shadows.

I force a light tone. "You bellowed?"

"Bre and I are going down to the Kettle after this round." She gestures toward the other Paexyrian. "It's low tide. A perfect night for it. You should come with us."

I've never been to the Kettle. I'm not entirely sure I even know what the Kettle is. But right now I am willing to overlook that fact if it means a change of scenery from the strange air in this bar.

"Sure," I tell her thickly. "Count me in."

"Arwen?" Yara leans forward to meet her flight leader's eyes three stools down. "What about you?"

Arwen does not even break eye contact with Alaric. Their mouths are so close, they share each breath as she murmurs a suggestive, "We have other plans."

"I'll bet you do," Yara snorts. Then, she raises her Titan gin into the air, a silent toast to the couple who are now sharing more than mere air, their lips fused together in a kiss so passionate it makes me avert my eyes and breathe deeply.

Looking away does nothing to soothe me. My bloodstream is still churning with untapped lust. Pulses of pure desire spike straight through my center, demanding release now, this instant.

I have to get out of here.

Soren is a silent shadow at my back. I steady both my shoulders and my voice before I glance up at him. In the fading twilight, his face is carefully blank, but his eyes are active as they scan back and forth across my features. I hope like hell he is not reading my emotions in this moment.

"What?" I ask under my breath. "Do you have some objection to me going?"

"Not at all. I just want to make sure you're prepared for an evening at the Kettle."

"Whatever it is, I'm sure I can handle myself."

One brow arches. "I'm sure you can, skylark."

I do not care for the mocking note in his voice. My spine stiffens. "No one said you had to come. I do not require constant supervision."

"And miss seeing your reaction to one of Hylios's chief attractions?" He leans in a shade, stare never leaving mine. "Not a chance."

CHAPTER
EIGHTEEN

The moment the Kettle comes into view, I understand how it got its nickname. The network of steaming hot springs in which dozens of people lounge does indeed resemble vats of boiling water on a hearth. Unlike the sulfuric pools at Blister Bight, these are free of fymandridae.

The Paexyrian's group has expanded to include a duo of the new arrivals from Daggerpoint. We walk in pairs along the curving line of the exposed sandbar that leads beyond the city walls—a path that will disappear as soon as the tides wash back in.

It is a popular destination tonight. The main pool is especially crowded. By the time we come to a stop on the edge, the sun has nearly set; only the feeblest vestiges of orange remain streaking across the sky. Any minute, stars will begin to stir awake in the aether. Despite the swelling darkness, I pick out the shape of many piles of clothing peppered across the sand by our feet.

My eyes widen.

Everyone within the cluster of tidal pools is stark naked. Young and old, male and female. Bodies of all shapes and sizes. And they do not appear even slightly modest about their nudity. In fact, as my gaze meanders around the bubbling surface, I see sev-

eral pairs—and even trios—are taking full advantage of their un-
clothed state, touching one another in a way no amount of steam
can disguise. Everywhere my eyes land, acts typically confined
to the bedchamber are on full display. Teeth nibble their way
down neck columns, hands slide over slick flesh, mouths meet
with unabashed hunger.

The sight does nothing to ease the relentless ache stirring
deep inside me. If anything, it only exacerbates the feelings I am
so desperate to escape.

Oh, hell. This was a mistake.

I swallow down my startled gasp, but not quickly enough.
Soren's low chuckle from my right makes it clear he's heard.

"I did try to warn you," he murmurs. "If you want to
leave . . ."

"No. We're already here."

I take a thready breath, attempting to steady myself. I am not
the quivering virgin he seems to think I am, nor some cloistered
prude with no concept of passion—even if I have never before
seen such a blatant exhibition. So, though my hands shake, when
the members of our group begin to disrobe I do not hesitate to
reach for the laces at my boots.

Yara hurriedly whips her uniform off, then jumps into the
water with a joyful whoop, her compact form creating a mighty
splash that earns her more than a few disgruntled looks from the
reposed bathers. Bretiax enters with far more elegance, her
shapely legs striding confidently into the shallows. The wheat-
haired soldiers from Daggerpoint follow after them enthusiastically, eyes never drifting far from the feminine forms that soon
disappear into the steam.

My heart pounds hard as I unstrap my thigh sheath and push
my pants past my hips to puddle around my ankles. It pounds
harder still as I pull the shirt up over my head and drop it beside

my discarded boots. I hear the faint rustle of Soren doing the same behind me, but I ignore him, focused fully on stripping the last remaining scraps of fabric from my body before I lose my nerve.

As my underthings fall away, baring me to the moonlight, I hear a sound that makes my toes curl in the damp sand. It comes from deep in his throat—not quite a groan, almost a growl. My breath hitches as an abrupt lash of lust cascades down the bond, strong enough to bowl me over. My knees wobble under the sheer force of it, then give out entirely.

Before I hit the ground, a hand closes around my bare biceps, steadying me. I glance over at Soren in shock, eyes wide, breaths choppy. He immediately tamps down his maegic, muting the bond between us with brute force, but traces of it still swim in his eyes as they hold mine. He looks less in control than I've ever seen him.

"I'm—I'm sorry." He shakes his head as if to clear a daze. His voice is gravel again. "Are you all right?"

I manage a nod. Though, in truth, I feel anything but. It is unlike him to slip up like that. Lingering effects of the siren song, no doubt. I should be glad it is not only me feeling so off-balance, but I am too preoccupied with other thoughts. Namely: keeping my eyes above chin level.

I try, I truly do. But in the end, I cannot prevent them from flashing down to Soren's chest. My stolen glance lasts no longer than the length of a heartbeat. Still, that is plenty long enough to get an eyeful of golden skin and corded muscle. The dark whorls of his Remnant mark, furling fluidly over his left pectoral.

Soren's sharp exhale makes my eyes jerk back up. I expect him to be looking at me in that mocking way of his, perhaps accompanied by a teasing comment about me yet again spying on him in the nude. Thus, I am wholly unprepared to find his eyes are not playful in the slightest. They are half-lidded . . . and making their own slow trek down my naked form.

Gods.

His stare locks on the Remnant between my breasts, lingering for what seems an eternity. In the silvery shades of moonlight, the mark looks especially dark against my skin. His fingers flex, an involuntary reflex, as his eyes rove over the rosy peaks of my nipples, then shift lower. A rush of warmth blooms wherever they touch. My rib cage . . . The shallow indent of my navel . . . The curve of my waist . . . The slope of my hips . . . The apex of my thighs . . .

Thighs that I am pressing together as though I might stave off the sharp craving coiled there, between them. His hold on my arm gradually tightens as his gaze caresses every part of my flesh, the strong lengths of his fingers wrapped in a way that is not painful, but almost.

It is just the siren's thrall, I tell myself, heart slamming against my rib cage like a blacksmith's hammer. *Ignore it. Pull back.*

But I do not, nor does he. His eyes continue their intent exploration until no part of me is left untouched. The longer he looks, the harder it is to keep still. I fight the growing urge to squirm, forcing my breaths into measured inhales. Forcing my mind to form logical conclusions.

Who cares if he looks?

It means nothing.

I have never been one for excessive modesty, and besides, everyone around us is equally bare. Any moment now he will make a lighthearted comment and shatter this newfound tension . . .

And yet, when his gaze finally returns to mine, my knees

nearly buckle again. His expression mirrors the one I saw at the bar, when he was caught in the throes of siren song. Dark, driving desire. A whole ocean's worth, hidden just below that polished surface he so often shows the world. As the intensity of that look steals through me, I think one would have to be either very brave or very foolish to plumb the depths of such a man.

Surely, you would drown just trying.

"*Oi!* Rhya!" Yara yells from what seems a very far distance, though she is only a few paces away. "Are you coming in, or what?"

I rip my stare from Soren's and my arm from his grip. Whirling around, I find Yara peering up at me, her elbows propped up against the edge of the pool, her eyes dancing with humor as they shift from me to the man at my side.

"Did I interrupt something?"

"Don't be ridiculous," I scold, stepping down into the water. It is deliciously warm against my heated skin as I sink up to my chin, my hair floating all around me in a pale cloud.

Soren says nothing as he follows me in. But I think I hear the rattle of a resigned sigh before Yara grabs my hand and drags me deeper into the steam.

IT'S LATE.

The night is clear and while the moon is well on its way to being full, it does nothing to diminish the stars. They are out in full force, a tremendous array of constellations overhead. I stare up at them, feeling like the only living soul left in the realm.

Despite the late hour, I am reluctant to leave the warm waters of the Kettle. Floating in the darkness of one of the more secluded pools on the fringes, my mind is quiet, my body utterly relaxed. The moment I climb out, I will be forced to face the storm of feelings I've been pushing down since the Frostlander battle. Selfishly, I want to put off that confrontation with my own conscience as long as possible.

That will not be for much longer. The tide is coming in. Soon, the sandbar will be swallowed up by the waves, eliminating access to the city, crashing in over the rocky edges of the thermal baths. Most of them have already emptied out, their occupants fleeing home hours ago. Even Yara and Bretiax have vanished.

Not exactly a surprise. After an hour of our group of six joking and laughing together—mostly at Arwen's expense—in one of the main pools, the two riders had made it clear the rest of their evening would be occupied by other pursuits. Ones of the purely physical variety. Their new Daggerpoint men were promptly dragged away, assumedly to a more private location in the city proper where they would receive what Yara called, through a fit of unrepentant giggles, a "proper Paexyrian riding lesson."

Sad as I was to see them go, I was grateful I would not become a firsthand witness to whatever she deemed a hearty Hylian welcome. Gods know, I'd already withstood enough gratuitous carnality this day to last a lifetime.

Alone in the quiet, I listen to the slosh of the incoming tide and let my waterlogged limbs float freely beneath the surface. I wonder if Soren's left as well, or is still somewhere in the main pool. I lost sight of him sometime in the aftermath of the others' departure. I feel not a trace of him through the bond. His maegic is fully muted from me.

Perhaps he found a partner of his own and headed back to the villa.

The thought makes me inexplicably tense, though I cannot explain why. It is no business of mine who he brings through the warded doors of his bedchamber. For all I know he keeps a full harem behind that thick slab of crystal.

I've heard you've quite the appetite . . . Melité's voice purrs in my memory. *You like to sample a wide variety of flavors . . .*

I press my spine harder against the rocky edge of the pool, attempting to ground myself in the present. Clinging to my fraying sense of calm, I close my eyes on the stars and pull in a huge gulp of air. My emotions are uncomfortably close to the surface, however I try to force them down. My heart aches like an open wound, each beat pumping with contradictory feelings. And between my legs, at the very core of me, a different sort of ache—one stirred awake by siren song and building in strength all evening, no matter how I try to suppress it. One I am desperate to relieve before it consumes me from the inside out.

Through slivered lids, I scan the steaming surface for witnesses, but there is no one around to see. This particular pool was mostly unoccupied even before the mass exodus. On a sharp exhale, I allow my hand to slip between my parted thighs. My teeth score into my bottom lip, containing a gasp as my fingers find the source of all my pent-up pleasure.

Yes.

Gods, yes.

This is what I crave, what I've been craving for hours. Blissful release from the torturous uproar within. My fingers circle, chasing gratification with an impatience that normally might embarrass me, even alone beneath my bedcovers. But in this moment, I feel nothing except pure need.

I am so caught up, it takes me a moment to detect the gentle churn of unseen currents flowing around me—starting at my feet, moving up my legs, climbing from my fingertips to my arms, then winding around my shoulders. It is like being wrapped in an embrace. My back arches against the stone as warm tendrils of water slide over my damp skin with languid caresses, massaging every ounce of tautness out of my submerged shoulders, sluicing down the length of my spine as it bows under rolling waves of mounting satisfaction.

In combination with my fingers, it feels unbelievably good.

Unnaturally good, I realize with a start.

My hand stills as my eyes crack open, searching for him. For though Soren has long since shrouded his presence from me, I know with instant surety that he must still be here somewhere. This is his doing, this fluid glide of water across my skin, this kneading of muscle and sinew I feel all the way down to my marrow.

Calling a swift breeze, I sweep the steam from the surface and finally spot him. He is clear across the pool, some twenty paces away. Hardly more than a shadow. Still, I can see the faint silvery gleam of his irises as his maegic courses over my skin, never pausing in its quest to alleviate every bit of my tension.

Did he know that I'd been—

My cheeks are aflame. Of course he knows. Gods, how embarrassing. And, if I'm being entirely honest, frustrating. Need still swims within me, unsatisfied. But I cannot continue now. Not with him here to witness it.

Can I?

As though feeling my indecision, his tendrils of water keep at their soothing strokes up and down my body. He is not touching me; he is not anywhere near me. And yet, this phantomlike contact makes my heart pound so hard, I'm certain he can hear it.

My mouth opens to call out to him, fully prepared to tell him he has to stop, that this is wholly inappropriate. No words escape. Instead, a shallow huff of air slips from my lips as a thready breath hitches inside my throat. At the sound, our eyes lock across the moonlit pool. The moment they do, faint silver turns star bright as he stops muting his maegic. It floods into me, furls through me—sweeping away all my best intentions to stop whatever is happening, along with all my mortification that he is bearing witness to this most private of moments.

Not only bearing witness, in fact, but . . .

Participating.

There is no longer room for embarrassment, though. The need coursing through my bloodstream is too strong to feel anything else. I am caught in a current of desire and can no longer hold it back. Even if I could, I no longer care to try. My fingers begin to move again, sending spikes of pleasure rocketing through my frame.

I hear a sharp intake of air from Soren as he senses what I'm doing beneath the surface. In the same instant, the water resumes its play across my skin, moving with new intent. Not mere relaxation anymore, but a sinuous seduction. I feel his maegic moving all over me, underneath me. Flowing down my back and up my limbs.

My whole body spasms as a warm rush of water slides between my parted legs, weaving its way to the precise spot where my fingers are rotating with ever-increasing speed. Doubling the sensation in a way that makes a cry catch in my throat.

Gods.

My breaths are shredded pants, coming fast. The ache within climbs to new extremes, higher and higher, moving toward an unquestionable peak. I feel its swift approach and do not attempt to stop it. Instead, I call it forth, eager to feel that moment of release.

Desperate for it.

I am nearly there all on my own. Yet when I see the unexpected movement of Soren's arm across the pool, the rhythmic jerk of his fist beneath the surface as he strokes himself to the same precipice on which I am poised . . .

I shatter to pieces.

It is brilliant. Blinding. I throw my head back as I fall apart, teeth bearing down to contain a cry as waves of sheer exaltation wash through me. Soren's throaty groan of release rings out at the same moment his maegic swells down the bond, infusing my very soul with stardust.

It takes several long moments for the pleasure to ebb. When it does, I am left with the hollow echo of disbelief. I can hardly wrap my mind around the shocking intimacy of the moment we have just shared.

He did not touch my skin, did not kiss me, did not even come within a stone's throw of my body. Still, I feel flayed open, as though he has split my rib cage with a sword and peered inside my chest cavity.

All the feelings I pushed aside when caught up in the moment of blinding satisfaction come crashing back. Embarrassment, surely, but also an intractable sense of guilt. I tell myself I have done nothing wrong. I have committed no betrayal.

So why is my skin aflame with mortification? Why does my pulse pound twice its normal speed? Why is my head even more tangled with contradictory emotions than it was in the wake of the Frostlander battle?

The godsdamned siren song, that's why.

It must be. There is no other explanation for my wanton display, for caving to my basest bodily instincts. Soren and I had both been momentarily lost in it. That's all this was. A lapse in judgment, stirred by forces beyond our control. An aberration, never to be repeated. As soon as we awaken tomorrow, fresh eyed and clear headed, things will go back to normal.

They must.

There is no other option.

If Soren senses my brimming disquiet, he does not comment on it. He seems caught up in his own thoughts as we climb from the pool and locate our discarded clothing. He says nothing as we dress, though he whisks the water away from my skin before it can settle into the fabric with a wave of maegic that whispers across every part of me. My cheeks burn as I recall the feeling of that touch beneath the water. I am grateful for the darkness, so he cannot see the blush.

We make our way back to the city side by side, our footfalls soundless as we walk along the narrow sliver of sandbar that remains. Soon, it will disappear altogether. Our silence lingers as we cut through the stone passage, and throughout the winding walk along the canals that leads to the royal grounds.

With each step up the many stone flights to the villa, my thoughts grow more murky, my feelings more tangled. I do not know what to say to the man at my side any more than he seems to know what to say to me. We are swimming in uncharted waters.

Should I make a joke about it? Laugh it off, as though it was nothing? Or would it be better to pretend it had not happened at all—a mutual agreement to move on without ever addressing our shared submission to the most hedonistic of impulses?

I have no answers.

It is not until we reach the door to my suite that he finally breaks the heavy quiet. His voice is oddly serious.

"Rhya."

My hand freezes on the handle. I am too cowardly to turn and look at him; afraid of what I might see in his eyes when I do. "Don't."

He pauses. "Don't what?"

"Don't say anything. I'm not . . ." I swallow hard and lean my forehead against the wood panel, where carvings of coral and seashells press back at me. "I can't. Okay? Not now."

He moves close to my back. So close, I can feel the heat of his chest. I still, terrified he is going to touch me; equally terrified he won't. But he holds back, maintaining a small sliver of space between us.

"I only wanted to say good night," he whispers, breath stirring the hair at my nape. There is another pause—this one longer. I think he might not say anything else. But then . . .

"You aren't ready for the things I want to say to you," he says finally. "So, I'll wait."

I suck in a breath.

He'd wait?

His voice warms a shade, returning to something more like his normal sardonic tones. "Gods know, I've had enough practice at it."

With that, he walks away, long strides carrying him down the hall to his chamber. I remain there, frozen in place with my forehead digging into the wood, until I hear the click of his thick crystalline door. Only then do I haul in a breath and step inside my suite.

CHAPTER
NINETEEN

How was the rest of your evening?" Yara asks the following morning, eyes scanning me up and down. "You look like you haven't slept."

I rub at my bleary eyes, fully aware they bear the shadowy traces of sleeplessness. For hours I tossed and turned, plagued by memories of the day before. The battle and its aftermath. Seeing the floating Frostlander bodies in my mind, a relentless parade of images. Envisioning the sunken fleet rotting on the bottom of the bay forevermore, an unending reminder of my own ruthlessness. Questioning what on earth was happening to me since coming to this city, and why I seem so incapable of denying my basest caprices when it comes to my power.

Or, apparently, my body.

"Shouldn't I be asking you that?" I direct the question back at Yara, skirting her need for an answer. "You're the one who spent the night . . . How shall I put it? Properly welcoming the men of Daggerpoint?"

"Just doing my part to give the bridegroom's half of the wedding party a warm reception."

"I have never seen such creativity in fulfilling one's civic duties."

She giggles lightly. "You'll see far more than that if you come out with me again tonight. Have you been to the pleasure clubs yet?"

I shake my head.

"Right. I forgot Soren's been keeping you all to himself, locked away in his villa."

"I am not locked away. I come and go as I please."

"Do you?"

"I'm here now, aren't I?" I pin her with a look. "Are you going to introduce me to the Paexyrian way of life or not?"

She grins, but gives me no more trouble as we walk around the open-air stables and unfenced grazing lands where the winged steeds spend much of their free time. I try to listen as Yara prattles on about flight formations and aerial maneuvers, but most of my focus is on the cluster of Paexyri just beyond the stables, where a natural spring bubbles gently. I've seen them from a distance, of course, but up close they are even more spectacular.

Yara rolls her eyes at my childlike awe when she calls Umyr close, but is quick to give me pointers for how best to approach— head bowed, eyes downcast, hand outstretched with an offering of something tasty, be it a sugar cube or a clump of sweet seagrass. It is important to display respect and to show you are not a threat when approaching for the first time. To a Paexyri, trust is paramount. If they do not trust you inherently, you'll never get close enough to pet their velvet nose; you'll certainly not get a chance to climb astride their back and take to the skies.

Umyr acknowledges me almost instantly. Even Yara is surprised—and, I would guess, a tiny bit wounded. It had taken her a fortnight of bribes and bows to gain the chestnut beast's acceptance, reputedly freezing her ass off in the frozen tundra atop a Llŷrian mountain where the Paexyri fly wild. But the moment my eyes meet Umyr's glossy brown ones, I see the under-standing there along with a keen intelligence. It takes no more than a few moments for her to accept my offering, her soft muzzle butting against my palm, her nostrils flaring with warm breath.

"Horses have always liked me," I tell Yara, shrugging as I run my hand along Umyr's flank. I hesitate when I reach the joint where her huge wing joins her torso, but she shifts toward my touch as though she craves it. I grin as I feel her feathers against my palm; they are far softer than I expected, each longer than my forearm.

"She's not a *horse*," Yara mutters. "She's a Paexyri."

"I know that."

One of the feathers comes loose in my hand, ready to be shed. I hold it up to the sky to properly study its colors. The sun-light filters through the finest strands at the tip, turning the red shades to bright flame.

It is a glorious morning, drenched with warm sun. Not a cloud in sight. For the first time since my arrival, the Hylian cli-mate lives up to its reputation.

Smiling, I call a thin tendril of wind and send the feather spinning in a lazy spiral high overhead. It casts strange shadows across Umyr's strong back as it moves under my command, tum-bling and turning like an acrobat onstage. My control has im-proved by leaps and bounds since that first day in the aviary.

"I suppose it makes sense," Yara mutters, eyeing me as I send the feather dancing toward her. She swats at it absently as I tickle the side of her face with the tip. "Creature of the air that you are, it's only natural you'd have an affinity with flying beasts. You really should think about joining our ranks."

"Recruiting without my input, are you?" a new voice cuts in.

The feather flutters to the ground as I whirl toward Arwen. She's hopped the fence and is striding our way across the pasture, eyes fixed on me, expression frosty as ever. In contrast, Alaric is grinning warmly by her side. They stop six paces from us.

"Last I checked, I had final say over who joins the Paexyrian." Arwen's tone is flat. "Just because you've taken a shine to some untested interloper—"

"It's not just me. Umyr likes her," Yara interjects, muscular arms crisscrossing her chest. "That's all I need to know."

"I like her, too," Alaric says kindly, though he barely knows me. I smile at him and am rewarded with a brown-eyed wink of support.

"It does not matter who *likes* her." There is no heat behind Arwen's snarl. Her chin jerks haughtily as our gazes meet. "Though I suppose you weren't entirely useless with the water cannon during the battle yesterday."

I fight the urge to roll my eyes. Of course she only respects me when it comes to my skills at indiscriminate slaughter.

"I wonder what you could do for our flight speeds . . ." Her head cants to one side in an evaluative manner that reminds me of Soren. "Do you think you'd be able to manipulate the wind currents at altitude?"

"I've had no occasion to try," I tell her truthfully.

"Pity." She looks over at Alaric as he takes her hand, lacing their fingers together, and scowls at him. "What did I tell you about displaying affection in public?"

"That it's wholly unacceptable," he replies.

"Correct." Her cheeks tinge with a hint of red. "So, do you care to explain why my hand is currently in yours? As we are, in fact, in public?"

In response, he leans in and kisses her soundly. She stiffens for approximately three seconds, then goes totally pliant and sinks into the kiss like she's powerless to stop herself. Only the sound of Yara's poorly suppressed laughter pulls her back to reality.

"Is something funny?" she snaps, cheeks pink as a sunrise, lips slightly swollen.

Yara's shoulders shake with silent chuckles. "Nothing at all, flight leader."

Alaric is grinning even wider than before. The sight of that grin inspires one of my own. His joy is infectious. He is absurdly handsome, like he's stepped out of an oil portrait and come to life. I do not fail to notice he is still holding Arwen's hand, despite her periodically tugging in a halfhearted attempt to extract herself.

"Lovely weather we're having today, isn't it?" His chocolate eyes twinkle. "If it holds like this, it will be perfect for the wedding next week."

It is a valiant attempt to change the subject. Little does he know, this is a point of contention between me and his blushing bride. Arwen's eyes narrow on me again. "See that it stays this way, airhead."

"No promises, sea urchin."

"Sea urchin?"

"Spiny. Occasionally poisonous. But inside . . ." I shrug. "Pure mush."

Yara makes a strangled sound.

Alaric coughs to cover a laugh.

"Mush!" Arwen shrieks, outraged. "My insides are not mush!"

Her cheeks are redder than ever.

"There is a certain resemblance," Alaric puts in quietly, brushing his lips against the side of her head. "Don't worry. I find your spines quite charming."

I brace myself for Arwen's retaliation, but her attention has shifted over my shoulder to something on the other side of the pasture. I turn to see what she's looking at and lock my knees when I spot Soren striding across the grassy stretch toward us. He looks windswept, his cheeks ruddy, his dark hair slightly wild. His broad frame is encased in clothing I've never seen him wear. It almost looks like a male version of the Paexyrian flight uniform, with a leather vest instead of a corset layered over a shirt of such deep navy, it is almost black, and breeches fit for riding.

A full-body tremble moves through me as our gazes tangle together. I have not seen him since last night. I'm unsure how to act around him in the aftermath. But he smiles easily at me as he comes to a stop at my side, then shifts his focus to the others like it is any normal day.

"Yara, Alaric," he greets, then looks at Arwen. "Daemon incarnate."

"Another lovely nickname," Yara murmurs, earning her a glare from her flight leader and a chortle from Alaric.

"Someone is just begging for stall-mucking duties, aren't they?" Arwen asks sweetly.

Yara winces.

Arwen's eyes shift to her brother, scanning down his form, taking note of his clothing. "You went to see Zephyr without me?"

Zephyr?

"You were occupied." He jerks his chin toward Alaric, mouth tugging up in a knowing smile. "Besides, I needed to clear my head." His eyes flicker to mine. "I had some . . . tension . . . to work out."

My stomach flips.

"I would've made the time," Arwen grouses. "It's been ages since I paid a visit. And I know Atyr misses him."

Soren is still staring at me. Ignoring his sister, he asks, "Are you finished here?"

"I believe so. Why?"

"We have a lesson to get to at my villa. Unless you are no longer interested in the things I plan to teach you?"

For whatever reason, the question makes my cheeks flame. I quickly avert my eyes to Yara, brows lifting in silent inquiry.

"Don't stick around on my account. You'll only get me in more trouble." She shoos me away playfully. I turn to go, but pause when she yells, "I meant what I said about the pleasure clubs! You want to tag along tonight, meet me here around dusk. Yeah?"

Soren tenses at my side for a fraction of a second. He recovers so quickly, I'm certain I imagined it.

"Thanks, Yara," I call back, looking anywhere but at him.

I wave goodbye to Alaric, avoid eye contact with Arwen, then start walking. My gaze moves to Umyr one last time as I cross the pasture. She retreated at some point during our conversation, but her intelligent eyes are on me even now. I give her a deep nod of respect and she spreads her wings—the Paexyri equivalent of a wave goodbye—in response before trotting away to join the other winged mounts who are drinking from the spring. Harpina, Thisobei, and Bretiax are lounging on rocks close by, signing and laughing.

Soren falls into step beside me, immediately matching his longer strides to mine. I'm feeling oddly tense, but his voice holds only familiar amusement when he speaks.

"The pleasure clubs with Yara? I know you're nearly immortal, skylark, but that is taking your life in your hands . . ."

"Just another day in Hylios, then."

He laughs as we turn onto the path through the lemon grove.

"True enough. Though Yara does have a certain magnetism for trouble."

That I can believe. "Trouble or not, she has been welcoming thus far. She gave me a tour of the stables this morning. Introduced me to Umyr. It was incredible." I grin at the memory. "Of course, Arwen was far less enthusiastic about my potential recruitment to the Paexyrian."

His gaze lingers on the side of my face, studying me as we make our way up the stone steps toward his villa.

"What?" I ask eventually, feeling self-conscious under the weight of his stare.

"I did not realize you had such an interest in mounted flight."

"I don't. Not necessarily." I shrug. "Though . . ."

He waits a beat, then pokes me lightly on the arm. "Are you planning to finish the thought or shall I start guessing?"

I shoot him a surly look. "My interest is more in flight as a general concept, I suppose. I saw a painting in your gallery last week depicting the fallen Queen of Taranis. It sparked my curiosity."

"Queen Arianrhod." He nods. "The Golden Goddess, they called her. She was legendary in combat. Beloved by her people. A sylph so at home in the skies, there were apparently no paintings of her ever commissioned with her feet on the ground."

"Yes. Well . . . I've been looking for books about her in your library, but I haven't found any."

"Mmm. Most of the Sky Court was destroyed when Taranis fell during the Cull. Books included, unfortunately. I did manage to rescue a few tomes from the rubble, but they require translation." His brows quirk up. "Unless you happen to speak the ancient Taranian tongue of your ancestors?"

I blink at him. "No."

"Shame."

"But you've actually been there?" I blurt. "To the Court of Clouds?"

"Yes. Several times." His eyes cut to mine, inquisitive. "I could take you someday, if you'd like."

I suck in a breath to contain my excitement. "Really?"

"Sure. Though the portal there was destroyed years ago. The closest one is a two-day ride through the most war-ravaged stretches of Westlake, followed by a trek through the mazelike pillars of Lordale. Assuming it, too, has not been sacked by now. There are no guarantees in the Midlands." He pauses. "It has been more than a decade since I last paid a visit to the ruins there."

"What was it like?"

"A beautiful pile of rubble," he scoffs, though a sad note creeps into his voice as he continues. "I scavenged what I could. There was not much. A few relics. A few baubles. I'll show you if you'd like to see them."

"That—" I swallow down my bubbling enthusiasm. "That would be wonderful."

He stops abruptly on the path back to the villa, where it forks between the terrace and the bathhouse. His stare is appraising.

"What?" I ask, pulling up short. "What is it?"

"I'd planned to teach you about weather patterns today," he murmurs. "So you might begin to use the atmosphere to your advantage. But I think I've just come up with a lesson that will be of far more interest to you. Assuming you're up for a short trip outside the city walls, that is." He leans closer, voice pitching to a low whisper. "I promise to return you in time for your night of debauchery."

My brows are high on my forehead as I weigh his words. After a few seconds, I give a small nod of assent. His face lights up in a smile so bright, it takes my breath away. Before I can catch it again, Soren grabs my hand and starts striding down the path that leads to his bathhouse.

THE PORTAL SPITS us out halfway up a mountain.

Soren drops my hand as I double over, winded from the disorienting passage. It was an easier venture than my last through the leylines but still took a toll on both mind and body, even with Soren there to guide me through. The wound on my palm—twin to the one he sliced into his own—is already stitching back together, leaving a crust of dried blood behind.

I look around, trying to get my bearings. The portal behind us dims, gradually disappearing back into the rock face. We are in the Cimmerians. I'm certain from the air alone—crisp and cold, carrying the scent of pine sap. This part of the range, east of the Avian Strait, is made up of peaks slightly lower than those I traversed with Pendefyre and his men, all those months ago. That diminutive difference in elevation has tremendous consequences, for the landscape around me is not ice capped but startlingly verdant. Evergreens soar up toward the bluest of skies, stubby grasses carpet the ground, fuzzy moss drapes over boulder formations that surround the glade.

"Where are we?"

"Not far from the Acrine Hold. There is a path, though few know of it, that leads down through the mountains to the strait." Soren strides several steps forward, eyes scanning all around him. He is looking for something—or someone—but he speaks again before I can ask. "This part of the range has many names. The Faery Ring. The Giant's Necklace. The Cimmerian Crown. See how these five peaks form almost a perfect circle around us?"

I pivot in a full rotation, eyes scanning the surrounding

summits. They do indeed appear to encircle this stretch of land where the five opposing slopes converge into a flat plane of sorts.

"What do you call it?"

"The Vale." Soren's voice grows fainter as he moves away from me, his tall form disappearing into the thick foliage. "It was apparently a site Emperor Belenus once considered for the imperial palace."

I trail after him, pushing aside the branches in my path. "Perhaps if he had, it would still be standing. The palace did not fare so well at Lake Lumen during the Cull, if my childhood lessons were at all accurate."

The emperor's grand palace was one of the mortal kings' first targets when they staged their bloody coup. If any of it remains, it has long since been swallowed by the glowing waters of Anwyvn's most famous lake.

"Or perhaps this place would merely be a ruin as well," Soren counters from somewhere out of sight. "Which would be most unfortunate, given our purposes here today."

"Which are . . . what, exactly?"

He materializes before me without warning, stepping out from behind a tree with such stealth, I have to swallow a bleat of panic. He smirks, voice dropping low. "The emperor did not make his home here, for this place already had a king."

My features are still scrunched in confusion when his hands hit my shoulders. He slowly spins me around to face the opposite direction. His chest brushes my back as he leans forward to speak directly into my ear, his words hushed so as not to startle the great winged stallion that is making landfall in the clearing we've just vacated, each pump of his feathers sending plumes of dust and pollen into the air.

"Zephyr," Soren says. "Winged King of the Vale."

Tears spring to my eyes as I take in the sight of him. Pure

black, from his heavy hooves to his long mane. And *gargantuan*. His wingspan is easily double that of Umyr's. His body would dwarf even Atyr's impressive bulk. He trots neatly to a stop just behind the tree line, tucking his wings close to his sides. His ears twitch as though he is listening for us in the quiet.

I can think of no words in the common tongue to encapsulate his sheer resplendence. I am afraid to move a single muscle, afraid the slightest movement will alert him to my presence and send him soaring back into the skies. When Soren pushes me forward a few steps, I dig my bootheels into the ground, resisting.

"You won't scare him off. Trust me, he would not have appeared at all if he did not want to meet you."

With a sigh I relent, allowing him to propel me forward on jellied legs. My heart is in my throat as the distance between me and the immense Paexyri shrinks. As we near, I see I was wrong at first glance—he is not all black. The very tips of his wings are dusted with gold and there are several thick streaks of it threaded through his tail and mane.

"I don't have a bribe," I whisper haltingly.

"You don't need one." Soren sounds amused. "You are the Remnant of Air. You are forged of the very maegic from which he sprang more than a millennium ago. Every facet of your being, from your scent to your power signature, is as familiar to him as the wind beneath his wings."

Despite his assurances, I still tremble with hesitation as I step into Zephyr's shadow. His black eyes bore into me, *through* me, seeming to reach my very soul. My hand shakes visibly as I lift it slowly from my side, palm facing upward. I don't realize it's the one caked with dried blood until I see the sudden flare of his nostrils. His wide muzzle drops down into my hand before I can pull it back. He inhales deeply, scenting me, then chuffs out a warm breath that makes me grin.

"See?" Soren's voice holds a matching smile. "He knows you already."

I spend the following few minutes studying the Paexyri king up close, marveling over his glossy coat and the graceful slope of his spine, running my fingers through his feathers, laughing as he nips at my braid and flicks his tail.

"Thank you," I say when I am finally able to turn my attention back to Soren. "This was amazing."

His eyes crinkle with mirth as he crosses his arms over his chest. "Did you think this was the only reason we came?"

"Well . . . Yes, I . . ." I blink in bewilderment. "Why else?"

His gaze shifts from me to Zephyr and back again. A slow smile spreads across his face, breaking like the first light of dawn over the sea.

"To fly, skylark. We've come to fly."

CHAPTER
TWENTY

Soren boosts me up onto Zephyr's bare back, then settles behind me with a fluidity born of long practice. He's practically vibrating with excitement, sharing none of the anxiety that thunders through my chest. But then, why would he? By his own admission, he's spent more hours flying atop Zephyr than he could count over the past two centuries, starting when he was barely tall enough to mount him. This very morning, in fact, he was here clearing his head with a ride over the Cimmerians.

Despite the lack of saddle, my seat feels secure with Soren at my back, his long legs hooked beneath the shoulder joints, his arms caging my body as his fingers calmly grip the mane. My own white-knuckled clutch only tightens as we break into a canter, then lift off the ground, propelled by the rhythmic pump of two colossal wings.

Soren laughs as I shriek, amused by my terror. Had there been any breath in my lungs, I might've cursed him. My stomach is left somewhere on the ground as the earth shrinks from view more rapidly than I would've thought possible. In seconds, we've ascended high into the sky and are making slow orbits around the five summits of the Vale.

"Breathe, skylark!" Soren yells, barely audible over the roar of the wind. "Zephyr won't let you fall!"

I suck in a desperate gulp of air, trying to get ahold of myself. Tears gloss my eyes—no wonder the Paexyrian squad wear goggles—and I blink them away, trying to take in the scope of the view from this altitude. There is the Avian Strait, far below us— a tapering pass through the mountainous boundary that divides the Northlands from the rest of Anwyvn. Beyond, I can see the war-ravaged battlefields that characterize the Midlands, from Aranthon's rolling plains to the distant forests that distinguish Eastwood to the boggy mires on the border of Westlake where I almost met my end with a noose around my neck. In the east, the Endless Ocean sprawls down the coast, stretching from the southern shores of Daggerpoint all the way to the Southlands. Though I cannot see it, somewhere beyond my sight line lies Dymmeria, that dark desert kingdom where Efnysien cowers.

We circle inland, looping one of the tallest summits, where the air is so thin the deepest breaths barely fill my lungs. My eyes skim over the speckle of rooftops I know must be Coldcross, past the glacier-bound stretch of Frostlander territory, and finally to the indistinct outline of a plateau I can only just begin to make out at the farthest limits of my eyesight.

Dyved.

A violent pang moves through my heart.

Caeldera.

Another pang.

Pendefyre.

A third, this one strong enough to cause true pain.

I have not allowed myself to think of him, these past weeks. Not often, and never deeply. Worries that once plagued me relentlessly—*How is he sleeping at night? Is he eating enough?*

Has his obsession with charging the wards waned?—no longer suffuse my every waking moment.

I do not let them.

I actively put them from my head.

At first, I did.

Now, as I squint toward the horizon, I realize *actively* is no longer the descriptor I'd use. I am not certain when exactly it happened, I only know I no longer guard constantly against such thoughts creeping in unbidden.

What at first was a deliberate matter of self-preservation morphed, at some unidentified point in time, into unconscious habit. And for a surprising amount of days in a row, I have not sought out his maegic, nor tried to sense our thin-stretched bond across the vast distance that stretches between us.

A flush of horror furls through me when I think of the Remnant bond—not the one connecting me to the man currently pressed so tight at my back, but the one turned threadbare by circumstance.

Would it atrophy from lack of use? Would that tenuous connection from flame to air fade away? Sputter into ash and scatter irrevocably out of reach?

No, I assure myself, pulse pounding fast, breaths coming short. It cannot. Pendefyre told me so himself, a long, long time ago.

Whether we like it or not, the Remnants are eternally linked.

By power. By prophecy. By fate.

We are four weighted scales hung from the same beam, forever seeking a balance only the others can deliver. Independent, but irrevocably tethered.

Somewhere deep beneath my aching cage of ribs, a twisted string of flame still burns. I can almost imagine it there. Can almost feel it, too, growing hotter with the renewed heat of un-settled emotions. A stoked blaze that gathers in my blood until the cold wind surrounding us seems as far removed as the ground below.

"*What is it?*" Soren asks, mind to mind, sensing my distress. "*What's wrong?*"

We've begun to channel subconsciously, the connection slid-ing into place so easily I do not notice our maegics merging to-gether until his voice sounds in my head.

"*Nothing,*" I lie thinly, jolting out of my convoluted thoughts. "*Nothing at all.*"

He knows I'm not being truthful, but does not push the mat-ter. He distracts me instead with a lesson on flight dynamics, en-gaging my mind with such a flood of information, within a matter of seconds I no longer feel my attention pulled toward trouble-some western horizons.

Then again, with Zephyr banking at perilous angles and ca-reening around mountaintops, it would be difficult to concentrate on anything but the present even if I tried.

We stay in the skies for a full hour—the final part of which Soren spends instructing me to really *sense* the wind cur-rents flowing around us, so someday I might mimic them without a Paexyri mount to ferry me along. The prospect of solo flight feels far out of reach—Queen Arianrhod, I am not—but I do as he says, honing my focus on the sky as it rushes by on all sides.

I am abuzz with pure exhilaration. My maegic sings through me, each pump of my heart in total harmony with Zephyr's beat-ing wings, as though we truly are connected at a spiritual level. I close my eyes to the realm below and channel all my energy in-ward, where my endless storms swirl.

My Remnant feels intensely awake. Awake in a way I have

never felt before. For this is where it belongs. I simply had not known it until now.

Before I felt the breadth of the heavens at my fingertips, I did not realize how I longed to reach for them. Before I breathed the thinnest air, I did not understand how much my lungs craved its crisp relief.

This, here—in the wind, in the air, in the sky—is as close as I have ever felt to knowing where I come from. As close as an orphaned halfling from the shores of Seahaven has ever come to calling somewhere *home*.

Tears streak down my cheeks for the remainder of the flight, and they have nothing to do with the biting air in my eyes.

AT SOME UNSPOKEN command, Zephyr guides us back between the five summits into the Vale's circle of shelter. Hooves clatter against the earth with a bone-shaking jolt as we touch down, galloping around the glade before slowing to a stop by the tree line. Soren dismounts first, then reaches up to help me down. His hands remain at my waist even after my boots hit the earth.

"Well?" His hair is windblown, his cheeks ruddy, his eyes warm as the Hylian hot springs. "What did you think?"

"It was a thrill," I confess, hearing my own wonderment. "Truly. One of the most incredible experiences of my life."

"I'm glad."

"Thank you, Soren."

His lips part, then close on a swallow. As though he wanted to say something, only to change his mind at the last moment. "Don't thank me," he says instead. "Thank Zephyr."

With that, he steps away from me, turning to murmur words of gratitude to the King of the Vale. I watch the two of them—how

Soren rests his forehead against Zephyr's nose, how his hands stroke gently along the strong sinews of the stallion's neck; how a velvet muzzle butts insistently against the left side of his broad chest, where his Remnant sits beneath the fabric.

Their bond is plain to see. Witnessing it inspires a muddled mix of emotions. Respect. Appreciation. Awe. Even envy, for I have never been so deeply connected to another living soul in all my years. Nor have I ever been touched with such reverence.

A sad state of affairs to find oneself jealous of a horse.

Cheeks aflame, I tear my eyes away from Soren's gentle touch on Zephyr's flanks.

We do not return by portal right away. Instead, we sit for a time beneath a large evergreen, our backs propped against the rough trunk. In my peripheral, Soren fiddles with a birch stick, peeling strips of white bark off in long ribbons. Most of my focus remains trained on the clearing. I thought Zephyr would immediately leave us, but he seems content enough to stay, grazing on the stubby grass and vibrant mosses.

"Why does he remain here instead of in Hylios with the others?" I ask eventually.

"Would you choose a stable over this open sky?"

"No. Probably not."

"Each Paexyri has a different temperament. Some are more suited to saddles and battle strategies. Others, like Zephyr, do not answer to any commands but their own. There are times when he does not appear even for me when I visit this place."

I study his distinctive lines for a time—the proud carriage, the keen eyes—and am struck with a distant chord of recognition.

"He looks a bit like Onyx," I murmur almost to myself.

Soren chuckles. "He would. Onyx is his colt. So it would be

more accurate to say Onyx looks like Zephyr, not the other way around."

Head whipping to the side, I gape at him. *"What?"*

"Don't look so shocked, skylark. Zephyr occasionally mates with the wild mares that roam the beaches of the Leeward Port. His offspring are only half Paexyri, resulting in a rather apparent lack of wings on Onyx." He twirls the stick in his fingers absently. "But I'm sure you've noticed how swift his gait, how long his range. They far exceed that of a normal horse."

That is true. No ordinary mount could run tirelessly for days on end. Yet in all the many occasions I have spent astride him, Penn has never said a word about it.

Is it possible he himself does not know Onyx's lineage?

"How did a half-Paexyri colt end up in Caeldera?" I ask.

"I gave him to Pendefyre about a century ago. A gift to celebrate the new alliance we'd struck between our two kingdoms." Soren says this in a casual way, as though it is nothing of importance.

"Penn . . ." I shake my head. "He never told me."

His hands still on the birch. There is a brief moment of stilted silence. "Why would he? Stories that paint me in a more generous light rarely seem to be circulated within the volcanic walls of the Fire Court."

"That's unfair."

The twig snaps cleanly in two. "Is it?"

"Many still speak of how you aided the city during the Battle of Fyremas. I saw myself how valiantly you fought, defending people who were not even your own."

He looks at me then—a look so intent, it makes my mouth parch and my stomach flutter with nerves. "Tell me, skylark. Why is it you are able to recognize the valor in my actions while defending Caeldera, but you can see only horror when it comes to your own?"

"That's not the same," I say immediately.

"No?" He tosses the snapped stick aside. "Your defense of Hylios protected my people from harm. How is that any different from what I did on Fyremas? Or, for that matter, what you yourself did?" His eyes narrow in frustration. "Why can you defend Pendefyre's court without thought, but view yourself as a monster for protecting mine?"

"It was not without thought." I swallow thickly. "Trust me, I do not ever take lives without thought. Each death weighs heavily on me. Or . . . they did."

He waits for me to go on, not interrupting. Merely listening.

"What scares me most is that it is becoming easier. The taking of lives. The weighing of morals." My voice shakes, though I take pains to steady it. "I look at my hands—the same hands I once used to heal—and see only the blood that stains them. I look in the mirror and do not recognize the woman I am becoming."

"Rhya—"

I cannot bear the softness of his tone. "Must we talk about this?"

"We can either talk about this or we can talk about what happened last night at the Kettle."

My teeth click shut so harshly, I nearly bite off the tip of my tongue. I would sooner carve it from my mouth voluntarily than discuss last night with him.

"Well?" he prompts.

Infernal hells.

I suck in a steadying breath. "I am not like Arwen or Yara or any of the other daring Paexyrian. I am not a warrior by nature. I do not want to be. I don't believe in killing recklessly, or crow-ing when the enemy is felled. And yet . . . I cannot help but worry, the longer I am immersed in this world of yours, the more I will lose my grip on the virtues that once guided my life."

Soren contemplates this for a long time, thoughts simmering in his eyes. "Morality is well and good, as lodestars go," he says finally, his voice quiet. "Shame, on the other hand, is not."

Shame?

My spine goes stiff. "I am not ashamed."

"You live like you are. And I would wager it dictates your choices just as much as your sense of right and wrong. Maybe more."

I shake my head. "No. No, that's . . ."

Not true, I want to say.

But the lie will not come out.

"Who was it?" Soren asks darkly. "Who was it who taught you to hide the best parts of yourself away in fear that they might be judged?"

I flinch.

His jaw tightens, a muscle leaping in his cheek. "You were born extraordinary, then forced to live as less than ordinary. To camouflage at all costs. But you, Rhya Fleetwood . . . you were made to stand out. To rise above every convention, every average, every metric. There is not a single ordinary bone in your body."

I want to retort, but I am too tongue-tied to speak. In my head, I hear a familiar refrain. My mentor's voice whispering in the oldest of my memories.

Best keep your mark covered, Rhya.

Best not allow anyone too close, Rhya.

Best try to blend in, Rhya.

"I was not there with you, so I do not know when, exactly, you learned to cower and conceal," Soren goes on. "I do not pretend to know what it was like to be raised as you were, a maegical being in a mortal land—"

"A halfling," I correct coarsely.

"What?"

"I was not a *maegical being*. I was a halfling, marked for death from my first breath. My ears were bad enough. An anomaly, a disfigurement. My Remnant mark was the direst of secrets. An execution order carved into my very flesh, should the wrong person see it." I clench my fists, nails scoring deeply into my palms. "You are right. You cannot understand. You will never understand. And if I was raised to hide . . . So what? My mentor, Eli, did that to keep me safe. He protected me without a second thought to his own fate. You may brand that secrecy as shame, but that shame is what kept me alive. That shame is what led me here, to this moment with you. I will not condemn Eli for inspiring it."

"You can find fault without condemnation. My own father, gods rest him, was not a perfect man." He blows out a breath, leaning more firmly against the trunk. "I worshipped him. And he in turn loved me tremendously. Yet that same love did not extend to my mother, whose heart he broke seemingly in slow motion, one ill-concealed affair at a time, until she was too bitter to love anyone at all. Even her children."

I sit with that for a moment. Digesting his words. Feeling, not for the first time, that there are deep ocean currents running through the very heart of this man. Ones he rarely allows to reach the surface.

"I did not know your mentor," he concedes. "Eli, was it?"

I nod.

"I am sorry you lost him. More, I'm sorry I will not ever get the chance to meet him. To thank him, for keeping you alive all those years. And for shaping you into the rather miraculous creature you've become." He pauses for a beat, shoulder pressing against mine—a solid, supportive weight. "You say you cannot recognize the woman looking back at you in the mirror. That's no surprise. A butterfly cannot ever recall how much it has changed since the cocoon, nor can she see the beauty of her own wings. Only those standing by watching, waiting, can appreciate her evolution."

My heart convulses as though he's wrapped his fist around it. No one has ever, in all my life, said something like that to me. Hearing it unlocks something deep inside. The gnawing sense of self-doubt I have been too scared to face head-on; the growing shame that has indeed been festering inside me for months now—not just since the Frostlander battle but since Fyremas. His words spiral through me, deeper and deeper, until they reach that pit of doubt and self-disgust, dislodging them and settling in their place. Filling me with something warm and strong and sure instead.

I breathe deeply until the emotions he's stirred are subdued enough to speak. "I just don't want . . ." I swallow hard, voice clogged with unshed tears. "I don't want Eli looking down at me from the aether with disappointment."

"Impossible." His shoulder presses harder, underscoring his words. "No one is perfect, Rhya. Not even the dead, who we all have a nasty habit of placing on pedestals and enshrining in heavenly light. If he is worthy of your descriptions, he will not find fault in your choices. For he will know, even up there in the skies, that they are guided by your heart."

"He loved me," I say, my voice breaking as a single tear rolls down my cheek. "He is the only one who ever loved . . . *me*."

Soren is silent. But I feel something through the bond—something I am too overwhelmed to process—as he reaches over and brushes the teardrop away with the pad of his thumb. A second later, he is on his feet, one hand extended down to me.

"Enough heaviness for one afternoon. Debauchery awaits."

THE MOMENT OUR boots hit the crystalline bathhouse floor, Soren's entire demeanor shifts—frame stilling with tension, jaw locking tight.

"What is it?"

"Someone's here," he mutters, moving soundlessly toward the exit.

I trail after him as quietly as I can manage, not daring to ask anything else as we move across the stone bridge into the gardens where the night-blooming flowers pinch their white petals closed against the late afternoon sunshine. I strain my ears, trying to pick up on whatever so alarmed Soren, but can detect nothing unusual. It is not until we round the bend in the path that leads up to the terrace that I hear something banging from the vicinity of the kitchen. It sounds like . . .

Pots and pans?

Soren shoots me a look as we cross the terrace toward the archway that leads inside, lifting his finger to his mouth to indicate I should keep quiet. I roll my eyes in response.

Does he think I'm about to start caterwauling?

His lips twitch, but flatten into a severe frown as we step over the threshold and prepare to confront the intruder. All at once, the tension bleeds out of him.

"Vaughn!"

The half-brother.

The half-Titan.

I stand in the archway, frozen in place as Soren strides toward the fae man who is currently making his way through what appears to be every scrap of food raided from the larders. The table is littered with several varieties of fruit, dried fish, olives, bread, cheese, and a whole roast waterfowl—the drumstick of which he is tearing into with a set of broad white teeth. The thick bone looks like a toothpick between his fingers.

Man is not the correct word to describe him, I think as I watch the two brothers embrace, hands pounding backs with spine-snapping enthusiasm. He is a man and a half, impossibly tall, towering three full heads above Soren. His build makes the barrel-chested wheelmen of the Twins look frail, with hands that could crush a cantaloupe with one squeeze and shoulders so broad, I wonder how he ever fit inside the cramped pantry.

He does not resemble Soren or Arwen, with their piercing beauty. His is a blunter visage with prominent features and a square jaw. His hair is a shade between blond and brown, and quite long, though he's tied it back from his face with a leather cord that matches the material of his vest, breeches, and fur-lined boots. He is dressed for a hunt through wolf-infested woods, not the posh waterways of Hylios.

Soren pulls back, neck craned to grin up into the massive man's face. It is an odd sight. Usually the King of Llŷr towers over everyone. "What the hell are you doing here, little brother?"

"You think I'd miss Arwen's wedding?" Vaughn guffaws. "I know better than to piss her off after centuries of practice. Or have you forgotten the decade-long snit she nursed when I skipped her seventy-fifth naming day?"

"Fair enough." Soren's eyes move to the mess of foodstuffs piled all over the kitchen. "It's been some time since you stepped foot in Hylios, but you do recall you have your own villa several levels down?"

"The one sandwiched between the scaly sisters of doom,

you mean? Forgive me if I'm in no hurry to reacquaint myself with Melité and Tethys."

Leaning back against the edge of the countertop, Soren shakes his head. "Be nice. They're your half-sisters."

"They're also half the reason I stayed away so long." His sigh is martyred. "Bloody sirens. You should hear the screams that echo from Melité's bedchamber windows at night. I can't decide if she's delivering torture or pleasure to her victims." He pauses. "Probably both, knowing her."

Soren snorts softly.

"Besides"—Vaughn takes another huge bite of his drumstick, talking on despite the mouthful that muffles his words—"your pantry is always so much better stocked than mine."

"And yet, you always seem to have more than enough Titan gin on hand."

"I don't recall you complaining, last time I brought over a cask from Prydain."

"I'd be stunned to know you recalled anything, given the amount of it you guzzled on that occasion."

Both men break into reminiscent laughter.

I venture hesitantly into the kitchen, making it only a handful of steps before two sets of eyes—Soren's undiluted blue, Vaughn's startling green—snap to me. I stop in my tracks.

"Erm . . . hello," I say awkwardly.

Vaughn's head whips from me to Soren and back, eyes widening. "Skies, brother, she looks just like—"

"Vaughn," Soren clips, cutting him off.

My brows go up.

I look just like . . .

Who?

Not Enid, I hope. Soren told me that I bear only a passing

resemblance to the previous wind weaver, who claimed not just his heart but Pendefyre's as well.

Had he downplayed matters to spare my feelings?

It certainly would not be beyond the realm of possibility that we share certain characteristics and coloring. Yet I confess, I do not much care for the thought of that. Looking like a woman Soren once loved leaves me strangely uneasy, for reasons I do not mull too thoroughly. It takes all my self-control to keep a glower off my face as I hold Vaughn's surprised gaze.

The giant man sets down the drumstick bone with a thud. He recovers quickly enough, burying his shock beneath a broad grin of welcome. "You must be the wind weaver I've heard so much about."

My brows rise even higher. I glance at Soren—who is pinching the bridge of his nose as if to stave off a headache—then back at Vaughn. "Good things, I hope?"

"That depends entirely on who you ask."

"Ah." My mouth twists. "I've tried to tell her off, but Arwen just won't stop singing my praises."

Vaughn laughs uproariously, then crosses toward me without warning, closing the distance in two strides. He moves with surprising speed for such a behemoth. Before I know what is happening, he's hauled me into his arms and lifted me clear off my feet in a hug that squeezes every particle of air from my lungs. I fear my rib cage might crack under the strain. When I expel an involuntary *oof*, Soren looses a low oath.

"You're crushing her."

"And? She's a Remnant, isn't she? Just because she looks fragile doesn't mean she is." With one last bone-crushing squeeze, he sets me back on my feet. His huge hands rest on my shoulders, each the size of a ham. "It's good to finally meet you, Rhya."

I drag in a desperate gulp of air that makes my bruised chest ache. "Nice to meet"—I wheeze—"you, too."

"Gods," Soren hisses.

Vaughn only chuckles, then retreats to grab an apple off the table. Half of it disappears in a single chomp. "So, Rhya, how are you enjoying your time in the Water Court? Puts a damper on the Fire Court, I'll bet."

"*Vaughn.*"

The half-Titan ignores his brother's menacing warning. "Can't imagine why you'd want to go back there."

I don't know how to respond to that. In lieu of an answer, I grab an apple of my own and take a bite. Luckily, Vaughn does not seem to notice he is carrying on a one-sided conversation.

"Couldn't convince me to live in Caeldera, not for all the gemstones in those Dyvedi mines of theirs. I'd sooner winter over in Melité's clammy cave or with the ice giants atop the Cimmerians."

I choke on my apple.

He pounds me on the back so hard, I fly forward into the table—a collision Soren prevents at the last moment by throwing out an arm to stop me slamming against the edge.

"Though hoarfrost monsters aren't a worry for you, are they, Rhya?" Vaughn goes on, oblivious. "Given the way you fried them on Fyremas. Soren described it in detail in one of his letters, but I still would've liked to see that for myself."

I'm too busy catching my breath to do more than nod weakly.

Soren smoothly intervenes, drawing his brother's attention away. "Where's Wotek?"

"Left him on Prydain. You know he hates ship travel." Vaughn's strong features contort into a frown. "Don't blame him, being crated in the hold for days on end . . ."

"Who is Wotek?" I ask, voice somewhat hoarse.

Vaughn glances at me. "My bear."

"Your *bear*?" I blink, bewildered. "You have a bear?"

"I'm too big for a horse." He shrugs. "Have to ride something into battle, don't I?"

Reaching over, Soren uses two fingers beneath my chin to click my jaw—which has fallen open in shock—closed again.

"Of course, I wouldn't need to ride at all if I weren't so small." Vaughn scratches at his thickly bearded jawline. "No one else on Prydain requires a mount to keep up."

I stare at him. He is the farthest thing from *small* I've ever seen.

"I'm only half-Titan," he explains, recognizing my confusion. "My mother was a true colossal. Makes one wonder how our father managed to bed her all those years ago, logistically speaking."

Soren grimaces. "Some things are best left a mystery."

"Alas, no amount of her blood could make up for his shortcomings." Vaughn grins. "Emphasis on *short*. I'm the runt of Prydain. It's why I'm called Vaughn. Means 'little one.' An inside joke among my kind."

"How tall are the rest of the Titans?" I ask.

"The youngest are at least double Soren's height. The oldest easily triple it."

Skies, that's on par with the ice giants.

"I heard stories about Titans when I was growing up," I confess. "I did not realize they were anything beyond bedtime tales designed to scare children into behaving."

"That's no surprise. We don't get many visitors on the Isle of the Mighty." Vaughn picks up an entire baguette and tears the end off in one clean bite. "Titans are not the friendliest bunch, overall. But you can't really blame them for craving isolation from the rest of the realm, given its history. Fae problems tend to creep across the rough waters of Titan's Way, dragging them into battles they'd rather watch from afar."

"But you're half-fae . . ."

"That's why I'm here, standing in my brother's kitchen—"

"Eating all his food," Soren mutters.

"—talking to you." Vaughn takes another bite of bread. Half the baguette is gone already. "I have a vested interest in what goes on here in Hylios, and in the rest of Anwyvn. But the other side of my family tree displays very little in the way of concern for those rooted on the mainland. If every last fae and mortal slaughtered one another on the field of battle, the Titans wouldn't blink."

"But what of the blight?" My brows are arched nearly to my hairline. "Does it not concern them that the land is sickening year by year? That the birth rate is stagnant? That the crops are dying?"

He shrugs. "They have been around since the time before the Cull. They have seen empires rise and fall, have withstood famines and droughts and natural disasters. Our bloodiest wars do not seem to warrant any more attention than a game of sticks and stones played by the neighbor's children. They set themselves above it."

Soren scoffs. "Because they think themselves gods, directly descended from the blood of deities . . . despite no evidence to support that myth."

Vaughn tosses a chunk of bread at his brother's head. "How else do you explain our divine strength, if not as a gift from the skies?"

"By the same logic"—Soren dodges swiftly—"how do you explain such scarcity of brains paired with that overabundance of brawn?"

My eyes dart between them as they trade barbs, grinning at each other the entire time.

"You may enjoy talking in circles to dizzy your enemies, big brother, but as it turns out, you don't need all that much brainpower to pummel people into submission one-fisted."

"Ah yes," Soren drawls. "Titan diplomacy tactics. Never without bloodshed."

"Or gin. Speaking of . . ." Vaughn's smiling face turns my way. I freeze with my apple halfway to my mouth. "Have you ever had Titan gin before, Rhya?"

I shake my head warily.

"Excellent." He reaches down into the rucksack by his feet and produces a large bottle. The liquid inside is clear but swims with flecks of what looks like gold when he holds it to the light. "Tonight, it will be my honor to corrupt you."

Soren's groan is audible even over the pop of the cork being unstoppered.

TWENTY-ONE

My final week in Hylios passes with twice the speed of the two that came before. There is never a spare moment. Vaughn's larger-than-life presence infuses the once quiet royal grounds with so much energy, it is difficult to believe I once spent evenings on the ocean-facing terrace with a book and a glass of wine, only Soren's occasional presence to interrupt my serenity.

As the wedding creeps closer, each evening inevitably dissolves into an impromptu celebration—one every soul in the city seems more than eager to partake in, though none so enthusiastically as Vaughn.

Yara is a close second.

From that first day onward, when he declared his intentions to corrupt me, the half-Titan has kept his promise, thoroughly enjoying his role as rowdy ringleader. He is always spearheading something, whether it is an evening at Ledge for a sampling of every concoction on the menu or a late afternoon at Vintners' Cove in which he bribes the barge operators to bring up several treasured casks for private consumption.

His own villa, a quainter version of Soren's on the lower half of the royal grounds, is too small, he argues. Too isolated. He prefers the palatial elegance of his brother's home. And so, more often than not, that's where he can be found—splashing in the spring, bathing in the crystal bathhouse, and eating everything in the cupboards.

On the rare occasion you cannot find him in the crowd, towering heads above all others, his near constant laughter makes it easy to pinpoint him. It booms like a cannon across the city no matter the hour or occasion.

When he is not using his elephantine frame to stir up trouble, he is exercising it—chopping wood in the olive grove or lifting boulders repetitively overhead or throwing axes at the targets I use for projectile practice. Usually, he prefers the built-in weapons of his powerful fists, but a few times I see him swinging a broadsword so sharp it could cut me clean in half, using a series of wild moves the men of the Ember Guild would undoubtedly be interested in adopting for their own training regimens.

I can envision Jac, in particular, enjoying Vaughn's company— both at the sparring pits and at the local breweries. Height differences aside, there is something mirrored in the two men's dispositions that makes me miss my old friend.

Friends.

All of them.

Mabon, Cadogan, Jac, Farley.

I harbor a tiny sliver of hope that a favored few will be relieved from duty at Dyved's front lines long enough to accompany Pendefyre to the wedding—assuming he is still coming to the wedding. A month ago, I wouldn't have dared even that sliver, given the state of things in their kingdom. But with the Frostlanders' attention turned toward Llŷr—and half their fleet decaying at the bottom of the Bay of Blood, thanks to my efforts with the water cannon—perhaps the western side of the Northlands can take a much-needed breath.

I suppose I will find out in short order.

The wedding will be upon us before we know it. I cannot decide whether I am more excited or nervous to reach what once seemed a very far-off deadline. Whenever I think about it too much, my gut swarms with so many nervous butterflies it becomes difficult to breathe.

Thankfully, Vaughn is highly qualified at keeping me distracted. He stocks his daylight hours with healthy activities, if only so he can counteract them with drink and questionable decisions come nightfall, be it at the Kettle until he is chased out by incoming tides or in the low lighting of the pleasure clubs, where the pounding music and sumptuous decor provide a backdrop for the darkest desires Hylios has to offer.

My one and only visit to the clubs—the night I'd been dragged by Yara, Bretiax, Harpina, and Thisobei after an afternoon at the stables—I saw things that made the influence of Melité's siren song appear positively tame by comparison. I fled home almost as soon as we arrived, with burning cheeks, a fluttering pulse, and a heat in my veins that did not subside until I was alone in my bed, seeking release with my fingers between my legs.

I was ever so grateful that Soren and Vaughn chose to skip that particular venture, spending time with Alaric and Arwen at their villa instead. My mortification was deep enough without additional witnesses.

Though his house has never been so full of life, I see less of Soren than I have since my arrival in his city. Even our daily lessons fall somewhat by the wayside, for he is constantly in demand. Between his half-siblings, visiting dignitaries from every corner of the kingdom, Daggerpoint soldiers, and the Paexyrian squad, he has precious little time to offer me even in the rare

moments we find ourselves alone to discuss my maegical progress.

I keep up on my own, of course, but it is not the same. There is
no more escape to the Vale for rides on Zephyr; no more afternoons
on the skiff or mornings at the cove. This makes me puzzlingly restless, no matter how I fill my schedule with activity.

Yara brings me along for several patrols on Umyr, taking it
upon herself to teach me about high-altitude flight. She finds a
spare uniform for me, crafted of supple pale gray leather with a
fitted corset that cinches in my waist, padding at the thighs, and
boots that lace up beyond my knees. She even provides me with
a pair of goggles that are slightly too large, but better than nothing, given her fondness for speed.

Bretiax often flanks us on Isyr, her piebald Paexyri, communicating with signs as we soar over the craggy Llŷrian coastline. I've grown comfortable enough to release Umyr's mane for
short spans to sign back at her, using the simple symbols they're
teaching me day by day.

Ascend.

Descend.

Bank left.

Bank right.

Look back.

Return home.

Sometimes, our flights are the only times I can hear myself
think. For the villa is a constant parade of people eating and
chattering and laughing on every available surface, from the
kitchens to the terrace to the lush garden pathways to the now
fully occupied suites that line the back hallway between mine
and Soren's. They are everywhere, touching priceless artifacts in
the gallery like they're meaningless trinkets, flipping casually

through books with pages so old they've gone translucent. On more than one occasion, I catch myself biting back words of chastisement.

This is not my home.

These are not my guests.

It is not my place to interfere.

At first, I assume Soren is enjoying the festivities as much as his brother is. As the days slip by, however, the constant company begins to chafe at his deep reserve of self-control. He never says a word about it, but I watch a vein appear at his temple, pulsing with increasing frustration each time he returns to his once tranquil refuge and finds it stuffed floor to ceiling with strangers Vaughn has dragged in with him.

I, too, grow to miss the peace and quiet once the shine of new connections dulls to a pervasive intrusion. When at last the day before the wedding rolls around, I grit my teeth when I return from my morning flight to find a kitchen littered with empty bottles and food tins, the terrace crowded with unfamiliar Hylians eating lunch.

Boots crunching on crumbs no amount of sweeping can keep up with, I retreat to the library. But even in that tranquil sanctum I can hardly hear myself think over the ruckus that echoes down the halls. I collapse onto a chaise by the fireplace, then send out several tendrils of wind toward the desk in the corner. In seconds, I've whisked a stack of blank parchment across the room. I use a bit more care when transporting the inkpot—Soren will be peeved if I desecrate his beloved handwoven rugs with black spatters.

I settle back against the cushioned seat with the stack of parchment braced against my knees and contemplate what I want to say. My grip on the quill is so tight, I'm surprised it does not bend in half as I begin to scratch out my message. A futile endeavor, I know. But that knowledge does not stop the flood of forlorn words.

Dear Carys,

I know you will likely not reply to this letter, as you have not replied to any of the previous three I have sent. Hell, I am not even certain you are reading them. For all I know, you are tossing them straight into the fire, watching my words burn to ash. But I will keep writing, my dear friend, for the thought of you holding my scribbled missives in your hands—even if it is only to crumple them into balls and cast them into the flames—somehow brings me solace.

I miss you.

There it is, plain and simple. I miss your teasing jokes and your summery laugh and your words of wisdom. Even if you do not miss me, I have decided you cannot stop me missing you. You cannot stop me worrying about you, either.

In his letters, Lestyn assures me that you are well enough whenever he looks in on you. He says you and baby Nevin are both enjoying the spring weather that has finally descended on the crater—a long overdue thaw for Caeldera.

Apparently, the abundant sunshine has allowed the herb garden in your courtyard to flourish? Lestyn was thrilled when he wrote of it, though he did complain he can hardly keep up

with the weeding. I know you've been helping
him tend it . . . and, if I know you the way I
presume to, tending him as well.

Thank you for that.

It is surely brazen of me to ask you for
anything, but I hope you will continue to keep
an eye on him, for he has no one else to do it
and, though he acts the sage adult, he is after all
only thirteen. Without intervention, I fear
Osain, that old crone, will beat the intuitive
spirit out of the boy altogether.

He could use a friend.

(And, I think, so could you.)

Now you've surely tossed this into the fire,
furious at my meddling. Ah, well. I will keep
writing anyway, for I have never been diligent
enough to keep a consistent diary, and spilling
out my thoughts to you makes them feel slightly
less confounding.

Skies, Carys, there is so much I ache
to talk with you about. I wish I could tell
you everything that's happened, these past
weeks since I left Caeldera. Everything that's
changed. If I'm being honest, my head has
never been so confused. Nor has my heart.
Still, a part of me is unshakably convinced it
could all be sorted out in one single afternoon
sipping tea in your shop. You were always far
better at understanding me than I ever have
been myself.

I know you may never forgive me. Trust
that I suffer no foolish hopes in that regard.

But my friendship will not wane, even if we never speak again except in discarded letters and distant memories.

Kiss Nevin for me. And hug Lestyn, if you can manage to make him stand still for longer than a breath.

All my love,
Rhya

Finished, I scatter a pinch of sand across the letter's surface to set the ink. Whether or not I receive an answer back from Carys, I feel marginally more myself having emptied the contents of my heart onto the parchment.

Next: Lestyn.

I am overdue to respond to the boy's most recent letter, which chronicled his deep boredom without any sick Caelderans to tend, for the infirmary is reportedly empty, as are his afternoons.

The sound of shattering glass from the direction of the terrace makes my quill jump, ruining the parchment before I've written more than a handful of lines. Sighing, I ball up the ink-blotted letter and toss it blindly toward the bin.

Soren's hand darts out and catches it as it sails through the air.

"Oh!" I loose a startled gasp, nearly knocking over my pot of quill ink. "You scared me. I didn't hear you come in."

"How could you over all the racket?" His jaw is tight with tension, a muscle leaping in his cheek. The paper in his fist compresses with a crunch. "I'm going to bloody kill him."

I suppress a laugh. "No, you aren't."

"Why not?"

I rise to my feet and cross to stand in front of him. "Firstly, because he's your brother and you would miss him. Secondly, because I fear he would pop your head like a grape in one great fist if you were to interfere with his fun."

Some of the tension bleeds out of his stare, replaced by the humor that has been gone for several days. I've missed seeing it there. His ability to laugh—at himself along with others—is one of his chief attributes.

"So little faith in me, skylark," he murmurs, shaking his head. "Haven't I taught you anything? Brute force only goes so far. He would have to catch me first."

"Well, our lessons have been rather lacking of late."

He arches one dark brow. "Is that disappointment I detect in your tone?"

"Definitely not. I'm merely saying . . . I just meant . . ." I press my lips together, suddenly wishing the earth would swallow me up. "Never mind."

"Oh, no. Too late to walk it back now. You've missed me. Admit it."

"I will not admit any such thing!"

"Coward."

"If I missed anything, it would be our training," I say stiffly. "Not *you*."

He's grinning at me now, all traces of the throbbing tension at his temple vanished. His voice drops down to a whisper as he leans in. "I've missed you, too."

My heart spasms in a ridiculous manner. Before I can set him straight with a scathing retort, he tosses away the parchment and takes my hand. He's led me most of the way across the library before I locate my powers of speech.

"Where are you taking me?"

"Away from this nonstop noise and wedding nonsense. Somewhere we can hear ourselves think for a change." He does not break stride as he shoots a smile at me over his shoulder. "I've been most neglectful of your lessons these past few days. I can't have my star pupil slipping, can I?"

"But you can't just leave. There are a dozen people on your terrace for a dinner feast! And tomorrow—"

"Will be more of the same." He groans. "Pomp and circumstance, small talk and frivolity. Arwen will forgive me if I miss yet another prenuptial celebration." He shakes his head, voice dropping lower. "Right now I don't want to be with anyone. Can you understand that?"

"I can. But bringing me along somewhat undermines your desire to be alone."

He's quiet for a long beat. "I do not want to be alone. I want to be alone with you."

I stumble over my own feet.

Soren catches me before I fall on my face, his grip strong and sure in all the ways I still feel hesitant, leading me down the hallway to destinations unknown. And though I know I should be sensible, that it is unwise to anger Arwen when she is only just beginning to tolerate my presence without a sneer . . . I cannot deny how my heart sails at the prospect of escaping the circus for a few hours of solitude.

Or . . . solitude with Soren.

Somehow, though, his company never grates at me the way others' does.

"OPEN IT."

I stare at the wooden box, wary. "Why do I feel something nefarious is about to jump out at me?"

"Because you have issues with trust."

"Or, perhaps, because *someone* revels in every opportunity to catch me off guard, be it with water globes or impromptu flight lessons."

His scoff is dark. "You will not be complaining about my methods when you've fully mastered your maegic. Already you have come so far in such a short time."

I cannot contradict that statement. He's right. Despite the past few days without our lessons, I feel in command of my power in a way I never have before. The confidence I have gained over my skills cannot be negated.

Was it really only three weeks ago that I arrived in this city, too afraid to call the wind? Quivering at the thought of tapping into my maegical reserves?

Sucking in a breath, I cross to the box he set on the sand when we arrived. We aren't far from Hylios—if I squint, I can make out the towering walls of the capital to the northeast—but we might as well be a whole world away. The secluded cove he's brought me to is a short walk from a cleverly concealed portal tucked in the thick trunk of an oversized palm tree.

I tried in vain to peek at the mysterious box when he retrieved it off one of his many artifact shelves back at the villa, managing no more than the briefest glimpse before he tucked it under his arm. Now, up close, I can finally make out the details. It is made of lightweight wood with silver hinges. The top is scored with a symbol I recognize instantly, for it is nearly identical to the one etched into the skin of my chest.

The Air Remnant.

My pulse picks up speed as I lift the lid to reveal a length of what I think is rope, nestled on a bed of blue velvet. Instead of jute or hemp fibers, it is crafted of coils of pure gold. It gleams even in the low afternoon light, catching the fading rays of sunshine. When I lift it out, I expect it to be stiff, the metal resistant to movement, and yet it is pliable as a silken cord in my hands. One end frays into a tassel of many braids, some so thin they are very nearly gossamer; the other tapers into a slim handle with a knotted bottom that fits perfectly in my palm.

Like it was made especially for me.

"The hallowed Whip of Light," Soren says. "A gift from the Goddess of Skies. Created from one strand of her golden hair, and capable of wielding lightning—or so say the legends."

I want to look at him, but I cannot pull my eyes away from the gilded weapon. My voice is hushed, reverent. "Wherever did you get this?"

"I told you, I found several relics in the ruins of the Court of Clouds. This was one of them."

"It's beautiful."

"It's yours."

My eyes snap up. "What?"

"It belonged to Queen Arianrhod herself, two centuries ago. Now it belongs to you."

To me.

My hand tightens possessively, as though he might reach out and take it away from me. Which is ridiculous, as he's only just gifted it. But the whip has a thrall of its own—one I am finding it hard to resist.

"I cannot possibly accept something so valuable," I say, forcing out the words.

"You can. You will." Soren moves close and places his hand over mine, tightening until the heavy, solid gold handle scores against my palm. "It belongs with a wind weaver far more than on a shelf gathering dust."

"But—"

"Rhya."

My mouth clicks shut at his tone.

"I have been waiting for an opportunity to give you this gift since I first saw you unleash that electrical storm on Fyremas. Months of anticipation for this single moment." His eyes narrow a shade. "Do not spoil it out of some misguided feeling of obligation."

I suck in a sharp slice of air. "Okay."

"Okay?"

"Yes. I'll keep it." My lips twitch. "Mostly because I think if you try to pry it away from me, my fingers may react of their own accord. With violence."

His eyes edge with silver as he laughs. "Now that that's settled . . ." His hand, still holding mine, spins me neatly around so my back is pinned to his front. "How do you feel about giving it a try?"

"Here?" The word comes out in a panicked squeak. "Now?"

"Look around. There's no one to harm but a few electric eels. And somehow, I don't think they'll mind the extra charge."

I allow my eyes to swing around the cove from the shallows where the waves gently kiss at the shore to the deeper waters where, every so often, a flash of white zaps from the turquoise depths.

No wonder the shorebirds and seals give this place such a wide berth.

"What do I do?"

He pauses to think, for once not ready with an answer. "It's a conduit of sorts. From what I've read about Queen Arianrhod, she used it for precision strikes in battle. With each crack of the whip you should be able to send a paralyzing bolt of lightning at an enemy. In theory, at least. You'll have to trust your gut to guide you in putting said theory into practice."

That sounds less than ideal.

Soren senses my hesitation, reading me easily despite my

firm mental shields. "What did it feel like the last time you used your lightning?"

"The only time, you mean."

He sighs, his breath stirring the hair at my nape, sending a shiver down my spine. "What did it feel like?"

"Like my skin was about to explode. Like every nerve ending in my body was immolating. Like I was about to die and I did not truly care, because if I was dead I wouldn't be in pain anymore."

He is silent, mulling that over. Eventually, he lifts his hand out in front of us and, with a surge of maegic, calls forth a globe of water from the cove. As it comes closer, I see he's captured one of the electric eels within it.

My eyes widen as it halts five paces from us, hovering in mid-air. "What are you doing?"

"Research." I can hear the smile in his voice. "Look at it. Really look. What do you see?"

I study the vibrant yellow eel, its serpentine body undulating as it makes slow loops around its floating cage. It is horribly ugly, with a gaping mouth full of razor-sharp teeth, slitted nostrils, and dark beady eyes inset in its head.

"I see . . . a very unfortunate-looking neck scarf."

He huffs out a chuckle. "Okay, then what do you feel?"

My lips are parted to deliver another snarky retort when, suddenly, the eel releases a high-voltage electrical charge. The whole globule of water lights up like the sun, pulsing with power. Free arm knifing around my midsection, Soren hauls me backward a few steps as the air turns static all around us.

"Skies!" I don't know whether to laugh or screech as he sets me back on my feet. "I certainly felt *that*."

"And?"

"And what?"

"Did it feel like your lightning? Or different?"

"Different but somehow similar. Like a lower chord of the same song . . . Softer, smoother."

"Because it's using the water as a conductor. When you last used your lightning, it came out of you as it does a storm cloud, in violent arcs that spread across the sky. Pure, untempered power." He steers the eel away, depositing it back into the shallows where it disappears with a flip of its tail and another white-hot pulse. "With a comparable conductor, you might be able to suppress the surge and send it straight down the whip in a concentrated charge. Just as we did on the *Selkie*, the first time you used your air currents."

"Finesse," I say wryly.

"Precisely."

His maegic whispers through me, his mind settling over mine in a blanket the moment I drop my guards to admit him.

"I will be your conductor, skylark. Put me to use."

I fight another shiver. *"You make it sound simple."*

"It is simple. Your power is a natural extension of your will. Yours to manifest, yours to shape however you see fit."

"And if I hurt you in the process?"

Even mentally, his smirk is audible. *"I can take it."*

Gods, he could be cocky.

I grip the handle tightly as I close my eyes and search deep inside my maegical reserves. The swirling hurricane within is somewhat subdued by Soren's presence in my head, its maelstroms soothed into a quiet I only ever experience when we channel. I let it wash through me, a balm to my soul, as I call forth the storm to the forefront of my mind.

And I see it.

Feel it.

There, deep in the darkness.

A flicker.

A flash.

My power.

My lightning.

"Step back."

He does not question my order, complying instantly. I am momentarily afraid the distance will sever our mental connection, but our bond has strengthened significantly from those early days. We are just as tethered at ten paces as we are when pressed tight together.

I open my eyes as all the fine, feathery hair on my body lifts to stand on end. The charge gathers beneath my skin, volts skating down my limbs, pulses pricking at my nerves. I swing my arm at my side, shaking off some of the tension that tightens my muscles. Preparing myself as much as I can for what is to come. My body tingles from the roots of my hair to the tips of my toes as the buzz grows to a voltage I struggle to contain.

Now or never.

Before I can talk myself out of it, I swing my arm up high over my head, then snap it back down. The whip lashes out with a violent crack and, as it does, I watch a bolt of lightning ripple down my arm, then race outward along its taut gold length. The result is a singular arc of brilliant light that shoots like an arrow straight over the cove into open sky. It dissipates in a blink, the light almost faster than the eye's ability to track it. The initial crack of the whip has faded long before the boom of thunder resounds back to us, vibrating from the clouds down onto the sea, strong enough to make the sands tremble beneath my boots.

Gods, that feels good.

The sensation is incredible. Never before have I experienced such a surge of power—not the morning I fought the arachnida nor the afternoon of the Frostlander battle when the dizzying rush of the water cannon swept away my morality. Not even the night of Fyremas, when my lightning turned the tide of battle against the ice giants.

My own self-satisfaction is underscored tenfold by an immense flood of feeling down the bond.

Soren.

He is proud of me.

More than merely proud, he is . . .

Awed.

By me.

I turn to him as the lightning cools from my skin, feeling like I might explode into a million pieces. My hair floats all around my face, platinum wisps awhirl. I am pure electricity, a hum of static in the shape of a woman. I do not know how to tamp it down, nor how to release it. My emotions fray, all inhibitions zapped to aether.

I expect him to be ten paces away, but he's right there, a whisper from me, so close our chests graze. Our eyes lock instantly. His are pure sapphire. I'm sure mine are a wild storm. I have no idea what my expression looks like in this moment, but his . . . His radiates so much intensity, I can hardly take it in. Seeing it amplifies the currents of electricity running rampant through my bloodstream, pitches up the sibilation inside me to new heights.

Skies, I could drown in that look and die happy.

The deluge coming out of him makes it difficult to breathe as we stare at each other. One, two, three endless seconds. The whip hits the sand at my feet. I do not bend to pick it up. I cannot look away from him, not for anything. Not even for a priceless relic. And he knows it. For my own emotions are laid utterly bare, exposed by the bond as we continue to channel.

There is no hiding from him. Not now. He can feel everything inside my heart, each desperate pound, each aching beat that seems to sing his name over and over, a constant refrain I can no longer deny. One that, if I am honest, has been playing there for a while now, at first the faintest stirring, now a tune I would know in darkness, in distance, in death.

Soren, Soren, Soren.

The tingles of electricity that still race up and down my limbs are gathering at the tips of my fingers, urging me to reach out. To reach for him. To close that infinitesimal gap that separates us before another moment passes. To remove that impossible distance dividing his body from mine and finally—

We both feel it at once.

A ripple through the bond, strong enough to shatter the moment.

Heat.

Fire.

Burning leaves on an autumn wind.

I reel back as though I've been struck.

"Fuck," Soren growls, pure frustration.

Fuck, indeed.

Our maegics disconnect as I slam my mental guards back up. I take several hasty paces away, unable to look at him. Unable to look inside myself, for fear of what I will see there. Instead, I stare down at the sand, attempting to slow my racing heart. Attempting to come to terms with the new duality inside me, where two warring tethers are wrapped around my rib cage, slowly pulling me apart.

One, a soothing tendril of deepest ocean.

The other, a burning furl of smoke and flame.

I have not felt the second for three long weeks, but there is no denying what its abrupt strengthening means, even before my eyes shift out to the bay where a ship with russet-brown sails embroidered with a familiar sigil—the flaming mountain—cuts smoothly toward the sea gate. My bond to the Remnant of Fire simmers with an awareness I have not experienced since I left Blister Bight.

I press a hand to my heart, wishing I might suppress its ache.

Pendefyre is in Hylios.

CHAPTER
TWENTY-TWO

We hasten back to the city by portal. Even so, we are not quick enough. By the time Soren and I reach the harbor's edge, somewhat breathless from our silent sprint along the ramparts, the Dyvedi faction has already disembarked and an altercation is brewing.

A line of Paexyrian face off with a line of Ember Guild. Yara, Thisobei, Bretiax, and Harpina glare relentlessly, looking fierce as ever in their flight leathers and strapped to the teeth with weaponry, from their throwing stars to their sleek silver bows to their curved scimitars.

Cadogan, Mabon, Jac, and Farley stare back. They are also heavily armed, Jac with his double-bit battle-axe, Farley with his bow, Mabon with his crossbow, Cadogan with his broadsword. They do not seem daunted by the feminine fury directed their way. Mabon and Cadogan stand shoulder to shoulder, opposites in appearance yet fully aligned in their sedate expressions. Farley is grinning wide, auburn hair wind-tousled, looking for all the world like he is enjoying the drama. And judging by the love-struck look in Jac's eyes as they roam up and down Bretiax's lithe, leather-clad body, he does not find animosity even a remote deterrent to affection.

Soren falls back as I approach, apparently preferring to watch the face-off from afar.

Farley spots me first. "Ace! Hell, is that you?"

In a breath, I am surrounded by the familiar faces of my friends. Warmth floods me as my eyes shift from one to another. I've hardly allowed myself the space to miss them since we parted. But there is no way to disguise the surge of joy I feel as Farley's arms tug me into a tight embrace, as Jac chucks me lightly beneath the chin with his fist, as Mabon clasps my hand with his large one, as Cadogan gives my shoulder a fond shake.

"You're here," I say, ignoring the thickness of my voice and the way my eyes prickle. "You're all here."

"You thought we'd leave you with only this rabble for company?" Jac teases, jerking his thumb over his shoulder at the Paexyrian.

Yara huffs in annoyance.

"I for one never miss a wedding," Farley puts in, green eyes dancing as his voice drops. "All the better if it's in a new city. So many potential conquests to acquire . . ."

"We've barely made landfall and already he's thinking about his cock," Cadogan mutters.

Mabon snorts. "That surprises you?"

"Any more days at sea, he might've crawled into your hammock looking for love." Jac elbows the stocky bald soldier.

Mabon shakes his head tiredly in response.

"He should be so lucky," Farley retorts. "Given the snores that echoed from your side of the crew quarters, my hammock would've been a reprieve."

I hear a few of the Paexyrian smother laughs.

Jac replies by way of a suggestive finger raise.

"Gods help us." Cadogan sighs, then looks at me. "Are you well, Rhya?"

"Look at her." Farley gestures vaguely at me. "Of course she's well. She's damn near glowing."

Was I?

"Don't you flirt with me, Farley. I'm not one of your . . ."

The words dry up on my tongue. For at that moment, my awareness is tugged toward the end of the dinghy dock where a tall figure is standing with his back to the city, his eyes on the sea gate as it slowly ratchets closed under the power of the churning waterwheels.

Even in silhouette, I know him instantly. The rigid lines of his frame. So much strength kept under such unflinching control. My feet carry me to him without thought, a moth to flame. I hardly notice the Ember Guild falling silent in my wake, hardly feel the weight of the Paexyrian stares riveted to me as I move down the dock.

My footfalls strike like anvils, a match for the one that is compressing my chest as the distance shrinks. Half of me aches to fly to his side; the other half screams that I am walking in the wrong direction entirely. I'm not breathing, not blinking, not even thinking as I come to a stop five careful paces from him. My mind blanks.

He knows I am there. I watch the breadth of his shoulders expand on a massive inhale, steeling himself before he turns to face me.

Gods, I wish I'd braced myself.

For the moment our gazes meet, the fire I've spent the past few weeks allowing to smolder into ashes reignites, sparking up from my stomach into my throat. His dark eyes are aflame with a heat he cannot quite bank, even as he strains to mute his maegic from searing down the bond that connects us.

"Pendefyre," I whisper, voice as fractured as my feelings.

His jaw tightens.

He says nothing.

But those eyes, those flaming eyes . . . They are speaking plainly as they chart a course down my body, taking me in as though I am a stranger. I cannot blame him for that. Last he saw me, I was a weary skeleton in a wet novitiate's uniform. Now tight dove-gray leather is sculpted over every curve of my body. Two daggers fill the built-in sheaths—the glyphed one he gave me months ago, and a new one gifted to me by Vaughn on his second day in the city after he accidentally knocked me into the canal with a bit of overenthusiastic gesticulation that clipped me midchest. My new golden whip hangs in a neat coil at my belt.

It is more than altered attire, though. My long hair flows loose down my back, freed from its orderly braid. My formerly pale skin is tinged with a hint of tan from all my time spent in the sunshine, and a good deal of it is exposed by the sleeveless corset. The dark whorls of my Remnant peek out the top of the tight-laced bodice. And the body within it is no longer lacking food or sleep. Three weeks of resting on a down-feather mattress and silken sheets, plus steady access to Soren's cooking, has nourished me in a way I have not experienced since childhood. Perhaps not even then, for though Eli and I never went hungry, we were never entirely able to make ends meet, either. Especially as the crops began to fail and the game grew scarce.

For the first time in my life, I am healthy.

Penn, on the other hand, has never looked worse. He is still handsome as ever, but there is a drawn pinch to his features, along with a scoring of deep shadows beneath his eyes. He has not been sleeping, nor eating, from the looks of it. Not much, and certainly not well.

Questions rush through my head as my gaze roams over him—ones I have not allowed myself to ask in our weeks apart, knowing the want of answers would torture me.

Is he still bunking at the barracks? Does he still visit the ward chamber each night? Who is there to pull him back from the brink, if not me? Has he no regard for his own life? How fares the rest of the city? What has changed since we last spoke? And what will change now that we are finally face-to-face once more?

My lips press together, straining to keep the torrent of questions from bursting forth. I wish I could read his emotions through the bond, but he is keeping them well in check, even if it takes visible effort. His hands fist tightly at his sides; his jaw locks like a vise.

"I . . . You . . . I did not think . . ." I suck in a breath, then start again. "I was not certain you would come."

He flinches, a tiny quake rocking his broad frame. "I do not run from my obligations. I said I would come. I have come."

The cold detachment of his tone is a lash straight to the heart. He is angry, but there is something else just below the surface of that furious front he is putting on.

Pain.

Torment.

Desolation.

Gods, guide me through this without falling to pieces.

My throat is thick. I swallow against the lump lodged inside it. "Of course. I just . . . I never heard back from you."

"I did not realize you wished for a response." He speaks through clenched teeth. "Your singular letter three weeks ago, informing me of your location, certainly did not leave me with that impression."

My eyes press closed for a beat, guilt berating my heart. "I'm sorry, Penn. I did not mean to—"

"I do not need your apologies. It is done. In the past. We do not need to discuss it further." He sucks in a calming breath, reining in his temper before it sparks out of control. "I did not come here to retrace old ground or rehash old arguments. I have more important things to speak with you about, if you will listen."

"I have never once shied away from the things you had to say to me," I remind him.

He is the one who's always withheld.

"I know that." Flames leap in his eyes as they hold mine. A muscle begins to tick in his cheek, as though he is waging war inwardly. "Rhya, I must tell you . . . You must realize that I . . ."

The pound of boots stalls his tongue. The force with which they are coming down the dock is impossible to miss. I turn to watch Soren—who, since the start of our acquaintance, has only ever moved in absolute stealth—stomp toward us in a manner designed specifically to interrupt. There is an easy smile on his face, but it cannot compensate for the ice floes in his eyes, cold enough to chill any perceived warmth of welcome.

"Pendefyre."

"Soren," Penn returns. "Your timing is inopportune as ever."

"One could say the same about yours." Soren's smile turns sharp. "Your ship appeared on my horizon at a most unfortunate time. I was in the middle of something important."

A flutter of nerves explodes in my stomach.

"Feel free to get back to it," Penn says. "Rhya and I can manage without your company."

Soren's scoff holds the faintest edge of bitterness. "Oh, I'm afraid that won't be possible. Not while you are here, at least. The matter is . . . delicate. It will require all my attention."

Skies.

My cheeks flush red. I pray Penn will not look at me and question why.

Thankfully, he is busy staring hard at Soren, his mouth a severe line. "Did you or did you not insist upon my presence at this wedding? Now that I have complied, you insult me for deigning to do so?"

"How right you are. Apologies. It seems my manners have fallen by the wayside today." Soren takes a breath and strives for civility. "I welcome you and your men to Hylios. I've arranged staff to see to your lodgings and provide whatever you require during your visit." He glances over his shoulder to where the Ember Guild and Paexyrian are still facing off. It does not appear much of the ice has thawed despite Jac's most charming grins. "Assuming they survive until nightfall."

Penn grunts. "Your hospitality is appreciated but unnecessary. We will sleep on the ship with the crew who traveled with us."

"Nonsense. You are here in an official capacity as both King of Dyved and Remnant of Fire. It is only fitting that you stay on the royal grounds with the other honored guests." Soren's glacial gaze cuts to mine, freezing me down to the bone. "One big happy family. Are we not?"

"YOU LOOK LIKE you need this more than I do."

At Arwen's murmur, I glance up in time to see her top off my glass with a long pour of gold-flecked Titan gin, not stopping until it threatens to flow over the rim.

"Thanks," I whisper.

She nods, taking a slug straight from the bottle's mouth. Alaric watches her, grinning indulgently, then takes a long sip of his own.

I'm glad someone is enjoying himself.

The rest of our gathering shows no signs of smiling anytime soon. Soren and Penn glare at each other from opposite heads of the table. Mabon and Jac flank the Dyvedi king while Vaughn and Arwen flank the Llŷrian one, leaving Alaric and me with the rather unfortunate position smack at the center, a sliver of neutral territory between opposing factions.

I raise my glass to my lips and take a long swallow, relishing the fire that burns down my throat. Its heady rush is not enough to quell the discomfort that pumps through my bloodstream as I look around the terrace of the guest villa where the Ember Guild is staying, then out at the city beyond.

Located at the base of the royal grounds, almost at sea level, it boasts a view of the central canal, where hundreds of Llŷrians can be seen on bridges and barges and all manner of boats, the darkness no deterrent to their frivolity. Chatter carries back to us across the waterways along with the scent of tybae leaf and the distant pound of drums from the pleasure clubs. If I had to wager, I'd bet Farley followed that beat straight into the heart of depravity. Hopefully Cadogan will keep him from getting into any real trouble.

My eyes move back to the table, which is as far a cry from the city's collective merriment as one can imagine. The platters of food at the center sit untouched. My spine remains ramrod straight despite the cushioned seat beneath me. The atmosphere is rife with tension—and only grows more so as the unofficial war council gets underway.

I'd anticipated that Penn would not squander the opportunity to discuss his plans for war while in Hylios. I had not realized he would suggest a meeting so soon after arriving, or that Soren would agree to it. Certainly not on the eve of his sister's wedding. Yet no sooner had he shown the Dyvedi men to their sleeping quarters than the demand was made and quickly met.

Arwen was promptly summoned, for no discussion of battle tactics could happen without the commander of the Llŷrian armies in attendance. And with Arwen came Alaric—there in his role as her future husband, but also as the ruler of Daggerpoint and admiral of the fastest fleet in all the Northlands.

To my surprise, Vaughn appeared not long after, his ruddy face atypically clear of humor as he introduced himself as the official emissary of Prydain Isle, liaison to the Titans. He was an intimidating sight, with his immense size and inconceivable height, even to battle-hardened warriors like Mabon and Jac. When he took his seat beside me at the table, though, he reached over and ruffled my hair with a hand larger than my head.

"Do you want to start?" Soren shatters the thick silence, watching Penn through slitted eyes. "It is you who called this conclave, after all."

Penn's hand tightens around his glass. "If you are under the impression that Efnysien's actions do not warrant a conversation—"

"I did not say that." Soren cuts him off.

"Yet you are reluctant to discuss the terms of his elimination."

"I did not say that, either." Soren grabs the bottle and pours himself a helping. "Out of everyone at this table, I am the one with the fullest understanding of the threat we are facing in the Southlands."

"I don't know about that," Arwen mutters. There is a dark look on her face—not the disdain she so often sends my way, but something more nefarious. Disgust, I think . . . but also fear.

I quail at the notion of whatever scares Arwen.

Soren's eyes flash briefly to his sister. His jaw tightens before he throws back his gin in a single gulp.

"Perhaps you could enlighten those of us who are unfamiliar with the history here," I wade in quietly. "I, for one, am not sure I understand the full extent of Efnysien's crimes beyond the bloody massacre he orchestrated on Fyremas."

Arwen and Soren trade a loaded look, holding a conversation with their eyes alone. Whatever messages they convey, whatever memories they share, are entrenched in darkness.

"We do not need to speak of it," she says tightly, downing more gin. "It's no one's business. Certainly not those who were not even born when it transpired."

"Arwen," Soren snaps. "Enough."

"If that was directed at me, you have my deepest apologies," I drawl with faux sincerity. "How inconvenient that I have not yet begun to fossilize like the rest of you."

She attempts to glare at me, but her lips twitch. If I didn't know better, I'd think the sea urchin is actually warming toward me—despite her best efforts.

"Can we get on with this already?" Jac puts in. "The night is waning."

"Agreed." Vaughn's large fist bangs the table like a gavel, making all our glasses jump.

Soren's voice is fluid as ever, but there is an uncompromising current running through it as he stares at Arwen. "Rhya has earned a seat at this table. She has as much right to know the history as any of us. If you do not want to relive it, sister, that is your liberty. Feel free to take your leave. But do not make the mistake of demanding she take hers."

"You would have her stay?" Arwen sounds outraged. "Over me?"

His head cants to the side—a deceptively passive look, designed to mask feelings that are anything but. "You assume your role in my affairs carries more weight than Rhya's. Why? Because you have been around for longer?" His eyes glitter. "Do not ask me to choose between you and her. You may not like the results."

I bite my lip to contain a bleat of surprise.

Penn stiffens in his seat. A sound comes from low in his throat—one that makes me too nervous to look at him. If the displeased emotions rolling down the bond are any indication, he is not happy about Soren's declaration of loyalty to me.

Nor is Arwen. She scowls mightily, but says no more.

"Right!" The glasses jump again with another fist-pound. "Now that that's settled . . ." Vaughn's bright green eyes find mine. "Our stepbrother is a monumental prick."

"I've gathered that," I say dryly.

His mouth tugs up in a half grin as he leans back in his chair. The wood groans under his weight. "He always had a dark side, even before he perverted himself with blood maegic. The difference is, now he's a kingdom away. Out of sight, out of mind. But those of us who grew up with him here on these very grounds . . ." All levity flees his face. "It was like being raised alongside a snake. A poisonous one."

Soren takes up the threads of the tale. "His mother, Duvessa, brought him from across the North Sea when she came to marry our father. She possessed great beauty and supposedly ensnared the king within the span of a single meeting. He did not even know she had a son until her ship arrived here in Hylios."

"Doubt that came up in conversation when she was seducing a proposal out of old Manawydan," Vaughn mutters. "Sorceress that she was, the old man never stood a chance."

"We were children. We did not yet know how to recognize evil, even as it walked among us." Soren runs a hand through his hair, mussing the strands. "We welcomed him in with open arms. One more sibling to swim and sail and spar with."

Arwen's scoff is sharp.

My apprehension mounts.

"From the first moment he stepped within these walls, Efnysien was unnaturally fixated on those of us with special abilities,"

Soren goes on. "Be it Vaughn's Titan strength, or Melité's and Tethys's siren song, or my and Arwen's water powers. He coveted that which he did not have, for he was born with not a drop of fae blood flowing through his veins."

"So far as we know," Vaughn notes.

"Mmm. His bloodline, his parentage . . . if our father learned of it, he never revealed it to us." Soren's sigh is one of frustration. "And though I have ordered scouts across the sea several times over the years, they found no records of either him or his mother."

"He watched us. That's what I remember most." Vaughn shudders. "Always creeping in shadows, peeking around corners. Those odd eyes peering from the darkness. Foul little lurker."

"We all intrigued him, to an extent." Soren's voice turns flat, dispassionate. "But it was Arwen who fascinated him beyond reason."

My eyes move to her automatically.

"Tell me there's more gin," she pleads, desperation in her voice.

Alaric slowly slides his arm along the back of her chair and tugs her closer. His voice is inaudible, but whatever he whispers in her ear makes some of the tension bleed out of her stiff shoulders.

Vaughn reaches under the table and produces a fresh bottle, twice the size of the last. "I always bring reinforcements."

"You are my favorite sibling." She manages a smile, but it lacks the saucy self-confidence I am accustomed to seeing.

"His fixation only grew as we got older," Soren continues. The glass in his hand is gripped so tightly, I think it is in danger of shattering. "As we matured into adults, he made it clear he felt things for his stepsister that were . . . Not the way a brother should feel for his sister."

"That's putting it politely," Vaughn says gruffly. "He attacked her. He came close to rap—"

"He *tried*," Arwen snarls. Her face is furious, but her eyes hold a weak sheen of silver. For the first time, I feel a trace of her maegic swell in the air—not nearly as strong as Soren's, but there all the same. "I stabbed him through the hand before he could do more than tear my nightgown."

My stomach turns to lead. All my previous assumptions about the bad blood between Efnysien and his siblings pales in comparison to this. Suddenly the gin in my glass does not feel strong enough to endure the rest of this evening.

"I banished him," Soren says bluntly. "He has not been welcome in Hylios—in any part of Llŷr—in the hundred years since."

"You should have killed him," Penn puts in, face twisting with wrath. "Then, we would not be here now, discussing how best to dispatch him."

"I wanted to rip his head from his shoulders, trust me." Soren bares his teeth in a bitter grin. "I was convinced to spare him by some of our other siblings—"

"Bloody *sirens*," Vaughn hisses.

"—whose pleas for mercy momentarily stayed my hand." Soren's jaw is tight as he goes on. "A mistake I have taken pains to rectify many times over the years, all without success. Most recently, following the events at Fyremas, after which I spent two months giving fruitless chase across blood-soaked stretches of mortal territory, only to be brought up short again and again by an impenetrable barrier of black sand." His eyes shift to Penn. "Which effectively brings us to the present. Your grand plans for revenge."

Penn's lip curls in distaste. "Do not patronize me, nymph."

"Tell me, fire salamander," he shoots back, the barb making

both his siblings smirk. "Do you think I have been merely sitting on my hands these past decades, too lazy to seek out someone who attempted to hurt my sister? Do you think he still breathes because I have been too busy to bother strangling the air from his lungs?"

Penn does not respond except to take a sip of his gin.

"No," Soren answers for him, leaning back in his seat. "I have tried many times to infiltrate that dark desert. It cannot be done."

"I do not accept that."

"Whether or not you accept reality does nothing to alter it."

"And what would you have me do?" Penn's words thrum with rage. "Allow another century to pass, hoping the matter resolves itself?"

"No. I would counsel temperance," Soren counters. "Do not rush into the Husk Desert on a fool's mission with visions of victory clouding your sense of reason. Instead, wait for Efnysien to poke his head out from the sand again. When he does, we will be ready to hack it off."

"That could take another decade." Penn's outrage is thick. "Just because you are too cowardly to try again—"

"Call me a coward all you like. You think your idiocy makes you brave? It doesn't. It makes you *dead*. Fodder for the black sands, where you will stumble into an abyss pit or be picked clean by the arachnidae or consumed by the wraiths long before you even glimpse the gothic spires of the Symmetria Keep."

The candles on the table burn brighter as Penn's fury erupts. His jaw is clenched tight, attempting to lock down his anger. It flows down the bond despite his efforts. I wonder if Soren can sense it, too; if he realizes just how close this discussion is to igniting.

"I will march south with or without your aid," Penn says,

nostrils flaring on a harsh exhale. "With it, we remain as we are now. Allies. Without it . . ."

"You would risk the treaty between Llŷr and Dyved over this half-baked quest for vengeance?" Soren's tone drips with derision. "If you do that, you weaken the united front of the Northlands. You open us all up to attacks from more than Frostlanders and Reavers and Cimmerian monsters. The mortal kings are ever grasping. Their invasion will be swift and brutal."

A ripple of unease moves around the table.

"How long do you think we will last against another uprising from the Midlands?" Soren asks, head shaking. "How do you think your citizens will fare, facing a second Cull?"

Penn's breaths are labored with the effort to remain in control. "There is no threat of that if you make the right choice. If you march with me to the south, a united front."

Soren's eyes edge with silver as they narrow on Penn. "And if you fail? What then? What of Caeldera when your corpse desiccates beneath the gray sun of the Southlands?"

"Then I suppose it will not matter our alliance is broken, for I will no longer be around to enforce it," Penn says coldly. His gaze flickers to me for a heartbeat, simmering with flames. "I wonder if that is not the outcome you are hoping for regardless. It seems you move with haste to fill whatever roles I vacate."

Absolute silence descends.

Soren shatters it after what seems a lifetime. "If you are fool enough to let treasure slip through your fingers, you cannot blame another for picking it up, brushing it off, and making it shine again."

The conversation has somehow skewed off course. The air has grown even more tense than when they were discussing their precarious treaty.

"Maybe we should retire for the night," Alaric puts in, a

much-needed voice of reason. "It's getting late and we seem to have reached a momentary impasse. We will all have another chance to speak again after tomorrow's wedding festivities."

"It wouldn't be a proper party without some discussion of bloodshed." Vaughn chuckles at the prospect.

"So long as there is no *actual* bloodshed," I murmur.

Mabon cracks a smile—his first since his arrival in Hylios.

Jac grunts his agreement. "I'm with the big man. Let's reconvene after the wedding."

"Why after? I can discuss attack strategies in a gown just as well as I can in my flight leathers" is Arwen's low input.

"After," Alaric says firmly, looking around the table. "I plan to enjoy my wedding night with my bride, if you don't mind."

Jac and Vaughn both grin.

I suppress a smile of my own as Arwen shoves her husband-to-be, noting there is no force at all behind the blow.

Finally, it is down to Soren and Penn. The two of them stare at each other from opposite sides of the table.

"After the wedding," Soren says finally. "We will revisit this with fresh eyes."

And cooler tempers, I hope.

Penn nods tightly. "Fine."

With that, the war council disperses. Alaric and Arwen go first, his arm looped low around her waist, his mouth at her ear. Vaughn is on their heels. Soren hesitates a beat, eyes flashing over to me for a lingering look I cannot quite decipher, before he follows them off the terrace into the dark.

Jac's gaze darts between Penn and me before he vaults to his feet. "We'll just . . . go track down Farley and Cadogan. They said something about visiting those pleasure clubs the Paexyrian ladies were talking about earlier. That one, Yara, seems like a handful. Two redheads in one place can't be left unattended for long."

Visions of Yara and Farley move through my mind.

Gods, what a pair.

Mabon does not move.

"Mabon," Jac mutters pointedly.

"What?" The stocky soldier's dark brows shoot up his forehead. "I'm here to stand guard over our king, not indulge myself. I have no interest in whatever goes on in those clubs."

Jac looks like he wants to reach out and throttle the man. "Yes," he hisses. "You do."

"I do not."

"You do. You said so yourself, just a few moments ago."

Mabon scoffs. "I said no such thing."

Jac's stare sharpens to daggers. "Man, for the love of the gods—"

"Mabon," Penn interjects lowly. "Give us a moment, would you?"

Mabon is instantly on his feet, realization dawning quickly. There is a sheepish look on his typically self-assured face. "Right. The pleasure clubs sound . . . intriguing. Let's go, Jac."

The two men vanish so fast, you'd think they were under enemy fire.

Leaving me alone with Penn.

CHAPTER
TWENTY-THREE

At first, Penn says nothing.

In silence, he reaches out and pours us each another serving of the triple-strength gin. It is beginning to go to my head. I have not eaten any dinner, I remind myself.

Best sip slowly.

My hand trembles as I lift the glass to my mouth.

"Are you scared to be alone with me?"

I start so violently, gin sloshes over the rim. "Afraid of you? Of course not. Why would you think that?"

"You're shaking."

"Perhaps I'm cold."

"It's twice as warm here as Caeldera, and you never trembled in my presence there."

My gaze moves to his. "How is Caeldera?"

"Progress is slow. We have cleared the majority of the rubble from the inner keep. Now we begin the painstaking process of rebuilding." He takes a long sip, eyes holding mine over the rim of his glass. Even in the darkness, they glow with banked flames. "It will take years. But one day, it will be as it was. Better, even."

"I have no doubt."

"You will see the progress for yourself when you return."

Tongue-tied, I take another gulp of my drink.

"It was difficult to leave, even knowing it is well protected by those who remain behind." He pauses. "Not that there are many citizens left to protect. More have fled. They, like you, seem to have started new lives in new places."

My shoulders tense. "I did not flee, Penn. That's not fair."

It is like he does not even hear me. His expression turns as dark as his tone. "Nothing is the same since you left."

The breath evacuates my lungs. "Pende—"

"No. Let me get this out." He pushes aside his glass and leans over the table so I cannot escape his eyes. "Rhya, I watch my kingdom slowly knitting back together, watch the light beginning to return to the eyes of my people, and I realize . . . none of it matters without you there by my side to see it."

My pulse kicks up to a patter.

"In every crowd, it is your face I search for. At every table, it is you I seek to sit beside. Every triumph, every failure . . . you are the one I wish to share them with. But you are no longer there. You are a ghost in the corner of my eyes, gone the second I turn to look. And your absence . . . Gods, Rhya, it haunts me. *You* haunt me. Around every corner, down every corridor. Dreaming or waking, you are there, burned into my eyes like a brand."

"I never meant to haunt you," I whisper. "I thought, in staying away, I might grant you peace."

He pushes to his feet so fast, the chair tumbles backward to the ground with a clatter. "Peace? There is no peace without you."

He takes two strides in my direction and falls to his knees before me. My stunned mind struggles to process what is happening as he grips my chair by its legs and drags it around to face him. On the shadowy terrace, his ember eyes seem the only source of light.

"Rhya . . ." His hands lock on my hips, holding tight enough to bruise. "I have not known peace since the moment you went through that portal. I fear I will never know it again. Not until you are back with me in Caeldera."

I gape at him, incapable of speech.

"Do you understand what I am telling you?" He shudders with the effort to keep his powers in check, his broad shoulders shaking with each breath. His hands are warm as brands even through the leather. "Rhya, I . . . I never should've let you go. I cannot be without you, not for another day, not for another moment. Come back. Please, *please* . . . come back to me."

With that halting confession, he lays his head in my lap.

I go utterly still.

I have no idea what to do, what to say. For this is everything I've wished to hear from Penn for so very long. Everything I dreamed he might one day confess to me as I tossed and turned at night, as I agonized over *maybes* and *somedays*. As I chastised myself for daring to hope for an ending in which we might end up together.

"*Rhya,*" he whispers—nearly a whimper. "Please."

His pain brims over, rushes through me. Tears spring to my eyes as it mingles with my own wildly vacillating emotions. Before I can stop myself, my fingers are threading through his thick, burnished chestnut hair. He groans as he feels my touch.

I mean it to be soothing—but Penn is not in the mood to be soothed. In a blink, his grip on my hips tightens and I feel my body dragged down to the floor, the edge of the chair scraping my spine, my skull cracking against the hard terrace tiles. I barely feel the pain as Penn's body rolls on top of mine, his weight compressing the breath from my lungs as he settles between my legs. My gasp of shock is swept away by his mouth, which claims mine in a bruising, feverish kiss.

Skies.

Heat sears through me, unstoppable. It is the same as it always is between us—sweet combustion, delicious torture. I feel like crying as our lips dance together, a violent clash of tongues and teeth that blazes me down to my bones.

But how can I be crying?

This is everything I have wanted, everything I have wished for in my most far-flung fantasies. The formidable Pendefyre of Dyved, submitting to me. Relinquishing his precious control, pulling me into his arms, and never letting me go again. Mine to hold—not just for a few stolen seconds in the darkness, not just for a momentary lapse of judgment.

Mine.

Is he mine?

Am I his?

My body is alight with such pleasure, it takes my mind a moment to catch up. For reason to crash back in, a wave of pain to douse the passion. Tearing my mouth from his, I push at his shoulders until he rolls off of me.

"Wait! *Wait.*"

His breaths are as ragged as mine. "What? What is it? What's wrong?"

"Penn . . ." I shake my head as I sit up, feeling a million contradictory emotions at once. "This . . . We . . . We cannot do this."

"Why the hell not?"

"We cannot just dive back into each other. Not after everything that's happened."

He stares at me, face stricken, hair messy from my hands. "Rhya—"

"There are things we must talk about," I insist softly, trying to get my spinning senses under control. Praying he will not touch me again, for when he does, my thoughts go up in flames. "I need a moment to process."

"To process what? I've just told you—"

"That you want me back in Caeldera. Back by your side," I echo thickly, scooting back a few feet so I can breathe properly. "Yes. I got that part."

"Then why are you confused?"

"What, exactly, does that mean?"

"I do not know how to make it any clearer."

"Then . . ." I shake my head, trying desperately to slow my pulse from a thudding tattoo to a more measured tempo. "What has changed these past three weeks?"

"Changed? Changed how?" He studies me, brow furrowed, eyes dark with displeasure. "It seems you are the one who has changed most during this separation."

My chin jerks. "That may be true. But that was not my question, as you well know—even if you are attempting to deflect it."

"Gods, you've spent too much bloody time among people who speak in circles," he mutters. "Not everything requires endless discussion."

"I think I have earned a conversation. An explanation, at the very least."

Scowling, he gestures at me to continue.

"What will be different between us if I return with you?"

"If?" He bites out the word. "Do you intend to stay here, then? With him?"

"Do not drag Soren into this."

"I am not dragging him anywhere. He has inserted himself between us gleefully." He wipes a hand down his face, as if that might clear the hurt from his expression. "It pains me you cannot see how he is toying with your emotions."

"And it pains me that you think I cannot make a decision

about my future without being misled by the men in my life." Suddenly, I am on my feet. Too furious to stand still, I begin to pace in tight loops across the terrace. "Gods, Penn, you accuse Soren of toying with my emotions. What is it you are doing? Showing up here, acting the wounded party, asking me to return to Caeldera with you . . . And, all the while, I have yet to hear you express what our life will look like, should I make that choice. Will we be together? Or will things go right back to how they were before I went through the portal at Blister Bight?"

"You expect me to be an oracle, predicting the future? I cannot do that, Rhya. All I can tell you is how I feel now, in this moment." He steps into my path, halting me in my tracks. I did not even hear him find his feet. He does not touch me, but his eyes hold me captive, their burning depths ablaze with the intensity of his emotions. "This fire you have lit inside me will burn and burn and burn until it has consumed me from within. I know you feel the same. Your body does not lie. The bond does not lie."

I cannot deny the words. They are the truth—but not the whole of it. I cling to my hard-fought logic even as my foolish heart begs me to yield. To fall back into his arms and let his fiery touch erase all my hesitations.

"Passion alone is not enough to sustain a partnership," I whisper. "At least . . . not the kind I want."

His eyes narrow. "And what kind is that?"

"The kind in which I am an equal in all aspects. Encouraged to participate, not relegated to the sidelines like a child."

His pause is rife with self-restraint. "I have only ever sought to keep you safe."

"I know that. I do. But, Penn . . . I have learned to keep myself safe. My powers are strong, and grow stronger every day."

His head shakes once, a jolt of disbelief. "So you do not need me anymore. That's what you are saying."

"No, I'm saying that I do not want to love someone because I *need* him. I want to love someone because I *choose* him. And because he chooses me in return. The real me. Not the version he wants me to go back to, not the potential he hopes he can forge me into one day. Just . . . me, as I am now. Rhya."

He looks at me as though I am speaking a foreign tongue, as though he cannot begin to understand what I am trying to convey to him. Each second I spend waiting for a response drives the blade a bit deeper into my heart.

"What is it you want me to say to you?" he asks finally. "Tell me the words, I will speak them. Hand me a script, I will read it. Whatever assurances you need, I will give them to you . . . So long as it means you are with me on my ship in two days' time, charting a course back to my city."

A fissure of pain splits through my chest as the blade strikes clean through. I do not want to tell him how to win me. I do not want to hand him the cipher he needs to crack the secrets coded into the subtext of my soul.

I want him to know, in one look across a room, how I am feeling. I want him to catch my gaze in a thick crowd and make me feel as though we are the only two in existence, so connected there is no question of it. I want the gentle caring I'd seen between Uther and Carys; the bone-deep sense of *knowing* that radiates between Alaric and Arwen.

They seem to move in the same orbit, like two tethered stars, Soren told me once.

That is what I want—and I will accept no less.

Not ever again.

Years ago, Tomas kept me like a secret. His hidden shame.

Now Penn keeps me like treasure. A dragon safeguarding gold. And yet, neither of them has ever kept me the way I truly desire.

Like a vow.

Like a promise.

Not hidden away, nor sequestered in an airless vault. A love that feels like the wind. Wild and free. Infinite as the aether.

"Say something," Penn begs, voice gruff.

"My head is spinning," I admit truthfully. "It's been a long night already. I need a bit of time to wrap my thoughts around this."

"This?"

"Returning to Caeldera. Returning to . . . you."

A muscle leaps in his cheek. "You've had weeks of time."

I did not use it pining over you, I think but do not say, for I know it will only hurt him. "Penn . . ."

"You love me," he whispers, head shaking slowly back and forth. His eyes are an inferno of devastation. "I know you do."

I do.

I do love him.

There is a part of me that will always love him, until I am naught but ashes, my soul returned to the skies. But as I stare at him now, I cannot help wondering if love alone is enough to last a lifetime.

Can you call it love if it only comes in a half measure?

He was right to say that I'm changing. I hardly know who I am anymore. I cannot predict the woman I will one day become. How can I expect him to know me, truly, when I do not know myself? How can I demand he unravel the mysteries of my psyche when, even to me, they are a storm of unknowns?

It is not fair.

Not to me, not to him.

I haul in a breath and force myself to take a step back. "Pendefyre—"

"No. Don't."

My brows rise. "What?"

"Whatever you are about to say, don't." He speaks through clenched teeth. "I realize now, looking at you, that I have rushed this. Words are not my forte. Expressing my emotions is not a strength. I can admit that. I meant to do this slowly. Properly. I had a speech prepared, had a million points to make . . . But the moment I saw you . . ." His hands are tight fists at his sides. "I'm sorry. Take all the time you require, Rhya. When next we speak of this, I promise I will do a better job at articulating the depth of my feelings for you."

Something about Penn's halting vulnerability makes my eyes burn with unshed tears. It is so unlike him to lay himself bare, I can hardly believe I'm about to walk away. Still, I know I must—for both our sakes. If I stay, we will end up right back where we began, allowing our bodies to make promises our hearts cannot uphold. A momentary solution for a perpetual problem.

Arching up onto my tiptoes, I press a kiss to his warm cheek. It lasts no longer than the length of a heartbeat.

"Good night, Penn. I will see you tomorrow at the wedding."

I wait for him to say something else. For him to do something else. To catch me by the arm, to call me back. To pull me in and tell me, without an ounce of hesitation, that our future will be more than a tightrope walk between repression and release. That he has learned in our time apart that some risks are worth taking, for the rewards are beyond compare. That Caeldera will be my kingdom as much as his if I come back—to protect, to rule, to safeguard in every way.

My home, with my king.

But he merely stands there, hands balled into tight fists at his sides as he watches me turn and walk away from him, disappearing into the darkness like a ghost.

THE LLŶRIANS CONSIDER midsummer a lucky day for a wedding. The luckiest of the year, in fact, for it has more hours of sunlight than any other and thus, any couple whose union is forged on the solstice will forever walk together bathed in the light of the gods.

Arwen and Alaric are married at high noon, when the sun is at its peak in the skies, on top of the sea gate, with the whole city gathered to watch them exchange vows. Vaughn officiates, his massive form clad in a rich teal tunic threaded with gold, his voice loud enough to carry the solemn rites outward across the ramparts to the farthest canals and bridges for all to hear. Even the squadrons posted at battlements within the walls can surely make out his deep boom.

The Paexyrian fly overhead, whooping their support from above, shooting immolating arrows in choreographed arcs that explode into dazzling fireworks over the harbor. Soren is up there somewhere, too, though Zephyr soars on the wind so fast, he is no more than a black smudge against the azure.

Everyone cheers as Alaric bends his bride deeply over one arm, the other arm punching skyward in pure victory as he kisses the woman he's waited so many years to call his own. Before the cheers have faded, the couple climb onto Atyr's back and ride off together, their hair rippling in the wind, the train of Arwen's long dress a pale flag flying out behind them as they disappear from view.

It is the most beautiful ceremony I've ever seen.

But my heart feels hollow as I add my voice to the chorus of cheers, my mind blank as I lift my hands to join the thunderous applause. I did not sleep last night. After my heated discussion with Pendefyre, I'd wound my way up the many steps of the royal grounds, a silent shadow in a city of revelers.

Soren's villa was a crush of strangers, the terrace crowded with guests drinking Daggerpoint lager and dining under the starlight. For once, the expansive kitchen was fully staffed, hearth ablaze as delicacies were prepared to feed the masses. Well-muscled porters trekked back and forth across the sloping lawns, ferrying furniture. They've spent days setting up long tables throughout the gardens for the elaborate feast that is to take place after today's ceremony.

No one noticed as I slipped into my suite and shut the door. Curled into a ball, I sat on my balcony, staring out at Hylios's midnight beauty, unmoving. Penn's taste lingered on my lips; his words played on a loop in my head.

There is no peace without you.

I cannot be without you.

Please, please, come back to me.

I hoped, if I sat there long enough, some of my uncertainties would crystallize into a solid decision. But I was still sitting there when the sun crept up over the horizon, with no more answers in either my head or my heart. I felt more confused than ever as I dressed for the wedding, pulling on the gown I'd spotted a fortnight past in the window of one of the many boutiques that line the canals.

We were meant to be buying me another set of flight leathers, but Bretiax had pulled me inside when she saw my lingering gaze and insisted I try it on, with Harpina's gentle encouragement. It is nearly identical in style to the one Soren once gave me, plunging deeply at the bodice to expose my Remnant, then flowing to my ankles in a frothy sea of sapphire and silver fabric. I'd thought it was too scandalous for a midday wedding, but both women assured me it was perfect.

Now, as I look around at the crowd, I'm glad I listened. Everyone is dressed in their finest despite the bright sun that beats down overhead. Even the Ember Guild looks quite dashing in their maroon dress uniforms, with embroidered sashes across their chests and boots polished to a shine.

"Say what you will about the Llŷrians," Jac says, grinning at me. "They know how to celebrate."

"Thought it was called the Water Court because of the canals." Cadogan shakes his head. "It's because the citizens drink like fish."

Farley presses a hand to his temple. "Not so loud, for the love of the gods."

"You have no one to blame but yourself for that hangover." Mabon cracks a grin. "Tried to drink Yara under the table, the fool."

I grimace. I'd seen Yara down her body weight in Titan gin and remain standing. "If I had some herbs on hand, I would mix you a tonic for the headache. There is a hospital ward near the barracks; I'm sure the healers there have something that will help."

Farley waves away my words. "It'll pass as soon as I start drinking again. Hair of the hound that bit, as they say. Hopefully, they'll serve something strong at the feast." He pauses. "Will Yara be there, do you think? I am entitled to a rematch. My dignity depends on it."

My lips twist. "I'm sure she and the other Paexyrian will be in attendance."

When I left the villa this morning, it was in the full swing of final preparations—flowers being carefully arranged, candles being positioned just so, fine silver being set out beside bone china. The tables in the gardens are set with fifty places, enough to accommodate Alaric and Arwen's closest friends and family members—a group that, surprisingly, includes me.

The Ember Guild is also to attend. Evidently, Penn's role as King of Dyved and Remnant of Fire is enough to warrant a place at the table. And where he goes, so do his men.

"When does it start, again?" Mabon asks.

"In two hours," Cadogan says.

Jac waggles his brows suggestively. "Just enough time to give the newlyweds a chance to consummate."

I shove him. "Don't be crass."

"Just trying to fit in with the Hylians. The things we saw at those pleasure clubs of theirs . . ."

I hold up a hand to stop his words. "I do not need to hear about it."

"You're blushing," Cadogan informs me.

"So are you," I retort, noting the stain of pink on his high cheekbones. "Don't tell me the least romantically inclined member of the Ember Guild finally had his head turned by someone last night?"

Cadogan's blush increases. "That's absurd."

"Your face does not match your words."

Mabon snorts. "She's got you there."

"Let's just say, we crossed paths with the siren sisters." Jac is grinning hugely as he elbows Cadogan in the gut. "He's as hot-blooded as the rest of us under all that stoicism. Who knew?"

"Elbow me again," Cadogan hisses, still red as a beet, "and you will find yourself taking a swim in the nearest canal."

Jac appears unconcerned. "Perhaps a siren will pull me out."

"I think Melité might be more inclined to drag you to the depths," I warn.

His sigh is dreamy. "But what a way to die . . ."

"Ah!" Farley cries suddenly, hand flinging out toward the other side of the harbor. "I think I see a tavern over there! If we hurry, we can beat the crowd to the bar."

"Do you ever think of anything except fucking, feasting, or falling down drunk?"

Farley shoots Cadogan an exasperated look. "Do *you* ever think of anything except battle formations? We are at a wedding, for gods' sake. Forgive me if I do not plan to squander this brief reprieve from sleeping on a bedroll, freezing my bollocks off by the North Sea, waiting for Frostlanders to attack in the night."

"He has a point," Mabon puts in quietly. "We might as well enjoy our leave. Our ship heads back to Dyved tomorrow."

My heart sinks at the deadline. I still have not decided whether I will be on board with them.

"Enough of this back-and-forth," Jac declares. "I'm in charge, and I've decided we have time for a round or three before the feast."

Mabon scoffs. "Why are you in charge?"

Ignoring him, Jac slings an arm around my shoulders and squeezes. "What do you say, Ace? Will you show us your new stomping grounds? For old times' sake?"

I mull it over for a beat, then shrug. "Oh, why not."

We head off in search of refreshments. I can't help smiling at their expressions as they take in the undeniable splendor of Hylios. The sun is shining down, warm and bright, bathing the white stone buildings that line the canals, refracting off the domed blue rooftops. Colorful flowers explode from every facade, their vines bursting with fresh blooms.

I bring them first through the floating market by flatboat, laughing as they sample imported delicacies from places none of us have ever heard of—Cadogan choking on a shrimp skewer in his haste to swallow, Mabon's face screwing up in a horrified mask as I explain the cracker he's just consumed is made from dehydrated sea lion testicles. Even our hired sternman chuckles as the fearsome Ember Guild warrior spews over the side.

My spirits soar higher as we disembark by a busy tavern I visited several days ago with Yara, Thisobei, and Vaughn. The proprietor has a stake in Vintners' Cove, and serves the best wine in the city. Every table is filled with happy Hylians, all drinking and smoking from long-hosed braziers, but we manage to carve out a space to stand by the bar with a view of the canal.

It does indeed feel like old times, albeit with a few glaring exceptions. Uther's absence among us is a blow that still takes my breath away.

As is Penn's.

He did not come to the wedding. I can feel his presence through the bond, not so very far away, so I know he is still in the city somewhere. Surely he will make an appearance at the feast . . . If not to celebrate the couple or speak to me, then to re-visit his plans for a southern invasion with Soren.

I sip my wine, reminding myself that the complexities of my personal relationships pale in comparison to the other decisions that will be made during this royal assemblage. For by the end of it, Dyved and Llŷr will remain allies in arms or fracture irrevo-cably apart.

I cannot predict that outcome any more than I can predict my own future. And so, for a time, I allow myself the chance to drink and laugh with my friends, shored up by their tales of cam-paigns on the northern coast, of clandestine missions through Cimmerian snow.

I've missed them.

Gods, I've missed them.

Just as I will now miss people here if I set sail tomorrow . . .

I think I do a good job of smiling and laughing. Feigning normalcy, despite the tumult inside. But every so often, I'll catch Mabon's dark eyes on the side of my face, or see the way Cadogan's pale blond brows furrow with concern, and I know they are not entirely fooled by my act.

CHAPTER
TWENTY-FOUR

Alaric and Arwen sway to the music, staring deeply into each other's eyes. They are surrounded by other dancing couples who move their bodies in time with the quartet of fiddlers. Yara and Farley, both a bit bleary-eyed from their drinking rematch, appear to be holding each other up as they rock back and forth, paying no mind to the rhythm. Harpina and a stunningly beautiful Hylian woman are much more coordinated on the edge of the dance floor, clad in gowns of the same orange hue. Jac has somehow convinced Bretiax to let him lead her onto the floor—he does not know how to sign, but evidently his charm surpasses the need for words. Even Mabon has been dragged away, incapable of resisting Thisobei's mischievous invitation.

Only Cadogan remains seated with Penn and me at our once crowded table, and we might as well be invisible to him. His eyes are riveted to the siren sisters reposed on a wide chaise across the gardens. Even from here, I see they are surrounded by admirers on large colorful pillows in the grass.

Melité and Tethys are supposedly muting their seductive song, but it seems to saturate the atmosphere regardless, working a slow spell over everyone at the feast as the afternoon fades to streaks of pink twilight, then slips into the silvery blue of a rising full moon. Silent servants move along the tables, lighting candles and torches, illuminating the paper lanterns strung from the thwacking palms.

All traces of the elaborate meal have long since been cleared. I fidget in my chair, wishing I could vanish as easily as the canapés had. Penn, on the contrary, is stock-still in the seat across from mine. Just as he's been since he first dropped into it two hours ago.

Inches away, he might as well be leagues. I tell myself to shatter the heavy quiet, but I'm even more tongue-tied around him than I was last night—especially when I feel the weight of a bold blue stare locked on us from the main table some distance away, where the King of Llŷr is seated beside his brother.

Strangely, I sense nothing through the bond from Soren. He is muting me—and has been, I realize belatedly, since we left the cove yesterday after my lightning lesson. Since that electrified moment when our eyes met and . . .

Skies, I must not think of that.

I study the tablecloth as though it is the most fascinating piece of artwork, willing time to pass faster. The feast itself was not so bad. Sure, the exquisitely prepared food tasted like ash on my tongue and my appetite had been nonexistent. But when I was actively chewing, I was not in danger of blurting out half-formed thoughts that will only further muddle a murky situation.

I'd happily force down another plate if only to have something to do with my mouth. Perhaps Penn feels the same, for he grunted no more than a handful of words to his men throughout the meal. He's never been one for expressing himself freely. And last night, when he'd finally found the fortitude to try . . .

I was the one to withdraw.

That must've crushed him. He can barely meet my eyes now. When Farley made an absentminded remark earlier about the journey home, Penn physically flinched in pain. As though the possibility that I might not return to Dyved with them tomorrow was more than he could bear.

This fire you have lit inside me will burn and burn and burn until it has consumed me from within . . .

I take another sip from my goblet, all the while knowing there is not enough wine in the world to ease the tension thickening the air around me like a cloud. Over the rim, my eyes snag on Penn's.

Say something to him, you coward, I chide myself. *Anything is better than this conversational void you have fallen into.*

"I have something for you," he rumbles softly, before I've quite mustered my courage.

"Oh?" My hand shakes as I set my goblet back down. "What is it?"

He reaches into the pocket of his luxe maroon doublet and extracts an envelope closed with light green wax. My heart leaps into my throat when I recognize the insignia pressed into the seal.

"Carys?" I ask, voice thick.

Penn nods as he slides the letter across the table to me. "She wanted me to pass it along to you."

I stare at the letter, suddenly afraid to touch it. Months of wishing for Carys to speak to me and, now that she has, I'm paralyzed by what she'll say. What if she asks me to leave her the hell alone, once and for all? Or, gods, what if something terrible has happened since I left? To her, to the baby . . .

I assume Lestyn would've told me any major news, but worries flood me anyway. My eyes are still locked on the envelope when I choke out, "What—What is it?"

"No idea. I haven't read it." Recognizing the panic on my face, he quickly adds, "It's nothing bad. When she gave it to me, she was in better spirits than I've seen her since—Well, you know."

I do.

Forcing my gaze up to his, I take pains to clear my voice. "How is she?"

His eyes soften around the edges, solemn with thought. "She's getting by. Taking it day by day. She misses him." Gravel creeps into his throat. "We all miss him."

Uther.

Pain lances through me. My words drop to a whisper. "I wish more than anything that I could go back to that last moment with him. Tell him—"

"Don't. Don't punish yourself for what happened that day, Rhya. It was not your fault." His stare grows intent. He leans slightly forward in his seat, as though determined to make me hear his next words. "Nothing about Fyremas was your fault. If I failed to make that clear . . . If I somehow made you believe otherwise, that day at Blister Bight . . ." His jaw tightens, locking in the rest of his words.

He's sorry.

I'm glad to know it, even if he cannot admit it plainly. My bottom lip quivers as I reach out and take the letter. My fingertip traces over the inky loops of my name in a familiar feminine hand. The paper is thick and slightly textured. Carys makes it herself, presses flower petals into the pulp before it dries. I've watched her do it more than once. Even helped occasionally. Before I can stop myself, I'm lifting it to my nose and breathing deep.

Lilacs and honeysuckle.

The same sweet, springy scent that infuses her dress shop.

The lip wobble increases until I sink my teeth down to stop it. My fingers tighten on the parchment as I lower the letter to my lap. I want nothing more than to rip it open and devour the contents, but I have a feeling whatever is inside will require privacy. I cannot fall apart at a wedding feast with scores of strangers around to see my blubbering.

"Thank you for bringing this to me, Penn. I never thought she'd write me back." I inhale with deliberate slowness, sinuses tingling with unshed tears. "I didn't dare to hope she'd . . ."

"Rhya. She loves you. Just as—" He pauses again, this time for so long I have no choice but to meet his gaze. The instant I do, his throat bobs roughly. Swallowing down words he is not ready, or not willing, to say. "She wants you back in Caeldera. Back where you belong." Another heady pause. "We all want that."

Ignoring the way my stomach pitches, I steer the conversation forward. "And the baby? How is he?"

"Growing stronger by the day. He's got his father's fortitude. And his mother's lungs." For the first time since he arrived in this city, all the tension bleeds out of Penn's shoulders. He relaxes back in his seat, voice turning singularly gentle. "I've been spending some time with him, now that he's a bit more alert. I think . . ."

I wait when he trails off, not interrupting. Hardly even breathing. I know Pendefyre well enough to realize that even a slight interjection at this juncture will snatch away whatever he is about to confess.

"I think Uther would want that," he continues finally, fingers flexing on his water goblet. "He was my cousin, as you know. My blood. My kin. So, while Nevin is not mine, and while I could never seek to overtake Uther's role in his life . . . I feel a certain responsibility to look out for him."

My heart convulses wildly at the vision of Penn raising Uther's son. His strong arms guiding a child's first steps . . . His protective instincts put to good use . . . His dim life of repression lit up by a baby's bubbling laughter . . .

I press my eyes closed, as if to imprint the images there forever.

"I just hope I am up to the task," he confesses quietly, snapping me back to the present. "I always thought, if I ever became a father, it would be . . ."

It damn near kills me to bite back a prompting question. But I am terrified to break the spell of his words, now that he is finally offering them so freely.

"Actually, the truth is, in over a century of life, I have hardly allowed myself to consider that I might someday become a father." His gaze grows intense as it finds mine again. "That I might meet someone with whom I'd create a new life. An heir. A . . . a family." Any trace of the soft, relaxed demeanor I saw moments ago is gone. His spine is ramrod against his seat, his shoulders stiff beneath his doublet. "The inherent limitations of my power prevented me from even entertaining the possibility. Until . . ."

Until?

I am no longer breathing at all. The very air seems to still around our table—the palm trees overhead no longer thwacking in the night breeze, even the taper candles ceasing their flickers. Around us, the wedding frivolity carries on throughout the gardens, but it feels very far away. As though we are in a bubble of our own making, sequestered from the rest of the living world.

This is a topic we have never broached. A topic I did not even dare to think of, let alone address with him.

Marriage.

Children.

Legacy.

Love.

Pendefyre has never confessed to wanting any of those things. He has always acted as though the price they demand is too high to pay; has always stated, unequivocally, that tying himself too tightly to anyone would result in a conflagration of direst consequence.

Has he changed his mind?

I cannot bring myself to ask any more than he can bring himself to say. Poised on the edge of a knife that threatens to slice straight through my future, I do the only thing I can do.

I wait.

"I—I don't—" Penn takes a breath that broadens his whole frame, then takes a sip of water before he attempts again. "I do not know what my future holds, in that regard. I cannot say if I will ever take a wife, or sire a child of my own. Not now. Perhaps not ever."

Of course not.

"In the meantime," he goes on, not seeming to notice my flinch, "I will do my best to help raise Nevin. I will try to honor Uther's legacy any way I can, and support Carys however she will allow. I will keep them close enough to protect."

But not to love.

He still cannot allow himself to make that leap. Still cannot convince himself that loving is not the same as forfeiting; that to surrender one's heart can be done without losing one's free will.

I wonder, not for the first time, if he will ever be able to love freely, or if his affections will forever remain trapped along with his power in a cage of rigid self-control. The one person he ever truly allowed himself to care for, body and soul, is long gone. The fading shadow of a memory. A ghost who haunts his every new beginning, reminding him of the worst repercussions that can come of mixing passion and power.

Enid.

The thought of her no longer pains me, as it once did. Instead, it offers a shred of enlightenment about Penn's complex past. And, in a concurrent stroke, illuminates some harsher realities about his future.

I exhale, long and low. As I do, I feel the world come rushing back in—light and laughter and sound returning in one great whoosh. There is the thwacking of the palm fronds overhead, the faint sway of the glowing paper lanterns, the stomping of boots on the dance floor. There is Yara's snarky commentary, and Vaughn's resounding laugh, and the warbling whine of a fiddle.

We are back in breathable air.

Back on stable conversational ground.

Setting aside the perilous prospect of *us*, I clear my throat. "You describe this new guardianship as a responsibility. I think it can be more than that, Penn. If you let it. It can be a source of good, and joy, and harmony."

He stares at me, seemingly at a loss for words.

"Don't doubt yourself or your capabilities. Nevin is lucky to have you."

He blows out a breath. "I am hardly a perfect role model."

"Children don't care about perfect." I smile at him, thinking of my own wizened, occasionally crotchety mentor. "The man who raised me wasn't, but I still miss him terribly each day. I—"

Reminiscences of Eli are snatched away as Yara's screech of mirth cuts across the gardens. My head whips to the side in time to watch Farley, drunker than I've ever witnessed, falling in a dead faint to the dance floor.

"*Timber!*" Yara claps her hands, laughing uproariously at her downed partner. "Down he goes!"

I glance back at Penn, mouth agape. "Should we—"

"I'll get him to the guest villa." He's already halfway out of his chair, expression stormy. "The buffoon needs to sleep it off in a bed."

I don't know whether to feel concerned or amused as I watch Penn cutting through the sea of swaying couples to Farley's prone form.

"Do you think he needs help carrying him down the steps?" I ask Cadogan.

When I receive no response, I turn to face the soldier at the end of our table. He's in the same position he's been for the past few hours: body eerily still, unfocused gaze trained at the siren sisters. His tidy mop of bright blond hair is uncharacteristically mussed.

"Hey!" I snap a finger to get his attention. "Cadogan!"

He blinks twice, as if to clear a fog, then meets my eyes. His brows quirk in confusion. "Sorry, did you say something?"

Skies.

"Farley's taken a tumble on the dance floor. Too much Titan gin, not enough common sense. Pendefyre's gone to carry him down to your villa. Which you would know, if you'd been paying attention to a single thing that's happened this evening."

"Ah." A hint of a blush creeps up the side of Cadogan's neck. "Right. I was . . ."

"Entranced?" I finish wryly. "I can see that."

He runs a hand through his messy mane. It's an odd sight, him so disheveled. He's usually the picture of self-discipline. "I'm sure Farley will be fine," he mutters. "Pendefyre won't even punish him. Tomorrow's journey home will be punishment enough. Nothing worse than a hangover on the high seas. He'll spend most of the sail to Caeldera heaving over the side, I wager."

I grimace. "Poor Farley."

"No more than he deserves." A shade of his typical solemnity creeps back into Cadogan's expression as our stares hold. "And you? Will you be sailing with us tomorrow?"

A lump lodges in my throat. "I . . . I don't know yet."

"Mmm. Well, you'd better make up your mind soon. We leave at daybreak." He looks back at the sirens, mouth instantly going slack. "Even if there are reasons we wish we could delay . . ."

His words are a stark reminder that I still have not made a decision about my rapidly approaching future. I am running out of time to choose. I can feel each second ticking away, each passing moment slipping through my fingers like sand in an hourglass.

A part of me wants nothing more than to pick up the pieces of my old life again. To settle back into the familiarity of the crater, with its roaring falls and jewel-toned lake. Mornings in the infirmary, healing patients who need me. Tea with Carys as baby Nevin naps. Evenings with Lestyn, poring over medicinal texts. Sparring lessons with Jac. Rounds of twyllo with Farley.

And Penn.

Everything . . . with Penn.

I can see it so clearly: a fresh start in Caeldera, mine for the taking. But each time I think of leaving Llŷr, my heart feels as though it will be torn in two.

Gods, what is happening?

Why do I feel this way?

When did the path beneath my feet diverge in two?

I need clarity. I need advice. I need someone, anyone, to tell me what to do, for I feel woefully unequipped to make the decision on my own.

Almost before I'm consciously aware of it, my senses are reaching out for a familiar presence. Seeking out a person I've grown accustomed to turning to with a near constant torrent of questions about everything under the sun. A person who is always available with answers to all of life's many curiosities. A person whose insight—and whose presence—has been woefully absent from me all day.

Soren.

It's almost amusing: weeks ago, if someone had asked whether I could ever trust such a man with my innermost confidences and deepest shames, I would've laughed in their face. How strange, then, that he is the only person whose counsel I want at this crossroads I've come to. The only one whose opinion about my future truly seems to matter.

I want, with a shocking desperation, to know how he feels about the prospect of my leaving his city. If I'm honest with myself, it is more than a mere want. It is a need. Without it, there is a hole punched straight through my list of pros and cons, a missing weight upon the scales that sway in the winds of my destiny.

I must speak to him.

I must know if . . .

I must . . .

But I do not feel him anywhere. I do not see him, either, when I turn to look. Not at his seat at the head of the main banquet table, not on the dance floor. Not anywhere my eyes move. I reach out with my senses, testing the limits of our bond, stretching it across the city from wall to wall, twining through the labyrinth of canals all the way to the sea gate.

Still, I cannot feel his presence. It's as though he's vanished off the face of the earth. As though he's retreated from me until my decision is made.

The one time I actually crave his snarky commentary, he decides to respect my autonomy? The one time I desire him to push my boundaries beyond reason, he regards them with utmost politeness?

Skies, I could throttle the man. My hands curl into frustrated fists in my lap. The movement knocks the thick envelope resting there to the ground.

Carys's letter.

Perhaps it holds some insight. Perhaps my old friend has some sage words of wisdom to impart, some lessons from afar to help make an impossible decision slightly easier.

I sweep it up like it holds the solution to all my troubles, my grip tight enough to bend the parchment. I push out of my chair so suddenly it startles Cadogan from his siren-induced haze.

"Are you all right?"

"Fine," I lie, heart thudding madly. "I just need some air. I'm going to walk the ramparts for a while."

"Do you want company?"

I shake my head. "I will be back soon."

He looks troubled, his old instincts rearing up inside him. But I am no longer under the protection of the Fire Court. He is not sworn to guard me as he was back in Dyved. His mouth presses shut and, with a short nod, he lets me go.

I wind a slow path around the edges of the dance floor, not entirely sure where I am headed. A quiet place. Somewhere I can read the letter in peace, away from the drunken revelry. The aviary, maybe?

The gown floats around my legs like water, lightweight silver threads catching the candlelight with each step. My eyes move across the crowd, studying every face—most of them unfamiliar to me. Regardless, everyone smiles as our eyes meet, relaxed by the thrall of good food and better wine. Spirits are high.

Folks always love a wedding.

My eyes move quickly past the half-sirens holding court by the spring. The dense throng of admirers has only grown since I last looked their way. I'd finally been introduced to Tethys a few hours before. She is no less attractive than her twin, with the same voluptuous body and voluminous curls, but her temperament is somewhat softer. Tethys has a tendency to fade into the shadows while Melité actively seeks the spotlight.

When she feels my gaze, her black eyes move to mine. No whites are visible around the irises—they are two glossy pools of octopus ink that, like her smile, lack all warmth. Her skin, though luminous, never loses that eerie blue sheen that brings to mind the scales of a fish. She cants her head in greeting, exposing the long column of her neck, and I see a series of deep gouges on either side.

Gills.

I force a wan smile in return and keep moving. My eyes continue to scan the crowd until I reach the far side of the gardens. It's less crowded here, but I hear the occasional love-laced sigh sounding from the foliage as I move onto the darkened path. More than a few couples have snuck off for a bit of privacy— Bretiax and Jac among them, I realize as I round a bend and spot them pressed tight together by a large jasmine shrub, hands exploring each other's bodies in a way that requires no shared language skills.

My cheeks heat as I avert my gaze. Hurrying my pace, I follow the mellow glow of lanterns to the aviary, praying I will not find it occupied by another groping pair. I'm nearly there when I trip over something that sends me sprawling face-first onto the path. I curse as I catch myself, palms planting on the mossy earth.

My oath is quickly overtaken by a series of deep chuckles. "That was elegant."

Dusting dirt from my skirts, I turn toward the familiar voice. My eyes track the long lengths of two booted legs—the source of my trip—up the wide planes of a chest in a dark teal tunic. It's

Vaughn, his huge form slumped against the base of a palm, his back pressed to the trunk as he nurses a heavy goblet of what I'm guessing is Titan gin, judging by his red-rimmed eyes.

"Vaughn. Sorry, didn't see you there."

"Not me you're looking for, though, is it?"

My nose scrunches in confusion. "Pardon?"

"He's not here."

"What? Who?"

"Soren. He's not here." He pauses to take a sip. "He's who you're looking for, isn't he?"

I stare at him. "I was just getting some air."

"Right. That's what he said, too." The ghost of a smile crosses his face. "If you feel like *getting some air* together, you could probably find him at the sea organ. It'll be abandoned tonight with the celebrations raging in the center of the city."

My mouth parts to retort, then closes again before a single sound escapes.

"Don't tell him I sent you," he orders gruffly, still grinning. "Unless it goes well. In which case, I expect full credit."

"I have no idea what you're talking about."

"Sure you don't. Forget I said anything."

His laughter rings in my ears as I start down the path again. I forgo the aviary altogether, abruptly too restless to stop moving. My pulse is pounding far too quickly for no reason at all. A panicky sort of energy sizzles through my veins. One I cannot account for.

I'm simply going to clear my head, as I told Cadogan. I want a quiet place to contemplate my correspondence. I have absolutely no intentions of tracking anyone down. Least of all someone who does not wish to be found.

Soren wants to be alone.

I should respect that.

I *will* respect that.

My thoughts are a tangle of contradictions as I walk aimlessly through the moonlit gardens, watching fyrewisps flash a rainbow of hues among the heavenly white florals. I'm not paying much attention to my overall direction, sandled feet taking turns at random. Before I know it, the gardens have fallen away and I'm passing through the lemon grove, then opening the warded gate that leads out onto the upper ramparts.

The night presses close as I make my way along the top of the walls, passing by several guard posts, where uniformed Hylians stare soberly out at the dark sea as sounds of distant celebration echo from the city below. Otherwise, there's hardly a soul around. Like Vaughn mentioned, most everyone is gathered at the crux of the canals tonight.

My favorite bench by the Westerly Beacon is, unsurprisingly, unoccupied. I settle onto it, thankful they've lit the torches atop the walls even if there's no one else around to use them. For a few moments, I stare out at the ebony ocean, listening to the crash of swells against stone, imploring my nerves to settle. I still feel strangely jittery as I work one fingertip beneath the wax seal of the letter, prying it loose. Allowing the parchment to furl open, my eyes drink in the fluid elegance of Carys's words.

Dearest Rhya,

I have two favors to ask of you in this letter.
The first is that you forgive me for not writing back sooner. I assure you, your letters were not cast into the flames, as you feared, but savored, word by word, sentence by sentence.
I have loved reading of your new life in Hylios. The shops you described sound amazing. I imagine

I could learn a lot from Llŷr's most talented craftsmen. I hope I'll get to visit someday. In the interim, maybe you can send a sample of the glyphed fabric you described so I can study it for my own designs? I haven't touched my needles in ages, but lately I've had the urge to pick them up again.

I confess, it's been difficult to see through the fog of grief. I think it will always be difficult. That fog will never lift, not truly.

But my eyes are beginning to adapt.

When I looked around a fortnight ago and realized you were no longer in Caeldera, I was disappointed in myself. I cannot help feeling that I played some small part in your leaving. Or in your staying away.

In my sorrow, I withdrew from our friendship. I closed the door and kept it bolted against all chances at reconciliation. I cannot deny my actions or undo them. I can only attempt to explain my reasons, for they are not what you think.

I do not hold you responsible for what happened to Uther. Not for any of it, darling girl. The idea of you carrying the burden of his death breaks my heart. And, frankly, if Uther knew you were blaming yourself, he would be furious.

Twice now you've saved the lives of me and my son—the day he came into this world and the day his father fled it. Without you, neither Nevin nor I would still be here.

Our savior, twice over.

That is who you are to my family.

That is what you mean to me.

Please do not ever allow yourself to think otherwise.

I must also thank you for sending Lestyn into our lives. At first, his unexpected appearances barely registered in my mind. But over these past few weeks, I've made more of an effort to get to know the boy. When I discovered he'd lost his parents on Fyremas, and learned he'd been sleeping at the infirmary most nights . . .

Well, I simply couldn't allow that to go on. After some persuading, he's agreed to take up the second bedroom in the apartments above my shop. Temporarily. (Or so he believes.)

I intend to keep him with us. He needs a guardian in his life besides Osain, that great curmudgeon. And, to be honest, I need a distraction from the grimness of my thoughts.

Thankfully, the nonstop prattling of a thirteen-year-old proves a perfect remedy. These days, laughter fills rooms where, for months, there has only been quiet. Already, he treats Nevin like a little brother. We are, in this strange new reality, building a different sort of family. Not the one I'd pictured for myself, perhaps, but one I need all the same.

Which brings me to the second favor I must ask you.

I know you're likely bracing for me to beg you to return home to Caeldera, or to give our beloved, pigheaded Pendefyre a chance to explain why he's been acting like the king of fools when it comes to you.

(I'll save that for my next letter.)

For now, I simply want you to promise me something. Promise me you will not waste time. Not an hour of it. Not a minute. Promise me you will live, Rhya. Fully, freely. Regardless of what anyone else says, or thinks, or expects of you.

If losing Uther has taught me anything, it is that life is cruelly short, and unimaginably hard. The losses never cease coming, no matter how intolerable. We cannot stop them. All we can do is try to make them worthwhile while we are still here on this earth. We can reap such immeasurable joy, it outweighs the inevitable pain.

I think of my husband, and though the agony has not dimmed, I would not wish it away. Even knowing I would lose him so soon, looking back at my life, I would not make any different choices.

How blessed was I to know a love so powerful, it is embedded in my very bones? How lucky to have shared a connection so deep, it remains even when my beloved does not?

That is my greatest wish for you, Rhya.

To live so authentically, and love so completely, no ending can erase your mark on this world.

Find a purpose that fills your soul, and people who patch the cracks in your heart. Find a joy that makes all this inevitable suffering worthwhile. Find a love that burns so bright, it lingers even when the world turns darkest.

Do it now.
While you still have time.

All my love,
Carys

My heart is thumping twice its typical tempo as I carefully fold the letter and tuck it into the pocket of my gown. Between my ears, a buzz of static erodes all rational thought as I rise slowly from the bench and start walking.

I cannot think.

More accurately, I do not let myself think. I am caught up in the urge to act upon my dear friend's advice.

To *live*.

Live *now*.

Before my chance slips away with the dawn.

CHAPTER
TWENTY-FIVE

I hardly recall the long climb down the ladder that descends to canal level, my gown's hem hiked high to keep from tangling on the rungs. But suddenly, there I am, on a darkened bend at the base of the Westerly Beacon. The roar between my ears matches the tremendous thunder of my pulse as I cut through the passage that leads outside the walls. It is so loud, I'm surprised I can hear the faint stirring of strange musical notes that call out to me, ushering me forward.

When I emerge into the night, I find myself staring at a wide marble staircase, approximately twenty-five paces in length, leading straight down into the sea. The steps are open at the fronts and hollow at the centers, allowing a rush of water to flow inside with each crashing wave, activating a cleverly designed network of organ pipes. The result is a haunting song of the sea that changes with the incoming tide—each swell creating a new melody, each step producing a different pitch.

I blink at the sea organ, eyes sweeping along the length of it.

There is no one here.

Not a soul around.

I want to laugh. I want to scream. What the hell am I doing

here? Gods, I was foolish to come, seeking answers to questions I'm too terrified to ask myself, let alone . . .

I turn to go.

"Planning a late-night swim?"

I spin around, eyes sweeping the area again. It's not until I walk to the edge of the musical steps that I finally spot him. He is lying on his back halfway down, his supine form mostly concealed by the marble. Just inches below him, waves pour into the lower half of the organ, producing deep notes of melancholy. If he is getting splashed, he does not seem to mind.

"I must warn you," Soren goes on, voice even more fluid than normal, "I am not in any state to rescue you."

My eyes narrow as I sit cautiously on the top tread, several steps above him. "Are you drunk?"

"I was an hour ago. Less so, now. I should've brought the bottle along." He frowns up at the moon. I cannot quite keep pace with his rapidly shifting emotions. Despite his clear intoxication, he is still successfully blocking me out. "How did you find me?"

"I was sworn to secrecy, I'm afraid."

He mulls that over for a moment, then mutters, "Vaughn. Meddlesome mammoth."

I've never seen him like this before—so cavalier, so uncalculated in his responses. I find it both unsettling and intriguing. "Is it wise to be lying there like that, on the edge, while inebriated?"

"Worried I'll drown, skylark?"

"*Can* you drown?"

"Can *you* die of suffocation?" He snorts softly. "What sort of question is that?"

"I don't know! You're the Water Remnant." My cheeks heat. "I thought maybe you could breathe underwater."

The unbridled sound of his laughter rings into the night. When it tapers off, he raises his arms, knits his fingers together, and folds them beneath his head in a cushion. "It's my half-sisters who have the gills."

"Forget I asked." I huff lightly, gathering the long train of my gown so it doesn't slip down the steps. "Why aren't you up at the villa celebrating with everyone?"

"I didn't feel much like celebrating."

My brows sail upward. "I thought you liked Alaric. I thought you supported this match."

He is quiet for a long time. "That's not why I don't feel like celebrating."

"Ah." My mind races, considering all variables. "You're upset about Arwen going away."

"Arwen." He nods. His voice is thick. "And you."

The breath snags in my throat.

"That's why you've come here, isn't it? To tell me you're leaving. To tell me goodbye."

My tongue is not complying with orders to produce coherent words. "I . . . That's not . . . I'm not . . ." I shake my head vigorously to clear it. "I'm not certain what I'm going to do."

He sits up suddenly, planting his boots against a mostly submerged slab of marble. He does not seem to notice they are getting soaked. He does not turn to meet my eyes. He speaks to the sea instead, his words so hushed I can hardly make them out over the mournful soundtrack of the sea organ.

"But he's asked you to return with him. Pendefyre. He's asked for you back."

"Yes," I answer truthfully.

Tension ripples through his shoulders, quickly steadied. "If you're planning to leave, just go. There's no need for some long drawn-out goodbye."

My features contort into a wince. He sounds so unlike himself. So . . . resigned. Almost *defeated*. I cannot bear to hear him like that. It causes me physical pain, sets off an ache inside my chest cavity I cannot endure for longer than a few agonizing heartbeats.

Before I know it, I am sliding myself down the steps one at a time, my silken skirts slipping against the marble as I make my way to sit beside him. I do not say anything as I come to a stop. I merely lean my side against his, pressing my bare shoulder to the thick fabric of his ornate navy tunic.

He takes an audible inhale as he feels my weight. "What are you doing?"

"I told you, I don't know yet. The ship—"

"I don't mean tomorrow," he clips. He still does not look at me, not even for a moment, keeping his spine ramrod as he stares out to sea. "What are you doing right now?"

"Sitting here with you."

"I don't need your pity."

"Good, because you don't have it." My eyes bore holes into the side of his face, willing him to glance over. "You're angry with me."

His jaw tightens. "No."

"And you're lying about it." My voice turns incredulous. "I thought you promised never to lie to me. I thought you claimed you would always be truthful."

His expression twists into a bleak mask that, even in profile, makes me uneasy. When he finally shifts his focus to me, I almost reel back. The full force of that look is terrifying. A Soren I have never seen before. No levity, no mirth. No easy laughter. He shows me the deepest fathoms of his pain, his fury, his frustration, holding nothing back as his eyes pierce mine.

I am suddenly grateful the bond is muted. I do not think I could bear to feel those emotions firsthand.

"You want the truth?" he mutters, the words hoarse. "Truly?"

My heart thuds harder, faster. "Always."

"The first night you arrived here, I told you I would always be honest with you, but you had not yet earned my secrets. Do you remember that?"

I nod.

"You have earned them now."

My heart stumbles. *I have?*

"But the things I want to say to you, Rhya . . . These words I keep locked inside my heart . . . I fear if I allow them to the surface, you will run from me and never return. I fear the last glimpse I ever have of you will be on the bow of a brown-sailed ship, fading into the distance, forever out of my reach."

Shivers of trepidation move through my bloodstream. I push past them, determined not to shy away. "You cannot know that. I have never run from you before, no matter what you told me, no matter how far you've pushed me. And you have pushed me greatly, these past few weeks. Mentally, elementally"—I swallow hard—"physically."

His eyes flash, silver joining the sapphire in a way that suddenly reminds me of the gown I am wearing. As though he shares my thoughts, his gaze moves down my body, taking in the plunging cleavage, the exposed whorls of my Remnant . . . Moving past the flowing fabric that hugs my curves to the delicate silver sandals on my feet where they rest on the step beside his heavy black boots, periodically splashed by warm waves.

"Physically," he repeats, the word nearly a growl.

I had meant it in regard to the water globes he is constantly battering me with, or the way he sometimes uses his broad frame to corral me down a path, or his propensity for grabbing my hand and tugging me along behind him. But as our gazes hold and hold, all those physical acts are pushed aside as the memory of that night at the Kettle threads its way into my thoughts.

My teeth score my bottom lip as I recall the way he drew pleasure from my body without ever once putting his hands on my skin. It is a memory I have replayed again and again, this past week, late at night when no one is around to see the flush of my cheeks or hear the rapid patter of my pulse.

Soren reads the direction of my thoughts instantly. His eyes go half-lidded as they drop to my mouth and lock there. "I thought you did not want to talk about that."

"I don't," I breathe.

"Good. We've talked enough."

"What—"

His hand slides behind my neck without warning, jerking me close in one smooth tug. Our foreheads bump together with a jolt that might've been painful if I could feel anything except shock. My lips are still half-parted on a word I can no longer remember. All I can think about is the hairsbreadth of space that separates my mouth from Soren's.

I wait for him to close it, to crush his lips against mine.

He doesn't.

When I manage to peel my attention from his mouth, I look directly into his eyes. They are pure silver, like starlight shining on the sea. Our breaths mingle in the space between our faces, both of us breathing like we've just run the length of the ramparts.

"Is there something you wanted from me, skylark?" he whispers, so close I feel each word form before it reaches my ears. "Another lesson? A bit of insight?"

He will not be the one to make this leap, I realize as I hold his stare. He has made all the rest. This one—this choice—will have to be mine. With that realization, I shift slightly forward and, as I do, I allow my maegic to shift as well.

My mind brushes his, a hopeful question; his brushes back, an irrefutable answer.

The one I want.

The one I need.

Yes.

I surge forward even as he pulls me in. Our mouths meet with shocking urgency. And, just like that, Soren is kissing me. A kiss I have no words for, a kiss that is the opposite of everything I thought I knew about passion. Not the violent combustion of pent-up need, not the unstoppable flare of lust, but something else. Something deeper. A kiss so deep, I could swim in it forever and still never reach the bottom.

Pretenses fall away as our maegics meld together. Water and wind, air and ocean. We sink into each other, a deliberate drowning. Fast as a riptide, I am lost. Lost in the sea of him, infinite and all-encompassing.

He is just as lost. I can feel his unfettered need for me, the unfathomable scope of it, as he hauls me flush against him. His fingers dig into my skin, gripping me tighter—one hand collaring my neck, the other anchored at the small of my back. My own hands shake with desire as they lift to his chest, sliding up the strong planes to cling to his shoulders.

I'm shocked by the desperation that swirls inside me, a wild tempest of longing finally unleashed; shocked by how much I want him now that I am at last able to own up to it.

Throughout my life, I had dreamed many times of a deep, dark sea. A dream I'd returned to again and again, for as long as I could remember. Sinking, sinking, sinking. Never quite knowing what I'd find at the bottom. I would wake gasping—tasting brine on my lips, feeling salt on my skin, curious how my mind conjured such a vivid dreamscape. Wondering why, of all my dreams, it was the one I most longed to return to whenever I closed my eyes.

And here it is again. Only this time, I am not asleep. This time, as I sink, I am wide awake. I slip deeper and deeper, losing a bit more of myself with each moment. I should be afraid to lose sight of the shores of logic and reason, should be terrified as reality ebbs out of my grip. But with each devouring stroke of his mouth, Soren breathes life into me. With each drugging touch, he guides me into an abyss from which there is no end.

I do not want an end.

The dams have broken wide, unleashing a flood that soon carries us away. We are both caught in the current, unable to stop as we finally allow ourselves to taste, to touch. Indulging in fantasies long forbidden from even entering my waking thoughts. I feel less in control of my body than I was the night he fought back the tsunami, when his power pulled me to him; less in command than I was in the leylines, when I felt the tug of something—*someone*—familiar amid the oblivion.

I do not recall moving, yet here I am on his lap, my arms wrapped tight around his shoulders, my knees straddling him. When I feel the rigid length of his desire pressed against the sensitive heart of mine, my hungry whimper breaks the kiss.

"Skies, skylark," he rasps, mouth moving to my neck. His teeth scrape down the column of my throat. He nips sharply at my collarbone then kisses away the sting, sending a shiver through my bones. His lips curve in a smile when he feels it. As they skate lower, I arch against him, pressing as close as physically possible. In this moment, if I could climb inside him, I think I would do it.

I cannot prevent my hands from clinging to his nape as his mouth moves between my breasts, nor can I stop the shocked gasp that erupts from my throat as he begins to trace the spirals of my Remnant mark with the tip of his tongue, a devilishly slow exploration that makes me feel like I might combust.

"Soren, that's—" I moan. My airway is suddenly too tight to speak; I shift to mind-to-mind. *"That's sensitive."*

"Oh, I know."

He moves with startling quickness, flipping me over onto my back. I blink up at the full moon for a second, my sluggish mind trying to orient itself. My hand flies out, reaching for him— hating the sudden loss of his mouth, his touch, his scent. His grin is a white flash in the dark as he takes in the sight of me sprawled across the steps of the sea organ. But the look on his face changes as his gaze lingers on my body. Growing predatory with intent, it pins me in place as effectively as a set of shackles the moment before he strikes.

The sodden hem of my gown drags through the swells of the incoming tide, the salt no doubt ruining the perfect silk, but I cannot bring myself to care as Soren's hands bunch in the fabric, shoving it up over my parted knees. He kneels between them, hands skimming up the sensitive skin of my inner thighs, mouth trailing in their wake. He takes the thin material of my undergarments in his grip and, with one tug of his strong fingers, tears them clear off my body. Blindly, he tosses them into the waves.

"What are you—"

My mind fragments into pieces as he kisses me in a place I've never before been kissed, a place I did not even know one *could* be kissed. The pleasure is blinding. A volt of pure lust arcs through me. I bow up off the steps, an involuntary squirm, but his hands lock onto my hips, holding me firmly in place as he begins to feast on me like a starving man.

Gods, I'm about to shatter and he's only just begun.

My desire densifies the air around us, an electrical charge building in direct relation to the relentless pleasure he is inflicting, lash by lash, stroke by stroke, until I fear I will unleash a storm of electricity.

"*Soren,*" I cry. "*Soren, I'm going to—*"

"*Let go, skylark.*" His inner voice is raw with lust. His mouth never stops its delicious torture between my legs; if anything, it grows more ravenous. "*Let go.*"

His teeth clamp down, a sudden spike of sensation, and I explode into a violent release. The moment I do, bolts of lightning streak across the midnight sky overhead, a jagged display of power I do not even see, as my eyes are closed. His name sings down the bond again and again, harmonizing with the low song of the sea that vibrates from the pipes beneath us.

My blood continues to pound as the intensity of what has just occurred starts to wane, as the aftershocks of lust clear from my mind. Soren is still between my legs, pressing kisses to my inner thighs, when I manage to open my eyes to the moon.

"*Did I tell you I like your dress?*"

A startled laugh bursts from my lips. "No," I whisper aloud. My voice sounds as staggered as I feel.

"*I do.*" His inner voice slides through my head like the silk he so easily ripped into scraps. His eyes are bright as he comes up over me, one hand planting on the marble step beside my head, the other hovering just above my face, tracing the outline of my lips with one finger. "*Though I am eager to see what you look like out of it.*"

I crane my neck as his mouth comes toward mine, ready for the kiss, ready for more. So much more. His lips have scarcely pressed down when a keening toll blares overhead, stilling us both instantly.

The beacons.

For one frozen moment, neither of us moves.

"Something's wrong," Soren mutters, scooping me up and

setting me on my feet at the top of the steps. "Something's happened."

Together, we run back into the city.

WE SMELL THE smoke before we see the blaze.

Slamming to a halt at the edge of the canal, I cannot believe my eyes. The floating market is on fire, each barge engulfed entirely in flames. Civilians are running for cover. Vendors scream as their livelihoods are reduced to ashes. Some toss bucketfuls of water, but their efforts have little impact. The inferno is raging out of control.

Soren looses a low oath as he takes in the scene. His maegic surges, a potent current, as he draws up vast quantities of water from the canals and douses the barges. The fire splutters out with a crackle and a hiss.

I exhale in relief.

The panicked screams subside as those gathered along the edges of the market watch the rise of steam that drifts into the cloudless night. It is a bleak sight—most of the colorful barges blackened with soot, their proud banners naught but cinders. Only hours ago, I was here with Farley, Jac, Mabon, and Cadogan, sampling delicacies, spending coin, calling merrily to passing boats . . .

"How did this happen?" Soren asks one of the vendors, eyes roaming the wreckage. "This is no natural fi—"

His question stops short as a guttural bellow pierces the night—a cry of victory, and of vengeance. My eyes seek out the source of the sound and go wide when they find it. Standing atop the bridge that spans a nearby canal are two men with flaming torches held aloft. They are bare chested, their skin streaked with something dark.

Dirt?

Paint?

I cannot tell from this distance.

They stare at us for several frozen seconds, their eyes locked on Soren.

"For Shadowfall!" one of them screeches, tossing his torch into the canal. With a hiss, it extinguishes instantly. His companion follows suit. Then, before the tendrils of my wind or Soren's water can ensnare them, the two men pull daggers from their belts, lift them to their necks, and draw the blades across with harsh finality.

Blood spurts as they fall, dead, to the bridge.

A collective gasp ripples around the market.

"What the hell was that?" My eyes fly to Soren. *For Shadowfall?"*

He looks utterly grave. His gaze moves to mine for a brief moment. He says just one word—but that one is enough to freeze my heart in the cold grip of fear.

"Efnysien."

I have questions, but there is no time to ask them. We run to the bodies as fast as our feet can carry us. For once, it is Soren who struggles to keep pace with me. My heels have wings tonight.

He kicks at one of the corpses, confirming it is truly dead as I drop into a crouch to examine the other. They are mortal, judging by their rounded ears. Every inch of their skin is streaked with dark, dried fluid. Not dirt or mud . . .

"Is that paint?"

"Blood," Soren mutters.

My nose wrinkles as I bend closer, inhaling the sharp, metallic scent. It wafts off the corpses like strong cologne. Definitely blood.

A lot of it.

It does not take long to check the bodies; they are not wearing much of anything, barefoot and bare chested. Nothing of value in the pockets of their thin breeches, no sigils stitched into the fabric.

"How did they get in?" I look up to the ramparts, seeking signs of an attack. All appears quiet and still atop the walls. "Did they breach the sea gate? Or sneak in on a merchant ship?"

Soren's head shakes. "Every arrival has been accounted for, every manifest inspected multiple times."

"Then I don't understand . . ." My heart is racing. Something is not adding up here. "Why set fire to the market? And why kill themselves? Is it some sort of message?"

Overhead, the beacons continue to sound despite the fact that the fire is out. Soren's eyes shift up to the royal grounds, narrowed to pinpricks. As though he is trying to pull something into sharper focus. I do not know what he is looking for, what he is sensing . . . Not until I see the shadow of fresh smoke snaking up toward the stars. Not until I feel the rush of fury burning down the bond.

Pendefyre.

Soren and I look at each other, both feeling it. Both fearing what it means. Without another second of hesitation, we take off running again.

THE FIRE AT the floating market was a diversion, designed to cause chaos, to shift focus from the true target of this attack. And it worked. For at the first sight of flames, every member of the Hylian Guard went running to help . . .

Leaving the royal grounds undefended.

My heart pumps with dread as we sprint up the many sets of

steps, passing darkened villas, winding through silent olive groves. Smoke thickens the air as we ascend. The fire is close now.

But what is burning?

My eyes go wide as the stables come into view. They are ablaze, a raging inferno. I hear the sound of equine fear—neighs and snorts of distressed Paexyri—along with Yara's voice, yelling in the night. I want to stop, to offer my help.

I cannot.

Not now.

Both Soren and I feel Penn's burning wrath and know, without a spoken word, that whatever horrors are unfolding before his eyes far exceed a few smoldering stalls. This blaze is more than likely another diversion, designed to pull attention from the wedding feast.

We run on past the dark silhouette of Arwen's villa on the cliffside. As we cut through the lemon grove, we pass by two dead bodies lying face up on the path. They, like the ones we saw on the bridge, are covered in blood. I am again struck by the sheer amount of it as we leap over them. It is not applied in careful stripes, like the Reavers' black warpaint; they look as though they've fully submerged themselves in it. Their lips and eyelids are coated, along with every bit of visible skin.

Some strange intimidation tactic?

An odd form of camouflage?

It makes no sense.

Racing up the steps toward Soren's villa, taking them three at a time, we hurtle into the gardens—and into a scene ripped from my darkest nightmares.

CHAPTER
TWENTY-SIX

Everywhere I look, I see corpses—lying amid overturned tables, bleeding onto plush floor cushions, staring sightless at the skies from the abandoned dance floor. Most of them are enemies, their blood-streaked skin and sliced jugulars giving them away. But several of the fallen are clad in the blue-gray colors of Daggerpoint. A handful of others are navy-uniformed Hylians, swords still clutched in their slackened hands.

Melité helps a battered Tethys onto a chair. Someone has tied a makeshift tourniquet around her upper arm. Mabon wipes blood from a gash over his eyes, Cadogan at his side. On the grass, Harpina clutches her lovely dancing companion close against her chest. Her tears fall, an endless torrent, onto the woman's death-stilled features. Her wail of grief is a lance that goes straight through me. Bretiax squats next to her fellow Paexyrian, stroking her short blond hair with breathtaking gentleness.

Fresh horrors greet my eyes wherever they land. The more I see, the thinner my sense of morality grows.

Someone should pay for this.

Someone will *pay for this.*

I search the sea of slaughter for an enemy to battle, my body taut with the need to exact retribution. But there are no enemies left alive. Floral centerpieces crunch beneath my sandals as I run blindly forward, seeking familiar faces in the crowd. Where is Farley? Where is Jac? Where are Alaric and Arwen and—

"Rhya!" Penn is suddenly there before me, cupping my cheek with one callused hand. His other still grips his broadsword, which glows red from his battle-fury. "Gods, you're safe. You're here." He exhales roughly, not quite able to hide his panic. "When I arrived and did not see you, I feared the worst."

"I'm fine. I'm not harmed." My voice wobbles. "Farley? Jac?"

"I told Farley to stay behind, but he insisted he was sober enough to help. He made for the stables to help put out the fire." He shakes his head. "I haven't seen Jac."

"What happened?"

"I was not here. I did not see it happen. I heard the screams from the guest villa's terrace and came running to find the wedding party under attack by these blood-covered mongrels. Half of them took their own lives before I had a chance to drive my sword through their guts."

"We saw the same down in the city." I steal a glance at Soren, who stands a few paces away. He is still. Eerily still. Like the withdrawn sea before a devastating tidal wave. Tamping down my simmering worry, I force my eyes back to Penn. "I still don't understand where they all came from . . ."

"The portal."

We all turn at the quiet boom of Vaughn's voice. As he exits the dark garden I gape, seeing the blood sprayed across his face.

"Are you—"

"Not mine," he says grimly, square chin jerking. "Smashed a few heads together before they could do more damage." His eyes shift to my side, where Soren is standing. He wastes no time in explaining. "They came through the bathhouse. Tore out of it, a great flood of them. At least twenty, by my count. We weren't prepared." His voice is blunt. "How could we be? It's not possible. It wasn't before, anyway . . ."

Something very deadly is emanating from Soren. Something so vicious, so violent, it makes my soul quiver.

Still, he says nothing.

"These men are mortal," I interject, shaking my head as confusion crashes through me. "I thought portals only worked for high fae?"

"The blood," Soren grits out, teeth clenched.

I blink. "What?"

"They're covered in it, head to toe. They must've bathed in it just before they stepped through. A coating thick enough to mask them."

"All twenty of them?" That must've taken a huge amount of blood. Barrels and barrels of it. "Wherever did they get so much?"

His jaw is set like stone. "Whoever they drained must've been of a very strong bloodline. Strong enough to deceive a portal. Strong enough to carry them through from Dymmeria."

"*Dymmeria?*" Penn roars. Sparks fly from his fingertips, skittering across the dance floor. "Do you mean to tell me this is Efnysien's doing?"

Vaughn does not look surprised, only grimmer and grimmer as Soren nods. "This is my stepbrother's handiwork, of that I have no doubt. The men who set the floating market ablaze took their own lives, but they shouted something first."

"For Shadowfall," I whisper.

"A rallying cry for the uprising of Efnysien's dark army." Soren's hands curl into fists at his sides, as though he does not trust himself to move without striking something. "A second Cull. One aimed directly at the Northlands, with the intent of eradicating fae kind once and for all."

Penn is breathing hard.

"Just what we need. More godsforsaken blood purists." Vaughn spits on the corpse lying a few paces away from us. "Wish there were more to kill . . ."

"Where is Arwen?" Soren's eyes cut like blue blades around the carnage, seeking out his sister. "It is unlike her not to be here barking orders."

Vaughn shrugs his massive shoulders. "I don't know. I lost sight of her in the havoc. I'm sure she's around somewhere."

Soren looks to Penn, who shrugs, then swings his gaze around until it lands on the siren sisters. "Melité! Where is Arwen?"

"Can you not see Tethys is injured?" she sneers, affronted. "Why, of all your sisters, is Arwen the only one who merits your attention?"

He ignores her. A crease of displeasure appears between his brows as he returns his attention to Vaughn. "She's likely at the stables—"

"She's gone."

I whip around at the fractured rasp from behind me. My heart quails at the expression on Alaric's handsome face. He looks totally broken. A shattered shell of the man who, only hours ago, punched the sky in victory as he wed his love before the whole city.

"What do you mean, she's gone?" Soren takes two strides toward him, hand flying out to fist in his gold-embossed tunic. He shakes him lightly. *"Where the fuck is she?"*

Alaric does not even seem to notice he is being shaken. His eyes are farseeing, his face a blank. "They took her. Those blood-soaked men. Hauled her away, through the portal." He holds up his hands; they are streaked with gore, the knuckles bruised and swollen. "I fought them. *We* fought them. But there were so many, and they . . ." His head shakes, as though he cannot quite believe what he is saying. As though he would do anything to wake from this nightmare he is living. "It was clear from the first moment that she was who they were after. The rest of this—all this butchery—is gratuitous. He wanted *her*. He has always wanted her." The apple of his throat bobs roughly. "And now he has her. *He has my wife.*"

Soren releases his grip, hands dropping woodenly to his sides. He is frozen, incapable of speech, incapable of comforting the man who is falling apart in front of him. Not while he himself is doing everything in his power to keep from doing the same.

It is Vaughn who moves close, his thick arms that wrap around Alaric's quaking frame, his deep voice that speaks assurances I fear none of us, standing there watching, truly believe.

"We will get her back, Alaric. We will get Arwen back."

"How?" Alaric whispers, a strangled plea. "We do not even know where they have taken her."

Soren flinches, just once, then starts moving, his long strides carrying him across the ruined feast so fast I have to run to catch him. I do not understand where he is going until I see the sets of bloody footprints that lead away from the dance floor, smudging the flagstones. Signs of a struggle; signs of an unwilling captive being dragged away into the dark.

A lump of nerves turns my stomach to lead as we follow the trail down the path, deeper into the lush gardens, passing broken palm fronds and another dead enemy with a throwing star embedded in his eye socket, pausing only when we reach the narrow bridge to the bathhouse.

"You do not have to go in there," I tell Soren quietly.

But he is beyond hearing. He steps onto the bridge, heedless of my words.

"Soren . . ."

Still, he does not stop. Perhaps he needs to see for himself. With no other choice, I follow after him.

Inside the bathhouse, the evidence of struggle is even more apparent. Two more bodies, one with Alaric's gold-hilted dagger still protruding from his gut, lie on the white floor. Their blood seeps into the crystal, staining its luster. There was not much furniture to wreck, but the little that was inside is in pieces—the teak footstool fractured to splinters, the mirror smashed into sharp fragments, the delicate vanity tipped over on its side, sending myriad bottles of bath oil and scented petals across the floor.

Arwen put up quite a fight.

Smears of fresh blood—hers, I think—color the base of the wall. Not a deadly amount, but definitely enough to activate a portal. It is no longer aglow, already dormant after their ruthless departure. By now she could be anywhere in Anwyvn. There are no clues about where she's been taken, no handy maps left behind by the perpetrators with locations circled in red ink.

Soren's face is pale, almost gaunt. I want desperately to comfort him, to make him the same promise Vaughn made Alaric: that we will get his sister back. But I cannot bring myself to lie to him.

Before I can summon a single word of consolation, a gasp sounds from among the bodies across the bathhouse. One of them is still alive. In a blink, Soren is looming over him, one hand around his throat, squeezing so hard I think he will crush the man's windpipe.

"*Where is she?*"

A wheeze rattles from between the man's teeth.

"*Where have they taken her?*"

"Soren!" Dropping to his side, I yank his arm. It does not budge. "Soren, he cannot tell you anything if he is dead!"

His chokehold only tightens.

The blood-crusted face of our enemy is contorted in pain, whether from the grip at his throat or the blade in his gut. But his eyes are alert as they glare up at us through narrow slivers. He wheezes again as his life force flickers under Soren's unwavering strength.

I try again to pull him back, without success. No amount of tugging makes impact. He is too angry. Reaching inward for my maegic, I send razor-thin tendrils of wind swirling around his arm, twining around his fingers. One by one, I peel them back until he has no choice but to release.

The moment his hold breaks, his eyes snap to mine. I watch clarity wash back in, reason replacing the revenge that very nearly swamped him. He looks startled by his own slip.

"*I will handle this,*" I tell him, mind to mind. "*Trust me.*"

He gives a shallow nod and, with great effort, backs off enough for me to take over. My shoulders stiffen as I lean forward, aligning my face with the dying man's.

"You will die soon," I tell him, voice surprisingly steady. "Whether that death is quick and painless or long and drawn out remains to be seen."

Understanding flickers beneath the haze of pain in his eyes.

"Where did they take Arwen?"

He does not answer except to grin at me. His teeth are red; his mouth is full of blood. He does not have long to live.

I grab the handle of the dagger that protrudes from his stomach and begin to twist it slowly. His grin vanishes instantly, replaced by an agonized grimace. His shrieks reverberate across the round walls of the bathhouse.

"Like I said," I continue, voice very calm. "It is your choice how you meet the skies. I am a healer. I could remove this blade and stitch your guts back together—not enough to save your life, but enough to prolong it." I smile at him as the lies spill out, a terrifyingly cold grin that matches the frigid feeling at my Remnant. "Would you like that? To remain in this state for days? For weeks?" I bend closer, eyes never leaving his. "I don't believe you would."

He huffs a pained breath. There is panic in his stare as it shifts over my features, judging whether I am lying. I reach again for the handle—

"The Iron Isle," he chokes out, the words gurgling up his blood-filled throat. "But she will be dead," he croaks, using his last strength, "long before you . . . ever breach it . . . fae scum."

Soren stiffens.

"Thank you," I whisper, sending out more tendrils of maegic. Pulling every bit of air from his lungs. Watching his eyes turn bloodshot as he quickly suffocates. "For your cooperation."

His body twitches, then stills.

He is gone.

I sit back, forcing my eyes to Soren. I look for condemnation in his gaze, for traces of disgust at my brutality . . . and find not even a shadow of it.

Morality is well and good, as lodestars go, he told me once. *Shame, on the other hand, is not.*

I am not ashamed of what I've done. I am not ashamed of who I am becoming. Not anymore. And it seems . . . neither is Soren. His eyes are steady, holding a subdued shade of the same pride I saw when I wielded my lightning whip.

We stare at each other in the loaded silence for several long moments. He does not say a word, merely offers me a hand and helps me to my feet. He holds tight as we leave the bathhouse behind and make our way back to tell the others what we've learned.

THE DEAD OUTNUMBER the wounded, but I do what I can for those in pain. It is, in a way, good that I have so much experience with the aftermath of battle. I go to that detached place in my mind born from years of training, where all that matters is the task at hand: wrapping wounds, checking pulses, stitching gashes. I see to Mabon, then Tethys, then several injured Hylians, not looking up until I feel Pendefyre's heavy presence at my back.

"Rhya. Come with me. Jac's asking for you down at the stables."

"Is he all right?" I ask, instantly panicked.

His nod is short. His grave expression does not shift. "Yes. But . . ."

"What is it? What's happened now? Surely this night cannot get any worse . . ."

Penn's lips flatten to a frown, a wordless contradiction.

I cast one last glance at Soren, who is on the terrace conferring in hushed tones with Alaric and Vaughn, as Penn leads me away from the villa. My trepidation grows as we walk down the stone steps to the stables. Or, what remains of them. Farley is there, sitting in the dirt, looking dazed but unharmed. Jac's arm has been wrenched out of its socket and his face is pale with pain. He will need a sling once I fix the dislocation. But that will have to wait, for . . .

Gods, no.

My eyes fix on the body that lies between them, her vacant eyes staring up at the skies. Her soul has fled there already.

"No, no, no," I breathe, rushing forward. I fall to my knees at her side, take her cold hand in mine. "Thisobei . . ."

Of all the Paexyrian, I knew her least. Still, the loss weighs heavily on me as I stare at her face, once so prone to impish smiles, now forever still.

"Rhya."

My tear-glazed eyes attempt to focus on Jac. "Y-yes?"

"You need to see to Yara." His eyes, always so playful, are deadly serious. "You need to get her to . . . move away."

I do not understand. Not remotely. But I nod and rise to my feet, following the sound of ragged breathing until I find her sitting in the darkness at the center of the grazing fields. There are several bodies littered around her—Efnysien's blood purists, gutted without mercy during an earlier skirmish.

Umyr's head rests in her arms.

I weep as I see the beautiful chestnut bay Paexyri no longer breathes. Her vast wings are flattened against the ground, her thick mane limp and lifeless. Her glossy, intelligent eyes are unseeing. The blood that seeps into the earth from the death wound at her flank is silver as the moonlight that shines down upon us.

"Oh, Yara."

She does not look up at me as my voice breaks on her name or as I drop into the dirt by her side. Her hand continues to stroke Umyr's velvet nose, so tender it tears my heart.

"She stepped in front of a blow meant for me."

I flinch at the raw grief in her voice.

"Meant for *me*," she whispers again, quieter.

"Yara—"

"I wish they had killed me instead." Her throat is thick with tears. "I wish I was the one lying here, and she was still flying high, guiding my soul into the aether."

My head shakes back and forth as tears track down my cheeks. "Do not say such things, Yara."

"Why not? It is the truth."

"Do not wish for death. Not ever. No matter what." Tentatively, I reach out and lay my hand atop hers, stilling its constant motion with a soft squeeze. "Life is the most precious gift we are ever given. To squander it would be a waste. To stop living in the face of loss . . . it does a disservice to those who are no longer here with us. Umyr would not want you to follow her into darkness."

"I do not know how to live without her. There is no meaning with her gone."

How do you find the words to say goodbye to a love so great, there seems no purpose existing without it? How do you carry on, knowing the rest of your days will be only the palest shadow of something extraordinary?

You do not.

You cannot.

I have no wise words to offer her, no comfort that will ease the pain of such a loss. I can only wrap her in my arms, holding her as she holds Umyr, and let her tears dampen my skin until, at long last, they run dry. When she looks up at me, eyes red rimmed with desolation, her words are a vow.

"I will avenge her." She rattles out a broken exhale. "Even if it takes my final breath to do it, I will strike down those who took her from me. So help me gods."

I GLANCE AROUND Soren's kitchen. We are a macabre group. The mood is decidedly somber. We have suffered unexpected losses. Faces flash in my mind. *Thisobei, Umyr, Arwen.* Many are wounded, not only bodies but souls. The sound of Thisobei's winged dapple-gray mount rends the sky as she flies in low loops above the royal grounds, mourning the loss of her rider. Atyr's deeper brays reverberate along with hers, an unbroken refrain that makes all of us wince each time it fills the heavens.

I have never heard a Paexyri in the throes of grief before. I pray I never will again.

"We embark at first light." Soren's voice is matter-of-fact. "Two ships. Should one be unable to continue, the other must carry on."

"Why can't you portal there?" Mabon asks quietly. "Wouldn't it be quicker?"

"Would that we could. There is no portal on the island. They will have taken her somewhere in Dymmeria first, then moved her to the prison. There is no way onto the Iron Isle except by boat."

"My fleet is fastest," Alaric offers. His eyes appear only partially focused on the room around him. "I will have my men prepare our two best brigs. Anything that can be off-loaded will be, to lighten the load."

Soren nods. "We will not need the cannons. This mission will be one of stealth and speed."

"Maybe keep one cannon," Vaughn mutters, scratching at his blood-crusted beard. "Just in case."

Jac scoffs.

"The roiling surf around the prison makes anchorage impossible," Soren says. "See here?"

We all bend close as he taps one finger against the huge map he's unfurled across the tabletop. It shows the entire eastern coast of Anwyvn, from the mist-cloaked cliffs of Prydain to the protruding Daggerpoint peninsula, down the jagged length of Eastwood and, finally, to the deathly black shoals that surround Dymmeria. Off the southeastern coast of that dark kingdom, there is an island—hardly more than a dot of ink, to my eyes—drawn amid ferocious brushstrokes that indicate an especially turbulent sea.

"Someone will have to remain behind on the ships while the rescue party makes landfall. Alaric, you're a skilled skipper, perhaps—"

"No." The blond man shakes his head, a flat rejection. "I'm going ashore."

Soren does not push him. "Fine. We will have only minutes to get in, get Arwen, and get back out. The prison will be heavily guarded by Efnysien's men, if not he himself. And, if I know my stepbrother the way I think I do, it will also be fortified with some unpredictable surprises."

I don't want to know; I ask anyway. "What sort of surprises?"

"His youthful fondness for cruel pranks has blossomed into a proclivity for decoys and booby traps designed specifically to take lives." Soren runs a hand through his hair. "Trick doors, false walls, concealed blades designed to cut an unsuspecting victim in two . . ."

A foreboding silence descends.

"Oh, is that all?" comes Jac's sarcastic mutter.

"No," Soren says, very serious. "It is not. They do not call it the Iron Isle without cause. The bedrock is thick with ore. It will weaken anyone with even a drop of fae blood running through their veins."

The collective foreboding intensifies.

"A perfect maegical prison," I murmur.

"Precisely." Soren's lips flatten into a frown. "Our powers will likely not be at full potential while we are ashore." His attention shifts to Penn briefly. "Especially those of us who are not naturally at ease surrounded by water."

Penn's eyes smolder. "Worry about your own weaknesses. I will handle mine."

For the next few moments, we all study the map as Soren lays out specifics of the plan. How best to conceal our initial approach, where he thinks he might be able to calm the roiling surf so we can row ashore, what time we will have the best chance at infiltration without tipping off the guards.

I stare at the faded parchment, wishing I felt half as confident as he sounds. The Iron Isle is a seven-day sail from Hylios with good wind. And the wind in the Endless Ocean is notoriously finicky. Ships can get stuck in the doldrums for days, even weeks, on end.

Arwen does not have weeks.

She may not even have days.

But none of us speak of that as we discuss ideas and walk through possible outcomes, laying out contingencies and exit strategies with the limited intel available to us. What little we know about the prison's interior layout—painstakingly sourced by Soren's best spies over the last half century—is outdated at best, inaccurate at worst.

"I want to make it clear, this is a voluntary mission." Soren pauses to glance around at everyone gathered. "I cannot guarantee any of your safety should you choose to take part."

"She's my sister." Vaughn sounds affronted. "I'm coming along."

"Me, too," Yara puts in. Her face is a portrait of fury. "Not just for Arwen. For Umyr. For Thisobei."

"And for my Kazia." Harpina's eyes shimmer with unshed tears as she whispers the name of her lover.

Bretiax signs her agreement.

I clear my throat. "I'm in, too."

Jac, Farley, Mabon, and Cadogan keep silent, their attention on their king. They cannot—will not—agree if he does not. But their expressions clearly communicate that they have no desire to stay behind while the rest of us sail straight into the jaws of danger.

Penn meets Soren's eyes, holding them for a long time. No one seems to breathe as we wait for him to give his decision.

"Dyved sails with Llŷr," he says firmly. "We are allies in this war, whatever form it takes."

I let out a long sigh, undeniably relieved.

"Besides . . ." The dark flames in Penn's stare leap higher as he continues. "I would not squander a chance to introduce your stepbrother to the length of my blade, should the opportunity present itself."

"You will have to beat me to him," Vaughn cuts in, grinning wolfishly.

Soren expels a breath. "If we are all in agreement—"

"I shall sail with you."

We all turn as one toward the archway where Melité stands watching us. Her eyes gleam solidly black as she glides into the kitchen, hips swaying with preternatural grace. Even from across the room, I hear Cadogan's abrupt intake of air.

"Melité." Soren's lip curls with distaste at just the sight of her. "You are not trained for combat."

"So? You expect me to stay behind, doing nothing? One of my sisters is in captivity," she hisses, hostile. "Another is gravely injured."

That is a bit of an exaggeration. I tended Tethys myself and, while the slice to her arm is deep, it closed easily with the help of a few stitches. She will heal quickly.

"I will be on that ship at dawn." Melité's gills flare as she huffs. "You cannot stop me. And you may, in fact, find yourself grateful for my presence. For while *your* powers may be weakened by the ore of that prison . . . mine are not."

"She has a point," Vaughn mutters, grimacing. "The guards can't very well pick up their blades if they're clutching their cocks, caught up in the thrall of siren song."

Cadogan makes a choking sound.

Mabon claps him soundly on the back until he resumes breathing.

"Fine," Soren growls, voice threaded with annoyance. "Then I will see you all at first light. Gather your weapons and get some sleep, if you can. We will not have much time to rest once we are underway."

THE PERVASIVE QUIET of my bedchamber is punctuated only by the occasional brays of desolate Paexyri. Each time I hear them, my heart pangs. I know they will not stop until the funeral rites on the cliffside are concluded. Until the pyres for Thisobei and Umyr flicker out, their souls returned to eternal flight in the aether.

Everyone dispersed after the meeting broke up, heading to their respective quarters to prepare for departure, or tending to their dead. I wonder if the others are able to quiet their minds enough to sleep or if they, too, are plagued by visions of bodies being carried away, of blood being wiped off the flagstones. Of the horrors still to come in the south.

I lay atop my bed, fully clothed in my formfitting gray leather getup—boots laced, daggers holstered, whip coiled. My small pack sits by the door, at the ready. My eyes are fixed on the coffered ceiling as I count down the time until we set sail.

Three hours until dawn.

Two hours.

One.

I swing off the bed, no longer able to remain still, not even for another second. Before I make the conscious decision, I've crossed the chamber, scooped my bag from the floor, and stepped into the hallway. My eyes do not shift from the crystalline doorway at the end of the corridor as I cut a path toward it.

My mind stretches out, seeking Soren down the bond, trying to discern whether he is behind that thick barricade. If he is, I cannot sense him. Not there, not anywhere.

He is blocking me out.

That realization sends a ripple of unease through me. I raise my hands, laying them flat against the warded door. It emits a strong maegical signature, one unique to Soren. Only he can trigger the locks. And yet, as my palms rest against the smooth white surface, the glyphs gouged into its handle begin to glow, pulsating in reaction to my presence.

I do not even consider the consequences of what I am about to do. I send a shot of maegic straight into the slab. Instantly, the door cracks open under my touch.

Strange.

I push it wider, hesitation slowing my movements. The chamber beyond is entrenched in darkness, not a single candle to illuminate it. No one appears to be inside. I know I should turn around, that it isn't right to snoop—especially not in the one place I was warned to stay away from. But I'm already halfway over the threshold . . .

Nerves race up my spine as I step fully inside, allowing the heavy door to swing shut at my back with a low click. The room is large, triple the size of my suite, with a wall of north-facing windows that offer an unmitigated view of the moonlit sea. The furniture is opulent, from the wingback chairs that face the vast stone fireplace on my right to the elaborately carved bed that takes up a good chunk of the floor space to my left. It looks big enough to accommodate a Titan.

In the corner, there are soaring bookshelves stocked with

tomes and trinkets from Soren's many travels, surrounding a cluttered desk where several pots of ink sit beside tidy stacks of parchment. Unlike the rest of the villa, the walls in this room are not covered in artwork. Instead, a single mural spans one entire wall opposite the imposing four-poster bed. In the silver-blue shades of starlight that pour through the glass panes, I cannot make out much in the way of detail. I wander closer, wanting a better look at whatever warrants such a large canvas . . . and feel my mouth drop open on a gasp.

It is a scene of battle.

A scene of pure annihilation, in fact.

The foreground is full of bodies lying on black sand. Fae and mortal alike, tangled together in a tableau of horror. Monsters, too, I see as I peer closer. Arachnidae legs twitch skyward beside putrid white cyntroedi carcasses. Ice giants' hoarfrost hands lie slack with death, still reaching toward the equally large corpses of Titans who've succumbed.

My eyes shift higher, to the center of the frame. In the sky above the carnage, a sole figure fills the tempestuous sky. In her golden armor, she looks like a goddess. I think it is Arianrhod at first, but the hair is too light. Not honey blond, but the pale platinum that flows from my own skull. Blood pours in rivulets from a set of all-too-familiar storm-cloud eyes. And the look on her face . . .

On *my* face.

For it is my face, staring back at me. Impossibly, incomprehensibly, I am staring at a portrait of myself. And judging by the holocaust depicted at my feet . . .

I am no savior.

No, I am the very source of this doom.

Flying high above the grisly battlefield, my arms outstretched to either side as I command six huge tornadoes in the distance.

They cut a terrifying visage of destruction across the background of the canvas, black as the desert sands they pull up into the skies in tremendous funnel clouds.

The longer I stare at the mural, the harder my heart pounds.

It isn't me, I reason. *I have never commanded tornadoes. I do not own gilded armor. I have never done battle on such a scale, never even witnessed one like that . . .*

This is someone else.

It must be.

"So, the skylark found her way inside my cage after all."

I practically jump out of my skin at the sound of Soren's voice. Heart in my throat, I spin around in time to watch him strike a match. It flares in the dark as he lights the candelabra on the end table, illuminating the shadowy corner where he sits in one of the wingback chairs.

"Skies! How long have you been sitting there?"

"Since before you snuck in."

I exhale, flustered. "You should've announced yourself!"

"Forgive me, I thought I was free to do as I liked in my own chambers." A wry note fills his voice. "I will endeavor to make you more comfortable the next time you come snooping in places you were told to steer clear of."

He has a point. I swallow down my embarrassment. "I'm sorry. I know you said this was the one place I was not meant to go, but—"

"Rhya. Relax. I'm teasing you." He crosses toward me slowly. He is fully dressed for departure in obsidian breeches and a fitted tunic with carved stone buttons of the same shade. There is a beautiful silver-hilted sword sheathed across his back. It's the first time I've ever seen him carry a weapon of any kind; he usually relies on his power alone. But that may not be an option on this mission.

The thought makes my stomach clench with anxiety.

His strides are soundless, his voice nearly so. "What are you doing in here?"

"I was . . ." I shake my head to clear it. "I couldn't sleep. I thought you might not be able to, either."

He stops a handspan away. His eyes move from me to the mural and back, and a furrow appears between the dark slashes of his brows. "That, there, is the reason I did not want you in my chambers."

"The mural?"

He nods, jaw tensing.

"Why?" My heart is pounding too fast from what I saw in the painting as well as his sudden proximity. "Why would you not want me to see a piece of art?"

"I knew it would upset you."

"But . . . I don't understand."

"No?"

I suck in a quick breath. "It is not me. It cannot be."

He simply stares at me, saying nothing.

"Soren—"

He cuts me off. "What are you really doing here? You did not come to discuss my artwork or to check if I was resting."

My whole frame rocks back, startled by the sudden shift in topic. "I . . . I . . ."

"Rhya." His eyes trace my features. "There is nothing you cannot tell me. Don't you know that by now?"

My heart flips. I do know that. I think I do. Still, I cannot quite force out the words.

"What's going on inside that beautiful head of yours?" he murmurs, leaning a shade closer, compressing all the air right out of my lungs. His mind brushes mine, inviting a mental connection, but he does not push past my barricades without permission.

"I could not feel you through the bond. Not at all," I admit in a rush. "I was worried, all right? Earlier, you were so upset when you learned about Arwen . . . I wondered if you might . . ." My voice shakes; with effort, I steady it. "Because you were not here when it happened, I worried that perhaps . . . you blamed me."

He stills. "You?"

I give a tiny nod.

"Why the hell would I ever blame you?" His confusion is tempered with anger as his mind races, putting the pieces together before I have a chance to answer. "Ah. Because *he* did. For Fyremas." Soren's scoff is harsh. "He shoved the blame on your shoulders when his were too cowed by his own shame to bear it."

My flinch is apparent, though I try to hide it.

How easily he sees through me. How clearly he reads between the lines of all I do not say, seeing the damage I've internalized before I can even recognize it myself.

Soren's hands find my face, his large palms framing it. He tilts my chin up so I am looking directly into his eyes. They are very blue, even in the dark.

"I do not blame you, Rhya. And while there is a whole list of things I regret about this night . . . what happened with you will *never* be included on it. Not as long as I breathe."

My eyes sting as the weight of those words rocks through me.

His forehead drops down to rest on mine. I think he might kiss me, but he does not. We remain like that for several long moments, simply sharing breaths, until he finally speaks again.

"Efnysien sent his minions to strike at the things he knows matter most to me. The floating market, which is the beating heart of my city. The Paexyri, who are the living embodiment of our oldest maegic. And my sister, my closest blood relation, whom he has always coveted for his own." His fingers flex against my face, then slide deeply into the hair at my temples. "If there is one thing I am grateful for, it is that he does not know the depth of my feelings where you are concerned. For if he wanted to deal me a death blow . . . it is you he would have taken through that portal tonight. It is you he would have stolen away from me."

"Soren—"

His lips close the gap, kissing away my surprised gasp. Kissing me and kissing me and kissing me until all the air is gone from my lungs, until I lose the strength to stand on my own and, knees weak, sink into him like the warmest of seas. He holds me tight against him, hands deep in my hair, tongue sliding between my parted lips to stroke mine. My arms twine around his back as I bow against him, losing myself in the sensations that are crashing through me like a tide.

The pound of a fist at the door tears us apart.

"Soren!" Vaughn pounds again. "The ships are ready!"

My eyes meet Soren's in the dark. The silver striations are brighter than ever. His voice is raw with regret.

"Time to go."

CHAPTER
TWENTY-SEVEN

W hat's the holdup?" Vaughn barks at me. "Sun's rising already. Get your ass on board or I'll toss you up."

I do not doubt he will.

Still, my feet remain rooted to the dock, eyes shifting back and forth between the two black-sailed ships as the first rays of dawn bathe the harbor in shades of palest pink. The rest of our party have already divided themselves neatly into groups, with Soren, Alaric, Vaughn, Yara, Harpina, and Bretiax moving to the first as Penn, Jac, Mabon, Cadogan, Farley, and Melité make for the second.

I alone hesitate, unsure which I'm meant to board.

"Rhya," Penn calls, staring at me from where he's stopped halfway up the gangplank. "Come."

I take a step, then stop. My gaze flashes to the other vessel where Soren stands at the rail, arms crossed over his chest, focus intent on me. He says nothing—not with his mouth, in any case. His eyes are saying plenty.

Across the harbor, the sea gate is ratcheting open in slow degrees, every churn of the waterwheel stirring up more indecision inside me. But suddenly Jac is there, wrapping his uninjured arm around my shoulders and squeezing in reassurance.

"Don't tell me you're scared of a little sailing adventure, Ace. You'll find your sea legs in no time."

"I'm not scared. I thought maybe I'd go on the other—"

"Nonsense. They've got the big man dragging them down already," he continues merrily. He seems no worse for wear despite the sling slanting across his chest. "Can't afford any extra weight."

"I heard that!" Vaughn bellows.

Chuckling, Jac steers me onto the gangplank, straight toward Penn. And my moment of uncertainty is lost.

IT IS A strange voyage.

We sail southward, a pair of sleek, seaworthy brigs with double-masted square rigs and unfussy quarters belowdecks. The sails are unusual in design, dyed deep black to blend in against the night skies, and stitched with glyphs to mirror the midday sunshine during daylight hours. Perfect for a stealth mission.

Normally, ships of this size can accommodate a full score of sailors. But we have no need for additional bodies burdening our holds, nor extra lives that might be put at risk. Our crews are kept as lean as possible, with each allotted only two extra sailors to help heave halyards and navigate through the nights.

Our skipper, to my delight, is none other than Deke, who mans the helm on the upper deck at the stern with a weathered air of expertise I find infinitely comforting as we round the Daggerpoint peninsula, then begin to chart our way to Dymmeria. The rest of us get a crash course in all aspects of nautical travel, taking turns doing everything from preparing sparse meals in the galley to unfurling heavy canvas sails from the booms to scurrying up ratlines to swabbing the salt-crusted decks. We catch sleep when we can, in hammocks or narrow bunks, lulled into a fitful slumber by the endless whooshing of waves against the wood hull.

At night, we take turns at the astrolabe, using the stars as our guide. During the day, we use the spyglass to scan the horizon for anything of note, be it enemy ships from the smoke-hazed Midlands or the sea monsters that supposedly make these waters their home.

I have yet to see evidence of them, despite Deke's warnings. I do, however, see plenty of dolphins, who plunge and prance before our bow with gleeful abandon, their bottle-noses breaking tirelessly through the swells.

It surprises me how quickly I settle into seafaring life. While our mission was born out of joyless necessity, the passage itself unleashes a thrill within me no amount of apprehension can erase. I spend much of my time standing upon the sunny foredeck, soaking in the feeling of wind in my hair, the salt on my skin, thinking of my wild days of youth on the white shores of Seahaven, when life was so much simpler.

Sometimes, Jac or Farley or Mabon stands with me, but more often than not they are otherwise occupied, entertaining themselves up in the crow's nest or wagering over rounds of twyllo or sparring hand to hand on the quarterdeck. As for Cadogan, I do not think his eyes have left Melité for even a moment since we boarded. He trails her like an imprinted duckling, his clear adoration provoking a constant barrage of ribbing from the rest of the men. The siren herself seems slightly amused but mostly indifferent, keeping to her own company most of the time and never lifting a finger to help, be it in furling sails or coiling lines.

That is fine by me.

I have no great interest in befriending Melité. In all honesty, I avoid her whenever I can. Something about her sets my teeth on edge. But even her inky-orb eyes and austere attitude cannot dampen my spirits. At sea, I feel nearly as exhilarated as I did soaring high above the Vale on Zephyr's back, the heavens rushing around me.

Not all of us take to sailing like fish to water. Poor Pendefyre has no affinity for it. He has never been less in his element, for the sea is the antithesis of everything that makes him who he is, a direct assault to the maegic blazing through his veins. To be surrounded by it on all sides is surely as uncomfortable as I feel whenever I find myself entombed in deep earth.

On the rare occasions he emerges from his cabin, he looks rather green, his sea legs shaky, his temper foul. Everyone on the ship gives him a wide berth whenever he comes up for air or, on rare occasions, attempts to stomach a solid meal.

I wish there were something I could do to ease the passage for him, but my presence only seems to darken his mood. It blackens all the more whenever he spots me channeling with the Remnant of Water across the distance. For, though Soren and I are on different vessels, separated by a whole swath of ocean, we spend several hours each day at our respective bows, merging our powers in an effort to lend the ships unnatural speed.

As Soren's maegic churns the currents below, ferrying us ferociously through the waves, mine fills our sails with a wind that never wanes, carrying us along at a clip that stuns even Deke. Our connection has never been so visible, so on display for all to see. Comments are made, and looks exchanged. Our two deckhands, Chari and Xio, avoid me at all costs, muttering superstitions about testing the limits of nature under their breath.

I pay them no mind.

The heavy weight of Pendefyre's eyes on my back is somewhat harder to ignore. There is an unspoken accusation in that stare, a simmering jealousy that, if I let it, might pull my focus from the task at hand. Thankfully, I have Soren in my head to keep me going.

"Steady, skylark. Keep a consistent current. Too much will only shred our sails and leave us stranded."

Alone, I would have faltered after a few moments. But his reserves are far deeper than mine, lasting hours at a time before he breaks away, demanding I stop before I fully deplete myself.

"You need your strength for the Iron Isle. Rest, Rhya. A few hours at least."

I do not want to rest. I'm thrilled with the progress we are making. In combining our powers, we have effectively halved a weeklong journey into a four-day one. Each time the ship slows back to its natural speed, without our maegic to propel it, I'm hit with a wave of disappointment. The plodding tacks upwind feel unbearably slow in comparison.

More than that, though, I miss Soren's presence in my head as I lie in my narrow bunk staring at the cabin's wood ceiling, or sitting in the galley eating flavorless bannocks on a bolted-down stool. Not so very long ago, I chafed against the idea of having anyone inside my head. But now, with him . . .

When we channel across the distance, we are in total sync. In perfect harmony. Sometimes we keep silent, focused only on our task, but more often we speak back and forth through the mental bond to keep each other company during the long hours.

"The sea agrees with you," he tells me halfway through the second night, a smile in his voice.

"Is that a surprise?"

"Not to me." He pauses. *"I cannot speak for others."*

He has not failed to notice Pendefyre's scowls each time he catches sight of us channeling. But I do not want to talk about

Penn. My thoughts regarding the both of them feel like walking on a tightrope—one that will fall out from beneath me with a single wrong step.

My eyes sweep across the night sky, where vibrant whirls of green and blue swirl among the stars. *"They're beautiful."*

"Mmm."

"What are they called?"

"Auroras. The lights of the aether, where the Goddess of Skies meets the God of Seas, and turns the heavens incandescent . . . Or so they say in the old tales."

"Are there tales older than you?" I tease.

"Just wait until you have a century under your belt. Then I will be the one making jests at your expense."

My mind spins at the thought of that. A hundred more years of this. Somehow, the prospect of an immortal life does not seem quite so abhorrent as it once did.

"You know, there was a time you claimed you had no interest in immortality or your role as a Remnant," I remind him. *"If I remember correctly, you declared the prophecy was more than likely some fabricated tale conjured up by a senile oracle who'd spent too long in the opium baths."*

"A statement I stand by, having met the woman."

"What do you mean, you met her?"

"Precisely what I said."

I blink hard. *"You met the oracle who gave the prophecy?"*

"Indeed."

"How?" I ask, stunned. *"And . . . why?"*

"What can I say? I was fifteen years old and curious. I wanted the truth about the prognostication set to dictate my life. So I tracked her down in a paint-spattered temple by the North Sea and demanded an explanation for the rather inconvenient forecast she'd croaked out in the wake of the Cull."

"And?"

"And what?"

Gods, he could be difficult. *"What did she say, Soren?"*

"Nothing that made much sense," he hedges. *"Though my memory may be a shade hazy. Have you ever tried to hold on to your wits in an opium bath?"*

"I can't say that I have."

"Not easy, skylark. Not easy at all." Humor creeps into his voice. *"Though perhaps it's a good thing I do not remember with perfect clarity. That seer looked older than time itself, with wrinkles to match her years . . . and a propensity for walking around in the nude whenever she saw fit."* He pauses. *"Which seemed to be every waking hour of the day."*

I bleat out a laugh. *"Be serious, will you?"*

"If only I were joking." He heaves a mental sigh. *"By the time I dropped in on her, she was addled. Spoke mostly in riddles with no answers. At one time, however, she must've been sane enough. She spent hundreds of years in the emperor's employ, counseling Belenus on all matters before his demise."*

"And yet, she did not see the Cull coming and think to warn him," I say wryly. *"Makes one doubt her gifts."*

"My thoughts exactly."

"Did she tell you anything else? Reveal any more clues about how we are meant to restore the balance, should all four Remnants appear?"

There is a long pause. *"Nothing I comprehended at the time."*

"And now?"

"It's been a hundred and eighty-five years, Rhya. She is dead and gone, her insights with her. Though the memory of her wizened form may never fully fade from my mind's eye . . ."

I do not entertain his attempts to distract me. *"Soren."*

He sighs. *"Yes?"*

"If you are withholding something—"

"Fine. I can admit now that perhaps I was wrong about the prophecy." He cuts me off. *"But meeting a rambling, raving seer was hardly what altered my opinion on our joined fate."*

My brows arch high on my forehead. *"Oh? Then what did?"*

He is silent. Hesitant.

"When we first met, you planned to happily watch the world burn from afar," I pester, undeterred. *"What changed?"*

"I talked to you for ten minutes."

I suck in a breath. *"Me?"*

"You," he says quietly.

Skies.

For a few moments, we continue to channel, saying nothing more. I focus on the wind flowing out of me, a steady current filling the coal-hued sails that furl outward from the square rigging overhead, doing the same for our sister ship across the sea.

A sudden pulse of maegic down the bond catches me off guard. This one is not meant for the waves that thrash at the hull, nor for the deep currents that carry us along. It is exclusively for me, washing straight down the bond and wrapping around my soul. The maegical equivalent of a warm embrace.

A sigh slips from my lips. *"Soren—"*

"I have long despised my fate. I saw it as more a curse than anything, this endless existence," he tells me in a voice devoid of all self-pity. He is purely stating a fact. *"After these last few weeks, I am finally beginning to take a different view of things. I am finally beginning to look forward to an unending lifetime ... for I no longer imagine spending it alone."*

My heart is pounding hard, my knees threatening to give out. Gripping the rail to keep myself upright, I try to cover my own ridiculous reaction with a lighthearted remark. *"Has Vaughn agreed to move to Hylios permanently, then?"*

"Rhya."

"Yes?"

He waits. And waits. And waits, until I have no choice but to give a serious answer. I shake my head in the darkness and offer up the only thing I have: truth.

"You speak of forevers. But forever is a very long time."

He is quiet for a long stretch, processing this. I fear he might sever the connection without saying anything else. But eventually he responds, his inner voice low with meaning.

"There is no amount of time with you that would ever be enough."

There are no words I can muster to equal what he has just said to me. Instead, I send a pulse of maegic back down the bond to him—a soundless affirmation that, I hope, matches the one he gave me.

A moment later, he laughs as I send an errant tendril of wind to ruffle his hair. Even across the dark waves, I can hear his joy echoing to me beneath the green-streaked sky.

ON OUR THIRD day at sea, the strip of coastline that runs along the horizon off our starboard bow changes from the thickly forested tracts of Eastwood to an eerie expanse of peaks and plateaus that jut into the sky like disjointed fingers.

"The Reaches," Soren tells me when I ask. *"See that dark patch, farther south? Where there seems a near constant cloud cover? Those are the Shadow Steppes. The terrain there is nearly impassable. The silt storms never cease, whipped to a frenzy between the bluffs."*

As we sail closer, the air grows denser, the skies above darkening with the promise of inclement conditions. I cast nervous glances upward as we sweep along choppy blue waters.

If a storm breaks out here . . .

Sensing my tension, Soren strives to distract me. He points out landmarks as we pass by, his words a comforting current in my head, forcing out the anxious thoughts.

"Those high dunes there, off the starboard bow? The Shifting Isles, they're called. Huge shoals of desert sand that change constantly."

"Have you visited?"

"Once, and never again. The nomadic tribes that live there are not overly accepting of strangers." He chuckles. *"I suppose that makes sense. When your territory has a tendency to move overnight, you must fiercely defend whatever claim you manage to stake."*

"People actually live there?" I blink at the hazy island dunes, some nearly as tall as the walls of Hylios, marveling at the thought of such a transient existence. *"It seems mad to live thus, packing up your whole encampment at a moment's notice."*

"Life as a wanderer is preferable to that in the rest of the Southlands, from what I can tell. Just ask those who occupy the Soot Flats of Nythia or the Howling Plains of Carvage."

I think of Carvage, that sprawling, sand-scorched kingdom at the southernmost point of Anwyvn. Once, it was a thick jungle, teeming with life. The most fertile land in all the realm . . .

Until the Cull.

"Is Carvage not the rumored location of the Earth Court?" I ask. *"Or what remains of it?"*

"Yes. I have searched for the ruins several times, without much success. Even before the mortals sacked it, the House of Amaethon was supposedly difficult to find. The most isolated of

the four strongholds and the least accessible, tucked at the heart of Anwyvn's oldest forest. The few tomes I have found on the subject describe a sprawling network of treehouses built into the upper canopy, connected by rope bridges and ladders."

"It sounds enchanting."

"I'm certain it was. Just as I'm certain they thought they were safe there, in their wild jungle. It had sheltered them for millennia. But mortal axes made stunningly quick work of their sacred groves. Catapults spread fires quicker than they could be put out." A low chord of discontent thrums down the bond. *"After they killed every fae they could get their hands on, the invading armies ripped out the jungle by the roots, then salted the earth to prevent anything from ever growing there again. It is now naught but a patch of scarred dirt, barren and lifeless."*

I cannot fathom the amount of hatred it would take to justify such a measure. *"They sought to erase us. Every trace."*

"Some still do," he warns. *"This simmering war will come to a head. And soon. Can you not feel it?"*

I can.

It is palpable in the air as our bows cut through the increasingly chaotic seas that churn off the northern coast of Dymmeria. It is visible in the dark clouds that block out the sun overhead, crackling with distant lightning. For once, I cannot be blamed for the foul weather.

We keep far offshore, though the passage would undoubtedly be smoother closer to the coast. We don't want to be spotted by Dymmerian soldiers stationed inside the many ebony lighthouses that spike up from the black sands at the edge of the desert. Each time we pass within their sight lines, I do what I can to cloak us with mist and fog, borrowing Soren's strength to alter the air's density. It is more difficult than I anticipated, and results in a splitting pain through my temples that threatens to knock me unconscious. I cannot hold it for long, even with his considerable strength shoring me up through the bond.

"Can't say I like sailing in a fogbank," Deke informs me, his peppery hair catching the wind. "But I'm sure I'd like it better than our odds in a sea battle without any cannons aboard."

I laugh to cover my anxiety.

Vaughn was right. We should've brought a cannon or two, speed be damned.

The closer we get to the Iron Isle, the more precarious the seas. Now the fins that slice beside our bows are not the curved dorsals of friendly dolphins but the deadly triangles of sharp-toothed sharks. The delight I'd felt in the wide-open expanse of the Endless Ocean dims to a faint flicker, then disappears entirely.

We are all tense, no longer laughing as we take watch, our eyes peeled to the rough surface for any sign of the shoals that stretch offshore, swept there by the unending sandstorms that rage through the Husk Desert. They are nearly impossible to see, especially at night. We err on the side of caution, for we cannot afford to run aground.

Our speed slows to an infuriating crawl.

"How much longer, do you think?" I ask Deke as dawn breaks on our fourth morning. My eyes flicker west, where Dymmeria bends in on itself like a misshapen horseshoe. The Iron Isle sits somewhere at the center of that curve, but I cannot yet make it out amid the shadowy waters. The sea here is so dark it is very nearly black, the surface only broken by the occasional whitecap of a cresting swell.

"Should be there by dusk, just in time for the late tide." Deke's weathered eyes narrow on the horizon. "Assuming we don't get tripped up by—"

The words are halfway out of his mouth when the quake hits.

The boom sounds from deep within Dymmeria. I do not understand what is happening at first. Not until I see the distant dunes collapsing in on themselves like a pile of sugar heaped too high. Whole mountains of sand shake violently as the earth below trembles with astonishing force. They fall into the sea all at once, an avalanche that causes a splash so high, my heart stumbles inside my chest. It stops entirely when I watch that splash solidify into a solid swell.

A tsunami.

"Infernal hells!" I hear Jac yell from the foredeck where he and Mabon are sparring. *"BRACE!"*

My eyes swing around the ship, taking account of everyone. There is Penn, racing up from the crew quarters, strapping his bandolier across his chest as he moves. There, by the starboard rail, Cadogan is running toward Melité. There, in the ratlines, Chari and Xio are scrambling quickly toward the deck.

Where is Farley?

"Fuck!" His oath is distant. "Oh, fuck me!"

Skies.

He's in the crow's nest, of all places.

"Farley!" I scream. "Get down from there!"

But there is no time. The wall of water barrels straight at us with incalculable speed, roaring like a wild beast. There is no stopping it, though I can feel Soren's maegic surging as he tries his best to stave off its advance from the other ship.

It is too strong, and far too close.

Even for him.

My eyes search for him as I reach out with my own maegic. I will offer him whatever strength I have, I will—

The wave hits, slamming both ships sideways like children's toys in a bathtub, one after the other. Plunging our sails into the water. I lose my footing as the world flips over, pitching me off the deck and into the dark before I have time to draw a full breath. The impact is disorienting, the cold mind-numbing. My body spins out of my control, no match for the raging ocean that tosses us round and round at its whims.

I force my eyes open, ignoring the sting of salt as I look around, trying to get my bearings. Trying to decipher which way is up, which direction to swim.

Where, gods, where is the surface?

My lungs are screaming. The submerged sails float ghostly black in the gloom. Ropes and rigging threaten to ensnare me as I kick blindly, praying my head will break free of the briny waters. By the time I burst into the dim light of day, my head is dizzy from the lack of air. I drag deep gulps into my throat, looking around the frothed surface with frantic eyes. The brig is lying on its side, heavy sails full of water.

"Rhya!" Penn roars somewhere out of sight. "Rhya, where are you?"

"Here!" My voice cracks on the shriek. "I'm here!"

Mabon's bald head breaks the surface not far from me. Near the stern, where the exposed rudder flaps uselessly, I see Cadogan and Melité treading water. Chari and Xio are with them.

I do not see Deke anywhere.

"Mabon!" I yell. "Where's Deke?"

"Here," comes the skipper's gruff reply. "Right behind you."

"I'm here, too, don't you worry about me," Jac grouses from my left, clutching a floating barrel. He looks mad as a wet house cat, his dark blond mane a snarled mess. "Anyone seen Farley?"

"He was in the crow's nest." Treading continuously, I do my best to keep my head above the swells as my gaze traces the length of the mainmast until its tip disappears into the inky waves. "Gods, what if he's tangled up in the rigging? What if—"

"Skies, woman," a familiar voice wheezes. "Don't get hysterical."

The redhead's ornery tones have never been so welcome. I spin around and see him swimming my way from behind several floating wood boxes that were swept off the deck. His auburn curls are plastered against his forehead, but he appears unharmed.

"Farley! Thank gods."

"Thank my fast reflexes, you mean." He scoffs. "If I hadn't jumped clear when I did, I'd have been dragged straight to the bottom."

We all trade relieved glances. The brig is felled, but we are all alive and accounted for. On this ship, at least.

Mabon's thoughts mirror mine. "Wonder how the others fared . . ."

The overturned vessel blocks most of our view. Jac pushes up on the barrel, trying to get higher. "Can't see a thing over these damn swells."

"More importantly," Farley says, grabbing hold of an apple as it floats by and tucking it into his tunic, "how the hell are we going to right the ship?"

"She'll right herself, if you give her a moment," Deke replies. "Her keel is heavy enough to pull her back upright. Or . . . mostly upright. So long as the air-holds aren't compromised, that is . . ."

Even as he speaks, the capsized vessel is straining toward the surface, fighting against the weight of her waterlogged sails with a low shudder I think might snap her masts clean in half.

That will not do.

"Mabon," I murmur. "If I pass out, don't let me sink."

"*What?*" His voice sharpens with alarm. "Rhya, what are you doing?"

Ignoring his concern, I send out several thick tendrils of air that wrap around the booms and twine up the rigging. Then, with a momentous pulse of maegic, I heave them skyward.

The water is unfathomably heavy. Almost immovable.

Still waters do not easily shift, Soren told me once.

How right he'd been. The effort required to raise it more than a handspan at a time leaves me lightheaded and even more breathless than before. Yet as I watch the mast inching slowly out of the water, I cannot stop a smile from spreading across my face.

It's working.

Once I get it started, the ship does the rest on its own—popping back up like a submerged cork in a barrel. Water rains down from the damp sails, hitting the deck in a thunderous downpour. It gushes from the gunnels, seeps out from the rails of the deck, returning to the ocean where it belongs.

Chari and Xio, who wisely clung to the rigging as it sailed upward, wave down at the rest of us from the port rail.

Jac makes a crude hand gesture in return. "Now why didn't I think of that?"

"Because you're a dimwit," Mabon mutters.

Farley laughs.

"Well done, Rhya," Penn says, treading water beside me. I did not even see him swim up, so intent was my focus. "You really have mastered your winds."

I blink at the ragged edge to his voice. "Mastered? Not quite. It's still—*I'm* still—a work in progress."

"But he did this for you. Soren, he—" His jaw tightens briefly, as though it is a struggle to force out the words. "He helped you. His methods, they worked. This time . . . they actually worked."

I nod, feeling strong emotions lash out of him from the bond. I'm quite sure he is thinking of Enid in this moment. Of the last wind weaver they tried to aid, only to find her wild tempests too strong to rein in. The woman he saved from certain death only to lose shortly thereafter. Even after seventy years, the pain of that loss is sharp as a blade. But beneath it, there is something new. Something unexpected.

Undeniable sparks of relief are catching within him.

I am not Enid.

I will not be swept away by my own powers.

And for Penn . . . there is hope in that. Hope for me. Hope for himself. Hope for an entirely different sort of future than the one he has been relegated to, a slave to his own incendiary tendencies.

"I do not know whether I am more awed by your control or envious I do not possess it for myself," he confesses without even a shade of bitterness. His eyes are alight with warmth for the first time in days, a flicker of his old heat. "It's incredible. *You* are incredible."

"Thank you, Penn." I smile tiredly at him. "Ready?"

His dark brows furrow. "For?"

I do not answer verbally. Instead, I use a fresh current of air to boost him straight up out of the sea, onto the righted ship. His surprised shout as he hits the deck makes Jac and Mabon laugh. But their amusement turns quickly to shouts of their own as they, too, are lifted clear of the swells and deposited aboard.

"No offense, but I think I'd prefer to use the ladder," Deke declares, swimming away from me toward the port stern, where Chari and Xio are lowering a rope ladder for Melité and Cadogan to climb up.

"None taken." I grin as I turn to Farley. "And you?"

He grins back at me. "Always wondered what it would be like to fly."

Laughing, I lift him up as gently as I can manage. He whoops the whole time, delighted as a child. As soon as he is settled, I heave myself airborne. I am not properly flying, not really; it is more of an elongated leap. But my heart soars all the same.

The joy is short-lived. The moment I hit the deck, I hear a chorus of panicked shouts ringing in the distance. I run to the opposite rail where the others are clustered, shoulders tense as they stare out at the other ship. It has not fared nearly as well as we did, perhaps because of its closer proximity to the shore. It is still lying on its side, sails fully submerged. And every member of its crew is swimming madly in our direction, arms flailing, faces stricken.

There is Vaughn, his powerful strokes carrying him along quicker than the others . . . Alaric, with his natural swiftness . . . the Paexyrian trio, all together in a line . . .

Where is Soren?

"What are they doing?"

No one bothers to answer Jac's low question, for at that very moment the cause of their rapid evacuation presents itself. We all watch in stunned disbelief as several writhing orange tentacles, each thicker than our central mast, creep up from the surface. Three at first, then four, then six, then eight. They slide sinuously around the prone ship in a deathly embrace . . .

And proceed to squeeze.

The hull splinters with the ease of a matchstick. The resounding crack is enough to make us all jump.

"What is that foul thing?" Penn mutters, moving to stand close behind me. His blade is in his hand. I do not think it wise to point out it will be less than effective against such a massive sea monster.

"An octopaeron," Deke says grimly, making a protective hand sigil in the air. "Let us hope it is satisfied with the offering of one ship and does not turn its eyes this way."

Chari and Xio are muttering an incantation under their breath: a prayer to the God of Seas, pleading for his mercy. Even so, their hands are taking more practical measures—reaching for the tangled rigging so we might pull in our slackened sails and take off at a moment's notice.

The orange tentacles furl over the other ship until it is fully ensconced. The underside of each flexible limb is covered with huge suckers that, once affixed, can rip wood planks and tear through rigging with laughable ease.

No wonder the other crew wants out of the water.

Deke tosses another rope ladder over the starboard rail for them to scurry aboard. Vaughn makes it first, hauling his hulking frame over the side and collapsing against the deck so hard, I think he might smash straight through it. Alaric scrambles up after him far more elegantly.

At the same time, I send out my wind to pluck the Paexyrian from the swells one by one, depositing them onto our ship spluttering and dripping wet. Yara is cursing with a colorful variety that would impress any seaman as Farley helps her to her feet. Mabon does the same for a far less vocal Harpina. And Jac, in a show of uncharacteristic sweetness, fumbles through several rudimentary signs to make sure Bretiax is all right.

I bend far out over the rail, eyes scanning the surface for the rest of their crew. My pulse spikes as the seconds tick by and, still, I see no sign of them.

Deke drops into a crouch beside the sprawling half-Titan. "Where is your skipper?"

"Eaten." Cursing, Vaughn sits upright. "Along with our deckhands."

Farley gasps. *"Eaten?"*

"Unless the bloody red froth that bubbled up after that *thing*"—Vaughn spits the word—"sucked them under was wine . . ."

"And Soren?" I ask, trying to bury the thick streak of fear in my voice but not quite able to manage it.

"Is he not here?" Vaughn is abruptly serious. His head whips toward his brother-in-law. "Alaric, was he not with you?"

"He was at the stern with me, trying to hold back the wave before it struck." Alaric's voice is edged with tension. "I lost sight of him when we went over, but—"

"But what?" I stride closer. "Alaric, *where is he*?"

"The boom clipped him across the chest. He went flying. Cracked his head on the rail just before we capsized."

My heart hits the deck. "And you did not think to check on him?"

"I . . . I . . ." Alaric shakes his head. "This is Soren we're talking about! I have never seen a better swimmer. I figured he'd recover his senses the second he hit the water." His expression drops and he goes pale. "There is no way he is . . ."

Dead.

Gods, tell me he is not dead.

I run back to the rail, watching with horror as the last of the ship is sucked fully under by suctioning orange tentacles. Only a few splintered pieces of wood remain floating amid the swells. I see no bodies among the wreckage. Nothing but black water, everywhere my eyes turn.

Beside me, Penn clears his throat. "Rhya—"

"Shh!"

My maegic spirals outward, seeking Soren. I home in on the feeling of him. His signature—that cool, crisp current; that melodic, mercurial tide.

He is not here. Not at the surface. I search deeper, widening the radius of my sensory pursuit, trying not to allow my increasing panic to interfere.

There.

He is there.

Somewhere deep, somewhere dark.

Sinking down, down, down, like a stone toward the bottom.

In a flash, I am standing on the water-beaded rail. My boots slide against its beveled surface, but I grab the ratlines to steady myself before I pitch off-balance.

"What are you doing?" Penn yells, moving for me.

My eyes cut to his, the look in their depths stilling him in his tracks, then sweep down the line of faces turned up to me in shock.

"I'm going after Soren."

"He's at the bottom of the bloody ocean." Penn's face is a mask of dread. "Rhya, you cannot—"

"I can," I hiss. *"I must."*

His features contort—a flash of pure pain replacing the dread. Awareness floods his eyes as they hold mine for several long beats. For, in that moment, Penn knows. Irrefutably. As he feels my desperation for the man lost in the sea . . . as he sees my determination to save him from the depths, no matter the cost . . .

He *knows.*

The tides of my affection have shifted beyond his grasp. My heart, which once beat solely for him, has somehow changed alliances, surely as the moon reverses the ocean's steady course, irrevocably as a cresting waterfall over the face of a cliff.

I am Soren's in a way I have never been Penn's.

I know it.

I have, perhaps, always known it.

And now . . . so does he.

"Rhya," Deke calls, shattering the moment. "The octopaeron is still out there."

My eyes jerk to the captain's ruddy face. My hand tightens on the rigging. "Yes, it is," I agree in a low whisper. "And if that monster so much as touches Soren, there is no ocean deep enough where it will be able to hide from my retribution."

With that, I jump off the railing.

Into the deep, dark sea.

CHAPTER
TWENTY-EIGHT

I hit the water feetfirst, a breath-stealing plunge into the cold. Into the dark. I do not think about whatever monsters might be waiting for me as I begin to make my way down toward the bottom, kicking and clawing into the abyss.

The desert shoals ensure the sea here is shallow compared to some of the deeper stretches of ocean we have traversed on this voyage, but by no means is it a short swim. And by no means am I the strongest swimmer. The only thing I do have on my side is my maegic. A bubble of air surrounds my head, allowing me to breathe far beyond my lungs' normal capacity. I use the bond like a tether, propelling myself along the current that connects me to Soren.

Deeper, deeper.

Darker, darker.

My head begins to ache from overexertion. I have used so much of my power already, my reserves feel thin indeed. But I cannot stop. I will not stop. Not until I've found him.

Emotions are not a liability; they are a limitless resource, Soren is whispering in my memory, a phantom spurring me on. *You want to wield your power like me? You need to feel it. All of it.*

Panic is my fuel, distress my propellant. I feed them into my wind like kindling to a fire, until my power swirls through my chest in an unstoppable squall. I push on. Past the point of reason, past the point of all endurance, to a place somewhere beyond any previous limit.

He is still alive. I can feel his life force, though it seems to flicker periodically as the moments pass. Diminishing, even as I grow nearer. I speak to him, knowing all the while he cannot hear me in his unconscious state.

"Hold on. Just hold on. I am coming for you."

Only days ago, I asked him if he could drown. He laughed me off. Curse him for not giving me a straight answer. Curse him for his need to always turn things into a jest. Curse him for making me care about him if only to—

No.

No.

He will not die.

I swim harder, though my muscles scream for reprieve. The pressure at this depth is its own sort of entombment. Not quite as bad as being buried beneath the earth, but still distinctly unpleasant. My claustrophobia rears its ugly head, threatening to paralyze me before I make it another fathom.

Ignoring the buzzing at my temples, the thrumming of my heart, I press on. Passing schools of silver-scaled fish and drifting clouds of diaphanous algae.

Deeper, deeper.

Darker, darker.

Until, finally, my hand reaches forward in a blind stroke and strikes sand. At last, I'm at the bottom. I can see next to nothing at this depth. All is in shadow, a blue-green world leached of color. I feel my way to him, pulse roaring so loud inside my head I can hardly hear the ragged pants that come from my mouth on each winded exhale. I shove aside a clump of thick seaweed, plunge past a cluster of debris from the shattered ship, and then—

There.

There he is, floating like a ghost. Limbs deadweight, dark hair drifting in the currents. His skin is so pale it nearly glows. My heart cries out at the sight of him as I swim closer. I claw my fingertips into his tunic and drag his limp body into my arms. It is a struggle. He's heavy, even underwater. Waterlogged like . . .

A corpse.

His heart is not beating.

He is no longer breathing.

How long has he been without breath?

I cannot risk swimming back to the surface with him in this condition. He'll never make it. With a great torrent of maegic, I expand the small bubble of air around my head until it is large enough to contain us both. The weight of the water pushes in from all sides, but I do not waver, shoving it back until we are encircled in a dry sphere on the seafloor.

I take a thin breath. "Soren?" I slap his cheek lightly. "Soren, can you hear me?"

My frantic eyes roam his features, looking for signs of life. There is nothing, not even a flicker. I bring my lips to his, ignoring their lifeless chill, and breathe, forcing air into his lungs. When that does not work on its own, I use my maegic to aid me— flooding his airways, attempting to expel the water he's swallowed.

Still nothing.

His lungs remain unmoving, his heart with them. Our bond is eerily numb. And his life force . . . that remote flare I felt when I first found him here on the bottom . . .

It has sputtered out.

"Soren," I plead, trying again. Tears track down my cheeks, a relentless stream. "Please do not do this."

My maegic is waning, the effort of holding our air pocket intact taking every ounce of my energy. I am very near to passing out. And then where will we be?

Both dead.

"You cannot leave me," I tell him through the bond, forcing more of my maegic into his deathly still lungs. Into the very fabric of his soul. *"I will not let you flee to the skies. They are my domain, and they cannot have you. Do you hear me, Soren? I cannot let you go."*

But he does not hear me.

For he has gone.

Sobs tear at my chest, unchecked. The grief is impossible to swallow, impossible to breathe around. I ignore it, refusing to process the loss. Refusing to accept what it means. If I accept it, that means he is truly dead. Truly out of my reach. Never again to make me laugh or cook me dinner or look at me in that singular way of his that makes me feel as though no one else in the world has ever looked at me before and truly seen me. Never again to wrap me in his arms or press his mouth to my skin or rest his forehead against mine so we might share breaths. Never to be mine in anything but a memory.

No.

Pushing aside those morbid realities, I give more of my maegic. More of my very self. I feel my essence tearing away as I force it into him, feel my own life force rippling like I, too, might turn cold and blue, another corpse on the seafloor. It is not painful. It is something so far beyond pain, I have no words for it. An excruciating cleaving of the very soul.

I am shredding myself apart, bit by agonizing bit. Yet I cannot bring myself to stop. I will claw him back from the brink of death even if the effort takes me along with him.

"Take my breath, take my blood, take my beating heart. My very soul is yours, if only you come back to me."

His body convulses like he's been shocked by a bolt of lightning. Choking and spluttering as water surges up from his lungs, Soren snaps back into consciousness as though he's only been lightly dozing on the sofa in his library, not slipping into the afterlife.

His eyes flicker open, their sapphire depths swirling with incomprehension as he takes in the sight of me looming over him— soaking wet and sobbing, shaking with pain and relief and exhaustion. His chest rattles as he takes his first true breath.

He is breathing.

His shocked gaze shifts around the air pocket I've created, struggling to comprehend the dark sea that surrounds us on all sides.

Grief flows from my eyes in a torrent. I wipe it away and see it is not tears, but blood. With an exhausted whimper, my head drops down to rest in the crook of his shoulder. I weep from sheer relief.

A shaky hand reaches up to thread into the damp hair at my nape.

"*Rhya?*" His voice breaks on my name.

I suck in a breath, trying to slow my tears. "You're alive?"

"Signs point to yes, if the searing pain in my head and at my ribs is any indication." He pauses, voice lightening. "I also thought I was meant to be greeted in the aether by the angels, but there's only you here, so . . ."

My battered body tenses. "So help me gods, if you even think about making a joke out of this situation—"

"Skylark, look at me."

I pull back enough to comply. My face is a mess of blood, my eyes are stung red, my hair a snarl of salt and seaweed . . . but he is looking at me like he doesn't notice any of that. He is looking at me with such a heartrending flood of emotion, I know whatever he is about to say will make the tears that have only just subsided rush out again.

"Rhya, I—"

Two colossal orange tentacles wrap around the air pocket without warning. They're so large, they block out the dark ocean. All I can see are suction cups, pulsing periodically as they slide against my solidified bubble, searching for weak spots.

"Fuck!" Soren curses, sitting up. His hand presses to his side, where his ribs are shattered. "We've got to get out of here."

"Really? I thought we'd stay awhile, maybe have a chat with the octopaeron before it eats us alive."

"Now who's making jokes?" His eyes are deadly serious as they scan up and down my face, no doubt reading the exhaustion etched into my features. Before I can blink, he is flooding me with his maegic, his reserves shoring up my flagging ones.

"Soren, you're still weak."

"I'm fine," he grits. "You're about to pass out."

"That's—"

My words turn to a gasp as the tentacles suddenly tighten, the pressure of it nearly doubling. I refortify my air pocket, the effort of it setting off sparks in my peripherals. Four orange arms now engulf us. And where they converge . . .

I shudder, seeing the mouth of the gigantic beast. A circular opening fettered with ring after ring of razor-sharp teeth. It, like the suction cups, pulses periodically as it attempts to swallow us whole.

"If you can just hold your air shields, I'll do my best to propel us to the surface." Soren grabs my hand, twining our sandy fingers tight. "Together."

I shake my head, rapidly rejecting that haphazard plan. "No. Absolutely not."

"Why?"

"Have you forgotten you were *actively dying* about three seconds ago? You're not about to expend any more of your maegic. I can feel how weak you are through the bond. We aren't taking any chances."

"Do you have any better ideas?"

I look around, contemplating our bleak circumstances for a few wasted seconds. *Could I use my whip? Strike it with lightning?* Not without frying Soren, too. *Drive it off with my paltry dagger?* Not bloody likely.

My maegic will simply have to be strong enough for the both of us. I will hold out until we are at the surface. There is no other choice.

I look straight into his eyes as I move closer. "Don't let go."

His gaze flares with frustration, but he does not argue. He gives a shallow nod and wraps his arms around my back. His squeeze is only half strength.

I get as close as I can manage, ducking my head down to rest against his throat, where his thready pulse pounds. There is no need to explain the plan to him, no need to spell out my thoughts. He is inside my head, watching them form as if they were his own.

"Ready?"

His lips press a fleeting kiss to the hinge of my jaw. "Just in case we die."

I might laugh, if this were any other moment. As it is, I'm barely holding on to my consciousness. The octopaeron's tentacles cinch tighter and tighter, determined to make us its next meal.

I am not about to let it.

With the last dregs of my strength, I rocket us straight toward the sky with a purified stream of air. A soundless scream builds in my throat as the immense effort of it tears through me.

Gods, why did I think I was strong enough to do this on my own?

Our progress is hampered by the immense weight of the beast still wrapped around us as we ascend. Though I've forbidden him to help, Soren can't resist adding his maegic to mine, lending me whatever strength he can spare. His currents rip at the clinging limbs, prying them off one sucker at a time. One tentacle falls away, then another.

We are nearing the surface.

The water pressure eases, the leached colors saturating once more as we hurtle rapidly toward light. Toward *life*. I give one last mighty push—the last one I have in me, if I am being honest—propelling us upward so fast, the sea monster cannot sustain its grip.

"We're there," Soren says. *"We made it."*

We explode out of the sea, the force of our exit slingshotting us straight toward the clouds. The octopaeron's long tentacles reach fruitlessly after us, but we are all too quickly out of range. I cling tight to Soren as I carry us up into the skies, higher and higher, riding the wind currents like I've sprouted invisible wings. I do not think about the mechanics of flight. I do not need to. I was born for this, a creature of the aether, as at home among the skies as Zephyr.

I do not slow until I'm certain we are safe. Until I'm confident we will not be pulled back down into that watery void. When I take a breath and look around, we are suspended high above the sea, naught but clouds around us.

"Oh." I blink, surprised by our altitude. "I did not mean to . . ."

My words fail, for Soren starts shaking. At first, I think he is upset or afraid or . . . Oh, gods, is he injured? Was the ascent too much for him?

I quickly realize he is *laughing*.

"What in the realm could possibly be funny?" I ask, a hint of annoyance in my tone.

He pulls back enough so he can look into my eyes. They are crinkled up at the corners with mirth. "You never do anything by half measures, do you, skylark?"

I think about that for a moment. "What would the point of that be?"

The mirth fades, replaced by a serious look that makes my breath catch. "How close are you to passing out?"

"Why?"

"Because if I kiss you right now, I want to be prepared to plummet half a league into monster-infested seas."

My breath catches. I ignore the darkness pulsing at my temples, a dire warning. "I feel fine. Really. Never stronger."

"Liar," he whispers, mouth twitching.

He kisses me anyway.

It does not last long—it cannot, for I truly am in danger of depleting all my maegical reserves, even with him channeling me. But for a few glorious seconds, floating in the clouds, I do not think of anything on the ground. It is just me and Soren, hearts racing in time, lips moving together, arms twined so tight I think nothing will ever make me let go.

REALITY CRASHES BACK in with a vengeance the moment we reach the ship. No sooner have our boot soles touched down than I collapse in a heap of utter exhaustion.

Soren's arms catch me before I hit the deck.

"Rhya!" Penn calls from a great distance. "Gods, is she all right?"

I want to tell him I'm perfectly fine. Hadn't he just seen me flying? Unfortunately, my eyes slip closed and blackness consumes me before I can.

I dream in fitful flashes of nightmarish scenes. Battlefields full of dead, mortal and fae alike. And me, flying high above it all, vengeance in my heart as I survey a world ripped to shreds. My wrath knowing no bounds, my fury huge enough to sweep away kingdoms . . .

A fateful tempest.

A storm unbound.

When I awaken, I am in an unfamiliar cabin far larger than the one in which I've been bunking. The captain's quarters at the ship's stern. I hear the rhythmic slosh of waves against the hull outside.

We are underway.

I roll over and find Soren sitting on the edge of the mattress, staring down at me. One hand is planted in the blankets beside my head. There is a deep furrow of displeasure between his eyes. I reach up and smooth it away with my thumb. My arm feels like it weighs a ton.

"You look terrible," I inform him softly.

He scoffs. "Speak for yourself."

My hand falls back to the bed. I push myself upright against the headboard, wincing as my sore muscles protest. Everything hurts, down to my marrow.

"How long was I out?"

"About six hours." He studies me, eyes slivers of blue. The expression on his face is one I cannot fully decipher. "How are you feeling?"

"A bit sore."

"Only a bit?"

"Okay, slightly more than a bit." I blow out a breath, rubbing at my Remnant mark. It aches worse than usual. "Nothing that will not heal in a few hours' time. Nothing permanent."

His expression turns suspiciously blank.

"What? What is it?" My heart beats faster. "Has something happened?"

His mouth opens, then shuts again. As though he cannot quite find the words. "Rhya . . ."

"Are you injured?"

"My ribs are bruised but already on the mend."

"You should let me wrap them."

"They're fine. Barely a twinge anymore."

"Then what's changed?" I ask, leaning closer to him, eyes narrowing on his face. "What's wrong with you?"

"Nothing is wrong."

And yet, there is something decidedly off about him. I cannot put my finger on what. If my maegic were not so drained, I'd reach out with it and try to read him elementally. The bond always gives me a clearer picture of what is going on inside his head—and inside his heart.

It should not take long for my maegic to recover enough to feel him again. Still, I do not much enjoy even a short stretch of disconnection.

I drag in a deep breath. "Do not tell me we're abandoning the mission?"

"No. We should reach the Iron Isle within the hour."

"Then what is it?" I scan his empty features, searching for clues. "What's wrong?"

"I told you, nothing is wrong."

"Yet you are acting strangely," I insist, leaning closer to catch his stare. "I think you might have a concussion. You hit your head hard enough to knock you unconscious."

"Unconscious," he repeats slowly.

I blink. There it is again. That odd look, that unsettling tone. He is acting . . .

Unlike himself.

"Is that what I was, Rhya?" His head cants to one side, eyes gleaming with incisive light. "Was I only *unconscious*?"

My breath snags. My words dry up on my tongue.

Does he know, somehow, what happened on that seafloor? Does he remember that he was not merely without breath but . . . without *life*? That he was . . .

Dead.

He was dead.

There is no way he can know that. No possible way. I certainly have not told him. Nor do I plan to—not now, in any case. There is no reason to confide just how close he came to slipping away, nor how near I was to following him over that bottomless cliff toward eternal rest.

In truth, looking back at those dark moments, I am shocked by my own intense reaction to the prospect of losing him. My cheeks sear as I recall my own savage desperation, my mad bargaining with the gods, my reckless disregard for my own life . . .

Skies.

How did this happen? How did a few short weeks at his side flip everything in my world on its head? How has he become so irrevocably important that I do not want to carry on living if he is not here to do it with me?

I can scarcely own up to such truths myself, let alone lay them bare at his feet. And even if I could muster the courage, this is not the right time or place for that discussion. Not with Penn pacing right outside the door, along with half our friends . . .

No.

When we are back in Hylios and I've had proper time to process, I will be able to find the right words. After Arwen's life is no longer hanging in the balance, I will be able to confess how we almost lost ours at the bottom of the ocean.

"Rhya." Soren's brows quirk high on his forehead. "Are you all right? You've gone quiet."

"I'm . . ." I bite my lip, swallow hard, and start again. "How close did you say we are to the Iron Isle?"

"An hour, maybe less."

So little time. "Perhaps we should stall."

His frame goes solid. His voice goes dark. "*Stall?*"

"For a few hours. Long enough to gather our strength before we storm the prison." I pause, sucking in a gulp of air. "Neither of us will be much use if we're drained to the point of exhaustion."

He shakes his head. A lock of dark hair falls over his forehead, into his eyes; my fingers itch to push it back for him. I curl them into the sheets instead.

"No. If we hesitate, we'll miss the tide. We will have to wait a full day for another opportunity to make landfall under the cover of darkness."

I forgot about the tides.

The plan of infiltration we've sketched out is loose at best, but there is one incontrovertible factor. Sea level. We need it at its absolute lowest if we want even a chance to bring our dinghies ashore at the rocky cove on the eastern side of the island. According to Soren, it is a treacherous stretch of stone only exposed for two hours at a time.

We cannot miss that window.

Nor can we exceed it.

"A delay until tomorrow night's tide will do only one thing," he continues haltingly. "Assure Arwen's death."

"She will not—"

"I cannot lose her." His jaw tightens, locking in his volatile emotions. "She is all that I have."

I stare at him, a new ache in my chest. I want to say the words that will contradict that statement.

You have me, Soren.

You have me.

But I do not.

For all our many conversations since I tumbled unexpectedly from a portal and landed at his feet, for all that we have been through together these past weeks . . . we have not ever hit on the heart of the matter. Even as we channeled bow to bow throughout the course of this voyage, speaking of everything from geography to the gods . . . we never addressed the most important topic.

Us.

What we are. What we may yet become.

Not in so many words.

"We press on," he says decidedly, expression dark with determination. "We finish this. We get Arwen back. And then . . ." His eyes find mine, so bright with longing it spears me straight through the heart. "There will be time for other conversations."

My brows go up, silently asking a question I am too afraid to voice.

"There are things we need to discuss." His gaze shifts back and forth over my face, as though he is memorizing my every feature. Then, it drops down to the Remnant that peeks from the top of my leather bodice. "There are things I need to explain to you. Things you do not yet seem to understand. But this . . ." His focus flashes briefly to the door. "This is not our moment."

"Right," I breathe, disappointment crashing through me. "You're right. Of course you're right."

Soft light slants in through the windows at the stern. The sun is setting. It will be dark soon. But in this moment, with the cabin bathed in buttery twilight and Soren a handspan away from me on the bed, I do not think about what awaits us in the dead of night. All I see is him. His angular features, his savage beauty. All I feel is my pulse, thudding madly at my throat.

I tell myself to get up, out of bed. To find my daggers and my boots, to braid my hair and prepare for the battle to come. But I do not get up. I sit there, spine pressing hard against the headboard, knowing if I move a single muscle, I'll reach for him.

Soren exhales harshly, as though he knows my thoughts. As though he shares them. His hand slides behind my neck, warm and solid. He tugs me forward until we are a hairsbreadth apart.

"We will have our moment, Rhya. We will have *more* than a moment," he says, and it is a vow. "The things I need to say to you . . . The things I want to do with you . . ."

Longing cascades through me, irrepressible. Turning my bones to water. My voice is a breathy whisper, "What sort of things?"

His eyes go half-lidded. "Gods help me, I . . ."

His mouth is suddenly on mine, hard and fast. A hungry, reckless kiss that says everything we are both unable to express with words. I kiss him back, equally desperate for him. Pouring all my need into my fingers as they fist in the white linen of his shirt and pull him down on top of me. He growls low in his throat as we collide, his larger frame crushing mine into the thin feather mattress of the captain's bed. The thready sound vibrates through me like a mallet on a drum, striking deep chords of passion. Setting off an unstoppable lust that threatens to carry me away.

And though we've said there is no time, though we've adamantly declared that this fractured instant is not meant for us . . . neither one of us seems capable of stopping now that we've begun. The planes of his body are deliciously firm against mine, stealing my breath along with my inhibitions. The throbbing evidence of his need nestles in the crook of my thighs, hard and undeniable, and I feel my own amplify tenfold, an animalistic urge that shocks me to my core.

I hardly recognize myself—this desperate creature who fumbles for buttons and claws to get closer, closer, closer. I want to tear off every piece of clothing that keeps us apart with my teeth; want to shred the fabric from his limbs and erase every barrier that has ever come between us. I want nothing but him and me in this bed, stripped to the skin. Laid bare, body and soul.

With the bond still muted, I may not be able to read his thoughts, but Soren's actions make it abundantly clear he feels the same. His fingers work at the tight lacing of my leather bodice as mine skate under the hem of his shirt to trace the indentations of his muscles. That expanse of golden skin is finally, *finally*, under my hands. And it is glorious. I cannot hold back my fractured whimper any more than I can stop my body from arching off the bed as his teeth scrape a torturous path up the column of my throat, to my ear.

I feel the twitch of his smile even before I hear it in his voice. "If you mewl like that when I kiss you, I cannot wait to hear what other sounds I'll manage to inspire . . ."

Skies.

I gasp as his teeth tweak the lobe.

Lowering more of his weight on top of me, he grinds his hips into mine in a way that dizzies all my senses. "Will you sing my name when you shatter, skylark?"

I will sing anything he wants, if only he keeps touching me like this. My mind is a blank of pleasure as his hands part the supple leather of my unbound bodice, then skim the bare flesh beneath. His palm grazes the peak of my nipple, frustratingly featherlight.

I want more than that.

I *need* more than that.

He waits until he's elicited another pitiful whimper from my throat before he relents, palming my breast with expert attention, kneading and caressing until I am reduced to a squirming storm of want beneath him.

"Soren." My breath hitches. My fingers dig into his skin. "Please—"

"Please what, Rhya? What is it you want from me?"

He's enjoying this, the great tease.

He sucks my bottom lip into his mouth at the exact moment my nails score across the raised pattern of his Remnant, where the skin is excruciatingly sensitive. The effect is instant. His whole body shudders. He exhales against my lips, a pant of pure desire I feel in every corner of my body. All playfulness sweeps straight out of the cabin, replaced by a ferocious need that arises inside him with the swiftness of a summer squall.

When he kisses me again, it is with such unflagging passion, such savage desire, I know his control is hanging by the thinnest of threads; when he touches me, it is no longer with teasing caresses or playful swipes, but with a barely leashed ardency that turns my bloodstream to pure starlight. He grips my body with bruising need, clutching me close. And I do the same, equally brutal in my eagerness for him.

Time slips out of focus as we touch and gasp, peeling away layers with shaking hands. I get his shirt unbuttoned and push it impatiently off his shoulders, revealing his perfect chest. He uses his teeth on the laces of my pants, groaning low in his throat when I thread my fingers into his hair. When he presses his mouth to me through the thin leather, my whole body spasms.

Skies, if he kisses me there again . . .

I nearly come apart just thinking about it.

His hands are at my hips, peeling down my pants, when a fist pounds at the door to the cabin.

"Brother!" Godsdamned Vaughn. "The island is in sight! Whatever you're doing in there, wrap it up, would you?"

Soren groans, a sound of frustration, and drops his head against the crook of my thighs. "Fuck. Not again."

Sucking in a shaky breath, I force my fingers to dislodge from his hair. My body thrums with untapped passion. My heart is a riot beneath my rib cage. Just beside it, my Remnant is stirring awake, its momentary slumber cut short by the crashing sensations that rack me head to toe.

We climb off the bed, both breathing hard, and set our clothes to rights. My fingers shake as I do the laces of my bodice and comb through my mussed mane. There is nothing to be done about the redness of my cheeks, nor the sheen of lust in my eyes.

Soren is hardly better off. I have never seen him so unbalanced. He looks shockingly young as he buttons his shirt and rolls up his sleeves, his face a portrait of boyish inhibition. The polished facade is askew, knocked off its orbit by everything we have just done.

Everything we have *almost* done.

"We should go," I force myself to say, hardly able to look at him without my heart stumbling or my breath catching. "They're waiting for us."

I make it only a few steps toward the door before he stops me with a hand at my nape, pulling me around to crush his mouth against mine one last time. As I kiss him back, I memorize everything about him, committing the moment to the deepest recesses of my mind in case I never get another like it. His scent, his strength. The way we fit together like two halves of a broken plate, every jagged, ugly edge somehow perfectly aligned to create something whole and strong and healed.

The pounding comes again. "We'll miss the tide!"

"There will come a day when I have the luxury of kissing you without interruption," Soren murmurs against my lips, a ghost of his usual humor in his tone. "And, I hope, a day when I have the luxury of doing *more* than merely kiss you." His exhale is resigned. "But today does not seem to be that day."

CHAPTER
TWENTY-NINE

I avoid everyone's eyes on the top deck, but it's no use. They all seem to know exactly what happened inside the captain's cabin. It is there in the teasing edge to Yara's grin, in the knowing light of Jac's stare. Mostly, though, it is there in the dark resentment I feel emanating from Penn clear across the ship.

I swallow down my guilt and my embarrassment. This is hardly the most pressing issue facing our crew at the moment.

We gather at the wheel to discuss our strategy one last time. Deke is at the helm, the deckhands hovering nearby. Vaughn towers between Melité and the Paexyrian by the steps up from mid-deck. Penn is sandwiched between his men on the starboard side. I sit on the stern rail, one hand on the backstay to keep from pitching overboard into the rough swells. Soren stands near Alaric in the very center, addressing everyone at once as he walks us through the plan.

I try to focus on his words, but my eyes keep shifting out over the sea to the island in the distance. It is a foreboding sight, even from here. What little I can see of it, in any case. The dark stone walls are shrouded in a pervasive mist that makes it difficult to spot, even at midday. Now, as the sun disappears over the horizon, it is hardly more than a shadowy smudge.

Hopefully that will make it harder for anyone inside keeping watch to spot our approach. The success of our plan hinges almost entirely on the element of surprise; they won't know we are coming until it's too late to mount a proper defense.

Get in, get Arwen, get out alive.

Do not engage if it can be avoided.

The isle itself is not large. A fraction of the size of Hylios, at first glance it appears more like a large rock than a notorious fae prison. Dark stone walls, black as the sands of the Husk Desert, designed to blend into the natural cliff formations. There is no harbor to put into, no calm inlet in which to drop anchor. The sea directly around its perimeter is particularly violent, sending huge plumes of foam up into the air with each crash.

The brig cannot possibly get close. Not unless we fancy swimming home to Llŷr when this is done. And the whitecapped waves on the surface are not half so worrisome as whatever monsters lurk beneath.

I am less than eager to confront another octopaeron.

"Rhya."

I startle back to the present and find everyone staring at me. "What?"

"The initial plan was for you to use your fog to conceal the dinghies as we approach," Soren says, that troubled furrow back between his eyes. "But your powers are not yet returned to full strength."

"I'll do what I can." I press a hand to my Remnant. It still feels strange. Slightly sore in a way it never has before. And yet, beneath the soreness, I can feel my maegic returning, my inner storms beginning to swirl and spin with increasing strength. "I cannot promise success, only that I will try."

Soren nods, then shifts his eyes to Deke. "You will remain here, manning the ship until our return. If two hours pass and we do not come out, consider the mission forfeit. Get yourself home."

The bleakness of that order settles heavily on all of our shoulders.

"Maybe give us three," Vaughn mutters.

Jac snorts out a laugh. It fades quickly when Soren speaks again. "Three hours, that beach will be underwater. Even if we're still alive in there, we'll be trapped with no exit strategy."

The leather-faced captain's mouth presses into a frown. "Don't like this part of the plan."

"You don't have to like it, so long as you stick to it," Soren counters. His eyes slide to the two scruffy-looking sailors leaning against the port rail. "Chari, Xio . . . are you certain you are able to bring us in?"

"Navigated worse waters than these in the Desert Depths." Xio shrugs, their slim shoulders lifting quickly. "And Chari rows faster than a Frostlander."

Chari nods in confirmation.

"Good. I will do what I can to calm the waters long enough for you to bring us in." His focus moves to the Paexyrian. "Is the equipment ready?"

Yara grins hugely, a trace of her old spirit creeping through the film of grief in her eyes. "Oh, it's ready." Her thumb jerks toward Farley, Cadogan, Jac, and Mabon. "Whether this ragtag lot is up to the challenge of using it remains to be seen."

"Trust me," Farley says, winking at her. "When it comes to my equipment, I *always* rise to the challenge."

She rolls her eyes.

"Then we're prepared." Soren's gaze sweeps around the whole group one final time, somber enough to make my pulse skitter. "Last chance to back out. There's no turning around once we reach the isle."

No one says a word.

EVEN THE BEST-LAID plans often go awry. And ours is not best laid. For there are only so many elements we can predict, only so many hurdles we can anticipate.

From the very start, I have a knot of worry in my stomach that tightens with each passing moment. Our approach through the roiling waves leaves several members of our crew retching over the side before we've reached the sliver of rocky beach.

Ashore, circumstances are hardly improved. We endure a constant spray of cold sea-foam as we struggle for solid footing on the slippery stones, hauling the dinghies from the shallows as quietly as we can manage so as not to call any patrolling guards down upon our heads.

Not so very high above us, several narrow windows are aglow in the darkness. If I strain my ears over the crashing swells, I can make out the faint sound of voices from inside the thick prison walls.

Not speaking.

Screaming.

Gods, I hope that is not Arwen making such a sound. It is pain in its purest form, the embodiment of agony. I shudder as it rings out again and again into the night. So does Alaric. He looks like he's been punched in the gut, breathless with fear.

For the first time, it occurs to me that there might be other prisoners inside this godsawful place. Others captured by Efnysien for purposes I do not want to contemplate.

Near the base of the wall, Yara and Bretiax look up from their positions, flanked by Mabon and Jac. All four hold in their hands a claw-shot—a modified crossbow of sorts with a tight spool of wire mounted at the base. Instead of a standard bolt, it is rigged to shoot a sharp-toothed grappling hook from the end.

At Yara's low signal they all fire in sync, sending their hooks upward toward the top of the wall. There is a low crack as the stone is punctured, a sharp snap as the wires go taut. We all hold our breaths in the aftermath, waiting for the telltale shouts of warning, the thunder of boots running our way.

A minute passes, then another, and it does not come. The thunderous sea has muffled the clangor.

The base of each wire is secured to the rocks. One by one, we make our way up, leaving Chari and Xio behind with the dinghies. The thin wires dig harshly against my palms despite the thick climbing gloves I've donned to protect them. I call a current of air to buoy myself, speeding the ascent.

We've only just arrived, but already I can feel the malignant effects of the iron eroding my maegical reservoirs. These rocks reek with ore, thicker even than that within the copper depths of the Red Chasm back in the Midlands—and that deadly crevasse had been potent enough to bring me to my knees.

But I am stronger now, I reason, gritting my teeth as I haul my body upward. I am no longer that scared, skeletal halfling on the edge of a cliff, at the mercy of mortal soldiers. Nor am I the frightened girl who fled Seahaven in the night without even a pair of boots to protect her bloodied feet.

That girl had no real concept of who she was or what she was capable of. She knew nothing of the real world. Not its horrors, nor its enchantments. She had never taken a life. She had never wielded her power. She had never looked into someone's eyes and felt, down to her very marrow, that she would be quite satisfied to never look at anything else for the rest of her life, if only—

I shake my head, banishing the distracting thoughts as I heave myself up over the edge of the wall into Mabon's burly arms. Taking a deep breath, I look around. The thick stone beneath my feet hides all manner of evil. I can feel it oozing through the mortar like sap from a poisonous tree.

We move in silence, eyes peeled for threats. Atop the ramparts, it is wide enough for only two to walk side by side. Or, in Vaughn's case, for one. I find myself squeezed in next to Alaric, staring at the back of Soren's and Penn's heads as they lead us toward a guard tower. I cloak us as best I can as the distance narrows from paces to handspans, but summoning even a thin shrouding of mist takes twice the effort it did at sea. It is like pulling maegic through a sieve.

Soren gives a nod and, with a speed that stuns the senses, Penn jerks open the door. The two of them strike like lightning, dispatching the pair of scarlet-clad guards inside before they can even summon a scream. Their necks snap in perfect sync, their bodies falling to the stones with twin thuds. I stare at their slackened faces and the unsettled pit in my stomach stretches wider.

They are mortal. And yet, not quite. There is something distorted about them. Their faces bear a strange amalgamation of wounds new and old—some scars long healed, the others freshly stitched closed. Their sightless eyes are beady as a vulture's, and unnatural in color. Strangest of all is their skin. Even before their hearts ceased beating, it was not the tone of healthy flesh but the bluish gray of a corpse. Beneath the pallor, the veins appear black and mottled. It reminds me of meat gone spoiled at the butcher's shop—the rotten hunks only fit for hounds and hunting traps.

No wonder the soldiers of Efnysien's red army are so reviled. Just the sight of them on the field of battle would surely be enough to make any enemy troops turn tail. I wonder briefly what sort of hideous experiments led to such an appearance of flesh and form, then quickly decide I don't want to know.

We move single file through the chamber, exiting to the ramparts on the other side, where we continue our slow slink through the darkness. The prison is square in design, with four equidistant lookout towers at the corners. According to Soren's spies, the cellblocks are buried deep beneath the inner courtyard, in a light-starved dungeon where the ore is thickest. If Arwen is here—if she is still alive—that is undoubtedly where she will be.

She is alive.

She has to be. Efnysien has been obsessed with her for more than a century. He has been planning this for gods only know how many years. Why go to all the trouble of having her kidnapped from her own wedding, only to execute her immediately?

He would not.

No, he will make this last, draw out this ploy as long as possible. Not only to sate his own vile bloodlust but to strike at Soren. Efnysien knows how close they are. He knows that each day his sister spends in captivity takes its toll. If we do not get her back, I fear Soren will be forever changed. As for Arwen . . . I dare to hope she is tough enough to endure whatever horrors have already been inflicted. A spirit like hers is not easily broken.

We slow as we come upon the second tower, keeping to the shadows as we listen to the voices that spill out the narrow windows. At minimum three guards, from the sound of it. We cannot afford to leave them alive. If a single one of them sends up the alarm, every guard on this island will come running, and our one chance to reach Arwen will crumble into dust.

Farley and Harpina both draw their bows, ready to fire as the door is jerked open. But there is no need for arrows. Soren and Penn move in perfect coordination as they repeat their swift neck-snapping efforts, taking out a trio of scarlet-uniformed soldiers without a whisper. I avert my eyes from the black-veined skin and slackened faces, examining the tower instead. This one is slightly larger than the first. On the far wall, a set of steps spirals downward toward the inner courtyard—or, with any luck, the dungeons beneath.

"We'll take the final two towers," Penn tells Soren, voice low. His chin jerks to indicate the Ember Guild. "The rest of you go down, get Arwen out."

Soren nods. "I'm not certain how effective the bond will be once we're belowground. The ore . . ." He pauses, brows pulling together. "If you find yourself in trouble and cannot signal for us, get yourself to the boats. We will find our own way out."

I do not like that.

Not at all.

Penn isn't looking at me, but even in profile I can see how tightly his jaw is clenched. How the muscle in his cheek ticks with rage. The shadows beneath his eyes look darker than ever. I cannot sense his emotions, but I know just being here, surrounded by water, is sapping his maegic.

"We should not split up," I interject softly. "Penn, you are not at full strength. The effects of the water in addition to the ore here . . ."

"Do not concern yourself with me," Penn says, a hint of bitterness in his tone. "It is no longer your place. If it ever was."

I suck in a breath, heart panging.

Soren says nothing, but I can feel his anger billowing out, charging the air with new tension. He does not like to see me wounded—not even if it is a lashing I deserve.

"Is this melodrama necessary," Melité drawls from the corner, crossing her arms over her ample chest. "Or can we carry on ahead?"

My glare narrows on her. She is nearly popping out of her dress. I have no idea how she managed to scale the wall in such ridiculous attire. Though Cadogan does not seem to find fault with it. He is gazing at her with the same dopey-eyed affection I've seen since they first met.

"Gill-girl has a point. We need to keep moving," Vaughn mutters, stepping over one of the corpses as he strides toward the stairs.

Alaric is already starting down them.

Melité, whose eyes turned fully black with rage at Vaughn's flippant nickname, heaves a huge sigh that tests the structural integrity of her dress's thin shoulder straps, then follows. I cannot lie, I feel uneasy with her in our midst. I'm not certain why she insisted on coming along. Thus far, she has contributed nothing to the mission except the occasional haughty comment and aloof look.

I watch her hips sashaying out of sight behind Vaughn before Yara, Harpina, and Bretiax follow her down the spiraling steps. I know I should go, too, but my boots remain stubbornly rooted in place. My throat is tight with fear as I stare after Pendefyre. I do not want to part at all, but certainly not like this. Should something happen to either of us . . .

This cannot be our goodbye.

It is wrong, all wrong.

Whatever else has changed between us, one thing remains the same. One thing will always remain the same. Pendefyre owns a piece of me—one I have not gotten back. One I am not sure I will ever get back. His pain is my pain.

Even when it is pain I've caused.

His gaze moves to mine for a brief moment, then shifts to his men. "Cadogan, Farley, take point. Mabon, Jac, at their backs. I'll cover the rear."

They fall seamlessly into step—Farley shooting me a quick farewell grin, Jac waggling his brows, Mabon jerking his chin, Cadogan winking. My answering smile wobbles as they turn away.

"Pendefyre," I call after them.

He jolts to a stop and looks back at me, brows lifting.

"Please, be safe. Please . . . don't do anything reckless."

The agony in his eyes flares bright, then fades. He does not say a word. He does not have to. I know him well enough to recognize he is in the process of locking down his emotions, shoving them deep inside where they will not distract him from the task at hand. Ever the master of self-containment.

In this scenario, perhaps that is a strength, not a detriment. My own conflicted feelings are tearing me from the inside out.

When the Dyvedi contingent disappears out onto the ramparts, Soren and I follow the rest of the Llŷrian faction down the low-lit steps. There is nothing to break the shadows besides the occasional torch flickering in a bracket along the walls. Smoke hazes the stifled air, burning down my throat with each inhale. I swallow the urge to cough as we descend deeper and deeper.

Gods, I hate this.

No light, no air.

No wind.

"Breathe," Soren orders silently. *"It will stave off the fear."*

My nod is shallow.

I try to take measured breaths, to keep my heartbeats steady and even, but my pulse spikes in alarm when we reach the bottom and find ourselves in a dim, cobwebbed corridor. Water drips from the damp walls. The scent of dust and decay presses in on me.

"Pretend you are in the clouds, skylark. Feel the wind on your face, in your hair. You are not here. You are flying free."

His words bolster me as we move down a short passage, then turn a corner. We make it only a handful more steps before the way forward is blocked by a thick door.

"Locked," Yara declares, jiggling the handle.

"There goes our element of surprise." Vaughn grimaces. "This is going to make a racket."

He gently steers Yara aside, then braces his huge hands against the hinges. Loosing a muted grunt, he applies one short burst of pressure. There is a metallic groan, a splintering of wood. The door falls inward with a resounding thud that makes us all wince.

"Show-off," Yara mutters.

Vaughn merely grins and bows her onward. "Ladies first."

A silent Harpina trails close on Yara's heels. Bretiax reaches up to pat the half-Titan on the shoulder as she passes over the threshold. Alaric hurries through after them, followed by Melité, who seems in no hurry at all. Soren gestures for me to go before him, bringing up the rear with a hand at the small of my back. I've scarcely stepped into the next corridor when Yara's anguished howl splits the musty air.

Her petite body jerks, then sails backward into Vaughn. A thick arrow is embedded in her side. It is bleeding profusely.

"Yara!" I cry, racing for her—only to run straight into the immovable barricade of Soren's arm.

"Soren, she needs help! Let me by."

"This passage is booby-trapped," he clips. "No one move."

We all freeze instantly.

Two more arrows shoot into the space Yara's just vacated, a

mechanized whir their only warning sign. They ricochet off the thick stone walls and clatter to the floor. Our collective gaze follows them, scanning as though more traps might spring to life at any given moment. Soren exhales sharply and points at a flagstone just a few strides ahead. Upon closer examination, it looks a shade higher than the rest.

"There. See that? It's triggered to fire as soon as someone steps on it. She's lucky she wasn't killed."

Yara is breathing heavily, leaning back against Vaughn like she might fall over without him there to hold her up.

"Not feeling"—she wheezes—"particularly lucky"—her eyes press closed as pain washes through her—"right now."

"She can't carry on, not with that wound." My lips press into a frown as my mind races. "Bretiax, Harpina, get her up the stairs into the guard tower. Keep pressure on that wound and don't let her slip unconscious. If she worsens, get her to the dinghies. Can you do that?"

Bretiax hurriedly signs her affirmation, already moving to her friend's side.

"Bre, can you get her up those steps alone?" Harpina asks, her voice full of resignation. "I want to help, I do . . . but I should go on ahead. One of the Paexyrian should be there. For Arwen." She pauses. "And for Thisobei, gods rest her."

A lump forms in my throat at the raw grief in her voice . . . and the vengeance beneath it.

Yara nods weakly. "Go on, Harpina. Bre and I will be fine on our own."

Vaughn helps transfer Yara's weight onto Bretiax, maneuvering the redhead's arm over her shoulder. It is lucky Yara is so compact. Still, it will be a struggle to make their way up without Harpina's help.

"Melité," I force myself to say. "Maybe you could—"

"Absolutely not." The half-siren's lip curls in distaste. "I'm much more use in the dungeons than up in the tower playing nursemaid."

I bare my teeth at her in a grimace. "Yes, because you've been so useful thus far."

Vaughn snorts.

"We need to move on," Alaric murmurs, his handsome face a portrait of worry. "Someone will have heard that door break, as well as Yara's screams."

We all fall silent again.

I look at Yara. She is pale with blood loss. Her hand is at her side, where the arrow protrudes from her leather bodice. Two inches lower, it would have struck a vital organ. My worry must show on my face, for Yara rolls her eyes at me.

"Go! I'll be fine. Bre won't let me die. Will you, Bre?"

Bretiax sighs.

My lips twitch. "Very convincing."

"It's Arwen you need to worry about." Yara looks from me to Harpina and back. "You get a chance to gut the bastard who did this, you take it."

"I will," I promise.

Harpina's freckled nose wrinkles in annoyance. "I don't need your convincing, Yara."

"Good. I'm counting on it." The redhead attempts a smile, not quite managing through the pain. "Don't do anything I wouldn't do."

I nearly laugh. Is there anything Yara would not do? "We will see you soon, either at the tower or on the boats."

She nods. Bretiax shoots me a soft smile, then starts walking. Her slender form is bowed beneath the strain as they hobble back the way we came.

I look from Soren to Vaughn. "What are the odds of more traps in this corridor?"

"Probably the same as the odds of Melité pissing me off," Vaughn says.

The half-siren's gills flare as she huffs.

The pit of dread in my stomach spreads outward, eroding throughout my abdomen and chest cavity as we begin to move again, slower this time, our steps ginger on the flagstones. There is no easy way to avoid setting them off, but after a few near misses we learn to do it in a more controlled manner—sliding a toe out across the stone, applying pressure while your body remains safely out of range.

Before we've traversed the length of the passage, Vaughn has narrowly ducked a volley of arrows headed straight for his skull. Alaric dodges a swinging bar of spikes that drops from the ceiling by the skin of his teeth. Even Melité has to spring out of the way when a faulty floor panel plummets into a bottomless pit.

"Your stepbrother certainly has a flair for creativity," I mutter, leaping over the void into Soren's waiting arms. "A shame he didn't channel it into something a bit less evil."

Our progress is infuriatingly slow, grating on all our nerves. Every time we reach a corner, I brace myself for enemies lurking out of sight. But the prison seems almost abandoned as we move deeper and deeper, following set after set of damp steps into the earth. Only the occasional distant screech from the dungeons below disrupts the silence.

The air grows even staler as we near them. Musty and moldering in my lungs. Yet there is another scent here, too—one that grows stronger with each step until it waters the eyes and burns the throat.

The distinct, coppery tinge of blood.

We soon locate the source, stepping into a room I can only describe as a torture chamber. Tools line the walls, on racks and shelves and stands. Some I recognize from my Life Guild days. There are saws for limb amputation, tourniquets to control bleeding. Needles for stitching. And blades of every variety. Serrated, curved, pointed, double-edged. Some shine, freshly polished. Others are caked in gore.

Monster parts are littered about like decor. Hacked-off arachnidae legs rot in puddles of black ichor; cleaved cyntroedi mandibles rest beside harvested vials of green venom. An octopaeron eye floats in a tremendous glass jar. I can only imagine what depraved uses Efnysien finds for them.

At the center of the chamber sit three operating tables, similar in design to what a surgeon might employ. In a glance, it's clear these are not used for any sort of healing. They are not crafted of wood but massive slabs of granite, cleverly gouged along the edges to contain the blood before it spills. Beveled trenches at the foot of each table funnel into a vat in the middle of the floor.

A vat full to the brim with dark, red fluid.

Soren stills at the sight. "I guess that explains how he managed to confound the portals. There's enough there for a hundred journeys."

"Arwen." Alaric's voice breaks on his wife's name. His eyes bore into the center table, which appears to have been used most recently, if the smears of vibrant crimson are any indication. "Do you think—"

"This is far more than a few days' worth." Vaughn claps his brother-in-law on the back. "Come. Let's keep moving. We must be getting close. The screams are getting louder."

As if on cue, a muffled wail of agony echoes through the

thick stone walls. It does indeed sound closer than those that came before.

We move on, leaving the gruesome chamber behind. I keep one hand on the coiled whip at my waist, comforted by its golden weight in my hand even if my maegic is too muted down here for it to be of any use to me. I find it strange that no one is around and, from the edgy energy emanating from him, I know Soren feels the same.

Where are the guards?

Where are the wardens of this prison?

We see none. Not in the corridors, not on the stairways, not even posted at the thick door to the cellblocks.

Vaughn makes quick work of ripping it off its hinges. He looks at Soren as he sets the wood panel aside. "Does this feel . . ."

"Too easy," Soren finishes, teeth grinding together. "Definitely."

"Perhaps Efnysien is so cocky, he thinks this prison cannot be infiltrated," Alaric says, but his voice sounds unsure. "Between the guard towers above and the booby traps within, he must figure no one would be crazy enough to try."

"Mmm," Melité hums noncommittally.

Harpina says nothing, but I catch her making the sigil for protection from the Goddess of Fate out of the corner of my eye.

Soren looks at me. *"Stay close, skylark. I do not like this."*

"Really? I'm having a splendid time."

The ghost of a smile twitches at his lips. *"How are your nerves?"*

"Shot to all hell," I answer honestly. I expel a thin breath, wishing the confinement was not affecting me so harshly.

"We'll be out of here soon," he promises. *"Back in Hylios. Back in the sunlight. Think of that, not this place."*

I try to do as he says. To ignore the mounting panic. To put the dread out of my head. But it's no use.

It's not just me. We all feel it—that sinking feeling in our stomachs, that slow build of tension cinching tighter and tighter. Like hapless mice who've snuck into the den of a deadly predator, only to see the gleam of eyes in the darkness and realize, too late, that they never stood a chance at stealth.

My heartbeat picks up speed, matching my strides as we move into a corridor lined with cells on either side. The screams come in a chorus, moans and yells and nonsensical whimpers. I grip my dagger hilt with one hand, the other at the ready on my whip. My eyes trace the thick bars of iron, the dark shadows beyond. Most are vacant. The few that are not make my heart plummet to my feet, for their occupants are either dead-eyed and nonresponsive or raving and frothing. Regardless of their mental state, all of them share one commonality: they are horribly, horribly maimed. No doubt the result of many visits to the chamber of torture.

A man—I think it is a man—peers out as we pass without blinking, as though he does not even see us. As though he is already elsewhere, his broken body a shell for a soul long fled.

"Shouldn't we help them?" I whisper regardless, blinking back tears.

"There is no helping them," Melité snarls softly. "*Look* at them. That one is missing both its arms."

"Shut up, Melité," Vaughn growls, sounding shaken. He looks back at me, green eyes saddened. "We've no way to transport them all out of here, Rhya. And no room on the dinghies, even if we could."

I swallow thickly. "But—"

"Arwen!" Alaric's cry cuts the air like a knife, bringing us all running. He's at the end of the passage, rattling the rungs of a cell, paying no mind at all to the iron as it burns his hands. "She's in here, she's—Oh, gods, is she—"

"Move! I've got it." Vaughn shoulders Alaric out of the way. "You'll be no use to your bride if you singe your skin off."

Alaric does not even seem to feel the pain. His damaged hands fall to his sides, twitching slightly, but his eyes never shift from the half-Titan as he tears the iron door from its frame as easily as he did the wood ones. Alaric barely gives Vaughn time to step clear before he pushes into the cell, dropping to his knees beside a female form. She is curled in the fetal position, legs drawn up to her chest, arms wrapped tight around her head as if protecting it from being kicked.

Soren's breath catches in his throat. A pulse of pure despair bleeds through the bond, strong enough to overcome even the ore's dampening effects. I reach out and grab his hand, squeezing tight in a show of wordless support.

"Arwen? Arwen, can you hear me? It's me, love. It's Alaric." His bleeding hand trembles as he lifts it to cradle the side of her face.

She flinches violently beneath his light touch.

Soren's hand tenses in mine. He's seen it, too. His fearsome, fearless sister . . . *flinching.*

Arwen does not flinch.

My chest aches as more despair floods into me, mingling with my own.

"We've come to take you home." The halting tenderness of Alaric's whisper breaks something inside me. "I'm going to lift you. Okay? Maybe"—he sucks in a breath as he hesitates—"maybe you can wrap your arms around my neck. It's all right if you can't manage it. Just . . . try for me."

There is the smallest sound—a tiny whimper, barely audible. Then, her arms are winding tight around his neck and he's cradling her against his chest, his hold unbearably gentle. It is a sharp contrast to his fierce expression, to the wrath blazing from his typically mellow brown eyes.

I blink back tears as he carries Arwen from the cell. She looks fragile. Reduced to a shadow of herself. Her skin is pale, her body so weak she cannot even lift her head to look around at us. I have rarely seen her in anything but flight leathers or battle-ready garb. Yet here she is in a plain white nightgown, the kind you might wear as a little girl.

Soren skims his fingers along the side of her face, light as a butterfly's wing. His other hand is gripping mine so hard, I'm surprised the bones remain intact.

"Arwen."

Her eyes sliver open enough to find her brother's. He does not say anything else. I do not think he is capable of it. But then, there is no need for words, not between the two of them. Their stares hold in silent communication. Whatever they exchange in those three seconds is enough to make a shred of strength flicker across Arwen's pallid face.

I survey her with the eyes of a healer, looking for injuries. Finding none. Physically, she does not appear wounded. Mentally, spiritually . . . that remains to be seen.

"Can we get the fuck out of here now?" Vaughn looks around in distaste. "We don't exactly have time to spare and, even if we did, this place gives me the godsdamned creeps."

"Seconded," I murmur. My gaze drifts to the dark cell directly across from Arwen's. It's smaller than the rest. More of a cage, really, with a low ceiling and bars so thick, I'm surprised any air gets in. I cannot see anything inside and, at first glance, assume it's empty. But the longer my eyes linger on it, the harder it is to look away. Something is making the mark on my chest tingle with a foreign sensation I've never felt before. Not recognition, exactly, but . . .

Familiarity.

Alaric is already walking back in the direction we came from, murmuring to Arwen under his breath. Vaughn trails after them, Harpina at his side, Melité shadowing. When Soren moves to follow, my hand pulls him up short.

"Skylark? We need to move, there's no—"

"Don't you feel that?"

His mouth snaps shut and his brows draw together. I sense his mounting confusion as I drop his hand and step closer to the cage. My forehead stings as I bring it right up to the bars, the searing kiss of iron scorching my skin. I ignore the pain, narrowing my eyes on the shadows beyond. Trying to pull the occupant inside into focus.

"Hello?" I whisper. "Is someone there?"

A growl comes in answer.

It is a feral sound, like a wild wolf caught in a snare. Chills break out across my flesh and the hair at the back of my neck rises in alarm. I jolt backward several inches, pulse pounding hard.

"Soren, get the torch."

He crouches beside me, bringing the light close to the bars. Illuminating the crouched form inside.

Not a beast at all, but . . .

A girl.

She looks around my age, though it is difficult to tell. Most of her face is obscured by matted hanks of hair that have not seen a brush in gods only know how many years. It cascades practically to her feet. She is clothed in a nightgown similar to the one Arwen is wearing, but it looks frayed with age and streaked with filth. Her skin is nearly as dark as the shadows of her cage. But her eyes . . . they glow bright, green as the new shoots that erupt from the frozen earth each spring . . . and swirling with unchecked power.

My heart lurches as our gazes hold.

For beneath that telltale swirl, I see only madness. Madness and . . .

Rage.

"Rhya, we really should—"

Soren's words cut off sharply. Because at that moment, the ground begins to vibrate and the air begins to buzz. The bellwether of an earthquake. As I stare in shock through the bars, as I feel the surge of maegic swelling in the air, visceral despite the deadening ore in these walls . . . I know this quake will be like no other I have ever endured.

For we are standing at its epicenter.

And staring at its source.

"It's her," I choke out, hardly believing the words I'm about to say. "She is . . . She's . . . the Remnant of Earth."

CHAPTER
THIRTY

I think the whole prison will come down around our ears as we ride out the rampant trembles of the earthquake. Soren tucks most of my frame under his, as if that will protect me when the ceiling crashes in, refusing to move away until the last of the aftershocks have faded.

"No wonder the quakes have been so bad in recent months," he says, staring through the bars with the same shocked look I'm certain is etched across my own features. "She's been setting them off."

The girl growls again and chucks something violently against the bars. A rock, from the sound of it.

"Gods," I mutter. How long has she been here? Weeks? Months? Years? No wonder she's gone mad. I've been in this place for an hour and feel like my mind is under assault. "We need to get her out of here, Soren. Now."

His head snaps sideways to peer down the length of the corridor, which is littered with piles of fallen debris where the ceiling crumbled loose. Plumes of dust dim our visibility nearly to zero. "Vaughn!"

With a muffled oath and a few hurried steps, the half-Titan emerges from the gloom smacking dirt from his breeches. "I'm coming, I'm coming. Whole cellblock collapsed at the end of the hall. Bloody mess. Squished limbs everywhere."

"Vaughn."

He looks up at Soren's severe tone. "What? What could possibly top squished limbs?"

"Her." I point at the cage. My fingers get a bit too close to the bars and, almost before I have a chance to yank them back, a broad set of white teeth try to snap the tips off. "She's the Earth Remnant."

Vaughn takes one look at her and his mouth drops open. "So you're saying that quake . . . that was *her*?"

The girl snarls so ominously, I flinch back into Soren.

"It was her," he says, steadying me. "We saw it. We felt it."

Vaughn's voice turns skeptical. "And you presume to bring her back with us. On a ship. Across the sea."

Skies, I hadn't thought of that. But frankly, there is no time to waste playing out potential scenarios now. "Are you going to pull this door down or stand there debating with us?"

Vaughn sighs and steps up to the cage, muttering the whole time. "Just what we needed on this already harebrained adventure. A feral prisoner who will sink our one remaining ship before we've made it halfway back to Hylios. Can't wait for the return journey. Gods, say what you will about this family, it's never boring . . ."

"Watch your fingers," I warn quietly. "I'm getting the inkling she is not going to be cooperative."

Scoffing, he wraps his large hands around the bars and jerks the door off its hinges. Before he can even set it aside, he's pelted in the face with a rock.

"Fuck!" he roars, clutching his bleeding temple. "That's the thanks I get for getting her out of there?"

The girl scuttles back into the corner of her cage, pressing her spine to the stone wall. She looks like she's trying to make herself as small as possible. But there is not a lick of fear on her face. Only savage wrath, coupled by the bloom of insanity in her eyes.

"We're here to help you," I tell her. "We won't hurt you."

She stares at me, unmoved.

"I'm Rhya," I try, gesturing down to the top half of my mark that peeks over my bodice. "I'm a Remnant. See? I'm like you."

She has no reaction.

Is it possible she does not know what she is? I myself had been ignorant of my own power when Penn first discovered me . . .

I send out a pulse of maegic, trying to connect with her, but feel nothing in response. That could be due to the ore around us, or the very nature of our elements. For air and earth are natural foils, diametrically opposed in power and compatibility.

"Soren, can you try to connect with her?"

"I have been. Her mind is like a hedge maze. One made of lethal thorns." His eyes shift from the girl to the other end of the corridor where Melité, Alaric, Harpina, and Arwen have disappeared. "We don't have time for this. The tide is already coming in."

"I know." My teeth dig into my bottom lip. "But we cannot leave her here in Efnysien's hands."

"No. We cannot. Gods know, he has grown powerful enough already with constant access to her blood." He runs a hand through his hair in frustration. "But reasoning with her does not seem to be working. And dragging her out by force could prove deadly for us all, given her reactivity."

Vaughn drops into a crouch by the threshold, eyeing her warily. His temple is still bleeding. "Come on, quakes. Get out of there."

She does not move a muscle. Perhaps she doesn't like her nickname.

"You can't actually want to stay here," he continues, striving for a cajoling tone. "If you do, you're even madder than you look."

I take a few steps closer, stopping short when the girl bares her teeth at me in warning. "Vaughn, give her a minute. She's scared."

"She doesn't look scared," Soren notes wryly. "She looks like she wants us dead."

Vaughn abandons all civility, his voice turning blunt. "Two choices. You can come out or I can drag you out."

Another rock whips at his head. This one, he manages to duck. Barely. To his credit, he does not seem alarmed by the attack. In fact, a slow grin works its way across his broad face as he stares at the disheveled prisoner. Something like respect shines in his eyes.

"Option two it is."

He is remarkably quick for such a large man. I always forget that about him until I see him move. The girl also underestimates his alacrity; she does not even have time to resist before he's reached into the cage and plucked her out like she weighs no more than a feather.

"There now," Vaughn says, his arms a vise. "Settle do—
Ow!" He looses an oath. "Infernal hells! The she-devil bit me!"

"I did warn you," I remind him, smothering a laugh. But all my amusement fades when the ground beneath us begins to vibrate again.

Gods, no.

Not another quake.

"Contain her!" Soren shouts. "Before she brings this whole island down!"

"Trying!" Vaughn yells back, panting from the effort. "She's incredibly strong!"

Her powers must be manifesting as brute physical strength.

Enough to set off tremors that shake the realm at its seams. Enough to rattle the snows of the Cimmerians from half a continent away.

Even Vaughn, in his limitless Titan strength, is struggling to hold on to the girl. She fights like a wild thing against his grip, kicking and thrashing, snapping her teeth and scoring her fingernails deep into the flesh of his forearms.

"It's like holding on to a bloody rockslide," he hisses. His muscles flex under the immense strain of it. But for all her efforts, she cannot quite manage to escape him. He begins to march forward, ignoring the bloody scratches that mar his skin, paying no heed to the growls that promise retribution as soon as she gets the opportunity.

"If she's this strong down here, what will she be like on the surface?" I ask Soren as we hurry in their wake, my boots picking a careful path across the vibrating earthen floor.

His eyes cut to mine. "Let us hope we live long enough to find out."

FOR A BRIEF moment, I dare to hope we will make it out alive. Back to the ship, back to our lives. I dare to believe that this half-baked plan of ours will actually be a success.

Until we catch up to Alaric, Arwen, and Harpina.

They've stopped at the bottom of the stairs that lead up to the tower. Arwen is on her feet, though leaning heavily against her husband's side. She has one of Harpina's throwing stars gripped tight in her hand, gleaming silver in the flickering light of a torch. All three of them stare in silence at the pile of rubble that blocks our way forward.

"Must've collapsed in the quake," Soren says grimly. "We'll have to find another way up to the ramparts."

I inhale deeply, trying not to succumb to panic at the thought of being trapped down here forever. My throat feels uncomfortably tight.

Vaughn grunts, but does not otherwise chime in. He is preoccupied holding on to the Earth Remnant, who, while no longer actively clawing at his arms, is clearly still exerting her significant strength in an ongoing attempt to shake herself free of his grip. The frustration that contorts her expression is a mirror of that on Vaughn's face as their battle of wills drags on without a victor.

Quite the match, they make.

"We should fan out," Soren says. "Search for—"

"Over here," a melodic voice interrupts him. "There's a passage and a set of steps."

Melité.

I'd forgotten she was with us in the chaos of the past few moments. But there she is, hips swaying as she sidles out of the shadows. There's a serene smile on her face.

"Follow me," she murmurs, turning on a heel.

Soren and I trade a glance but say nothing. There is no other choice. Time is running short. If we stall down here any longer, we will be stranded when the tide sweeps back in and washes our escape options out to sea.

The staircase is narrow and dark, no torches to light our ascent. We make our way up steadily, Vaughn on our heels, his constant curses and grunts chasing us the entire journey. Just ahead, I can hear the hoarse metronome of Arwen's shallow breaths. And beyond, Melité's fluid tones, floating back to us from the top.

"Not much farther now."

I had thought my trepidation already at its apex in the dungeons, but it vaults to new levels as we step out of the stairwell and into the prison's inner courtyard. It is cast in shadow by the black stone walls that tower all around us. Against the dark sky, the illuminated guard towers cut a menacing silhouette.

Have Penn and the others already cleared all four?

If not, we will soon be spotted. There is nowhere to hide. Not even a tree to duck behind for cover. Just an expanse of flag-stones and unyielding mortar. About forty paces from where we stand, I spot a set of switchback steps along the interior wall, leading up to the ramparts.

"There," I say, voice hushed as I point them out. "Our exit."

We've scarcely made it three strides when Melité speaks again, halting our progression. "Oh, no. We won't be leaving so soon." A sinew of amusement runs through her serpentine tone. As though she is laughing at a joke we are not privy to. "Not until the family reunion is complete."

On my left, Soren stills. On my right, Vaughn does the same. Even the girl in his arms stops writhing, momentarily silenced by the half-siren's words.

A chill skitters down my spine.

"What is she talking about?" Alaric tightens his hold on Arwen's hand and looks at Soren. "What is she—"

"Our stepbrother is on his way, you see," Melité says sweetly. "And he will want to see you all when he arrives. Efnysien was so very happy when I told him we'd be paying a visit."

At the word *Efnysien*, Arwen gasps and goes pale as the blood rushes out of her face. The girl in Vaughn's arms has a less sedate reaction. She begins to struggle anew, doubling the intensity of her flailing. He grunts under the effort to contain her, his muscles flexing.

"*Quit.*" He flexes harder. "*It.*"

The ground beneath the Iron Isle gives an ominous rattle.

Melité laughs then, throwing her head back with abandon. If

you can call what she does a laugh. The sound is grating, almost mechanical. It tapers off as suddenly as it began when her inky eyes cut to me. "He would be here to greet you himself, if not for your little trick with the wind. We were not supposed to be here for two more days." Her gills flare. "No matter, though. His scouts knew to look for us thanks to me. They've had us in their sights since we passed into Dymmerian waters this morning. Even now, he is hastening here to greet us. He should arrive quite soon."

Skies above.

"Melité," Soren hisses, striding for his sister. "What have you done?"

"What have I done?" she spits, black fully overtaking her eyes. "What have *you* done? Hmm? Casting out your own kin. And for what? For *her*?" Her attention moves to Arwen, who is trembling in her thin nightgown, one hand white-knuckled as it grips her husband's, the other clutching the throwing star as though she'd like to hurl it at her sister's face. "Precious, perfect Arwen. Everyone's favorite. Everyone's obsession."

Arwen flinches.

Melité's next laugh is bitter. "No more. After what I have done for him, *I* will be his obsession. *I* will be the one deemed worthy of his affection, his praise. His love."

Soren's hand flashes out and he grabs Melité by the throat. "It was you. You who told him how to access the portal network. You who instructed him when to strike during the wedding." His fingers tighten, compressing her gills. "Why? Why would you betray us? We are your family."

Her black orbs glare at him, brimming over with hatred. "You have never been my family. Efnysien is my family. And my future. The Shadowfall is coming for you all, and with it the end of everything you hold d—"

Her vile words choke into silence as Soren squeezes her windpipe. He shakes her so hard her head snaps back. I think he will choke the life from her as we watch. The pure wrath suffusing his expression makes my heart fail.

"Soren," I call, stepping closer to him. "Leave her. She is not worth it."

"Rhya's right, brother." Vaughn's voice carries back to us as he makes his way toward the stairs. "We need to go. If what she says is true, we don't have long before company arrives."

Soren releases her with a disgusted snarl. "You have chosen your side in this war. You will live to regret it."

"But I will live," she wheezes, gripping her throat delicately. "Unlike all of you."

With that, she raises her arm up toward the sky. A silent signal. For what, I do not know . . . until the whoosh of two dozen torches being illuminated at once washes across the flagstones. In a blink, the entire courtyard is ablaze with light. We are surrounded by guards on all sides, their mottled skin even more inhuman in the flickering of the torches as they step forward. There are more of them than I can count. And, if Melité is to be believed, others are on their way.

Efnysien among them.

"Alaric, get Arwen out of here," Soren barks. "Follow Vaughn up to the ramparts. Now."

They do not hesitate, for this is no suggestion. It is as kingly an order as I have ever heard him give. I watch Alaric ushering Arwen toward the stairs, his hand firm on hers. Just ahead of them, Vaughn struggles to haul the Earth Remnant across the flagstones, his low oaths booming.

"Keep this up, quakes," he mutters over a feminine growl, "and I'll have no choice but to knock you out."

The answering flash of viridescent eyes is undaunted.

Soren's focus never shifts from Melité, even as he speaks. "Rhya . . ."

"Right here," I say, stepping up beside him. Our shoulders brush as I jerk the whip free from my belt, feeling steadier with its golden handle cupped in my palm.

"I'll take the left half," he mutters. "You take the right."

We are plainly outnumbered.

But when has that ever stopped us before?

I feel the surge of Soren's maegic—thinner than usual, but still strong enough to summon a globe of water capable of bowling over three men at once. Electricity sparks down my arm as I summon my storms to the forefront of my mind. The gathered charge feels weaker than I'm accustomed to. Diluted or no, the first crack of my whip sends a whole line of guards scurrying backward like cockroaches in the light. I grin as I watch them fleeing from me.

Soren is at my back, siphoning tendrils of water from the saturated stones, sending them down the throats of everyone who charges into his path.

"Now, now. This won't do at all." Melité makes a *tsk* sound. "We can't have the party breaking up so soon, can we?"

I look over in time to see her step between two mottled soldiers, each holding a crossbow. Her eyes are on Arwen and Alaric as they reach the bottom of the stairs.

"Him," she purrs, smiling.

My whip flashes out toward them, but it's too late. The soldiers fire. Time shifts into slow motion as the bolts arc through the air. I see the horror on Arwen's face as she looks over her shoulder, the split second of realization as she watches the inbound projectiles and can do nothing to stop them. She cannot push him out of the way, she cannot dodge in front of him. She cannot even cry out in warning.

Two bolts pierce Alaric's chest.

Straight through the center, where his heart beats.

Where his lungs pump.

A death stroke.

He falls to his knees, hands reaching uselessly for his wife, face a tableau of disbelief. Her wail splits the night as he slumps over, his gorgeous eyes unseeing, his pale hair turning scarlet as the blood pools beneath him.

Arwen's incoherent laments morph into a word. One word. One *name*, repeated over and over again, so full of agony I know, as long as I live, I will never forget the sound of it.

"ALARIC!"

Above her screams, the unfathomable cackle of Melité's sick laughter.

My fury rises, a blinding thing, unfurling inside me like a tornado. I crack my whip and send a zap of lightning straight for her. One of the mottled soldiers sees it coming and dives to shield her. He writhes as he is electrocuted, then collapses before her in a steaming, twitching heap of black-veined limbs.

Melité has the gall to mock me as she slinks behind the protective line of soldiers. "And here I thought we were becoming friends, Rhya."

I advance on them, whip cracking out again and again. Behind me, Arwen's continuous screams rip through my heart.

"Go to her," I tell Soren through the bond. *"Go to your sister."*

I can feel his solemnity, his endless grief, a milder echo of hers. This loss is one he shares. He and Alaric were close friends for decades, long before marriage made them brothers. He wants to race to her, but he is holding back. Hesitant to leave me to this battle alone.

"Go," I urge. *"I've got this."*

There is a brief pause. Then, *"I know you do, skylark."*

And I do.

I do have it.

I have never felt so in control, even with the iron's lecherous influence. I take out half a dozen soldiers in the time it takes Soren to cross the courtyard, covering him as he runs. They are husks by the time they hit the ground.

The second Soren's arms close around her, Arwen's screams taper off into violent sobs that tear from her throat.

"I'm going to kill her!" she shrieks, voice cracking. "I'm going to kill that sea-bitch with my bare hands!"

"I should like to see you try," Melité calls back, sounding bored.

With a roar, Arwen tears out of Soren's grip and barrels across the courtyard. She does not seem to realize she is barefoot and covered in blood, without even a dagger to fight with as she runs headlong toward a line of enemies. She is blind with grief. And with retribution. The need for it burns through her, searing in her veins. I can feel it lashing across the courtyard from here.

"Soren!" I call, alarmed. *"She's going to get herself killed!"*

"I've got her." His inner voice is labored as he sprints after her.

"Get her out of here, now. Go with Vaughn. Get to the ship. I will meet you there soon."

"I will not leave you here alone."

"I am not alone."

And I am not. I can sense Penn closing in on us, drawn by the surge of maegic and the sound of screams. Even now, he is running across the ramparts on the opposite side of the courtyard, coming down the switchback set of steps that mirror those Vaughn has just ascended.

"Skylark—"

"I'm going to kill you!" Arwen bellows at her half-sister, fighting against Soren's arms with nearly as much violence as the Earth Remnant had displayed. Harpina hovers close by her flight leader's side, her sleek silver bow twanging again and again as she covers them with unshakable focus.

"*Go,*" I repeat firmly.

He finally complies, lifting Arwen into his arms and sprinting up the steps, Harpina shadowing. Arwen bellows the whole way, her screams not fading until they are on the ramparts, out of sight.

I keep myself planted between the stairs and the remaining cluster of soldiers as they scurry into a fresh formation, surrounding Melité on all sides. Relief crashes through me as I spot Cadogan, Jac, Farley, Mabon, and Penn barreling down the opposite staircase, only to pull up short on the stone landing when they spot the shocking scene below.

"Right on time," Melité hums. As her voice lifts to call out, her siren song spins through the air like smoke. "Cadogan, my love. Come to me."

His handsome face contorts into a lovestruck mask as she pulls him into her thrall. I cry out to stop him, my voice carrying across the courtyard. Penn reaches for him. So does Mabon.

But it is too late.

Too late.

All we can do is watch in horror as he complies with her orders—taking a step out into empty air, plummeting from the landing onto the courtyard. His body hits the flagstones with a sickening crunch.

He does not get up.

Fresh grief explodes through my body. My scream is swallowed up by the collective roars of the Ember Guild. Everyone erupts into motion at once—Farley firing arrow after arrow, straight for Melité's heart; Jac reaching for his battle-axe as he pounds down the steps; Mabon's heavy crossbow twanging as he fires indiscriminately at the clustered guards.

Penn reaches the ground first, his face a mask of wrath. The blade in his hand blazes red, though its color is more muted than usual. Thankfully, he does not require maegic to fight like a daemon. He cuts a path through the soldiers, cleaving bodies in two, driving his sword home again and again and again until the flagstones are awash in rivers of clotted black blood.

I cross the courtyard in a single bound, vaulting through the air to Cadogan's crumpled form. My tears fall in a torrent onto his bloodied face as I gently roll him onto his back.

Please, gods, please do not be dead.

His handsome features are fractured irreparably—straight nose gnashed, full lips torn, expressive eyes swollen shut. He breathes, but barely. His chest rises and falls in halting shudders that tell me his ribs are likely broken. His legs are both bent at unnatural angles, as is one arm.

"Cadogan," I whisper.

"Is he alive?" Jac is suddenly there, crouching at my side. He reaches out as if to touch his friend, but pulls back before making contact. "Ace, is he alive?"

"He's alive."

There is a short silence. "Will he stay alive?"

Our eyes meet. His, like mine, are glossed with tears.

"I don't know," I answer truthfully, hating the tremor in my voice. "But if he's to stand any sort of chance, you need to get him out of here. Get him back to the ship." My gaze swings around until it lands on Mabon, who is still firing bolts at the guards. "Mabon! Get over here and help Jac carry him up the stairs."

He rushes toward us instantly.

"Farley!" I yell up to him on the landing, where he is still shooting off arrows. "Go with them! They need cover."

He nods, never taking his eyes off the courtyard as he nocks back another arrow and sends it sailing straight through the heart of a mottled guard.

I bend forward and brush my lips against Cadogan's forehead before Jac and Mabon hoist him into their arms. Farley shadows their progress toward the stairs, his arrows finding marks without reprieve. I do not even have the luxury of watching the four of them go, for Penn is still battling in the thick of it, his red-hot blade whirling so fast I can hardly keep it in my sights as he hacks a path straight toward the half-siren.

She is, I notice, no longer laughing or taunting. She actually looks a bit nervous as their ranks drop below twenty for the first time. Penn continues to cut them down, his blade vicious as it clashes and parries, the tangs of swordplay rebounding against the stone walls. I join him, battling at his back whenever he charges forward to engage new enemies, my wind currents knocking inbound arrows and bolts off course before they can graze him. My whip cracks out again and again, lightning to accompany the thunder of his strikes, turning the mottled soldiers to steaming skeletons.

We've culled the group to about a dozen guards when I feel Soren's mind brush mine from somewhere far in the distance.

"Rhya," he calls, his voice barely audible. *"Tell me you are on that second dinghy."*

"I'm on that dinghy," I lie, blasting an incoming volley of arrows off course with a pulse of air.

"Gods damn it, skylark, what are you thinking?"

"Cadogan was wounded." I allow the horrific visions of his fall to furl down the bond. *"They could not afford to wait any longer."*

"We're bringing the first dinghy back for you and Penn."

"Thanks. I don't much fancy swimming."

He does not seem amused. *"You need to get the hell out of there."*

"I'm not sticking around for the ambiance, trust me."

"Get up to the ramparts. Wait for us there." His worry is palpable. *"There are ships on the horizon, closing in."*

Skies.

Efnysien is close.

"Penn!" I yell. "We need to get out of here!"

But Penn is caught up in the fury of battle, his fiery temper raging out of control. I have seen him like this before; seen how he loses himself beneath the surge, how he cannot pull himself back from the brink.

I grab his arm and cling, even when he tries to shake me off. It takes a toll on my remaining strength to summon an air shield that will keep us momentarily safe from enemy fire.

"Pendefyre!" I send a sharp pulse down the bond—the strongest one I can muster without hurting him. "Listen to me. Penn, please. Look at me."

He finally manages to focus, his flaming eyes locked on mine. He blinks slowly, the haze of battle clearing. "Rhya."

"We have to go. Now."

"Not until I kill her. She has to pay. For Cadogan."

"You cannot kill her if you are dead," I snap. "There is a ship inbound with gods only know how many men aboard."

He stills. "Efnysien."

Perhaps I should not have told him that. He sees it as an opportunity, not a deterrent.

"You cannot take him on alone."

His jaw clenches. "This may be our only chance."

"It will not be." My fury mingles with frustration. "We will kill him, and her. But not this night." I inhale deeply, trying to calm my thudding pulse. "Your men need you. Cadogan needs you. Who will hold them together, if you are not there?"

He stares at me, uncompromising.

Three bolts bounce off my air shield and clatter to the ground.

"I do not want to lose you," I tell him, reaching out a hand and pressing it against his heart through the fabric of his shirt. "For once, please do not argue with me. For once . . . let me win in our butting of heads. Can you do that? For me?"

His eyes flare with heat and then, with sheer force of will, he locks down his scorching anger. I watch it ebb from his frame in slow degrees as he exhales, the tension leaving his stiff shoulders, the clench of his jaw relaxing slightly. He shoots one fleeting look at Melité, who has retreated into the shadows with her remaining contingent of protection, before he nods.

"Let's go."

Together, we sprint for the steps on the opposite side of the courtyard. I close my eyes as we leap over Alaric's dead body, not wanting to see how his kind eyes stare blankly at the skies. Several guards give chase, their pounding boots in close pursuit. I send a blunt blast of air over my shoulder, knocking them off the steps and onto the ground. Finesse is a distant memory. My maegic is flagging, pushed beyond the pale.

We rush along the ramparts toward the grappling hooks still embedded in the stone. Below, there is no sign of the rocky beach. No place for a dinghy to put in. Waves throttle the base of the walls with the force of a battering ram.

"Fuck," Penn clips, his jaw tense.

My eyes fly toward the horizon. I see the shadowy silhouette of our brig with its black sails and, far closer, the much smaller shape of a dinghy moving toward us at immense speed, no doubt propelled by Soren's maegic.

"That's them," I breathe.

"Should we jump for it?" Penn sounds grim. "Try to swim to them?"

I shake my head, eyeing the thrashing waves. They will break us like glass against the walls.

"I have a better idea." I gulp nervously. "But you'll have to trust me."

Penn's head turns my way. His eyes are very solemn, as is his voice. "Rhya. I would trust you with my life. I would trust you with anything."

Our gazes hold for a long moment.

My maegic gathers in the air all around us, swelling from a gentle current to a solid stream as I wind it around his broad frame. I give him no warning as I lift him off his feet. His shout of surprise makes a laugh spill from my lips.

"Rhya! What are you—"

"Don't worry," I tell him, grinning. "I'm right behind you."

With that, I sweep him higher into the air, then steer him out over the dark waves. My grin fades as the true weight of this task swamps me. I nearly bite through my lip in the effort not to drop him. I have never done this before—at least, not for so long a distance. And he is solid muscle. So very heavy.

Still, I cannot let him drop.

This is Penn.

I will not let him drop.

I watch the dinghy slow to a crawl as the men aboard spot my delivery sailing through the sky toward them. Black waves of exhaustion press in at my temples as I slowly lower his hulking form into the boat. As I release my hold, I collapse forward against the stone railing, sucking huge gasps of air into my aching lungs.

I'm about to pass out.

"*Clever.*" Soren sounds slightly amused by my methods, even from afar. "*Now get your ass off that island and into this boat.*"

"*I need a minute.*"

"*Rhya, you do not have a minute.*"

He's right. I can see, closing in, several foreign ships on the horizon. They are far larger than our brig and, if I had to guess, loaded with more than mere reinforcements. They surely have cannons, too, fully capable of blasting us out of the water.

"*Deke is already underway, sailing north. It will take all our combined powers just to catch up.*"

I push myself upright.

One last breath.

In through my nose, out through my mouth.

My mind is sluggish, my maegic drained. The poisonous ore has parched my inner reservoirs. The mark at my breast is icy with cold. I push through the fog of exhaustion as I step back from the rail.

Closing my eyes, I summon my frail wind. I don't open them even as I lift up off the stone rampart into the sky. For I do not need to see where I'm going. I only need to follow the thread that connects me to that dinghy. To the two souls who bob there in the darkness, waiting for me.

The first bolt of iron pierces me in the right lung.

The next tears a clean path through my stomach.

The final nicks my heart.

I fall, a bird plummeting straight down from the sky, flight abruptly ended. My body hits the ramparts hard enough to expel whatever air remains in my one functional lung. My head cracks against the stone, shattering my consciousness. And I am grateful for it.

The haze lessens the pain of my impending death.

I blink up at the night sky. There are no stars here. Only an endless expanse of black. It seems fitting somehow. A match for the blackness that encroaches at the edges of my vision, sweeping me away.

I hear the familiar cackle of Melité's laughter, ringing in my head.

I hear Soren roaring my name down the bond.

Then, the world goes dark, and I hear nothing at all.

CHAPTER
THIRTY-ONE

I am not dead.

But the moment consciousness returns, I begin to wish I were. For when I manage to peel my eyes open, I am no longer lying atop the ramparts. I am no longer on the Iron Isle. I am somewhere I have never been before, yet recognize in an instant.

Black sand.

Black sky.

The Husk Desert of Dymmeria.

A man stands over me, blocking out the anemic sun. Even at midday, it is mostly dark here. His face is the stuff of nightmares. The slitted nostrils, the deathly pallor. His gray-white limbs, like those of his men, are mottled black. In his case, however, those blackened veins are slightly raised like the gnarled bark of a tree. Like scar tissue. Like my Remnant mark. His eyes are blood red, reminiscent of a vampyre from the old tales. He has no hair. Not eyebrows nor stubble, not a single strand on his head. Tattoos mar his corpse-like skin, strange patterns that seem to shift and change even as I focus on them.

"You're finally awake. Good." His lips purse as he nudges me with the tip of one steel-toed boot. "I was beginning to think that iron had lodged a bit too close to your heart."

He bends down and twists the bolt that still protrudes from my chest.

My scream is a harrowing sound. The pain is unimaginable. I pass out again, only to jerk awake when he kicks me—a harsh blow to the ribs.

"Now, now, that won't do, Rhya." He pauses, studying my expression closely. "Oh, yes, I know your name. Does that surprise you? It should not. I know everything about you."

I cough violently and taste copper in my mouth. Turning my head, I spit the gob of blood onto the sand.

He drops fluidly into a crouch and shakes his head. "Don't be wasteful."

Scooping up the scarlet saliva, he places it on his tongue as though it is the finest delicacy Anwyvn has to offer. He practically moans as he swallows.

"How nice to have another flavor after all these years. I admit, I have grown rather tired of your earthy counterpart of late." He pauses, leaning over me. His face hovers only a few inches above mine. Up close, his red eyes are even more terrifying. "That is why your arrival is so perfect."

I head-butt him.

A shame he doesn't have a nose to break. He dodges before I can do more than graze his forehead with mine.

"Let's not get off on the wrong foot, little bird." His thin mouth attempts a smile, but there is no emotion behind it. Like his eyes, it is completely devoid of anything resembling feeling. "We are going to be spending so much time together, after all."

"Just"—I swallow down more blood—"kill me already."

"Kill you?" He laughs, a horrible sound. "Whyever would I do that? You are my honored guest. I plan to keep you for as long as I can." He pauses. "Which is to say, as long as your body holds out. My Zariah lasted half a decade. Though she was more spirited than most of my more . . . *breakable* . . . toys."

Zariah.

Is she the Remnant of Earth we saved from his dungeons? I find a shred of solace in the knowledge that she, at least, is free of this monster's clutches.

"A shame you and your friends managed to infiltrate my favorite place to play." He rises to his feet, soles sliding on the ebony dune. "No matter. We have a new sandbox, you and I. This one is a bit less accessible than the isle, should my stepbrother get any ideas about heroic rescues. We shall break it in together. How does that sound?"

I glare at him. I cannot speak. The iron pierced through my right lung is agony, scraping my insides with each breath. The one by my heart sends waves of poisonous pain rippling through me each time it beats.

"Dark Emperor," a new voice, hushed with reverence, offers as a scarlet-clad soldier steps into view. He does not appear quite as distorted as some of the others I saw at the prison. He could almost pass as any mortal soldier in the Midlands. "Excuse my intrusion, but—"

The sentence cuts off on a gasp as Efnysien's hand flies out and seizes the soldier by the throat.

"Did I or did I not say," he asks, voice utterly level, "that I was not to be disturbed with any unnecessary interruptions while greeting our new guest?"

The soldier makes a choking sound. His face is turning pale from lack of air.

"I'm relatively certain I did." In a decidedly serpentine move, Efnysien tilts his head to the side, evaluating the man in his grip.

I brace for the strike—the snap of a neck, the slash of a blade.

Still, I am unprepared for it. A cloud of black maegic amasses in the air, billowing like living smoke. It does not feel like my wind, or Penn's fire, or Soren's water. This is not Remnant power. Not natural. Not elemental.

It is something else.

Something evil.

I watch the snake of black slither down Efnysien's taut arm, then join his fingers in a deadly cuff around the soldier's windpipe. The man begins to convulse as it seeps into his skin. Already pale, he goes fully bloodless as the dark power suffuses his veins, hijacks his senses. His gasping mouth goes slack, his terror-widened eyes go empty. In the span of a breath, all semblance of life has been drained from his body.

And siphoned straight into Efnysien's.

The sorcerer's strange tattoos shift across his skin, *within* it, the patterns moving like shadows on a sundial as he absorbs the man's essence. His shoulders shudder, his chin tips back to the sky on a low groan. Sating his dark thirst. Not stopping until he's pumped every last shred of vitality. Until all that remains is a man-shaped shell.

It is enough to make my blood run cold.

An abomination.

An atrocity.

Without another word spoken, Efnysien releases his grip. The emperor does not even bother to watch as his loyal subject falls, dead, to the desert sand. His crimson eyes are already turning back to find mine.

I hope my face does not betray my fright.

He can kill by contact alone.

His very touch is death.

"It's going to be such fun, having you here," he says, as though we were never interrupted. "You'll see." He jerks his chin toward someone out of my sight line. "Isn't that right, my sea goddess?"

Melité's svelte form presses into his side. Her arms wind around his waist as she lays a kiss against his marbled neck, then angles her head down to stare at me. Her eyes are pure ink, her smile is coy. At her waist, my golden whip is coiled neatly on a braided sash.

"Rhya, Rhya. You know, now that we're being honest, I never did understand the fuss everyone made over your appearance in our lives. What's so special about *you*? Hmm?" Her eyes narrow a shade, gills flaring. "But the second you arrived, it was like Arwen all over again. Everyone fawning over your presence. My brother especially. *Pathetic*, the lot of them."

Efnysien's eyes flare victoriously. "Oh, Soren will be so upset at this turn of events. He never did enjoy it when I broke his favorite toys as a boy . . ."

My head is swimming from the pain and the terror. I must black out again for a moment because when I come to, Melité is crouched over me, holding a dagger—*my* dagger—to my face. Before I can react, she digs the tip into the flesh of my cheek and scores a slow line down toward my jaw, grinning as the blood spills into the sand. It hurts, but not half so much as my other injuries.

"Those stormy eyes of yours are so pretty," she says, her exquisite features contorted into an ugly grimace. "Always casting little looks across rooms at my brother when you think no one is watching. Always blazing with such defiance. Even now, when you're at my mercy. You can't help yourself, can you?" Her lips curve in anticipation as the blade inches closer to my eye socket.

I still, not even daring to draw breath.

"Should I pluck them out for you?" she asks. "It would save you the trouble of glaring at me . . . No more haughty looks . . ."

"Come now, Melité," Efnysien interjects. "There will be plenty of time to maim in the years to come. We want to savor it, do we not?"

She huffs out a resigned breath, then rises to her feet, skirts swishing as she stomps back to his side. "Fine. But I want her to suffer."

"Suffer she will, my vengeful one." He takes her place in my line of sight. His cadaverous skin and monstrous features are infinitely more horrifying than Melité's petulant beauty. I fight a gag as his tongue—foul black and forked at the tip—licks the side of my face, where the dagger carved its mark. His whole frame shudders in delight as he swallows my blood, eyelids closing to prolong the sensation. His tattoos shimmer again, the designs warping in a way I cannot decipher. His irises glow redder than before as they sliver open to meet mine.

"We'll start with these," he says smoothly, holding up a set of shackles.

I assume they'll be iron, but they do not appear to be crafted from the familiar dark metal. Instead, they are shiny black stone, and glow faintly in the weak light.

"Now, these are no normal manacles," he informs me, smiling like we are old friends. "These are harvested especially from dead portals. They contain traces of the leylines within them. Not enough to travel anywhere, of course, but enough to mimic the rather . . . intriguing . . . mental effects one experiences when lost within them."

Gods, no.

I have not forgotten how it felt to lose myself in the portal network. The way it frayed my mind, my very self. If these shackles do anything like that . . .

I will never survive it.

My heart's frantic beats scrape the iron bolt as my pulse kicks into higher gear. Fresh waves of pain wash over me, a relentless tide. My lips part, prepared to beg him not to put them on me, but I manage to swallow down my pleas at the last moment. I will not give him the satisfaction of begging.

"Here we are . . ." He fits the strange cuffs over my limp wrists, latching them shut with a firm clicking sound. The smooth stone is frigid against my skin, cold enough to induce frostbite. Otherwise, I feel no different.

Yet.

"They look lovely on you, Rhya. Just lovely. Don't you agree?"

I glare up at him, teeth clenched.

"Ah. Well. I'm sure you'll soon forget they're even there." He smirks, like he's party to a joke I do not understand. "Now that you're properly outfitted, I'd love to see if some of the rumors I've heard about wind weavers are true. Namely . . . that you are quite opposed to confinement."

My throat closes up.

No.

No.

No.

Not that.

Anything but that.

"I have crafted a new cage, made especially for you. I did not think I would have a chance to use it so soon. But now . . ." His lifeless smile sends a chill straight down to the fabric of my soul. "I think we should see how you fare inside it."

Without warning, I am lifted from the sand by two soldiers—one gripping my wrists, the other my ankles. My body is so weak, I can hardly even struggle as they carry me to the edge of a deep pit. My maegic is distant, the storms inside me dissipated to an intangible wisp. My mind feels muddled by more than panic, my thoughts fraying into tatters.

Is this the effect of the cuffs? Are they already working to poison my senses against me?

"It used to be a well before the water dried up," Efnysien says conversationally. "It goes quite far down. But don't worry about the arachnidae or sandwyverns. They will not be able to claw their way in, no matter how they try. The walls are fully lined with iron, you see."

I choke back a sob of pure terror as the men begin to swing me out over the edge of the pit like you'd heave a bale of hay or a heavy bag of flour, gaining momentum with each oscillation.

"I think we'll start with a month. That should give you some time to settle in before I check on you."

"Fuck you," I hiss.

He smiles placidly. "Two months."

Melité giggles somewhere out of sight.

"*Go. To. Hell.*"

"Oh, all right. If you insist." His smile widens, but his red eyes are utterly void. "Let's make it three."

At his nod, they release me. I scream as I plummet. The fall lasts forever. When I land at the bottom, I feel my wrist snap. The pain of it pales in comparison to the crossbow bolts, which tear my flesh as they jar loose, widening my wounds.

Breathless, I gape up at the faraway sky.

It reminds me of being at the bottom of the beacon back in Hylios. Staring up that endless obelisk toward a remote circle of light.

"Welcome to Dymmeria, Rhya." Efnysien's voice floats down to me. "We are so very happy to have you with us."

With that, the light disappears as an iron hatch slams shut.

I lie in the utter darkness. There is no light. No sound. No air. I am at the very depths of the earth.

I will die down here, I think, mind fracturing into pure panic. *I will desiccate and decay.*

I will never be found.

I will fade away into nothing.

As though I never existed.

"Let me out!" I scream to no one, voice cracking like glass. *"Let me out of here!"*

But he does not.

And there is no answer from the endless dark.

❧

AT FIRST, I hold on.

To hope.

To memory.

I push through the pain that persists even as I work the bolts from my flesh. Through the torment that remains even after my snapped wrist stitches itself back together. Through the clawing panic that never wanes, a constant reminder of my confinement. Through the muddling haze of the obsidian cuffs that make me question my own sanity.

I try to remember life before.

I try to keep the good things close.

Pretend you are in the clouds, Soren whispers in my opaque mind. *Feel the wind on your face, in your hair.*

You are not here. You are flying free.

Breathe, skylark. Just breathe.

I want to weep, but I have no moisture left in my body for tears. It dried up long ago, sucked out of me by the desert heat that, even down here, seems to wick every bit of water from the earth. Dehydration is a distant state; my very bones feel dry as tinder.

I am given only enough food and water to survive, delivered by guards who never show their faces or speak to me. There is no rhyme or reason to their schedule I can discern. Occasionally, they will toss down a moldy bit of bread, so hard I can scarcely gnaw through it. Other days, the hatch opens and a bucketful of water is dumped unceremoniously down the shaft. I slurp it from puddles off the floor before it runs into the drain in the corner where I relieve myself, tasting dirt and grime and blood with every desperate sip.

We'll be out of here soon, a familiar deep voice promises, rumbling like water over a bed of stone. *Back in Hylios. Back in the sunlight. Think of that, not this place.*

After a time, no amount of memories can warm my heart. My damaged body has healed itself as much as possible, but there is no cure for my ravaged soul.

A friend once expressed to me her wish for death. I can no longer recall her name, but I can conjure her face when I focus intently. Her red hair, blazing in the dark.

Do not wish for death, I told her. *Not ever. No matter what. Life is the most precious gift we are ever given. To squander it would be a waste. To stop living in the face of loss . . . it does a disservice to those who are no longer here with us.*

What a hypocrite I was.

What a naive little fool.

Death would be a mercy, compared to this.

But Efnysien does not know mercy.

HE COMES TO me eventually, as promised.

Three months, he said?

It feels like three lifetimes.

"Oh, dear," he calls down to me, voice taunting. "I must say, you're not looking so well." He sniffs audibly. "You're not smelling much better. You must endeavor to take better care of yourself moving forward."

"Please," I croak, clawing at the iron walls, singeing the skin off my fingertips. "Please, let me out."

"So hasty to fly, aren't you? No, little bird. I think another few months down here is exactly what you need."

"No! No, wait! Please, don't—"

The hatch slams shut with finality, plunging my world into darkness.

AFTER THAT FIRST visit, he comes irregularly, his appearances as unpredictable as the water deliveries. Sometimes Melité is there with him, her vicious laugh striking at my heart like a viper's fangs. Mostly, though, he is alone.

He speaks to me at length during these interludes.

"How many months has it been now, little bird? Eight already? Time does fly when you're enjoying yourself, does it not?"

Eight months?

It cannot be eight months.

Not that long.

Surely not . . .

But my grip on time grows as thin as the flesh that covers my bones. The cuffs cloud everything into incomprehension.

"DOES IT BOTHER you that they never attempted a rescue?" he asks the visit after that. "Never even tried, your valiant kings. They simply moved on with their lives, leaving you here to rot."

No.

No, that is not true.

They care for me.

They would never leave me.

They . . .

I think very hard, trying to pull their names into my mind, and choke out a sob when I cannot quite manage it. My memories are growing threadbare. Gossamer as cobwebs. The longer I spend down here, the more I feel myself unraveling. It is like that time I was lost in the portals.

Oblivion, someone called it.

I can see his face when I press my fingers to my temples and reach deep inside. Blue eyes, dark hair. A smile that could stop my heart in its tracks. I rock back and forth, trying to hold it. Trying to hold him. But he, like the rest, slips away.

THE NEXT VISIT is worse.

"I heard the juiciest news from the north. It seems one of your kings had a rather explosive incident at his court. Catastrophic, if the rumors are accurate. I wonder what set him off. . ."

Kings.

Two kings.

Two men.

A man of heat and flame.

A man of sea and starlight.

A distant toll rings in my head, there and gone in an instant. Flattened quickly by depression and despair.

Eventually, I do not even clamber to my feet when the hatch opens. Not for water, nor for the visits from my captor, which seem to grow rarer and rarer as weeks stretch into months, and months into years.

"My, my, little bird. Has it been three years already that

we've been together? It seems so much longer than that. I feel we've been in each other's lives forever. I can hardly remember a time before you came to be with me." He pauses. "What about you, little bird? How is your memory these days?"

Memory.

A fleeting thing.

Far out of focus.

Like the flap of a butterfly's wing on a distant wind.

Like the clasp of a warm hand on a cheek.

Like the feel of two lips brushing secret skin.

"Can you remember your life before you came here?" he asks. "Can you remember my name?"

I cannot.

But that does not matter. What is a name?

"Can you remember your own?"

Rhya.

Rhya.

My name is Rhya.

Wind weaver.

Light bringer.

Sky sylph.

I sing it over and over, clinging to that one piece of myself. That final piece. The only one that remains as everything else is stripped away.

"My name is Rhya," I whisper to the dark when the hatch closes again and he goes away. My voice is hoarse from disuse, scratchy as the legs of the arachnidae who sometimes try to dig their way up through my refuse drain.

Rhya.

Rhya.

My name was Rhya.

Wasn't it?

I hold on to that one detail for as long as I can. But I cannot hold on forever. And so my name, too, becomes a memory.

I become a memory.

Alone, at the bottom of the world, with only my madness for company . . .

I fade into the dark.

GLOSSARY OF TERMS

Anwyvn—A land shared by mortals and fae.

arachnidae—A variety of large, carnivorous spider native to the Southlands, with black ichor and paralytic venom.

Aurea Tree—A mythical golden tree at the heart of Seahaven's Starlight Wood.

Avian Strait—A narrow pass through the Cimmerian Mountains, the only known route into the Northlands and the site of many bloody battles.

Beacons of Hylios—A pair of monolithic lighthouses built into the perimeter walls of the Llŷrian capital.

Caeldera—The capital of Dyved; a city contained entirely within a dormant volcanic crater.

Cull—The uprising of mortal men against the fae race two hundred years ago.

culling priests—Holy men who hate the fae and preach on the need for blood purification in Anwyvn. Many claim to be descendants of the original priests who slew the emperor and his family.

cyntroedi—A variety of giant centipede, white in color, with toxic green venom, found in dark underground areas.

Dyved—A Northlands kingdom occupying the plateau in the north-western corner of Anwyvn, beyond the Cimmerian Mountains.

Ember Guild—A unit of highly trained warriors who answer directly to King Pendefyre of Dyved.

fymandridae—A variety of fire salamander indigenous to Dyved, viridescent in color, long considered a sacred symbol of the Fire Court.

fyre priestess—A member of a sect of holy women pledged to honor the God of Flame.

Fyremas—A Dyvedi holiday widely celebrated to mark the start of spring.

fyrewisps—A low class of fae, also known as will-o'-the-wisps or ghost lights, often seen floating in bogs or forests by travelers at night.

halfling—A human-fae hybrid from both bloodlines, typically powerless, only discernible from humankind by their pointed ears.

Hylios—The capital city of Llŷr.

ice giant—A legendary hoarfrost monster found mainly in the Frostlands and the Cimmerian Mountains.

leylines—A network of maegical threads deep in the earth that knit together the fabric of the realm.

Llŷr—A Northlands kingdom spanning the northeastern corner of Anwyvn, notoriously ruled by the bloodthirsty King Soren.

nymph—Slang for a fae with water powers.

Paexyri—Mythical mounts once ridden by fae in the time of maegic, said to run with twice the speed and stamina of a normal horse.

point—A derogatory term for fae kind.

portal—A maegical gateway in a place of power, allowing for instantaneous travel across the leylines of the land.

Prydain Isle—An isolated island kingdom in the North Sea, inhabited by Titans.

Red Chasm—A deep deposit of iron ore running through the Midlands.

Remnant—One of four reincarnated vestiges of elemental power.

sea gate—A retractable opening within the perimeter walls of Hylios, powered by large water wheels, that protects the inner harbor.

Starlight Wood—A forest of ancient trees on the western shore of Seahaven, long rumored to be a place of great fae power.

sylph—Slang for a fae with air powers.

tetrad—The four Remnants.

Thawe Bridge—A rope suspension bridge at the southern foot of the Cimmerian Mountains, connecting the Northlands to the Midlands.

Titan—A matriarchal species of giants native to Prydain Isle, immense in both strength and size.

Titan's Way—A strategic naval channel connecting the North Sea to the Bay of Blood.

twyllo—A game of cards and wagers popular in the Northlands.

ACKNOWLEDGMENTS

As I sit here attempting to encapsulate my deep gratitude to everyone who had a hand in *The Sea Spinner*, I find myself at a loss for words. (Which, as a writer, isn't something that usually happens to me.)

A simple "thank you" seems woefully inadequate.

To my readers who returned for another adventure in Anwyvn: none of this would be possible without your support. I only get to do my dream job every day because of you. I hope you know I never take that—or any of you—for granted. Bloggers, booksellers, librarians . . . You make my world go 'round.

This book would not be in your hands right now without the tireless efforts of my wonderful agents at Bookcase Literary Agency, Meire Dias and Flavia Viotti. You are my champions, my cheerleaders, my constant problem solvers. I don't know what I did to deserve you.

To my editor Sarah Blumenstock at Berkley: your guidance, wisdom, and immaculate eye for detail have made my writing sing off the pages like never before. Thank you for seeing my vision for these characters from the very beginning, and for continuing to see it as we approach the end.

I must also mention the wonderful Rebecca Hilsdon at

Penguin Michael Joseph, whose enthusiasm for this trilogy has never wavered. I feel so privileged to have you—and the whole MJ team—bringing this story to life across the pond. You've opened doors for me that I never dared dream of walking through.

To the wonderful marketers, publicists, and creatives at Ace who always go above and beyond: you are rock stars! Special thanks to Katie Anderson for her flawless cover design direction. And, speaking of covers . . .

To the immensely talented illustrator Tom Roberts, I owe my eternal appreciation. It is a genuine thrill to have your artistry grace my work.

I am lucky enough to say that this trilogy has now found a home in more than twenty countries. It would likely take me another five hundred pages to list everyone who has worked on this manuscript worldwide, from translators to editors to booksellers to formatters to narrators. But to each of my foreign publishers: I hope we meet someday so I can thank you in person. Until then, please know how honored I feel each time I see my books in your languages.

I cannot forget my fellow authors, particularly those in the romance community. You are a limitless source of knowledge, friendship, and motivation. Whether it's offering up a coveted blurb or sharing in everyday wins on social media, your energy is a driving force.

Last but never least, I must thank my friends and family members for their endless encouragement. (Yes, Atticus, I am including you in that statement. No, you don't need your own special shout-out. You are a cat.)

Parents, if you're reading this: I love you tremendously. And Grandma, if you're up there looking down on me, you should know . . . I'd never be where I am now if I hadn't pilfered that bodice ripper from your extensive collection at age twelve. You'd sure get a kick out of all this, huh?